VIOLENT AWAKENING

K.J. SUTTON

DEL REY

UK | USA | Canada | Ireland | Australia
India | New Zealand | South Africa

Del Rey is part of the Penguin Random House group of companies whose addresses can be found at global.penguinrandomhouse.com

Penguin Random House UK,
One Embassy Gardens, 8 Viaduct Gardens, London SW11 7BW

penguin.co.uk
global.penguinrandomhouse.com

Published in Penguin Books 2025
001

Copyright © K. J. Sutton, 2025

The moral right of the author has been asserted.

Violent Awakenings is a work of fiction. Names, places, and incidents either are products of the authors' imaginations or are used fictitiously. Any resemblance to actual events, locales, or persons, living or dead, is entirely coincidental.

Penguin Random House values and supports copyright. Copyright fuels creativity, encourages diverse voices, promotes freedom of expression and supports a vibrant culture. Thank you for purchasing an authorised edition of this book and for respecting intellectual property laws by not reproducing, scanning or distributing any part of it by any means without permission. You are supporting authors and enabling Penguin Random House to continue to publish books for everyone. No part of this book may be used or reproduced in any manner for the purpose of training artificial intelligence technologies or systems. In accordance with Article 4(3) of the DSM Directive 2019/790, Penguin Random House expressly reserves this work from the text and data mining exception.

Typeset in 9.2/13.75 pt Iowan Old Style Roman by
Six Red Marbles UK, Thetford, Norfolk

Printed and bound in Great Britain by Clays Ltd, Elcograf S.p.A.

The authorised representative in the EEA is Penguin Random House Ireland, Morrison Chambers, 32 Nassau Street, Dublin D02 YH68

A CIP catalogue record for this book is available from the British Library

ISBN: 978–1–804–94494–3

Penguin Random House is committed to a sustainable future for our business, our readers and our planet. This book is made from Forest Stewardship Council® certified paper.

PENGUIN BOOKS

VIOLENT AWAKENING

Praise for the Fortuna Sworn series

"A fantastic urban fantasy series that I highly recommend." – Beckie Bookworm

"A unique and compelling fantasy series that will grab you right from the start and hold your attention." – Mindy Lou's Book Review

"If you are looking for a new paranormal series, this is the one for you." – The Book Curmudgeon

"A captivating, fast-paced paranormal fantasy that is sure to sweep you away to a world unlike any other." – Lovely Loveday

"For fantasy readers who are looking for a little fresh and a lot fantastic!" – Tome Tender Book Blog

"The romance tantalizes and teases . . . leaving the reader begging for more." – This Girl Reads a Lot

"Prepare to delve into a dark and twisted world!" – Perspective of a Writer

"Sutton . . . managed to create a spin on not only the fae but other supernatural creatures that will fascinate you [and] leave you turning the pages as fast as you possibly can!" – My Guilty Obsession

ALSO BY K. J. SUTTON

The Fortuna Sworn Series

Fortuna Sworn

Restless Slumber

Deadly Dreams

Beautiful Nightmares

Endless Terrors

Other titles

Straight On 'Til Morning

The Door at the End of the Stars

Summer in the Elevator

Content guidance for this title is listed at the back of the book.

These violent delights have violent ends.

—William Shakespeare

Violent Awakening

PROLOGUE

I met my best friend's gaze and remembered who we used to be. Such young, silly creatures with carefree dreams and impossible hopes. I'd never imagined it could turn out like this. I'd never dreamed that sweet, freckled boy would become a Beast, or that sad, lonely girl would grow up to kill him.

"Tell me how to save you, Ollie," I whispered.

"You can't," he answered, his eyes bright with pain and all the days we wouldn't get to have. Then he said, his voice hardening, "Wake up, Fortuna. Wake up."

"Oliver, wait," I began to say, my own voice tinged with desperation. But it was too late.

Every dream had to end, and I was already gone.

CHAPTER ONE

COVINGTON, LOUISIANA

Red and blue lights flashed over the lawn.

Police vehicles filled the street in both directions. There were also two ambulances, but the sirens had gone silent, and they'd been parked for the past hour. Collith and I stood across the street, tucked into the shadows. We weren't the only ones observing the crime scene—most of the neighbors had come outside, drawn by all the movement and noise. They stood in robes and pajamas, looking confused and worried. But I didn't sense real fear from them, not yet.

That would change once the cops started bringing the bodies out.

"Did you catch a name?" I asked Collith quietly. I didn't look away from the house.

His voice was grim. "One of the officers knew them. This place belonged to Mark and Kiersten Henderson. Married couple, moved here a few years ago. No kids. Apparently they kept to themselves."

Mark and Kiersten Henderson. I repeated their names silently, memorizing them like a dark song lyric. The ice in my chest began to crack. I willed myself to go cold again, and my expression settled back into its hard mask. No kids, just like the rest. That was good. The only good thing about any of this, really.

I wondered, not for the first time, if it was a coincidence ... or if there was still something left of Oliver inside that thing I'd seen. That black-eyed, blank-faced creature with skin covered in dark lines, hulking wings rising over its golden head.

It doesn't matter, I reminded myself. Even if part of Oliver had survived, even if there was some lingering sense of humanity that made the Beast draw the line at hurting kids, our story only had one ending. Oliver was going to die, and I would be the one who killed him.

My resolve hardened. I refocused on the humans' progress. Silhouettes moved past the blood-spattered windows. There were at least over a dozen people inside, at least, which meant we still had a wait ahead of us. Collith used his own energy store when he worked an illusion, so the fewer minds he had to influence, the better. This was the fourth house we'd been to in the months since Finn's funeral, and we had learned a thing or two about how to make the process smoother. We were getting *better* at this, sickening as it was.

Finn. The thought of him sent another crack through me.

"Were they like the others?" I asked abruptly. I kept my eyes on that big, bright window.

In my peripheral vision, I saw Collith nod. "Fallen," he said. "I can smell the blood from here."

The ice in me cracked a third time, and now small bits and pieces slipped through. Guilt. Fury. Pain. Strangely, as I watched one of the police officers bolt out of the house and vomit on the front lawn, I started thinking about Oliver's freckles.

It seemed like such an insignificant, random thing to think about. But I was trying to connect that sweet, freckled boy to the abomination who had killed these people tonight. As another officer rushed outside, a memory came through. I stopped seeing the pale-faced, shaking policewoman, and a young boy loomed before me instead, replacing the nightmare playing out across the street.

We sat on the beach. Our small knees were buried in the sand, and the shore in both directions was empty, completely untouched except by us. The sky was clear and blue overhead, not a single cloud in sight. Seagulls flew through the wide expanse, their wild cries snatched away by a salt-laden breeze. To our right, the sea glittered. Waves reached for us again and again.

I was teaching the strange dream boy how to build a sandcastle. He sat beside me, his eyebrows knitted together with concentration. He didn't move like other children I knew. He didn't move like anyone I knew, really. He did everything slowly, as if it were all new to him, or he was afraid of making a mistake.

He'd finally started talking, but he didn't like it. His words came halting and uncertain. I had stopped asking the boy questions a while ago, since I never got an answer. It was like he'd just been born, or something. Now I eyed him anew, wondering if it was too soon to try again. After another minute, I gave in to my relentless curiosity.

"What's your name?" I asked.

The boy stared at our castle with a crinkled brow, a frown hovering at the corners of his mouth. I could tell he was thinking about it, harder than he'd thought about anything. For a few seconds, I watched him, certain he would remember it. But then the boy said, his voice faint, "I don't know."

I frowned, too. "You don't know your name?"

He stared at the castle, his eyes darker than they'd been a moment ago. "I don't think I have one."

Impatience sparked inside me. I put my hands beside his. "Well, that's silly. Everyone has a name," I said.

"Oh."

The boy sounded so confused, so worried, that I felt a jab of remorse. It wasn't his fault—none of this was. I gave him a kind smile. "It's okay. We'll just pick one out for you."

His eyes widened. "Can you do that?"

"Why not?" I shrugged, patting the side of the turret I'd just built. Parents usually picked names, but what if you didn't have parents?

The thought sent a pang through my entire body.

I'd forgotten, for a minute, that I didn't have parents, either. Not anymore.

I blinked rapidly, desperately fixing my gaze on the castle again. But the boy didn't move to help me, as he'd been helping every night since it happened. I glanced over at him, wondering why he was just sitting there. Then I got a look at his face, and a startled jolt went through my small frame. For the first time since the boy had first appeared in my dreams, I saw excitement in his expression.

That was when it clicked—he expected me to name him right now.

My mouth twisted with uncertainty. I'd never named something before, not even a pet. Dad had been allergic to everything, dogs, cats, turtles . . . No. I didn't want to think about Dad, not here. My mind skittered to the first memory it could find, and I remembered the movie I'd been watching before bed, surrounded by other foster kids in a living room that smelled like ramen noodles. The movie was a cartoon called Oliver & Company. *It had made me laugh, and I hadn't laughed since that night I was desperately fighting to forget.*

"Do you like the name Oliver?" I asked abruptly, meeting the boy's gaze.

"Oliver," he repeated with a tentative expression. Then, again, more firmly this time, "Oliver. Yes."

The seagulls called out again. Their cries echoed in my ears as I bent my head. We worked in silence for a minute or two. When a breeze tugged strands of hair into my eyes, I tucked them back and snuck another glance at the boy. His mouth was puckered in soft concentration. Oliver, *I thought again, studying the freckles that dotted his skin like sprinkles. The corners of my lips tilted.*

It fit.

"Fortuna. It's time."

Collith's voice penetrated the haze of images around my mind. I blinked that freckled boy away and reminded myself of the cold truth—that boy had died a long time ago. If he'd even existed at all.

Refocusing, I nodded at Collith to indicate that I was ready. We both knew it was a lie, and he had already offered to go in alone. Like all the other nights, I'd just shaken my head. Knowing what my answer would be never stopped Collith from saying the words, though. I still felt them hovering between us as we crossed the street and ducked beneath the crime-scene tape.

No one looked at us, which meant Collith had shielded us from view. We went up the sidewalk, passing several police officers and other uniformed people who must've been part of the investigation. If this was like the other three cases, which were all still ongoing, I knew what the humans would find—nothing. No fingerprints or footprints, no hairs or fluids.

There would only be feathers. Long, black feathers.

The humans were puzzled by them, but they were the one thing connecting all the victims together. Well, that and the way they'd all died.

Terribly. Violently. Darkly.

I would see their faces in my dreams for the rest of my life.

The smell hit me in the doorway. I couldn't detect the difference between human and Fallen like Collith, but I knew blood. It was as recognizable as my favorite perfume, or the aroma of coffee, or the cloying scent of Emma's joints. Most days, it felt like I'd been baptized in it.

But even as that familiar, terrible smell stuffed itself up my nostrils, I didn't let myself pause or hesitate. If I did, I might not be able to go through with this. I shifted my body to the side, allowing a man in a black coverall to pass, then went inside. I took a few steps into the room before I stopped and looked around, ignoring the spiderweb cracks that kept spreading through my chest. *Don't run, Fortuna. Don't you dare run.* I sensed Collith drawing to a halt beside me. He didn't say anything. I kept my face turned away, as if I were concentrating.

The house was smaller than it looked from outside. Everything was in its place—the old couches, the faded side tables, the colorful rugs sprawled over the wooden floor. But there were marks of a place that was lived in. A place that was *loved*. The vase of pink hydrangeas on the dining table in the corner, and a flowered blanket that rested in a pool on the floor, as if the person using it had jumped up from where they'd been sitting. There was no sign of that person now, though. This was not where the smell was coming from, I thought, forcing myself to keep looking.

We'd deduced that every family had been caught by surprise, because the messes we found were in the spots where they actually died, while the rest of the home was left largely intact. Oliver was good at this. *An efficient monster,* I thought bitterly, finishing my scan.

This wasn't the crime scene, but there were still two technicians and two police officers standing in here. As I turned my attention toward the doorway on the other side of them, I half-listened to their conversation. They were speculating on what kind of animal could've done this. It was so reminiscent of things I'd heard and read about my own parents' bodies that my stomach began to churn.

When it became clear the investigators were about to bag the victims up, I turned to Collith, and he nodded. He walked around the humans and through that wood-framed doorway, the white paint along the top of it peeling. I dragged my eyes back down and refocused, facing the yawning darkness as we walked deeper into the house. A moment later, we found ourselves in a narrow hallway. There were two closed doors on either side, and one at the very end—that door was open.

And that, I knew, was where the source of the smell came from.

With every step, the ringing in my ears got louder and louder. My heart felt like a wild thing inside my chest. I wanted to turn back. A scream built in my lungs, and I swore I could feel the physical pressure of it. I focused on putting one foot in front of the other, bringing myself closer and closer. The noise inside my skull was so loud it was painful now.

Then, when I reached the doorway of the kitchen, the ringing stopped.

The silence felt swollen, like a body rotting in a grave. I stood in the doorway, rooted in place. I had a vague sense of Collith saying something to me, but I couldn't make out the words. I scanned the room slowly, and my breathing was loud in my ears.

The female had died screaming. I wondered which had come first—the claw marks across her throat, which had practically beheaded her, or the dead male who lay slumped across from her. My guess was the latter. The female's face was twisted in a mass of anguish and terror. I'd felt pain like that.

Traces of her fear still lingered in the air, and it smelled like food that had gone bad. I breathed through my mouth as I turned my attention to the male. His death had been worse. Messier. His torso was barely more than a rib cage, with bits of torn flesh still clinging to the curved bones. I couldn't find his arms and legs amongst all the blood, but his head was on the floor at the other end of the room. A sour prickle filled my mouth as I examined the male's features, searching for anything that might seem familiar. But he was a stranger, though. Like all the others.

Whatever kind of Fallen creatures they'd been, these two hadn't been fighters. There was no sign of magic, and their body parts appeared human. When Finn died, he must've just begun to shift, because his fingers and teeth had been replaced by claws and fangs.

No. I wasn't thinking about Finn right now. I refocused again, blinking fast and hard. The blurred carnage solidified.

The photographers had finished documenting everything, and dozens of items throughout the room were marked with numbers. I tried to see the scene like they would. To picture how the whole thing had played out. But it was no use—every time I saw Oliver's latest victims, I remembered the first ones.

I'd protected my mind against the most powerful, ancient beings to walk the Earth, but against my own past, I was as helpless as a child. I stared down at a pile of intestines on the tiles, and all at once, it felt like I was traveling through time, landing amongst the broken, rusted, sharp-edged memories. I was eight years old again, kneeling on all fours, careless of the wet sensation seeping through my nightgown. The memory filled my mind until it was all I could see.

I'd gone back to her.

After I'd found my father, and seen that he was dead, I'd left that awful-smelling room and gone down the hallway. My mother was still there, slumped against the wall. I sank to my knees, staring at her horrified, blood-spattered face. Her skin was whiter than I'd ever seen it, like paper speckled with red ink.

"Mommy?" I said.

My voice was hoarse—I had stopped screaming a while ago, but my throat still hurt. Mom didn't move. I put my little hands on the holes, trying to make the flow stop. Like a Band-Aid. Bleeding was bad. I knew that much.

But no matter how hard I pushed down, the blood didn't stop. It squelched through my fingers. Help. I needed help. I raised my head, whimpering, and looked back at my mom's still face. "Mommy, tell me what to do," I pleaded.

Still, she said nothing. I knew she was dead, of course I knew that. But I had grown up with the knowledge that magic was real. I knew it could do incredible things, and so could the creatures my mother had told me about. Witches existed. Angels, too. I remembered Mom's stories about them, and how they'd once been guardians in another world. With a rush of painful hope, I decided to pray.

My mind launched into a desperate, silent appeal to anyone who would listen. Soon the cold began to creep into my bones, and exhaustion weighed down my eyelids. Never breaking in my string of promises and pleas to the one that could save Mom, I rested my full weight on the floor. Wetness had soaked through the entire bottom half of my nightgown, but I didn't care.

I looked down and watched a dark stain bloom across the white fabric. I kept my hands on my mother as it spread. Pressure, I thought. I had to keep pressure on her. My lips kept moving as I prayed on, and on, and on.

Time went by. Eventually, a man appeared in the hall. I was so focused on my job that I barely noticed. I only registered the faint tang of cologne, and my nostrils flared, desperate to replace that coppery smell wafting up from my mother. The man had something pressed against his ear, and he was saying something like, "Oh God, oh God, oh God."

There was a snap, and he put something in his pocket. He walked slowly over to us and spoke again. When I felt the man's hand on my arm, I jerked away and lowered myself down so my cheek touched the wall. I stared at my mother and touched her with the tip of my finger. She was still warm.

"Are you there?" I whispered.

When she didn't answer, I edged even closer, so close I could have kissed her if I'd wanted. The words to her favorite song popped into my head. Haltingly I sang, "Y-you may say I'm a dreamer, but I'm not the only one . . ."

I couldn't remember the rest. Mommy was so quiet now. Why didn't she help me remember the rest?

Suddenly a new sound shattered the night. This one I recognized—I had asked my mother what it was, once. A siren. It meant that someone needed help. Not us. We didn't need help. We were fine. I huddled against Mommy's shoulder and pressed my forehead to her temple. My stomach lurched when she didn't move. But she was fine, she would wake up soon. I just needed to protect her. The man beside me tried to talk again. His words were as meaningless as before. I kept singing, and soon, I forgot about him entirely.

I was still repeating that one line from the song in an aching cycle, since it was all I knew, when another man appeared. This one had a mustache, and his voice was a gentle rumble, like a giant's. He knelt beside me and my mother, the buttons on his uniform gleaming from the beam of a flashlight. There were more people behind him, I realized dimly. I hadn't even noticed them come in. Figures moved in and out of my parents' bedroom. They spoke quietly, but I heard the horror in their voices. The confusion. One of them said Damon's name, but not even that could pull me away.

"I know you'll miss her, and she'll miss you, but we have to take her," the police officer said, bringing my attention back to him.

I finally comprehended what he was saying. Terror overcame me, and suddenly I couldn't breathe. My grip tightened on Mommy's hand. "No. You can't take her. I n-need her," I hiccuped.

He didn't relent. "She can't stay here, honey."

"No!" I lashed out at him like a wild animal. The burst of adrenaline that hit my veins helped some of my sense return, and I finally remembered that I'd left my little brother in a darkened bedroom. I turned and looked toward the door with wild eyes. "Damon, where is Damon? I need to find Damon!"

The man tried to pull me down the hall, tried to soothe me with more words that swallowed me with their emptiness. I fought him and draped myself over my mother's remains. As if that would change anything. As if it would bring her back. And then I was screaming again, clawing at the man's arm as he picked me up. I kicked my legs out uselessly while he carried me out, filling my ears with his lies.

I wasn't okay. Nothing would ever be okay again.

"Fortuna. Come back. Come back to me." Hands cupped my cheeks.

I blinked up at Collith, dimly aware that I was gripping his wrists. There was a slight tremble in my fingers. Lately, I'd been slipping into the past so often it felt harder and harder to come back. "Get me out of here," I whispered.

His response was to wrap an arm around my shoulders and tuck me firmly against his side. His scent assailed my senses, and for just an instant, it blocked out everything else. I let myself close my eyes. The carnage was replaced by darkness, and Collith, and the solidness of his body against mine. And his voice, the soft sound of it filling that terrible stillness: "I've got you, sweetheart."

We left the room together, and I was breathing through my mouth now, trying to avoid the smell of death. The sound was small and ragged. Hearing it, Collith's grip tightened. Part of me wanted to close my eyes and press harder against him . . . but another part of me resisted. That had been happening a lot these days, I thought as Collith led us out. Every time we got closer, or it felt like I'd started to depend on him, I kept the smallest distance between us.

When we neared the entrance, I pulled away and raised my gaze, fixing it on the open door just a few yards away. The night sky beckoned like an old friend.

This time, I didn't look around. There were still a couple people here, and their low voices followed me and Collith outside.

At the first crime scene, I'd halted on the threshold, my heart lurching with alarm as something else occurred to me.

"Wait," I'd said, turning back. "The blood. Police officers will see it, and they'll take pictures—"

"Glamours linger after death," Collith had replied, his tone reassuring. "And by the time it fades, any evidence or witnesses are taken care of."

"Dracula?" I'd guessed. Collith nodded.

Tonight, I left without hesitation. The police lights flashed in our faces again. Even though no one could see us, they felt like a spotlight on my pain. I put my head down and hurried toward our rental car. Collith opened the passenger door and watched me lower myself into the seat before he circled the hood and went to the driver's side.

Once he was inside, pulling the door shut, I turned my face and looked out the window. There was nothing to see besides my own face reflected in the black glass. I'd lost weight, I thought faintly. Collith drove to the end of the block and turned, taking us away from that house of horrors. Within a minute, we were surrounded by farmland. I kept staring at myself, and my own haunted reflection was a reminder of everything that had happened to make me look like this.

There were so many cracks inside me now that I was on the verge of shattering. That happened a lot these days, too—getting to this point, this pain.

But every time I was at the edge, someone intervened.

At Bea's, when I opened my locker in search of eye drops and discovered a cupcake waiting for me, Ariel's subtle scent wafting out. At home, when I emerged from my room, red-eyed, and drew up short at the sight of Damon, Danny, and Matthew, all of them dressed for a hike, looking in my direction with expectant smiles. Some days, I'd get a timely text from Adam or Gil, inviting me to come train at the shop. Then there was Emma, leaving freshly baked cookies on the counter or asking how my sessions were going with Consuelo.

Without fail, my Shadow Court pulled me back again and again. Even those who weren't technically part of it.

At the same moment I had the thought, I sensed Collith's arm move. His fingers interlaced with mine, and then he lifted my hand, his lips pressing a brief, gentle kiss against the back of it. I watched him silently. Despite the cold that spread over my skin from that kiss, I felt warmer, a small spot of heat buried somewhere deep inside me.

I waited for Collith to say something, but he just turned his head, concentrating on the road again. Light from the screens in front of us cast a pale tint over his skin, and there was that stubborn lock of hair over his brow, I noted distantly. The one that always had my fingers itching to reach up and brush it back. But I couldn't even if I wanted to, because Collith hadn't let go of my hand. And I hadn't pulled away.

As I continued to study Collith's profile, the memory of his voice came back to me from those last minutes in the house. It had been my port in a storm of guilt and self-loathing. *I've got you.*

The warmth began to spread, threatening to thaw the icy wall I'd built. Finally tearing my gaze from Collith, I met the eyes of the woman in the window again. Streetlights and darkness rushed past, and she stared back at me with a look in her eyes that I knew all too well.

Fear.

No matter how hard I fought it, no matter how many times I tried to pretend it wasn't there, I felt it in my ragged breath, in my tight chest, as if there was a shadow behind my heart. Whispering to me with every hard, unsteady beat.

I *was* afraid. Not just that we would be too late again, and we'd be finding the remains of another family instead of saving them. Not just that I might let down Finn, and my parents, and everyone else that my twisted creation had slaughtered.

I was afraid I couldn't do it. Afraid that when the time came, and I was facing the creature Oliver had become—the one he'd *always* been, I corrected silently, a truth I would've seen sooner if I hadn't been so weak, so stubbornly *blind*—something would make me hesitate. The memory of that quiet, freckled boy. A shred of nostalgia or misplaced affection that might still live deep inside me, no matter how many times I reminded myself that the boy I loved didn't exist. He had just been another repressed memory. A monster.

In the cruelest of ironies, I'd been taking Oliver's advice a lot lately. A long time ago, back in the days of the dreamscape while we were still us, he'd told me, *Picture the worst possible outcome. Be cruel to yourself. Spare no pain. Do this again, and again, and again. Until one day, you'll find yourself immune to it, and the fear will no longer control you.*

So on nights like this, and most other nights, too, I pictured it. The exact moment when the light would leave Oliver's eyes, and the holy blade I planned to put in his gut was covered in blood. His blood. Maybe mine along with it, but that part didn't matter. I imagined it a hundred times, and then a hundred more, trying to prepare. To harden.

My stomach clenched with resolve, and I lifted my gaze. When the time came, I promised again, I would be ready.

But the woman in the window didn't believe me.

CHAPTER TWO

Sunlight glittered over the lake.

The water was so still that it looked like glass, but there was nothing still about the rest. Not the bugs, which flitted through the air and created small, ephemeral ripples. Not the birds appearing sporadically in the sky, swooping against the blue expanse and calling to each other in high, musical sounds. Not the gentle sway of the boat I sat in.

I leaned back and arched my pole back to cast the line. A moment later, the lure plopped gracelessly into the lake. My brow furrowed. "Damn it," I muttered.

"Release the reel button as the rod comes to eye level," a familiar voice said.

I nodded and reeled the line back in. "Like this?" I asked, trying again.

This time, the lure landed farther away. Finn squinted toward it, holding his own fishing pole over the edge. The corners of his solemn mouth tilted upward. "Good. Very good."

"Thanks." I smiled back and relaxed against the edge, holding my fishing pole in a loose grip.

After a moment, Finn turned away and gazed out at the lake.

I knew I was staring, but I didn't care. I drank in the sight of him as though I were waking up from a really long, really terrible dream. He looked the same, I thought. No, that wasn't true—he looked *better*.

I'd met Finn when he'd been a captive at the Unseelie Court, a creature that had been starved and beaten for years. Even after we'd been together for a while, after he was safe and fed and warm, I realized now that Finn had never truly recovered. I'd never gotten to know this healed, complete version of him.

Emotions swelled in my throat, a thick tangle of them, as if I'd swallowed too much at once. Sorrow. Pain. Guilt. To hide it from Finn, I refocused on my lure and watched how the light played on the water. Birdsong rode a breeze that smelled like pine trees.

"Is this real?" I asked finally.

My question was met with silence. I looked over at Finn again, and his expression made me feel a familiar wistful pang. The soft, thoughtful light in his eyes, the slight purse to his mouth. He was considering his response in the same quiet, careful way he'd done everything when he was alive. I guessed there were some things that never changed about a person, no matter how much blood and tears they shed.

"Depends on your definition of real," Finn said finally. Another bird flew overhead and its shadow passed over him.

I rolled my eyes, smiling, and turned back to our lines. "I don't remember you being so philosophical before. It's annoying."

"I was a wolf most of the time," Finn reminded me.

"Yeah, well, that never seemed to stop you from expressing your opinion," I countered. Finn's lips curved in the barest hint of a smile, and he opened his mouth to reply, but then my fishing pole surged forward. I swore and shot to my feet, tightening my hold on it. "Holy shit! I got one! I got one, Finn!"

"Jerk the line, make sure you've got him good," he urged. He stood and put his hand on my elbow to balance me as I yanked my fishing pole and a big, glistening fish shot into the air. A girlish squeal escaped me. Finn laughed while I frantically began to reel it in, and I was laughing, too, nearly losing my grip on the pole again.

Finn rushed to grab it from me, his white teeth shining. "Don't worry, I've got you—"

I jerked awake.

Reality came back in pieces. I was in a motel room. My skin still stung from the shower I'd taken a few hours ago, after I had scrubbed all the imaginary blood off my skin. Sighing, I slumped against the headboard and ran my hand down my face. The old clock on the nightstand revealed it was the Witching Hour. Maybe that was why I'd woken up. I wondered if Collith was awake, too, but I didn't hear anything through the thin wall between our rooms.

By the time we'd left that blood-filled house, it was almost two in the morning. The closest Door was several hours away, and I'd felt hollowed out after what we had just seen. Collith suggested stopping at a motel for the night, and I hadn't argued.

I'd searched for options on my phone while he drove. When I reached the drop-down menu for how many rooms we would need, my finger had hovered over the screen.

After a moment's hesitation, I chose two.

In the months since my return from Hell, things had been . . . paused between me and Collith. I never spoke about what had happened with Oliver, and Collith never asked, but he knew. He knew about Lucifer, too. Understandable, really, that he'd distanced himself. Collith wasn't even staying at the loft anymore, or at Cyrus's, and there were often weeks we didn't see each other.

But he texted every day.

It was strange, getting messages from Collith. Sending them back. We'd never had that kind of relationship before. Most of our time together had been narrowly escaping life-or-death situations, or arguing about whether I should kill someone. I'd only seen him flirt on a handful of occasions, and he'd teased me even more rarely.

Lately, Collith had been doing both of those things, and more.

He sent me book recommendations. Passages and poems he thought I'd like. Pictures of flowers in his garden. It wasn't constant, but the texts always seemed to arrive just when I was about to slip into the dark corners of my mind. I wasn't sure when it had happened, exactly—somewhere along the way, seeing Collith's name on my screen had become a highlight in my day.

Once in a while, usually late at night, I questioned the change in him. The shift that had happened in the way he treated me. It was almost as if he'd made his mind up about something, and now he was . . . waiting. And while he waited, he reminded me in consistent, subtle ways that he was there. Supporting me. Loving me.

If I weren't so fucked up and confused, I might have been tempted to let him.

As I'd held my hand under the shower spray, I'd blearily gone over the victims again. Laurie's people still hadn't been able to find any connections between them, either. The kills had to be random. Mindless. Oliver was on a bender, his humanity completely gone. Which meant there was no way to predict who he would hit next.

No way besides the dreams.

They started a few days after Oliver got free, and the dreams were how we'd found two of the four crime scenes. Monstrous, dark dreams that were worse than any of the nightmares my best friend had once protected me from. I felt myself tear into people like they were nothing more than paper, their flesh giving way beneath my hands, hot blood spilling over my fingers. Their screams filled my ears.

It wasn't hard to figure out that I was seeing the killings through Oliver's eyes. He might've had his own body now, but there was still a connection between us. A connection that, every time I thought about it, made my stomach churn.

I'd already asked Savannah if she could use this twisted bond to track Oliver. That would've been too easy, though, and magic was a fickle asshole. Savannah didn't know of any spell that could accomplish what I wanted, and she also didn't know enough about the strange power connecting us. My power.

The dreams were still useful, since I had been able to use context clues. Landmarks. House numbers. Once, I'd seen a name on an envelope. It was a strange feeling, dreading the moment I fell asleep and anxiously waiting for it, too. Praying that we would be able to find Oliver faster next time, maybe even fast enough to get there before he'd left, and finally end this. There was just the small matter of figuring out what Oliver's—

My thoughts were cut short when I heard a tap at the door. I got out of bed and hurried across the room. When I swung it open and saw Collith standing there, I was suddenly too aware that I wasn't wearing a bra.

"Hi," I said softly, giving him a questioning look. We'd agreed to leave at seven.

Collith's hazel eyes were inscrutable. He was fully dressed, as if he hadn't even tried to sleep, which meant we'd stopped here purely for my sake. "I heard you through the wall and thought I'd update you in person. I just got a call from our mutual friend," Collith said.

By *mutual friend*, of course, he meant Laurie. The Seelie King had been keeping his distance, too, since Finn's funeral. But he had even more reasons than Collith to stay away, and I hadn't tried to change his mind. Not when all I had to offer him was *I don't know* or *I can't right now*.

"And?" I said. Apprehension fluttered in my stomach. These days, updates from Laurie weren't a good thing.

Collith held out his phone. "Recognize this?"

As I took it from him, my fingers briefly brushing his, I stepped back and inclined my head in a silent invitation. Collith stepped past me, and I tried not to breathe in his scent, focusing quickly on the image Laurie had sent.

It was a bird's-eye view of a corn field, and right in the center, the crops had been cleared to form an earthen circle. And in the center of that, someone had carved a symbol deep into the dirt. When I registered the shape of the symbol, it felt like the air in my lungs froze.

It was the same as the mark on my back.

My gaze shot back to Collith's, and my voice was sharp. "Did he send anyone to this place? Where was it taken?"

"West Bengal. In the eastern Himalayas," he answered. "Laurelis sent two of his agents, and the area was abandoned. But they could sense magic had been there—strong magic."

"It's a mark Olorel created," I murmured, my brow lowered in thought. "That it made traveling between dimensions easier. Is he trying to go back to his world?"

A storm brewed in Collith's eyes, making them darken as he countered, "Or bring someone here?"

The possibilities were terrifying. I fell silent as I remembered the things I'd seen in Hell. When an image of Lucifer's creepy sister reared up, I hurriedly gave Collith his phone back. I caught a final glimpse of the field Lucifer had ruined just before Collith put his phone away. My frown deepened.

Whatever the mark meant, it was beginning to feel like all roads led back to Olorel.

For the hundredth time, I considered what I knew about him. My knowledge had evolved since I'd first heard his name. Back then, it was a three-day feast I'd needed to survive. I'd only been at the Unseelie Court to save my brother, and I didn't give a shit about what some ancient faerie had sacrificed.

Now I knew that Olorel had been one of the greatest powers in the universe. He could create tears between worlds, and he'd used that ability to save the rebels during the Battle of Red Pearls.

He'd used that same ability to make the Unseelie Court, a safe place where they could exist away from humans. The devil and his followers had been using Olorel's mark to reach across the dimensions for centuries—like that super fun time Belanor branded it on my back—and even Hell had a feast in his name. But when I'd asked Lucifer what they were celebrating, all he would say was, *It's a promise.*

Dread gripped me, and my gaze rose back to Collith. "Whatever Lucifer is doing, we need to stop him," I said. "So I guess the plan stays the same. Finding Oliver will lead us right to the devil. I know it, Collith."

He gave me a faint, solemn smile. "I believe you. We stay the course."

Something shifted in my chest. I believed him, too. And in that moment, it struck me just how much I'd grown to trust Collith. How much I depended on him. He'd become a part of my life gradually, sneaking into a thought or a breath, until now being with him felt as natural as breathing.

Suddenly I wondered if my thoughts were written all over my face. Uncertainty rushed in, and I realized I didn't know what to say. We were still standing by the door, so I reached for the knob and opened it, mostly just to stop myself from making some kind of clumsy, mortifying confession to Collith. "Well, thanks for passing on the update," I said.

Collith nodded, but he didn't move. I waited for him to walk out. He continued to linger there, his brows drawn together, his mouth bracketed by lines of tension. As the seconds ticked by, I realized that his silence had nothing to do with Laurie's update. Frowning, I closed the door again and forced myself to stay quiet.

"I'm afraid for you," Collith said finally.

The old me would've instantly gone on the defense or jumped to conclusions. But I knew it didn't come easy to Collith, revealing this. He guarded his secrets like most people guarded their heart after it had been broken a time or two.

"Afraid I won't be able to do it, you mean? When the time comes?" I said, keeping my expression neutral.

"You love him, Fortuna. You may not want to admit it, but if you're going to survive this, you need to." Toward the end of his response, there was almost a hint of pleading in Collith's tone. Then the tang of his fear whispered over my tongue. He was telling the truth, but that didn't do much to lessen the sting of his doubt.

"Do I seriously need to remind you that he killed my parents? He tore them apart just like he tore that couple apart tonight. He killed *Finn*." My voice cracked.

"Be that as it may, you love him." Collith wasn't backing down. He paused before he added, "Just as Laurie loved me even when he believed I'd stolen his power on purpose."

A dozen sharp retorts rose to my lips, and I pursed them so hard that it hurt. I welcomed the small pain—it made it easier to ignore the bigger ones. I didn't want to talk about any of this.

As soon as I had the thought, the urge to run gripped me. I fought it, because Collith deserved better than that. I was done running. I gave him a humorless smile and said, "Okay, what I'm really hearing you say is that we're all wildly dysfunctional, and we should make healthier choices in our relationships."

Collith didn't smile back. "You don't have to do it, Fortuna. You don't even have to be there," he insisted.

"Yes. Yes, I do." My voice was flat. My mind filled with a memory of Finn, and it was quickly followed by a rush of pain. I cleared my throat, glancing around the room as if I were looking for something. My gaze snagged on the TV.

"Will you stay for a while?" I asked impulsively. "We could watch a movie."

Before I had a chance to regret the offer, Collith said, "I'd like that."

I felt a strange rush of nervousness. I turned away quickly, relieved that I had something else to focus on. "Okay, great. Here's the remote. Let me just . . ."

Trailing off, I handed the remote to Collith and left him again. I proceeded to make a nest, of sorts, on the floor in front of the TV, then propped the pillows against the base of the bed. As I worked, I told myself I was imagining the amusement that seemed to radiate from the figure standing on the other side of the room. I couldn't bring myself to look at him. And why was it suddenly so hot in here?

Once I'd finished, Collith didn't wait for an invitation—he took off his shoes and folded his long body to sit on the motel's flowered bedspread. He held the remote in a light grip and began to absently flick through the channels. After a moment, I lowered myself down next to him, sitting close enough that his scent wafted to me again. Collith seemed wholly immersed in his search.

"Oh, it's *The Empire Strikes Back*," he said suddenly. "This one is my favorite."

Finding out that Collith was a Star Wars fan was like discovering Dracula's favorite author was Jane Austen. My discomfort forgotten, I smiled and looked over at him. "What? *The Empire Strikes Back* isn't anyone's favorite. That's weird."

Collith gave me an affronted look. "*The Empire Strikes Back* has everything, Fortuna. The soundtrack alone is incredible, but there's also plot, dialogue, stakes. It's a masterpiece."

"Wow," I said with raised brows. "I had no idea you were such a giant *nerd*."

"Takes one to know one," he countered. My lips twitched. Collith's gaze lingered on mine for another beat, and the undeniable heat of attraction filled the space between us. Then Collith went back to watching the movie.

Instead of turning toward the TV, too, I studied him. Collith seemed unaware of my attention. The blue lights flickered over the planes and angles of his serious, beautiful face. "This is the best part," he murmured.

I finally tore my eyes away from Collith. Leia's pale, upturned features filled the screen. "I love you," she said.

"I know," Han Solo replied, looking back at her with a promise in his gaze.

I struggled to focus. Collith's scent was distracting, and despite how exhausted I'd been in the car, I was suddenly wide awake, every part of me hyper-aware of the male sitting within reach. We were so close, and yet, the distance between us felt impossible. I wanted to close it, or at least take a single step.

For once, I had an idea of what that step should be.

Swallowing, I turned my head slightly, keeping my gaze down as I spoke. "I never apologized," I murmured.

I sensed Collith looking at me. "For what?"

My eyes rose to his. The memory of that night sparked, and I saw a flash of myself dropping the sapphire at Collith's feet. Regret seared my soul. "Helping Viessa take the throne."

He must've seen the shame inside me, because Collith shook his head, his brows drawn together. "I don't judge you for it, Fortuna. Any of it."

Another silence hovered between us. A thousand thoughts raced through my head, and it felt like my heart was rising and falling at the same time. "How can that be true?"

Collith gave me a sad, wry smile. Our past was in that smile, I thought. Every lie, every betrayal, every mistake. "Because there are a great many things I've had to apologize for," he reminded me.

That was true, too. We'd both made mistakes, and we'd both been hurt. My mind went even further back, back to the beginning, and I remembered the night I'd been whipped at Collith's feet. I felt a dull ache in my chest like the echo of an old wound. And when Collith leaned forward and pressed his forehead to mine, I remembered what he'd said afterward. *I made sure to feel every single lash*.

"You shouldn't touch me," I whispered. But I didn't move.

He didn't move, either, and his voice rolled through me like a gentle wave. "Why?"

"Because I'm . . ." I made a vague gesture toward myself, not sure what I was trying to say, exactly. "I'm . . . not safe. Anyone who gets close, anyone who . . ."

God, I wished I was better at this. I pulled away, wiping the tears off my cheeks with both hands. When had I started crying? Collith didn't try to offer comfort, but he shifted as subtly as he could, putting himself even closer to me. A silent offer or a show of support, I didn't know which. Probably both.

It wasn't the first time, but eventually, there would be a last. Inevitably, I thought about the other massive, invisible obstacle between us. I brought my knees in to my chest and rested my cheek on them, looking at Collith sidelong. "Are you going to take it back? The throne, I mean?"

He remained silent. And as I felt my heartbeat intensify, I realized the answer terrified me.

Mostly because I had no idea what I wanted it to be.

"I don't know," Collith said finally. Light from the TV flickered over his frown.

I hesitated. There was something else I wanted to say, but Viessa had always been a sensitive subject, especially after we'd worked together to unseat Collith. Not talking about her was one of the reasons we felt so far apart. I considered my words carefully before I said, "I do regret the coup, but . . . she's a good queen, Collith. She definitely thinks like a faerie sometimes, just like you did. In a way, your visions are the same. She's trying to bring the Unseelie Court into a new era. A new way of doing things. Some of the changes she's made I wish I'd thought of."

I shook my head wonderingly, a smile touching my lips as I remembered the last time I'd been to Viessa's Court. She'd completed the carvings on all the doors, and finished the pathways, too. She had also installed more lights. Those weren't the only changes, though. The new queen had also implemented policies that protected human lives and kept the nobles in line. She'd even started an education program to force the old ones into the ways of the twenty-first century. There had been many, many assassination attempts.

Fortunately, Viessa had Nuvian at her side, and I knew firsthand how good he was at protecting headstrong queens.

Collith made a sound in his throat, bringing me back to the present. His voice was quiet as he said, "Have I mentioned lately how extraordinary you are?"

Finally giving in to the urge to touch him, I rested my fingers on Collith's chest and searched his gaze. "I could say the same thing to you. Collith . . . how are you doing it?"

His brow furrowed. "Doing what?"

I hesitated. We had never talked about this, either. Which was why, once again, I made myself say the thing I'd been avoiding.

"You've been cut off from the Courts just like Lyari has. On top of that, you're a Nightmare, which comes with its own fun set of challenges. And yet, you haven't wavered this summer. Not once. Every time I've needed you, or disappointed you, or hurt you these past few months, you've been here. There should be more changes by now. How have you stayed . . . you?"

Silence met my question. Collith had the look on his face that told me he was considering his next words carefully. As I waited, one of his hands rose absently, trapping my own against his heart.

"I've been fighting the darkness inside me for a lifetime, Fortuna. There are still some things from my past that I haven't told you about. Choices that I'm not proud of." Collith's eyes darkened, but he didn't let go of my hand. He refocused and continued, "Most untethered faeries become goblins because they perceive themselves that way—weak, alone. The rejection from our own kind can drive us mad. But it wasn't that way for me. Being severed from my Court only made my mind clearer."

"That makes one of us." The words slipped out of me. I was too comfortable, too drawn to this version of Collith. The one who looked at me so openly, and laid himself bare without a trace of fear. My eyes dropped to Collith's lips, just for a moment, and then I caught myself and looked away.

But Collith saw.

He made a sound that made my core clench, and then he growled, "Fuck it."

When I turned to look at him again, he gripped the hair at the back of my head and closed the last breath of distance between us. I melted into Collith instantly, moaning into his mouth as we consumed each other. This, I thought distantly, this part of us had always worked. He tasted as good as I remembered, and the taste of him drove all sense away. I let my body take over. As I shifted to straddle Collith, sliding my hands beneath his shirt, I exalted at the ridges and strength that greeted my fingertips.

Instinct took hold of Collith, too. He moved with the speed of the fae, and suddenly I was lying on the bed, the bedsheets whispering against my skin. Still lost in his kiss, I wrapped my legs around Collith and rolled my hips. He lowered his head to tease and skim my neck while I tugged at his shirt again. Acquiescing to my silent demand, Collith pulled away to take it off. I made a satisfied noise and he reclaimed my mouth, making one of his own.

At the same moment I felt Collith reach for the waistband of my shorts, shouts came through the wall over the bed. The humans were so loud their voices overpowered the movie, which was still playing on the other side of the room. Collith and I went still at the same time. We stared silently at each other as the couple next to us argued about who got the last of the blow.

Collith collapsed on top of me with a sound of frustration. Smiling, I raked my fingers up the back of his head. "We always seem to wind up in motels together," I whispered.

Soft laughter sounded in my ear. Then, with a groan, Collith pushed himself up and rolled away. He bent to retrieve his shirt and stood. As Collith pulled it on, light from the TV shifted over the hard, defined lines of his stomach.

"The truth of the matter is, I want you everywhere," he said. "But you're rarely by yourself, and the constant presence of your Court helps me resist you. It just so happens that motel rooms are where we tend to find ourselves alone. Good night, Fortuna."

"Where are you going?" I blurted, watching Collith walk to the door. He thought he could say something like *that* and then just . . . leave?

"Back to my room." Collith must've seen my confusion, because he paused before adding, "Until this is all over, I think there should be some boundaries."

"Boundaries," I repeated slowly. "So when you say 'until this is all over,' what you really mean is . . . until Oliver is dead."

Collith turned in the doorway, one hand on the knob. His eyes were hard. "No. I mean until it's really me you want," he said.

I hesitated. "I . . . I *do* want you, Collith."

He searched my expression with an intensity that I hadn't seen in him for weeks. My body heated, and I felt the slow rise of hope.

At the exact moment Collith opened his mouth to answer, his phone rang. The sound pierced the stillness, and I jumped, yet my gaze never moved from Collith's. He reached into his pocket and sent the caller to voicemail. Relief whispered through me. I was afraid that if we didn't finish this conversation now, tonight, it wouldn't come up again. Not for a long time.

Once again, Collith opened his mouth to speak, and once again, his phone rang.

I felt myself deflate. "You should probably get that."

Collith's eyes flickered, and his mouth tightened—he knew I was right. With obvious reluctance, Collith pulled his phone out and glanced at it. Whatever he saw made him stiffen, and his reaction sent my pulse racing, too. Collith touched the screen and brought it to his pointed ear, turning away. I moved to the end of the bed and rested my elbows on my knees as I waited, pretending to watch the movie. While Collith spoke to the person on the other end, I thought about the other phone calls. The ones that always concluded with us walking through a sea of blood and body parts. But there couldn't be another scene so soon, I told myself. Not two in one week. That didn't fit the pattern, and Oliver had been consistent.

But apparently I didn't fully believe it, because the moment Collith faced me again, pocketing his phone, I pounced. "Who was that?"

"Dracula," Collith said.

A chill ran down my spine. In a burst of memory, I remembered that Dracula had come to the homestead a few weeks ago. I'd been in shock after Finn's death, and Collith had taken care of it. I hadn't even wondered about it until now. "Why would he be contacting you?" I asked.

Collith's expression was grim, and his eyes were a shade darker than usual as he answered, "Because we've been summoned."

"Collith." I spoke more sharply now. "Talk to me. Where are we being summoned?"

There was a note of resigned finality in Collith's voice. "To a meeting of the Order."

The alarm on my cell phone went off at 6:50 a.m.

I sat up and rubbed my eyes, surprised that I'd managed to fall asleep again after Collith left. I had tossed and turned for so long that I'd almost given up. Oliver was mostly to blame for the noise in my head last night . . . but some of it was Collith's fault, too.

Collith, who was probably waiting for me. Sighing, I dragged myself out of bed and went into the bathroom to brush my teeth and wash my face. Five minutes later, I stepped out of the motel room and found Collith leaning on the wall outside the door.

"Good morning," he said. It was a habit he'd picked up from Emma.

"Good morning," I said automatically, giving Collith a swift appraisal. He didn't look tired, but there was the slightest wrinkle to his clothes, which were still the same as yesterday's. *He could've sifted home to shower and change,* I thought, trying not to frown. Why hadn't he?

In an instant, I knew the answer—Collith hadn't wanted to leave me.

"No dreams?" he asked, completely oblivious to the way I couldn't seem to stop looking at him.

I shook my head. "Not this time."

"Good. You needed the rest."

"Yeah, I guess." With a soft smile, I started walking toward the parking lot. Collith fell into step beside me, his elbow brushing against mine. Birdsong floated through the quiet. When we got to the car, Collith opened the passenger side door for me again, flashing a small, crooked smile of his own. That familiar, stubborn lock of hair fell into his eye, and as Collith closed the door and rounded the hood, I watched him rake it back in an absent, habitual gesture. Then he got in and started the car, making sure the heat settings were how I liked them before he started driving. I felt another soft sensation inside me, a feeling that made me think of petals unfurling.

As we began the final leg of our journey to the Door, the morning sun was drowsy. It illuminated Collith as if he belonged in the light. I kept my face turned toward him, acting like I was absorbed by the brightening sky. Secretly, I mapped out the dips and lines of his profile. A small voice at the back of my head told me to stop it. To look away. But . . . I liked looking at Collith. The admission should've been frightening, and maybe something inside me did flutter a little. Only a little.

Still unaware of my scrutiny, or at least doing a valiant job of pretending to be, the object of my fixation slowed at a stop sign and turned on the blinker. It clicked into the stillness, marking every second that passed and neither of us brought up last night. Not just the kiss but what had come after that, too. Dracula's phone call, and the fact that our lives were about to potentially turn upside down again.

I'd asked Collith all my questions last night. The Order, it turned out, was a supernatural council formed of rulers from nearly every species. Witches, werewolves, vampires, fae, even nymphs. They only convened when it seemed like Fallenkind was being threatened or exposed. The most dire of circumstances, Collith told me, his voice tight with worry.

Although neither of us had said it out loud, I knew we were both thinking the same thing—the meeting was about me. I was the problem. Why else would our attendance be required?

"Do you think they're planning to kill me?" I'd asked.

"They can try," Collith said, his eyes glittering in a way I hadn't seen in a long time. These past few months, Collith had been a cool, calming presence in my life. Sometimes I forgot about the lightning that simmered beneath his skin.

The conversation floated through my thoughts for the next hour as we returned the rental car and made our way to the closest Door, which was through the bulkhead of an abandoned church. Within seconds, Collith and I found ourselves walking through familiar woods. Even now, neither of us said anything. Thick, green leaves rustled all around us and the air smelled like growing things. After a while, the path became even more beaten, and the branches retreated. A flock of geese appeared over the distant treetops, their wild cries echoing through the amber-tinted light. Collith and I arrived at the edge of the forest, and then I saw it—home.

Emma was outside, tending to the flowers she'd planted around the barn. She turned as if she heard us coming. It had been a good summer for Emma, despite how much she worried about me. There hadn't been any more health scares or trips to the hospital. I wanted to keep it that way, so every time we came back from a crime scene, I never went into much detail about what we'd found. Emma didn't ask, either.

While Collith and I finished crossing the yard, she got to her feet and brushed her hands off on the gardening apron I'd recently given her as a birthday present. "Good morning," she called.

I felt lighter, suddenly, and some of the darkness that had been crowding in my chest began to dissipate. "Good morning, Ems," I said.

She beamed at Collith as he walked over to her. Her thin, wrinkled arms rose to embrace him like they had been separated for months, though I was pretty sure she'd seen him a few days ago. Collith still bent to hug her back, just as he always did, and Emma's voice was muffled as she said, "I made pancakes. Would you like to join us?"

Collith straightened with a regretful expression. "I wish I could, but there are some things I need to do."

"What sort of things?" Emma demanded, and I pursed my lips, my shoulders giving a small twitch as I fought a laugh.

"Boring things," Collith said with a warm smile. He lifted his head, and I felt another tiny flutter when his gaze landed on me. "I'll see you in three days."

The reminder caused a knot of anxiety to form in my chest. In three days, I would be attending my first—and hopefully last—meeting of the Order.

Not trusting myself to respond in front of Emma, I just nodded. Collith walked over to kiss my forehead, then turned away. As I watched him go, I felt a gentle prickle on my skin. I turned to catch Emma watching me with that familiar, knowing look of hers. I swallowed a sigh and moved closer to her.

"I know I'm not a cute faerie, but could I get some pancakes?" I asked lightly.

"Of course you can." She wrapped her arm around me, careful as ever not to touch my skin, and we strode toward the door, moving into the building's shadow. The air instantly became cooler. I tipped my head back, taking in the familiar slope of the roof and the morning-tinted sky beyond it. A breath slipped past my lips and the tension left my shoulders, a single word singing through me. *Home*. For the first time in twenty-four hours, I felt safe.

But then I blinked, and our quiet barn became a scene from one of the murder houses. Red and blue lights shone over the yard and reflected in the glass windows. Uniforms swarmed everywhere and a faint, terrible scent clung to the air. I stood there, staring at my worst nightmare with frozen horror. Staring at the blood splattered on Nym's bedroom window.

I made a low, choked sound, but I didn't know if I was trying to shout or scream. Terror and denial raged through me like wildfire. No, this couldn't happen here. Not to them. This was a dream, just a terrible dream.

I made another sound, my mind latching onto the thought. A *dream*. Of course! It all made sense now. None of this was real, and I was asleep. I commanded myself to wake up. *Wake up, damn it!*

My fingers twitched. I couldn't move, couldn't breathe past the panic—

"Fortuna?"

Emma's voice broke through the high-pitched ringing in my ears. I blinked, and suddenly the awful scene was gone. The barn was exactly as it had been before. Still, serene, lit by the colors of morning as if someone had painted the siding pink while I was gone. Emma stood in the doorway, staring at me. A faint line had deepened between her brows, and I recognized it immediately. Worry.

Tasting Emma's fear on my tongue cleared my head, and faster than a blink, I gave her a weary smile. I trudged toward the barn as if I'd only paused from sheer exhaustion. "Coming," I said.

Emma didn't quite buy it, which was evident by how slowly she turned. But the older woman must've decided not to push me, because she went inside without another word. Trying to ignore a heavy sense of foreboding, I moved to follow.

My Shadow Court had sensed something, as well. As I walked to the open door, I felt their silent questions. The soft, hesitant touches that somehow felt like the barest brush of fingertips. I sent reassurances back and withdrew. I knew if I lingered, they'd see right through me. They would know how terrified I was. They would discover the truth that I had been keeping from everyone, including myself.

The truth that Collith might be right, and when the time came, I wouldn't be strong enough to save them.

At the threshold, I stopped again. Emma's footsteps sounded on the steps as I turned back and looked outside. Maybe to catch another glimpse of Collith, or scan the shadowed trees for something that didn't belong. Holding my breath, I searched the stirring leaves and the waking horizon. Nothing moved. Only birdsong drifted past my ears, followed by a gentle breeze that smelled like dew and freshly mown grass.

I exhaled and went inside.

CHAPTER THREE

Three days later, I stood outside the Seaside Motel.

We arrived in Maine near sunset, just as Dracula had directed when he'd called to say Collith and I had been summoned. As I stared at the quaint, slightly deteriorating building, knots of apprehension tightened in my stomach. I wondered what we were getting ourselves into, and if this would be a repeat of my other experiences when I'd met a Fallen monarch. It hadn't exactly gone well with Astrid, or Belanor, or Luther.

And now I was about to stand before an entire group of them.

Collith opened the door of the motel room for me, and I wasn't startled by the sight of a figure already standing inside. When Collith had come to the loft so we could walk to the Door together, he'd mentioned that we were meeting Laurie near the Order's headquarters. The Seelie King was a member, of course, so he was expected to be in attendance. I'd hidden my reaction from Collith, but it would be the first time Laurie and I had lain eyes on each other all summer. My heart had reacted at the thought of being in the same room as Laurie again, just as it did now.

He turned at the sound of our arrival, and the first thing I noticed was that he was wearing black.

I'd seen Laurie in black before, but never quite like this. His muscled legs were displayed in tight leather, and his dark shirt looked like it was from another time with its billowy sleeves and neckline ties. His piercing eyes were enhanced by the thick lines he'd drawn across his skin like war paint. They were striking, and jarring, and maybe a little frightening.

Which was exactly what Laurie had intended, no doubt.

"You have something on your face." Laurie leaned close, his brows drawn together as he examined me. His fingertips skimmed my cheekbone in the barest of touches, and a whisper of heat drifted through my stomach. A heat which promptly vanished when Laurie said, "Ah, I see now. It's *admiration*. Here, darling, let me get that drool at the corner of your mouth."

"We should get your head checked. You're seeing things." As I pushed his fingers away, trying to act normal so neither of them would notice my uneven pulse, I spotted a paper cup in Laurie's other hand. "Oh, thank God. Is there coffee?"

He took a sip and grimaced. "There's something. I'd say it tastes like dirt, but at least dirt has some flavor. Remind me why we couldn't meet at the Hilton? There's one down the street."

"Because we're only going to be here for an hour," Collith said, giving Laurie a hard look. "An *hour*, Laurelis. We can't be late for this."

Laurie rolled his eyes and flicked his wrist in a dismissive gesture, as if Collith were being totally unreasonable.

"What *are* we doing here for an hour?" I asked, my eyes darting between them.

Laurie looked at me as if the answer were obvious. "I brought what you're going to wear tonight. Get your head out of the gutter, Fortuna. Are we just pieces of meat to you?"

I didn't grace this with a response. "Bathroom?" I said, pointing.

Laurie nodded, his eyes gleaming. I walked past him and slipped into a dark room on the right. I flipped the light switch and turned. As promised, a black garment cover hung on a mounted hook. Just as I was about to close the door, Collith said something that made Laurie laugh. It rang out through the stillness, and I found myself smiling at the sound. I left the door open a crack and hurried to get undressed.

Once I'd returned to the main area, I faced the dingy mirror on the wall.

The dress was blue and silver. It looked like it was made of metal, with intricate designs carved onto every inch. When I'd put it on, I'd been surprised to find the material was soft. The sleeves were long and nearly transparent, clinging like a second skin. The design was cut in such a way that my entire back was exposed, but the train covered most of it. It dragged behind me, not like a wedding gown, but like a cape. A ridiculously long, heavy cape.

"This is a different look," I remarked, still studying myself.

Laurie shifted, and his face appeared next to mine. His rings flashed as he tucked a wayward strand of my hair back into place. "This is a different audience," he informed me. "We aren't just trying to intimidate some old faeries tonight. We want you to appear powerful but pure. Untouchable but righteous. It's not an easy thing to achieve. Luckily, you have me."

"Do I?" I murmured, looking at his reflection.

The words just slipped out. In an instant, I wished I could take them back, yet . . . I wanted to know the answer, too. Laurie went still, and our gazes met in the glass again. The room became so silent that I could hear sounds from outside—a seagull's call, and the rumble of an engine. My wild heartbeat, which had begun to quicken at what I saw in Laurie's eyes.

Before he could answer, the door behind us opened.

Collith's familiar scent greeted me, instantly comforting. He moved into my line of sight a moment later, his pale face filling the space on my other side. His hazel eyes seemed darker than they'd been an hour ago. He was on edge, and the fact that I could see it meant my own apprehension wasn't exactly unwarranted.

"The envoy should be here any minute. Are you ready?" Collith asked.

I fought an urge to swallow, knowing the faeries would hear it. I bent and picked up my train, then straightened and squared my shoulders. Resolve hardened in my stomach. "Ready as I'll ever be, I guess. Let's go."

"Fortuna." The seriousness in Collith's voice—more than usual, that is—made me turn. His jaw moved, the muscles flexing with tension. "If these creatures find out you're not only the creator of this beast, but that you're capable of making more things like him, they'll see you as a threat."

"Would they kill me on the spot or at least make it a nice, civil execution?" I asked lightly.

"That's not going to happen," Laurie interjected.

His voice was cool, but something in it reminded me just how deadly the Seelie King was beneath that pretty, smirking facade. I smiled at him faintly and put my hand on his arm in silent gratitude. It was the briefest of touches, just a slight press of my fingers, but Laurie's eyes burned as if I'd done so much more. My own eyes darted away, and I was careful not to look at Collith as I walked toward the door.

We left the motel in a tense silence. Collith and Laurie seemed to know exactly where we were going. They led me past the docks and down to the beach. Once we reached the sand, I paused to adjust my hold on the dress, making sure none of the ends would drag over the dirt. We began to walk alongside the shore. Despite the reason we were here, I couldn't help noticing the beauty of this place. The dying light cast shadows and color over the water, drawing my eyes to it. Farther out, I saw something that didn't belong.

I nudged Laurie, keeping my eyes on the lines of red amongst the calm waves. "What does that circle mean?"

His head turned, following the direction of my gaze. "A cruise ship supposedly went down there. It was blocked off for safety reasons," he said.

"Supposedly?" I repeated.

But this time, Laurie didn't answer.

We walked the rest of the way in silence. Laurie was texting, and Collith's eyes roamed constantly, following every movement, every sound. Eventually the sand ended in a dark outcropping, and I realized that a figure stood near it. The envoy Collith had mentioned, no doubt.

"What are the odds that you two will let me do most of the talking?" Collith asked us under his breath. Laurie snorted and I just gave him a sweet smile. He sighed and said, "Right."

As we approached the still figure, Laurie put his phone away. At first glance, the envoy seemed human. The fading sunlight touched her features and I noticed the crow's feet extending from the corners of her eyes. If I'd had to guess her age, I'd have put the stranger in her late forties or early fifties. She had shoulder-length blond hair and an hourglass figure, and she wore a brown pantsuit. I couldn't sense any power around her.

Honestly, if it hadn't been for where we were, I would've assumed she was like any other human soccer mom.

"Well met," the envoy said, giving us a warm smile that made me think of Emma. "Welcome to Raas. My name is Honey. I am the keeper here, and I shall be your host for the evening."

"So formal," Laurie murmured.

Honey beamed at him. "Laurie, dear, it's so good to see you."

I waited for them to hug, but Laurie just winked at her. Honey was blushing when she searched us for weapons. I'd left all mine behind tonight, since I was trying not to seem like a threat. The others had evidently done the same, since Honey turned away empty-handed. We all started walking toward the dark outcropping, and I held back all my questions, knowing I'd probably get answers in a minute. As we drew closer, I realized there was an opening in the rocks similar to the Door back home. Honey slipped into the darkness, and I did the same, followed closely by Collith and Laurie.

My eyes adjusted quickly, and unsurprisingly, I found myself in a cave. But after we'd taken a few steps, the darkness fell away, driven back by weak sunlight coming in through another opening in the rocks that was on the other side of the cave, almost big enough for a boat to fit through. There was no way to get to it, other than swimming—water glittered and lapped gently against the walls. Slick rocks peeked out from the surface like sirens as we went down the stairs.

A minute later, my three companions halted at the edge of an uneven path we'd been walking along, so I did the same. There was an air of expectancy around all of them, as if we were waiting for something. I held my dress and my questions, and I was rewarded when a sound eventually reached my ears. It was subtle, like a distant humming. I frowned, glancing at Laurie, but he kept his focus on the water.

I was about to speak when something came out of it.

I was so startled that I took an involuntary step backward. I quickly realized that it was just a machine rising slowly from the depths. It let out a hissing sound as it ground to a halt, water streaming down its sides. Seconds later, a pair of doors slid open and revealed an elevator, of sorts.

Two of the walls were made of metal, while the third was completely glass, allowing us to see the dark ocean beyond. Our group stepped into the confined space, and I felt my first flicker of true apprehension when the doors closed with a sound of finality. Guess there was no going back now.

The elevator descended smoothly. I stared into the dark water, half-expecting something to come rushing at us from the depths. Something with sharp teeth and cold eyes. But we plunged downward without event, and after a few seconds, the elevator came to another gradual stop. I turned and waited for the doors to open at what was presumably the bottom of the cave, but then it shifted to the left and we were moving again. I almost fell into Collith. A gentle, steadying hand touched my waist. I righted myself without taking my eyes off the doors, and the hand fell away, but I still felt the imprint of those cool fingertips like a wordless reassurance. *I've got you.*

Seconds later, the doors opened into a long, arched walkway.

"Stay close to us, please," Collith murmured, his voice edged with tension. For once, I just nodded in agreement. We moved forward, and I looked around curiously, allowing my dress to fall to the floor.

Knowing the long history of the Order, I'd expected a meeting place that was as ancient as its founders. But the structure was sleek and modern. These walls were also made of glass. We started down the walkway, and bright lights filled the tunnel, making it feel like this was just a visit to SeaWorld. Nervous laughter rose up inside me at the thought.

"The humans don't bother us here," Laurie said from behind.

Something in his tone made me turn, and I caught his glance toward the surface. *The red circle,* I thought. *I would bet my favorite gun that a cruise ship has never gone down here.*

"Let me guess. A faerie came up with that one," I remarked. Laurie just smirked.

We entered a chamber that had been divided into three rooms, and it was immediately apparent we were the earliest arrivals. The first room held a refreshment table and a bar, which was where Laurie stopped. An attendant stood behind it. She looked human, but the fact that she was here made me think otherwise. The second room was empty, with only a single document displayed on one of the walls. I began moving toward it, but then I noticed how the other walls contained faint shapes, like watermarks, each of them different. I traced the closest mark with my finger, frowning as I tried to discern its meaning. Collith appeared at my side, and he touched the image in the same spot, our fingers brushing in a flare of warm attraction.

He spoke without looking at me, his hazel eyes moving over the lines on the stone. "We couldn't possibly fit every species at the table, of course, so these images depict how they're all represented. For instance, the water nymph monarch speaks for all creatures of the water. The Queen of the Shapeshifters stands in for anything that can change its form, like dragons and weres—with the exception of the wolves and kitsunes, of course, stubborn creatures that they are—and the Vampire King is here for the parasites and predators, et cetera."

He gestured to each mark as he mentioned the representatives. I tried to commit the images to memory as best I could, since the knowledge could come in handy during this meeting. Maybe it would even be key to my survival, I thought grimly.

I noticed there wasn't a representative for the goblins, but I kept this observation to myself.

Moments later, Laurie returned holding three drinks in his hands, which he somehow made look effortless. He handed me a glass of wine and said, "Honey left to fetch the next guest. Shall we?"

I just nodded, my nerves returning in a rush at those words. *The next guest*.

Once again, Collith and Laurie positioned themselves on either side of me, and we turned away from the marks. As we continued walking, I tried to keep a loose grip on my wine, knowing that every detail about me would be noticed and assessed.

Somehow, even without a crown or a throne, I'd found myself playing the game again. The game that made me feel alive and terrible all at once, as if I were standing at the edge of a cliff with nothing but an abyss awaiting at the bottom. There was a reason I had walked away from all of this, but no matter how hard I tried, it always seemed to pull me back again. If I was going to survive this game, I needed to pay attention.

The third room, I saw as we approached, contained a strange table. It was enormous and round, with narrow gaps that led into the wide opening where the rest of the table was supposed to be. Dark water gleamed at the center of the opening. Probably a fountain, I thought, or the world's creepiest wading pool.

Most of the walls were more plates of glass, casting an otherworldly shimmer over everything. Only one surface was made of stone, and just like the document in the second room, a single item had been mounted on its surface. Since there was no one else here, I drew closer to the object, wanting to study it. This thing looked *old*.

Behind me, Laurie spoke in a bored tone, as if he were reciting from a textbook. "The Horn is one of the three holy items in this world, and it's supposed to summon the Host of Heaven," he said.

"The Host," I repeated, eyebrows raised. "You mean . . ."

He nodded. "Angels, yes. Full-blooded, unbanished, all-powerful angels. The kind of fuckers you *really* don't want to mess with."

"What are the other two items?" I asked curiously. How had I never heard of this before?

Laurie held up his fingers as he listed them off. "The Holy Lance, which was supposedly the spear that pierced Christ during his crucifixion. And the Holy Sword, also known as Cortana or Excalibur."

I studied the ancient instrument. "Seems kind of arrogant, doesn't it? Displaying the Horn like this?"

"It's completely useless to our kind. Only a true angel can blow the Horn. Not even the Court elders were able to make it sound." Laurie tilted his head, his expression becoming thoughtful. "But I think they hung it up because it looks like an enormous cock. These meetings are terribly dull, and we must have *some* way to get through it."

"Laurelis Dondarte," a voice said from the doorway. The

speaker sounded tired. "Must you always treat this sacred union with such disrespect?"

Laurie spun on his heel, already wearing an exaggerated expression of contrition. In a flash, he was across the room and standing before a frail-looking female in the doorway. Honey stood beside her. As Laurie bowed smoothly at the waist, brushing a feather-light kiss across the back of the old woman's hand, the envoy slipped away.

"Forgive me, Mother," Laurie said ruefully. "I'm a scoundrel trying to change his ways, but you know as well as I how hard change can be. I'm grateful to have you to remind me when I slip back into old habits."

The female scowled and snatched her hand away, flapping it at Laurie as though he were a gnat. "Oh, away with you. You don't even make an effort when you're lying."

Laurie evaded her easily, his mouth stretching into a wide grin. "You look lovely as ever. Lady Sworn, may I introduce Wichonne Babdock, the Mother of Witches. Mother, this is Fortuna Sworn."

"Well met," I said, giving her a respectful nod.

The Mother of Witches regarded me with a shrewdness that I couldn't help but admire. While her body might be deteriorating, it was clear that Wichonne Babdock's mind was perfectly intact. "I have heard much about you," she remarked.

"It's probably all true," I told her with a small shrug.

Amusement shone in the old witch's eyes. "It would seem so."

"I am many things, but I'm not a liar. Doesn't your kind have a saying about that?" someone asked, appearing beside the Mother of Witches with a glass of wine in her hand.

Mercy Wardwell. I hid a faint surge of annoyance, and bit back a comment about being surprised she could actually show up to something. Why was she here?

She'd never been my favorite person, considering she had a habit of spouting dark prophecies and making me feel like shit about myself. But the last time I'd spoken to Mercy, I'd called her for help, desperate to save Finn's life. The witch had practically hung up on me, then sent Savannah in her stead.

And ever since Finn had died, I'd been asking myself the question over and over—would he still be alive if Mercy Wardwell had come?

Out loud I said, "Actually, that was just something my dad said."

Savannah must've told her about it, I thought sourly. As usual, Mercy seemed to know exactly what was going through my head. The gleam of amusement in her eyes was nearly identical to Wichonne's as she replied, "Well met, Lady Sworn. Let us hope tonight's proceedings aren't quite so . . . lively as the other events you've attended."

Just as I started to respond, Collith shifted, and his arm brushed subtly against mine. Once again I bit back what I actually wanted to say and forced a tight smile. "Let's hope."

Mercy's lips were still curved in a faint smile as the witches moved toward the table. Desperate for a distraction, I turned to search the other rooms again. But someone else appeared in the doorway, blocking my view of whoever might be standing beyond it. He had blue-tipped dark hair and swords crisscrossed over his back. *No,* I thought when I noted the long grips. Those weren't swords—they were katanas. Somehow the male's black leather clothes didn't make a sound as he walked. His dark gaze met mine, and he looked at me for a single beat before his face turned away. I knew I'd been thoroughly dismissed.

"Who is that?" I asked under my breath.

Laurie followed my gaze toward the newcomer. The warrior was moving over to the table now, but he didn't look in our direction again. A female stuck to his side, her hand resting on the hilt of the katana at her hip.

"That's Katashi Nakamura," Laurie said. "He speaks for the

kitsunes. And that's his Second, Yaeko. She's one of the best fighters in the world."

There was nothing in his voice to hint at distaste, but I got the sense Laurie wasn't the kitsunes' biggest fan. "Even better than you?" I asked, putting my back to them.

He started to answer just as Honey returned with more arrivals.

A towering, barrel-chested male stood beside a slightly shorter female. The air around her was so thick with power that I didn't question for a moment which of the two of them was the ruler. I couldn't pinpoint their species, though. The female had short, black hair with blunt ends, and the piercings on her face glinted—her nose, her eyebrow, her chin. Her leather boots creaked as she circled the table and plopped into one of the seats. When she sat back, her jacket opened, and I caught a glimpse of what she wore beneath it. The female's T-shirt had a picture of a smiley face that was flicking everyone off.

Her voice was raspy as she said, "So it's true what they say."

This again. I raised my gaze, already knowing she'd be looking back at me. "They say a lot of things. You'll have to narrow it down for me," I answered.

She inclined her head, and her mascara-lined eyes moved down my body. "One of my wolves described a blond with big tits. Since you're neither, the rumors about your kind must be true."

"Lady Sworn, may I present the Matron of Wolves?" Collith said. "This is Anna Tombs."

My eyebrows rose.

"You were expecting an old crone?" she asked with a smirk. "I believe Wichonne over there has already got that covered."

"I heard that," the Mother of Witches called from the other side of the table.

"Good," Anna called back. She refocused on me and added, "Cora speaks highly of you."

The mention of Cora immediately made me feel lighter. I hadn't checked in with my young friend for a while. I smiled at the Matron of Wolves and asked, "How is she?"

"Coming into her own," Anna answered. She raised her eyebrows, and one of the silver hoops in her skin glinted. "Thanks to you, it seems."

"That's all her, actually," I said, my smile growing.

Anna looked at me as if I'd done something she hadn't expected. After a moment, she turned to the huge, silent figure standing behind her chair and smacked his stomach with the back of her hand. "This is my—"

The water in the center of the room pulled back as if someone had suddenly placed a drain in the ocean. I spun, already reaching for a weapon that wasn't there. My eyes widened as a figure hauled himself out of the hole.

Not a fountain then, I thought dimly.

Our latest arrival was completely naked, every inch of him made of hard muscle. He straightened and scraped his golden-brown hair back, his enormous cock swinging back and forth as he got to his feet.

No one seemed taken aback by the male's nudity. Another human-looking attendant rushed forward to offer a blue robe, and the male exuded boredom as he pulled it on, securing a lazy knot at his waist. He scanned the people who had gathered so far. His blue eyes landed on me and stayed there.

"Arriving with a faerie king on each arm. Who is this creature that she can enter our chamber with such arrogance?" the male asked, studying me more closely. He didn't look bored anymore. Behind him, someone else was coming out of the water—a second naked male with gills in his throat and a perfectly chiseled physique.

Before I could respond, a new voice floated through the room. The sultry tones dripped with amusement. "You've been swimming with the fish too long, Your Majesty, if you don't know who

Fortuna Sworn is. She's had the shadow world buzzing for the past year."

I'd know that voice anywhere. Already smiling, I turned to face Viessa Folduin, Queen of the Unseelie Court, who had, somehow, become one of my best friends over these past few months. Nuvian stood at her side, of course. I'd seen him a lot, too, but our relationship hadn't improved over time. Nuvian and I would never like each other, and that was fine with both of us. Viessa didn't give a shit, either.

Like the rest of my family, the Ice Queen seemed to have a sixth sense for the moments I was unraveling. She'd appear on a Friday night, only giving me five minutes to get ready before she whisked me away to some club on the other side of the world, where she dragged me beneath the strobe lights and forced me to remember the good parts of being alive.

I may not have approved of Viessa's choice in bedmates, but that was none of my business, and I had my own history of questionable choices in that department. We had something else in common, too. A secret that I'd put together in pieces, the more I'd gotten to know her.

The Ice Queen was just as lonely as I was.

When we were together, we weren't rulers or power players. There was no chessboard beneath us as we drank cocktails and laughed at the human antics happening around us. We were just... Viessa and Fortuna.

I knew we both valued our strange friendship, and that was why neither of us tried to be strategic now, even though it might've been in our best interests. We ignored the press of watching eyes as Viessa's arms wound around me briefly. I hugged her back, ignoring my usual instinct to avoid touch. For an instant, I felt the slightest whisper of ice on my skin, and the flavor of her fears skittered over my tongue.

We pulled away at the same time, giving each other small, secret smiles. Then Viessa nodded at the male still standing nearby, who was obviously waiting for an introduction. "Fortuna, this is Alexander of House Nørgård. He's one of the water nymph kings," she said.

"One of them?" I echoed, startled. "How many are there?"

Alexander's blue eyes drank me in like I was a shot of tequila after a long, terrible day. "There are seven, my lady. One for each sea. We draw sticks every time there's one of these meetings, and I drew the short one today. Or at least, I thought I did. May I just say, I wouldn't hesitate to give up my throne if you asked it of me."

I just gave him an empty stare. "Why the hell would I want a throne? Been there, done that."

"She has fire, as well as beauty," the nymph replied with a laugh. "No wonder there are so many kneeling at your altar, Lady Sworn."

His companion didn't seem nearly as taken with me. The second water nymph glared in my direction with contempt in his eyes. I was about to respond when Laurie tilted his head, that infamous silver hair glinting as he said, "I suggest you stop looking at her that way, fish boy."

I wasn't certain which male he was talking to until Alexander's eyebrows rose. "Why?"

"Because I know at least a thousand good places to hide a dead body," Laurie deadpanned. Alexander's amused expression didn't change, but his companion's nostrils flared with outrage.

"Pardon my friends. They're themselves today," I interjected, giving the Seelie King a look that said, *I can handle this, thanks*. He just looked back with a light in his eyes that made me realize how much I had missed him during the months we'd been apart.

I drew my attention back to the water nymph king, who looked like he hadn't missed a thing. He glanced between us with an inscrutable expression before he focused on Laurie. When he spoke, the humor in his voice was gone. "You don't frighten me, Pointy Ears."

At this, something dark and primal rose within my body. "Do not," I said quietly, "threaten him."

The air shifted as my power swelled, and everyone must've felt it, because the low conversations around us went quiet once more.

"Easy, cousin," Alexander murmured. He had placed a restraining hand on his companion's chest, but he didn't take his attention off me. His eyes flicked between mine, and his voice was full of wonder as he asked, "What *are* you?"

I looked back at him coolly. "Out of your league."

"Shall we sit?" Collith suggested abruptly, gesturing toward the table.

We weren't exactly off to a good start. This was all Laurie's fault, I decided as I sat down and rearranged my dress. The Seelie King claimed one of the chairs beside me, and I whispered from the corner of my mouth, "There's this thing called *tact*. Something you obviously were deprived of."

"And clearly I soaked up all that was left, since you have absolutely none," Laurie volleyed back under his breath. A laugh bubbled up in my throat.

"Are you two finished?" Collith cut in from my other side, keeping his voice low.

My skin prickled again. I pulled away from Laurie and glanced around, confirming that everyone was still watching us. Heat flooded my cheeks, but I raised my chin. Thankfully, just a moment later, the room's focus changed. I turned to see who the latest arrival was.

Dracula stood in the doorway.

The vampire's intelligent eyes immediately met mine, and I watched them crinkle at the corners. "It's lovely to see you again, Lady Fortuna," he said with an elegant bow.

"Dracula." I didn't move, but I gave him a warm smile in return. Once again, I could feel others in the room staring. I was a little surprised, myself—I hadn't forgotten about the time

Dracula gave me coffee spiked with vampire blood, but when you were in a room full of powerful, supernatural strangers and short on friends, beggars couldn't be choosers.

Dracula's gaze shifted toward the others seated at the table. "The Vampire King sends his regrets, and sends me in his stead," he informed them.

"No surprise there," someone muttered. I couldn't tell who.

"Now that we're all here, can we get to the matter at hand?" Alexander's companion asked snidely. His cousin, I remembered. "I prefer to spend as little time near land as possible."

"We're not all here." This was from Wichonne Babdock.

"What *is* the matter at hand?" Alexander drawled, leaning back in his chair.

The werewolf alpha raised her eyebrows. "Do you not watch the news? Wake up and smell the bloodbath. Something is eating people like they're an all-you-can-eat buffet. And whatever it is, the Beast apparently has no concerns about exposing our kind. There hasn't been a threat like this since Jack the Ripper."

I fought to keep the surprise and curiosity from my expression. Jack the Ripper had been Fallen?

Wichonne Babdock extended her arm and tapped her gnarled finger on the table. "Something is at work in the shadow world. The seers moan in my halls, and there have been tidings—"

"Not with the tidings," Alexander groaned. "Here we go again."

Mercy's eyes narrowed at him.

"Why are *we* here?" I interjected. "Collith and I are no longer associated with the Unseelie Court."

"Because you've been spotted on the Beast's trail," someone said from behind me. A ripple of awareness went through the room, and the tension heightened. I turned around to discover which new arrival had gotten everyone so worked up. When I saw who stood in the doorway, my stomach dropped in shock. *Holy shit*.

It was the shapeshifter from the black market. The girl who

had transformed into an owl and flown away after I'd freed her from a cage.

When our eyes met, she tilted her head in acknowledgment. "Well met, Lady Sworn. I am Nan, Queen of the Shapeshifters," she said.

I was still reeling, but a quiet voice in my head urged me not to reveal the fact that I'd met this queen before.

"Well met, Your Majesty," I replied.

I felt that telltale prickle over my skin, and I turned again, glancing across the table. The kitsune wasn't ignoring me anymore. Instead, he was looking at me thoughtfully, and there was a glint in his eyes that I didn't like.

"The Seelie King," he murmured. "The Unseelie Queen. The vampires. The witches. The werewolves. The Shapeshifter Queen herself. You have friends in high places, Fortuna Sworn. You may be more dangerous than the creature currently eating its way down the eastern seaboard."

Laurie shifted. It was subtle, but the small movement spoke volumes. This definitely wasn't going well. *Damn it,* I thought. Apparently I was a shitty liar, and we also hadn't been careful enough when it came to our pursuit of Oliver. Or *the Beast*, as this lot were calling him. There was no use denying it.

What could I tell them about Oliver without sounding insane? What if they didn't even believe it? Hell, what if they decided I was too dangerous to continue living, just as Collith had warned me?

Nan bought us some time as she started toward the last empty chair. Her movements were graceful and light, like a deer creeping through sun-dappled woods. I noticed that no one seemed to be guarding her, which meant she hadn't brought any protection. If I had to guess why, I'd say that Nan was the sort of creature no one ever fucked with.

Focus, Fortuna. I fought the urge to let out a nervous breath—every creature in this room would hear it. They could probably hear my heartbeat, too. They'd know if I lied. I had to do this the fae way, and dance the line between the truth and my own version of it.

Just in case God did care about my fate in some way, I mentally sent out a brief prayer. Then I opened my mouth.

As if he knew I was on the verge of confessing, Laurie quickly leaned forward. Collith, too, moved like he was about to speak, but Laurie beat him to it. "The creature is a beast of the Seelie Court. A witch's spell gone wrong that we have kept contained, until recent unfortunate events," he said.

The lie rolled so smoothly off his tongue that I was reminded, once again, of Laurie's darkness. Violence and deception were as natural to him as sex or breathing.

"*Recent unfortunate events?*" Dracula echoed, clearly skeptical.

Maybe Laurie wasn't as good a liar as I'd thought.

"It's a Seelie problem. We'll handle it," he said. Nothing about Laurie's posture changed, but some of the easiness had left his voice.

Dracula heard it, as well. The corner of his mouth tilted up, but I couldn't tell if he was mocking Laurie or just amused by him. His tone was courteous as ever as he replied, "I mean no disrespect, faerie, but my warriors would be much more efficient than your Guardians."

During the brief time I'd known him, I had learned that Dracula had no limits when it came to keeping Fallenkind a secret. He would torture, manipulate, and kill to glean information or eliminate a threat. If this vampire went after Oliver, the Beast's death would be agonizing and slow.

I'd also vowed to do it myself.

I darted a glance at Collith, and he saw the objection in my eyes. He refocused on Dracula. His voice revealed nothing as he said, "It won't just be King Laurelis's Guardians. He will have my considerable power, as well, along with Lady Sworn's."

"And why is that?" Katashi demanded, leaning forward in his chair. "You never mentioned why you've been hunting the Beast."

Once again, all the attention at the table shifted to me, and I realized the question would just keep coming up until I gave an answer. Collith and Laurie must've reached the same conclusion—neither of them intervened this time. Another silence fell while everyone waited for my response. I scrambled to think of something, anything that would steer them away from making a connection between my powers and Oliver's sudden appearance in the world.

In a rush of realization, it occurred to me that I *had* an obvious motive for following the Beast. It was actually the truth, too, so it wouldn't raise any alarms to a room full of lie detectors.

Just hold on, Finn. I just need you to hold on a little longer.

Forcing myself to think about the night I'd knelt in a pool of Finn's blood, the night I had held his broken body and filled his head with pretty things while he'd died, I met Katashi's gaze and said, "The Beast killed someone very dear to me. I'm following it because I plan to obliterate this thing from the face of the Earth."

No one spoke, but every figure was perfectly still. I knew they were probably listening for any hint of deception. They all must've heard the truth in my voice, my heartbeat, because there were no more questions or challenges.

"I say let him slaughter all the humans he likes. There's too many of them anyway," the water nymph king's companion said. I couldn't remember his name, if I'd even learned it.

"You sound like someone who's grown tired of having a full set of teeth," I said calmly.

The male's eyes flashed, and he turned in my direction, snarling. "How *dare* you speak to me that way, you insignificant maggot!"

As he spoke, he raised his hand to strike me. But he had to lean slightly over Laurie to do so, and Laurie moved so fast I didn't realize what had happened until a spray of blood appeared on the table, the floor, the wall. For an instant, the water nymph's body hovered there, and what remained of his neck spurted like a fountain. Then it slowly toppled over and hit the floor in a graceless heap.

"Holy *fuck*," Alexander said, leaping up from his chair. Responding to his magic, the water in the middle of the room shot into the air, splashing all over the floor and the edges of the table.

"Is he dead?" Viessa asked, leaning back to peer at the body. Nuvian stood behind her with his sword half-drawn, his body taut with readiness.

"No, no, I'm sure a healer can reattach his head," Laurie chirped, settling back into to his seat. An attendant was already rushing forward to tend to the mess.

Alexander turned to the Shapeshifter Queen indignantly. "I demand retribution—"

"You demand nothing." Laurie rested his elbows on the table and placed his chin on his crossed hands. "I was well within my rights, as per this council's own rules. He attacked me, and I defended myself."

"He didn't attack *you*," Alexander snarled, his overly bright eyes darting toward me. Collith and Laurie both went dangerously still.

Fuck, I thought. We'd had enough decapitations for one night. I opened my mouth to—

"King Laurelis is right," Nan announced.

Alexander stared at the shapeshifter silently, as if he was considering something. Another moment passed, the air practically vibrating with tension. We were a room of predators on high alert. From the corner of my eye, I saw Honey shift closer to our gathering, which confirmed that she was Fallen. No human would risk getting in the middle of *this*.

After another moment, Alexander Nørgård relented. His face was turned from me, so I couldn't see his expression as he slowly returned to his chair. The pressure in the air eased, and shoulders relaxed around the table. Guess the water nymph was smarter than he looked.

The kitsune's Second wasn't so smart.

"You're going to let that Seelie scum get away with murder based on a technicality?" she demanded.

It took a moment for her name to come back to me—Yaeko. The fox glared across the room at Laurie, her lip curling with hatred. I expected him to waggle his fingers back at her, but Laurie just gazed back at Yaeko with a familiar gleam in his eyes. It was the same way he'd looked at Ian O'Connell, once, shortly before Laurie had murdered him.

Oh yeah, I thought. There was *definitely* a history there.

The Shapeshifter Queen's eyes narrowed at Yaeko. "Technicalities are the foundation this organization was built upon."

Her power moved through the room again, and even I felt a whisper of wariness go down my spine. I definitely wouldn't want to be on the receiving end of *that* look. Apparently Yaeko wasn't a fan, either, because she didn't speak again.

Another silence fell over the room.

"Perhaps the simplest solution is to stay the course, Your Majesty," Wichonne murmured, tilting her gray head in deference. "If Lady Sworn and her companions intend to end the Beast, and they have proven to be capable of finding it, why not let them?"

The queen's mouth was puckered in thought, her index finger tapping absently. No one interrupted or pushed her. Not even when she said at last, her voice cold with warning, "You may continue your hunt for the Beast, but you are forbidden from interfering with the Order's efforts. If we find it first, we won't hesitate to eliminate the creature. King Laurelis, I will also grant you lenience for creating it in the first place. You have been a longtime friend to this organization and we know your strength of character. But if there's another incident like this, I will not be so forgiving."

Laurie gave her a respectful nod. "Thank you, Your Grace."

Dismissing the faerie king as if he were little more than a child, Nan's piercing gaze moved around the table. "While they act on behalf of this organization, King Laurelis, Lord Collith, and Lady Sworn are under my protection. Should harm come to them, any responsible parties will face the usual repercussions," she said.

Viessa leaned forward. "They will be considered an enemy of the Unseelie Court, as well."

Nuvian loved *that*—I could tell by the way his nostrils flared. I tamped down the urge to grin at him, reminding myself that I'd agreed to play nice. My eyes met Viessa's, whose lips deepened ever-so-slightly at the corners as though she knew *exactly* what I was thinking. Affection for the Unseelie Queen rushed through me. It caused a tight sensation in my heart, as if someone had pinched it.

Nan stood from her chair and looked at each one of us, her fingers steepled atop the table. When her eyes met mine, the creature I saw within those depths was something very old and completely unafraid. I caught myself wondering how on earth any goblin had managed to capture her.

"This meeting of the Order is adjourned," Nan said, cutting my thoughts short.

There was a collective shift in the room. The shapeshifter turned away and Anna immediately muttered something under her breath to her beta, who let out a chuckle. Whatever she'd said made the kitsunes stiffen with outrage.

I felt a tug of amusement, and I decided that I liked the Matron of Wolves.

My amusement faded instantly when Nan's scent reached me. As she passed, she gave a nod of acknowledgment. It was so subtle that I almost missed it. I understood exactly what that gesture meant—the Shapeshifter Queen considered her debt to me paid in full. Not only had she saved our asses, but she'd staved off all my other enemies while I hunted down Oliver and fixed the mess I had made. I'd say that definitely made us even.

Nan didn't head for the doorway. Instead, she slipped through one of the gaps in the table leading to that dark, unmoving pool at its center. With a regal tilt to her head, Nan stepped into the water. Then I blinked, and she was gone. Her dress floated on the surface while ripples spread toward the edges of the pool, the water disturbed by whatever had just plunged into the depths. One of the uniformed attendants moved to retrieve the gown. Although her expression revealed nothing, I detected the faintest tang of fear.

"What are the 'usual repercussions'?" I asked Collith under my breath as we stood. The room filled with the low murmur of other conversations happening around us.

Laurie stopped beside me and offered his arm. "Oh, you know. Long, diabolical torture and a slow, agonizing death. *No one* wants Honey coming after them. Not even me," he added.

My eyebrows shot up as we walked away from the table. "Honey?" I echoed. "The envoy?"

"I am the keeper, Lady Sworn." Honey appeared in front of us, and I jumped. She'd moved so silently. She gave me a warm smile and added, "May I escort you to the elevator?"

The fact that she wanted us to get a head start, and also planned to walk with us every step of the way, hinted that maybe Collith really hadn't been paranoid about the risks of coming here. Would the other members of the Order disobey Nan's direct orders?

They were Fallen. Defiance was in our blood.

As Honey waited for an answer, my gaze fell upon Laurie's hand, which hung limply at his side. A quiet jolt of recognition went through me—I knew that stance. Apparently Honey wasn't the only one who thought we were in danger, because Laurie was getting ready to reach for a hidden dagger. Honey might be good, but Laurie was better. I would've bet money he'd managed to keep at least one weapon hidden when Honey conducted her search earlier.

Seeing him on edge made my pulse kick up a notch, and I

realized if Alexander wanted revenge for his cousin's death, or if the kitsunes acted on their vendetta against Laurie, now was the time to do it. Here where there were no guards or Courts behind us.

"We'd appreciate that," I told Honey, keeping my voice low and steady.

She immediately led us toward the doorway. Viessa and I nodded at each other in passing, but the Unseelie Queen didn't try to stop us for chitchat. She'd probably seen the danger before I had. No one else attempted to say goodbye, or seemed to notice we were leaving. An act, of course. They could hear every footstep we made, every word spoken. But no one acknowledged our departure except the water nymph king; I felt his eyes on me as we retraced our steps through the three connected rooms.

Honey and Laurie made polite conversation along the way, but I was so eager to get out of Raas that I couldn't focus on what they were saying. We reached the elevator, which was open and empty, as if it were beckoning us and urging, *Get in*. I didn't even pause long enough to gather up my dress.

We'd just crossed the metal threshold when Alexander appeared—he must've followed us. Honey touched the panel while he kept walking toward the elevator. I recognized the look in his eyes all too well, and suddenly I knew he wasn't thinking about his cousin or any sort of revenge. Laurie must've seen it, too, because he made a sound of disdain beside me.

If I ever attended another meeting of the Order again, it would be too soon, I thought as the doors closed on the water nymph king's face.

This time, Collith and Laurie stood with their backs to the water. I did the same, but I couldn't help glancing behind me. My mind filled with a memory of the Leviathan, its wide jaws opening as it hurtled through the deep. I remembered Nan stepping into that hole without hesitation. What sort of creature had she become that she didn't fear what else might be in here with us?

"Okay?" Laurie murmured, bumping my shoulder with his. I must've made some kind of noise or movement.

I gave him a quick, distracted smile and nodded, fighting the urge to look back again. "Okay," I said.

But I could've sworn, just for a moment, that I'd seen the glint of eyes in the dark.

CHAPTER FOUR

"Well, that went better than expected."

The sound of Laurie's voice was jarring. All of us had been completely silent, even after we'd left Honey at the elevator. I shot Laurie a look of disbelief as I held up my skirt again, preparing to ascend the steps.

"Were we at the same meeting? You beheaded someone," I reminded him.

"Exactly. *One* person, and no one is going to miss that little pimple. I'd say everyone was downright civil," Laurie said cheerfully. He started climbing the steps beside me, despite his ability to sift. He kept his hands in his pockets, and every so often, his elbow gently brushed mine.

On my other side, Collith remained silent, a frown hovering at the corners of his full lips. I knew he was thinking about our task—finding Oliver before the Order did. I watched the slight nuances in his expression as he went from thought to thought. Planning. Weighing. Calculating. Once, I'd resented the way his mind worked.

Now I admired it.

I opened my mouth to ask if we had a plan, but in the next

breath, I realized that I didn't want to talk about Oliver anymore. I didn't even want to think about him. It had been a long day, and there wasn't anything we could do about the Beast right now. As I searched for something else to say, my mind went back to the meeting, and I remembered my curiosity when Dracula had arrived alone.

"Where was the Vampire King?" I asked abruptly.

Collith's expression was still distracted. "Other than Dracula, no one has seen him in centuries. It's widely believed amongst the Fallen that he may be the oldest of us, older even than the fae elders. Some think the Vampire King predates the Fall. I wonder what that might do to someone, living in the shadows for so long."

I knew what it did. Collith did, too. I could tell from the way his jaw tightened that we were both remembering the Dark Prince and everything he'd done to us.

I didn't want to think about Lucifer, either. I returned my focus to the conversation. "If no one has seen him, how do you know the Vampire King is real?" I pointed out.

"How does anyone know the Nightmare Queen is real?" Laurie's voice murmured in my ear just as we stepped out of the cave and into the night. Before I could answer, I felt his lips nip at the tender outer shell of my ear. I made a startled sound and shoved him away. Laurie's laugh rang out into the night.

"I don't think I've ever heard Fortuna squeak before," Collith said, watching us with a smile.

I rolled my eyes at Laurie. "You are *such* a child."

When we reached the beach, I expected the Seelie King to vanish. But he stayed at my side, talking easily with Collith. Not about the Order, or Lucifer, or Oliver—they talked about books and art, music and distant cities, politics and old films. I listened, interjecting now and then with questions. Both of them had been alive so much longer than I had, and they'd seen things I could only dream about. Maybe someday, I told myself silently. If we survived the coming months and all the enemies that were trying to kill us.

Collith and Laurie walked with me to town, where we found the Door and made our way through the woods. Night had fallen, but neither of my companions seemed worried about what might be tucked in the darkness. It was because they were together, I thought, watching their expressions in the moonlight. They didn't worry about creatures like wendigos or werewolves when the other was near. In spite of everything they'd been through, and their long, tragic history, Collith and Laurie had found their way back to each other.

Strangely, the thought stirred no jealousy in my heart.

Collith and Laurie walked me right up to the barn. As I reached to pull the door open, both of their scents wafted past, soft and fleeting. I turned to say good night. But when I faced them, the words faded in my throat. The water nymph king's remark came back to me, faint and haunting. *Arriving with a faerie king on each arm*.

I looked at Collith first, and I thought about how kind and patient he'd been this summer. I looked at Laurie and remembered every small act, every painful sacrifice. They both loved me and I loved both of them. We had never really talked about it, the three of us. What we were or what we could be. But it needed to be talked about, because my silence wasn't fair to anyone. I gathered a breath, and my heart rivaled the thunder of the wild horses Laurie had taken me to see once.

"I know you deserve better," I said, glancing between them again. "Both of you. I wish I could offer more. *Be* more. I just . . . I can't . . ."

I kept fumbling over my tongue, so eventually, I gave up and fell silent. Frustration simmered in my veins. Then Collith surprised me by smiling. A soft, tender smile. "You are exactly who you've always been, Fortuna, and that is more than enough," he said.

Laurie took my hand and pressed a kiss against the back of it. "Get some sleep, my lady. Our quest can wait one more night."

They each bowed to me, and I watched them walk away together. Seconds later, Collith and Laurie disappeared into the woods. If either of the faeries looked back, they were too far away for me to see it. I wondered where they were going. Knowing Laurie, they'd probably end up on the other side of the world somewhere. In a London pub, maybe, or a rooftop restaurant in Tokyo. Smiling at the thought, I began to step inside. At the last second, I drew back for a double-take—there *was* a figure at the edge of the trees again.

But it wasn't Laurie or Collith.

Mab stepped into the open, the long sleeves of her gown swaying in a breeze.

"It's happening again," she called, her voice drifting across the yard.

I knew faeries and their games—the old ones had become especially predictable. Mab wanted me to ask, *What's happening?* She hoped I would step right on top of the invisible net she'd placed between us.

But I wasn't playing tonight.

"It's been a long day, and I'm tired," I said. I didn't bother raising my voice. I didn't want to wake anyone up, and Mab's fae hearing was so sharp she could probably hear my heartbeat from across the field.

I started to turn away, and suddenly the ancient faerie was in front of me. A jolt of terror rushed through my frame. I felt my power snap up like claws, and only the knowledge that this was Laurie's mother stopped me from tearing through her brain.

"He's distracted," Mab said bluntly, her green eyes bright with anger. "At a time when he should be fully present, completely dedicated to his Court, Laurelis Dondarte's mind is elsewhere. And others are beginning to notice."

Normally I would be pissed at this point. But Mab's lithe form was wrapped in another black gown, her skin smooth and pale against the velvet backdrop of night. It was almost identical to the one she'd been wearing the day Belanor died. The gown was a stark reminder of what this faerie had recently lost, even if her son had been an evil psychopath. Mab was grieving, and I knew a thing or two about grief.

Which was why my voice was mild as I said, "Maybe he has a good reason to be distracted. Did that ever occur to you?"

"*You* are the reason. He's already sacrificed himself once, Fortuna Sworn, and even that didn't win you. How long do you intend to torment my son? Until he's lost his throne forever? Until he's dead?" Mab paused. "When will enough be enough?"

I looked back at her with the face of the Unseelie Queen, but Mab's words slid through my veins like poison. "Laurie is a big boy. He makes his own choices," I answered.

She raised her chin, her nostrils flaring. "His Majesty is many things. He is clever, and kind, and brave. But he has a weakness, and I fear that it will lead to his ruin—his heart. My son loves you. As long as you continue to let him, he will continue to abandon his duties to be by your side."

This time, I didn't respond. I went inside and shut the door with frantic, unnecessary force.

All the lights were off inside. I fumbled around for the switch, so affected by my conversation with Mab that I couldn't seem to remember where it was. Suddenly I was so eager to get upstairs that I decided to skip the light and head straight for the stairs.

But even though Mab was gone, the door between us firmly closed, her voice followed me into the barn. It trailed after me through the darkness.

When will enough be enough?

I dreamed of a glass ceiling.

Daylight shone through all the dirty planes, bouncing off green plants and vibrant trees. I was in a greenhouse, I observed numbly, staring up at all those sunbeams. No, wait . . .

Oliver was in a greenhouse.

He was the one staring up at that glass ceiling. His arms and legs were stretched out on either side of him, secured with ropes that had recently been doused in holy water—I felt the telltale burn across Oliver's wrists and ankles. His body rested against a stone surface. He was splayed like a lamb ready for slaughter, I thought. There was a slight wheeze to Oliver's breathing. Suddenly I could feel his pain like it was my own, as if I were the one who had just been stabbed in the lungs.

"You've displeased me, Beast," a familiar voice said.

Oliver was silent. Despite the pain, the rest of him had completely shut down, and his mind felt like a dark, hollow land. I stumbled around in search of him, but there was only emptiness. What had driven Oliver to this place?

"You know how this works," the voice murmured. "All of the pain can stop, and we can go about our lives. All you need to do is answer a simple question. Where is it?"

From somewhere near Oliver's head, there came a clinking sound. The moment I heard it, I knew what was coming. I could picture exactly what Lucifer was doing and which tools he was touching.

Just as the devil loved his witches, he loved his shiny toys, too. He liked how they dug into flesh, making it tear and bleed.

I knew all this about him, because I'd felt it, too. For one night, I had luxuriated in Lucifer's torture chambers and basked in Belanor's pain like it was paradise. I'd done everything I had seen Lucifer do with those tools, and more.

But why do this to Oliver? How had he "displeased" Lucifer?

Whatever the devil wanted to know, Oliver wasn't giving an inch. I could feel lingering whispers of pain throughout his body.

Lucifer must've stopped for a while to let him heal, and now here they were, back at it again. And I was about to get a front row seat.

If I'd had a stomach, it would have rolled at the thought.

Suddenly I couldn't bear to just sit there and do nothing, regardless of what Oliver had done. I wanted him to suffer ... but not like this. I wouldn't wish Lucifer on my worst enemy.

Lie, I urged Oliver. But we weren't in our dreamscape, and whatever connection we shared didn't seem to let us hear each other. Oliver didn't acknowledge me, and he stayed hidden in the barren wasteland.

"Very well." Lucifer's face appeared within Oliver's line of sight. Beauty sharpened to a blade, all angles and allure. His eyes met ours, and somehow, I felt colder. There was absolutely nothing within those depths as he continued, "I will remind you once again that this can stop at any point. The power is in your hands, Beast. Let us begin."

Oliver still said nothing, but I felt something stir in the wasteland. It wasn't fear—it was sorrow. Oliver gazed up at the glass ceiling and imagined what it would be like, flying that high. He'd only been amongst the clouds of the dreamscape, a place where nothing counted. Oliver would've liked to do one thing that counted before he died.

You're not dying, I tried to tell him. I knew Lucifer, and he would never kill the Beast as long as it was still useful to him. And if Oliver had valuable information, Lucifer would never give up trying to get it out of him.

I remembered the question he'd asked at the start of this dream that wasn't a dream. *Where is it?*

My focus sharpened. What was the devil looking for? Did this have something to do with the killings, or the mark Laurie's spies had found in those faraway crops?

Lucifer gazed down at Oliver with a calculating tilt to his mouth. I recognized that look. Suddenly I was glad Oliver was in that distant place. It would help him bear what was about to happen.

Barely a second after I'd had the thought, something sharp sliced up the length of Oliver's arm. His skin began to sizzle instantly, and smoke rose from his flesh as if Lucifer had touched him with acid. But Oliver held fast to his silence, twitching from the agonizing pain. The Dark Prince bent and put his mouth next to Oliver's ear.

"I'm going to skin you alive," he whispered.

And then Oliver began to scream.

CHAPTER FIVE

A week passed. Then, two.

There were no more dreams about Oliver, and Laurie didn't send word about any new findings. I continued seeing Consuelo, the therapist Emma had found for me after I'd made the crossroads deal. I trained with Adam and Gil at the garage. I worked at the bar, pretending that it didn't feel like someone had jabbed my chest with a red-hot poker every time Bea avoided looking at me—ever since she'd learned the truth about what I am, she hadn't been the same. Then Cyrus would call out from the kitchen, and the sound of his voice made the feeling fade.

Everything was so mundane, so close to the life I'd always wanted.

But... there was a shadow over it. A threat of darkness, hovering at the edge of every good moment. It felt like I was constantly holding my breath. Looking over my shoulder as I took out the trash at the bar. Scanning the trees for any sign of movement when I played with Matthew in the yard. Listening for sounds in the night while the rest of my family slept peacefully around me.

I couldn't escape the sense that something was coming, and I needed to be ready when it did.

My friends felt it, too. New clocks kept appearing around the loft, which seemed to be comforting to Nym, somehow. And no matter where I was, there was *always* a member of the Shadow Court nearby—they thought they were being subtle about it, but I hadn't explained to anyone how our bonds worked, mostly because I was still figuring it out myself.

The connections between me and my Court members were as powerful as mating magic. All I had to do was think about one of them, and focus on what I wanted to know. Then the answer came in soft flashes or gentle thoughts. I'd close my eyes and see Cyrus filling up his truck at the gas station. I'd hear the whir of a drill or a heavy metal song, and I knew Gil was at Adam's shop. I'd picture Nym and shudder against the waves of agitation that he always seemed to be drowning in. It was no wonder our bonding spell had been kept secret by the fae.

In the wrong hands, this power could be diabolical.

I didn't use my newfound ability often, since it felt like a violation of my family's privacy. They weren't exactly giving me the same consideration with this around-the-clock guard thing, but it was hard to be mad at anyone when I could literally feel their concern, their love like a living thing in my chest.

Tonight was the first time my Court members had eased up in weeks.

When I finished my closing shift at the bar, there was no one waiting for me in the parking lot. I gave a mental shrug and unlocked the van, waving back when Phil called goodbye. He was the only other employee still here—it had been a slow night, so the others were cut early. I checked my phone for messages, relieved when there was nothing except a meme from Gil. Along the top it said, *Why did the vampire refuse to work at the mirror factory?*

The answer was beneath a cringey picture of an actor from an old movie, his plastic fangs gleaming in a smirk. *He just couldn't see himself working there.*

Don't make me block you, I texted back. My lips twitched as I pocketed my phone.

Seconds later I was on the road, driving in the direction of home. My feet ached and I reeked of beer, since Angela had spilled some on my shoes earlier. Completely by accident, of course. Sighing, I rolled the window down and leaned my head back. My thoughts turned to Oliver, as they usually did these days, and how we could find him now that the dreams had stopped.

Then something walked into the road in a flash of long limbs and pale skin.

I gasped and slammed on my brakes, instinctively jerking the wheel. The van careened out of control. Pain ricocheted through my neck as my ears filled with the sound of squealing tires, and I screamed. All I could do was hold on as the entire vehicle spun like a carnival ride.

After a few seconds, there was a brief falling sensation, then another neck-snapping jolt. The airbags exploded and the horn went off, blaring through smoke and a distinctly chemical scent. I sat there for an instant, my mind slow with shock.

Before I could move or think, the passenger window shattered. There was no time to react—at the same moment a spindly arm reached inside, the overlong fingers tipped with black claws, I yanked my gun out of the middle compartment and flipped the safety off. The world exploded with sound as I pulled the trigger three times, shouting. The arm yanked back and I heard an otherworldly noise, something partway between a shriek and a roar. My skin crawled as I yanked the door handle and stumbled out, my ears ringing. Glass sprinkled down onto the grass. I kept my head up, searching for the *thing* that had run me off the road. The horn continued bellowing into the night.

The creature rushed at me in a blur of milky white skin and shrill noise. My spine slammed against the van and I gritted my teeth, shooting it again, twice. Its bony torso jerked and ruptured with every hit. The creature screamed and ran again, plunging into the darkness.

My entire body was singing with adrenaline. I only had three more bullets, and apparently none of them were going to do jack shit against this thing. Breathing hard, I took stock of the other weapons I had. It didn't look good. Just two knives and a small container of mace.

All my talk about being ready and now here I was, about to get killed in a ditch.

"Collith. Lyari. Laurie," I muttered, backing toward the driver's seat again. I'd left my phone in the cup holder. What were the odds it was still there? I held the gun up and kept my eyes on my surroundings, trying to reach backward. My breathing felt loud as I scanned the trees, patting blindly around the seats and the floor. Where was my goddamn phone?

It came from above this time.

I felt the entire van shake and the crackle of the roof caving in, and then the creature moved faster than my eyes could track, reaching in to grab me. Pain shrieked through my legs, and a split second later, I flew out of the van.

Gravel embedded in my skin as I hit the ground and rolled. I cried out, and I hadn't even come to a full stop before the creature was on me again. Its claws dug into my arms as it pushed me down, and I only had enough time to flatten my hands against its misshapen chest before it attacked. I screamed, jerking to the side as its jaws snapped, globs of foul-smelling saliva flying. This thing wanted to *eat* me.

My arms trembled with effort—God, it was strong—and I kept summoning my Court as I tried to get inside the creature's head. I hadn't used my powers in months, not like this, and I was slow with uncertainty. Everything in its psyche was pitch-black and cold, so cold that it hurt even as I fought for my life. I stared into the creature's round white eyes, distantly noting that it had slits where nostrils should've been. Its mind felt like something that had been in the dark for eons, starving, wasting away until all that was left was the hunger. A mind with no hope, love, or light.

Suddenly those jaws faltered.

My eyes widened, and my blood quickened. That was it!

Light, I thought.

Even the mention of it made the creature flinch, and when I saw that, I didn't hesitate. In the space of a single heartbeat, I imagined blinding incandescence, just as I had with Jassin when all of this began. The creature recoiled, making that terrible noise again. It shielded its eyes as if the light were real. I pushed myself up, wincing. The edges of my vision darkened.

But there was no time to worry about injuries while this creature was still alive. I gritted my teeth and stood to the sound of its unearthly screams. It was stronger than I'd anticipated. Most of my victims would've been dead, insane, or unconscious by now. I drew power from my Shadow Court to put more energy into the illusion. Sunlight, chandeliers, lightbulbs. Everything blinding and flickering, battering this thing from every direction.

It writhed against the road, the bitter taste of its terror exploding on my tongue . . . but it still didn't die. *Guess I have to fucking stab this thing.* Thankfully, the knife I kept tucked against my ankle had stayed in place. I fought another wave of dizziness as I pulled it out and flicked the holy blade open.

I was about to take my first step toward the creature when its head lopped off.

Its screams were cut short as its skull went flying into the dark. I froze in shock, staring with wide eyes at the creature's face, or rather, at the bottom half, since the rest had been chopped away. Lines of dark blood ran down its mouth, neck, and chest. Slowly, the rest of the creature's misshapen body toppled over, twitching.

Lyari stood on the other side.

The creature was clearly dead, but my friend didn't move. She looked down at what was left of it, holding her sword across her body. Her face was splattered with blood and the expression on her face was . . . feral.

We hadn't spoken in weeks. My voice was an uncertain whisper as I said, "Lyari?"

She lifted her head, and I blanched.

Her eyes were yellow. Bright, blinding yellow.

In a terrible way, they reminded me of Finn's in how they flared in the light. A moment later, I watched those eyes fill with shame. Lyari had undoubtedly seen my reaction. *Fuck.*

Before I could say anything else, my friend ran.

The fact that she fled on foot only caused another twinge in my chest. Lyari had either used whatever energy she'd had left to sift to me, or she'd lost the ability entirely. It probably meant she was weaker, too. I gazed into the darkness and thought about going after her. There could be more than one of these things out here.

But I could barely stay upright, and I couldn't leave while there was a dead monster on the road. Even if it was glamoured, someone might hit the body with their car and get hurt. I would need help getting rid of it—this thing was *huge*. I looked down at the headless corpse to guess its weight. From the moment I'd laid eyes on the creature, I'd been in survival mode. Now I actually had a chance to think about what it was and why it was here.

It could only have come from one place, I realized as I studied its anatomy in the moonlight.

This was a demon.

Now I just had more questions with no answers. Did Lucifer send it after me? And if so, why?

I told myself I'd have to think about that later. Swallowing a groan, I turned toward the van. My head swam as I struggled to consider my options. Option one, call Adam. He could help with the demon and tow the van. That would still leave me standing on a dark road by myself while I waited, though. And I *really* didn't want to wait here.

Option two, I could just start walking and call Adam on the way, telling him where to find the van on his own. Home was only a few miles down the road. If I left now, I'd be back sooner than it would take for someone to get here. That didn't leave me standing in the open like a target, during the Witching Hour, while more demons potentially prowled the hills.

But if I went home, someone could still hit the one we'd killed. I let out a soft curse, staring down at the corpse again as if another solution would magically come to me. I really, *really* didn't want to touch this thing. I glanced around the empty road, making a frustrated, helpless gesture. There were no houses around—only thin trees and shifting shadows. Seeing no hope for it, I bent and reached for the demon, grimacing when my bare fingers made contact with its smooth skin. I leaned back, making sure to brace myself, and put all my weight into pulling the creature away.

It didn't budge.

I swore again, louder this time. Okay, so I wasn't moving it. I couldn't chop it up into pieces, either, because it would take an hour to cut off a single arm with the little knives I'd brought. My panic mounted.

Focus, Fortuna. I winced as I turned away. I wasn't thinking clearly. It didn't matter what option I chose until I got a hold of Adam—that was the first step.

Every part of my body shrieked in pain as I went back to the van and searched for my phone again. Within a minute I found it in the backseat, miraculously intact. I scrolled through my contacts list and returned to the road. When the line began to ring, a relieved sigh slipped past my lips. I held the phone to my ear and wrapped my other arm around myself, tapping my foot in agitation. Adam didn't pick up. I tried Gil next and he didn't answer, either. Neither did Collith.

Everyone else I know will be asleep, I thought, flicking my thumb up the screen. But . . . there was one person who might be awake. One person who always answered, day or night. I bit my lip as I scrolled to a name.

It rang three times, then his silken voice filled my ear. "If you're hoping to make use of my cleaning team again, I'm afraid I really do need to start charging you, Fortuna. Or I at least deserve a couple nudes, since you'd probably object to the other forms of payment I have in mind."

For a moment, I was silent, my insides suddenly warm from a flash of crackling memory. I struggled to sound unaffected as I said, "Do *you* send people nudes, Laurie? That's not really the smartest thing to do if you're trying to lie low. Nothing is secret on the internet."

"Those pictures are my *gift* to the internet, and to humanity. You're welcome."

A tiny sound escaped me, a slight huff from my nostrils. Not quite laughter, but something very close to it. "Tell me, were you born with a big head, or did your skull change to adapt to that fancy crown of yours?" I asked.

Laurie didn't respond this time, and I knew he was probably wondering why I'd called. It's what I would be wondering. But after few seconds, all Laurie said was, "It's true, I do have a rather large brain. But its size is proportionate to my other vital organs."

This time the laugh started in my chest, but the feeling quickly faded. Talking to Laurie had made me almost forget the reason I needed help. I didn't want to tell him why I'd called; I wanted to keep joking and laughing. I wanted to ask him how his day had been, like normal people did.

We weren't normal people, though. Every moment I spent avoiding reality with Laurie was a moment I was putting someone else at risk. A small, sad sigh caught in my chest, but all that escaped me was the slightest breath. I turned my head and looked in the direction of home. The pavement gleamed with dew.

"I was just attacked by a demon," I said.

Laurie's voice sharpened. "At the loft? Is—"

"Everyone is okay," I cut in. "I was on my way home, and it came out onto the road. It's dead now, so I actually *could* use your help with clean up, sorry. It's way too heavy for me to move."

"I'll get it taken care of," Laurie said instantly, dismissing my apology. "Just share your location with me. Are you hurt?"

"I got away with some scrapes and bruises. Lyari saved my life." I finished sending Laurie a pin, and as I lifted my head, a sound echoed through the stillness. It made me think of a stick snapping under something's foot. Fear gripped my throat, and my grip involuntarily tightened on the phone. I turned in a circle to make sure nothing was trying to creep up on me from behind. "Hey, how long would you say it'll be until your people show up?"

"The Door isn't far from you. They'll be there in ten minutes, probably less. Why?"

Laurie had definitely picked up on something, I could hear it in his voice. I swallowed, wondering if I'd heard that snapping sound again or if I was still shaken from the encounter with the demon. Nothing stirred in the trees. I wanted to ask Laurie to sift here and stay with me until the rest of his team arrived. To pass the time with his jokes and his flirting. Maybe I'd even flirt back.

When I began to say the words, the conversation with Mab jabbed at my mind like a hot poker. *When will enough be enough?*

"I'm fine, don't worry," I said casually. "I'm almost home. I'm just worried about someone hitting that giant corpse."

To avoid making a complete liar out of myself, I finally left the demon and started walking. I could hear Laurie reassuring me, but I was too distracted to respond, my eyes still roaming the darkness in search of any hint of movement. I kept looking over my shoulder, too, half-expecting another demon to come up from behind, or for the one on the road to sit up and start running toward me. But it stayed where it was, a pale streak on the pavement, its long limbs splayed like broken tree branches, its blood gleaming like a distant mirage.

My footsteps felt overly loud in the mist-filled night. "I've seen that species of demon before, Laurie. In Hell," I said under my breath.

Laurie swore, and there was a faint rustling sound on the

other end, as if he'd gotten out of bed or was rummaging through a drawer. "At least now we know what snake boy has been doing in West Bengal. He must be getting them through somehow."

Hearing it out loud made knots form in my stomach. I relived every moment of my battle with the demon, and I knew the only reason I was alive was because I'd gotten lucky. No human stood a chance against the creatures of the underworld. If Lucifer was creating openings to Hell . . .

Thinking of the fight made me remember those final moments on the road, too. I fell silent for a moment, and then I said, "Lyari's eyes were yellow, Laurie."

He paused. "So she's begun the transition."

"Is that what you call it? Transitioning?" I repeated tightly.

"What do you call it?" Laurie asked, and I imagined him tilting his head.

My first instinct was to say something disparaging. I thought of the goblins that had held me hostage for days, then tried to sell me on the black market. I remembered the sound of their laughter while I'd huddled in that small, rusted cage.

My mind went further back. During her lessons, my mother had spoken of goblins with the same neutrality she'd used for every other species. It was only when I met more Fallen, like Sorcha, that I learned of how our world actually viewed their kind. Then I'd encountered goblins on my own, and those interactions only seemed to prove the stigma. Goblins were the worst of my customers at Bea's. They were obnoxious. Rude. Messy. They were also incredibly shitty tippers.

I hadn't known they could be different until I'd met Seth.

I thought of him next, and the goblin's earnestness. He'd been forced out of his Court for daring to want a better life. He'd endured my rejections again and again. Most people would've gotten angry. Most people would've given up. If Seth had, I would have missed out on a true friend, and knowing an incredible person.

"I'd call it change," I said finally.

Laurie made a thoughtful sound and replied, "I believe there's a saying or two about change."

I walked past a mailbox, and I recognized it instantly. I was getting closer to home, to safety. I'd been so focused on the conversation with Laurie that I'd forgotten my terror. But even now, I couldn't stop thinking about Lyari, or reliving the moment when the light had reflected off her yellow eyes.

"She keeps running from me, even before tonight," I murmured. "Maybe I should respect that. Maybe I'm just a painful reminder of who she used to be. How do you know when to keep holding on, and when it's time to let go?"

Laurie laughed, and I almost laughed too as I realized who I was talking to. All he said was, "Do you love her?"

"Yes. Of course I do."

"Then you should try again."

A small, faint smile touched my lips. It was such a Laurie response, and for some reason, the thought hurt. I blinked quickly, and I was afraid he would hear something in my voice if we kept talking. "I should go," I said.

"Actually, your timing is strange. A couple hours ago, I just got another address for you and Collith to check out. It's not a crime scene," Laurie added, probably knowing that was my next question.

My heart slowed at those words. "Did you find that mark again?"

"No. This is something else." Laurie paused again. "My team has been investigating sightings of a creature . . . a human-sized creature with wings, as it's been described. There are police reports, posts on social media, footage online. You won't see much on the news, of course, because the sightings are being dismissed as a hoax. Any source that legitimizes the claims seems to mysteriously disappear, so you can imagine how difficult it's been to obtain information."

Dracula had struck again. If he had any idea where Oliver was, that information might have been helpful. Maybe the vampire knew more than he'd let on at the meeting of the Order.

But I'd have to think about that later. Right now, there was another lead on Oliver. "Text me the address," I said to Laurie. "I'll let Collith know."

He fell silent for a moment. It was the sort of silence that felt like something unsaid. And then Laurie asked, "Why did you call me, Fortuna?"

I frowned. "I told you, a demon—"

"If all you wanted was a cleaning crew, Collith could've asked me. You've used him as a go-between before," Laurie pointed out. "Or you could've used magic to wake a member of your Court. Every single one of them would rush to your side without hesitation."

I opened my mouth to argue, but the words wouldn't come. Deep down, I knew it was just an excuse. I could see the barn off in the distance now, but the sight of that familiar sloped roof didn't bring me relief. The other end of the line was quiet as Laurie waited for the truth, and I couldn't see a way out of giving it to him. Despite Mab's warning, part of me didn't want to. I was so tired of lying and being lied to. Just like Oliver, I longed for something that counted.

As I spoke, I pictured myself stepping off the edge of a cliff.

"Because when something happens, you're always one of my first thoughts afterward. The good things. The bad things. When I'm scared, or when I'm on top of the world. The truth is that I've been wanting to call you all summer, because I missed you, and just the sound of your voice makes me feel better. Is that good enough for you? Is that what you wanted to hear? That I think of you as much as you think about me?" I demanded. My insides quivered while I waited for Laurie's response.

"I did warn you," he said. I began to frown in confusion, but my expression cleared when I realized what he was talking about. The conversation came back to me, every word as familiar as the notes of an old song. It was one I'd replayed more times than I cared to admit.

Please. Don't do this.

Do what?

Make me fall in love with you.

To be clear, I fully intend to do exactly that.

"I also told you I wouldn't survive it," I reminded Laurie, swallowing as a rush of fear hit me. I held the phone tighter.

This prompted another pensive sound. "Perhaps that's why we need him," the Seelie King remarked.

My eyebrows drew together. "Who?"

"Collith." Laurie's voice was soft now. I tried to picture him again, and I imagined him standing next to his bedroom window, a slant of moonlight falling across his face. I didn't know how to respond to his answer. But then Laurie spared me by saying, "Good luck with your hunt. I hope the intel is good."

He didn't offer to come, and I didn't ask.

"See you around?" I didn't mean to say it like a question, and once the words were out, I found myself holding my breath.

"See you around." Laurie didn't hesitate, but his tone was impossible to interpret. I pictured him raising his eyebrows as he added, "Oh, and Fortuna?"

Apprehension fluttered in my belly. I approached the barn and tipped my head back to gaze up at the window. Yellow light spilled from the glass panes and guided my way to the doors. "Yeah?"

"You're still a terrible liar."

"What do you . . ." I spotted movement in the corner of my eye, and panic exploded in my chest. I turned just as the call disconnected. Laurie had hung up on me. I scanned the yard and let out a startled breath when I saw him. He was walking away, but I'd recognize that stride anywhere. Arrogant. Graceful. The stride of a king.

With a faint smile, I started toward the barn again. From the corner of my eye, I saw that far off pale figure pause at the tree line and linger. Watching over me, just as he probably had the entire time I'd been walking home.

He was still there when I went inside and closed the door.

Twenty-four hours later, a full moon glowed outside the car window.

Collith and I were in another rental, on our way to investigate the lead on Oliver. Thanks to Zara, I was fully healed from my encounter with the demon. Adam had towed my totaled van away, once again leaving me without a vehicle, but I wouldn't need one until my next shift at Bea's. Tonight, Collith and I were somewhere in Georgia.

The smooth, black road ahead of us gleamed dully from the moisture in the air. One side of the highway was bracketed by dark forest, and the other was open fields. I sat in the passenger seat again, since Miss Daisy didn't like the way I drove. My temple rested against the glass as I studied the shapes on the moon's surface.

Even now, months later, it was still strange to look up and see stars instead of the red skies of Hell. Collith had been to the underworld, I remembered. It wasn't exactly something I could ever forget, and the fact always hovered at the back of my mind. But Collith wouldn't know about the red skies, would he? Had he ever left the cells beneath the tower?

Despite our conversation in the motel room, there was so much we still didn't talk about. So many secrets and pain and half-truths. Collith never asked, and I didn't, either. Maybe it just hurt too much, or we were afraid of driving the other person away. We'd already done this routine once before, after I'd made my crossroads deal and brought Collith back from Hell. It hadn't done us a lot of good then, and it wasn't helping now. If I wanted things to change, I had to keep trusting him. I needed to keep breaking our long habit of silence.

"You've never asked me how," I said suddenly. "How I could fall in love with the devil himself, after everything he's done."

If Collith was thrown by the suddenness of this, he didn't show it. He waited, just as he'd been waiting all summer. Right on cue, the shame hit. It urged me to stop. It shrieked at me to bury every feeling, every memory, rather than expose them to the light. I fought the instinct and continued, "Believe me, no one is more disgusted than I am."

Now Collith spoke. He gave me a swift, hard glance, and his voice was low. "I don't judge you."

"I don't see how. But the sick truth is, he reminded me of you." I smiled faintly. "Maybe that's part of the reason I fell for him. I knew he had secrets. I knew he had a dark side to him. I knew he'd probably hurt me, too. Apparently I have a type."

I fell silent, thinking for the thousandth time how badly I wished I could go back. Redo all the reckless, idiotic choices I'd made. My rush of self-loathing slowed when Collith asked, "You said that was only part of the reason. What else made you fall for Lucifer?"

My lips pressed together, and I felt my eyebrows furrow—thinking of him hurt. But I forced myself to, because I wanted to explain it to Collith. I wanted him to understand why I'd made such colossal mistakes, even if maybe I didn't fully understand myself.

I forced myself to relive those days in the tower. My time with Lucifer was vivid and hazy at the same time, as if it had been a previous life. I remembered the visceral pull toward him. I remembered how being with him made me lose all sense of time and anything else that existed. Anything else that mattered.

My voice was soft with regret as I said, "Everyone knows his power is desire, but they don't truly understand. It's not just the sexual kind, although he certainly uses that to his advantage, too.

Lucifer reflects what you want most in how you feel, which is even more intoxicating.

"When he seduced Eve, she was trapped in the Garden and knew nothing of the world outside its walls. Maybe she was even afraid of it. But after, once he'd gotten his claws into her, she became brave and reckless. She broke the rules and left everything familiar and safe behind.

"Then there's me." I swallowed. I could feel Collith looking my way, and I wanted to stare out the windshield. But I met his gaze and continued, "I'm scared of myself and what I can do. How using my power causes a rush of . . . euphoria, even when I'm hurting someone. I've always struggled with it. I wish I could be just one thing. A human, or a Nightmare. But I can't seem to stay in one world. I can't be what I am and pretend to be human, too.

"Around Lucifer, that struggle went away. Around him, I felt . . . normal." A bitter smile touched my lips. "The entire world may judge Eve, but I'm no better than she was. It was only toward the end that I started to break free of Lucifer's influence. After . . . after I disemboweled Belanor."

I winced and looked away. Collith's voice was soft as he told me, "You're not giving yourself enough credit, Fortuna. You didn't give yourself to the dark. You came back. You said it yourself—his power is intoxicating, and you were exposed to it for months."

"I wish it were that simple. I wish I could blame everything on that. But it wasn't just magic, Collith, or physical attraction. There were times I thought I saw . . . I thought I caught a glimpse of someone," I murmured. "A real man, instead of some ancient monster. He was so sad, and broken, and lost. Something about him made me want to offer comfort, in spite of everything he'd done. How twisted is *that*?"

The sound of my laugh was harsh in the small, dim space. A commercial came on the radio, and a voice floated between us, the upbeat tone at odds with the tension.

"It's not twisted at all, Fortuna. Your compassion is one of the reasons I love you." Collith's expression didn't change as he said this, and he didn't look over at me. Then he added, "I'm sure it's why he fell in love with you, too."

I made a soft, bitter sound and looked away, back toward the starry sky. "Lucifer doesn't love me. I was a means to an end, and once he got what he wanted, he tried to kill me," I said.

Collith's fingers tightened on the steering wheel. "I spent a lifetime with the Dark Prince. I know how his mind works, and it's nothing like how you and I think. He doesn't consider violence or pain as betrayals. To him, they're just tools. Reality. Hell is not a place any living creature is supposed to survive, and now he rules it. He didn't get there by holding onto his humanity."

"It almost sounds like you're defending him," I said.

Collith made a soft, humorless sound. "Lucifer took my body apart more times than I can count. When I think about the two of you together, *I* want to rip something apart with my bare hands. And if I get the chance, I won't hesitate to kill him. But helping you is more important than my ego."

A response had been gathering in my throat. It faded by the time he finished, and a strange tightness filled my chest. I ignored it. "So you're saying he must love me because I'm alive right now?"

Collith's eyes flicked in my direction. "You're a weakness, Fortuna, and the devil doesn't like weaknesses. He also doesn't like loose ends. You're both."

I turned my face away, looking out the window again. "Or maybe he's just not done with me yet," I murmured.

This time, Collith didn't reply. But I felt his fear, just as surely as he felt mine.

Neither of us spoke after that, and the only sound in the car was low music floating from the speakers. I tried to focus on Oliver and what I was about to do. Collith and I had brought a cache of holy weapons in case we did find him—knives, swords, guns. I pictured it, over and over, just as Oliver had once instructed. I'd had months to get used to the idea of his death, but the image of killing my best friend still made something inside me recoil.

If God really was orchestrating all of this, he was a sick bastard, I thought. I rested my temple against the window and kept going, picturing the moment again. Lifting the gun. Pointing it at Oliver's face. Pulling the trigger.

"Bang," I whispered.

I didn't mean to say it out loud, but thankfully, Collith pressed on the brakes at the same time and said, "This is it."

He pulled the car over, and we both got out. The air was balmy, and it pressed in on every side as we started down a private driveway, instinctively keeping to the shadows. There was a barn to our left, and it looked abandoned. There were no other buildings in sight. No neighbors, either. It was the perfect place to hide if you were a huge, violent beast from another dimension.

But Collith didn't seem to be stopping, which meant he hadn't sensed anything inside the barn. Every time the moonlight passed over his face, I saw the rigid set to his jaw. I shared his tension, and I knew the reason for it even though he hadn't said anything—we hadn't been able to form much of a plan, since there was no way of knowing where we would find Oliver tonight. We also didn't know his weaknesses or his healing capabilities.

I'd just figured I would shoot him in the face with a holy bullet and go from there.

Without warning, Collith slammed me against the side of the barn. I gasped and his hand clapped over my mouth. His hazel eyes burned into mine, and there wasn't any part of him that wasn't fused to me. Collith bent his head, and I felt his cool breath as he whispered, "We're leaving. You didn't tell me how big he was, Fortuna. Taking that thing on with just the two of us is fucking suicide. I'll lead it away, then loop back around. Meet me at the car. I'm not asking."

I was about to argue when Collith darted into the open. He moved with the speed of a faerie, blurring across the lawn. The Beast spotted him immediately, of course, and a rumbling snarl tore through the night. I caught a glimpse of an enormous, winged shadow against the ground before I edged around the corner of the barn, trying not to breathe even as my heart raced. I kept my back against the wall, my eyes wide as I strained to hear anything else. Should I go after Collith? What if he needed help?

My gaze rose to scan the sky, and in doing so, I caught sight of the car off in the distance. I thought of Collith's parting words. There was no cover between the barn and where we'd parked. If I made a run for it, I'd be exposed.

I waited another beat, but I still didn't hear anything. Knowing Collith, he was probably leading the Beast as far from here as possible. I could stay and cower, or get to the car, ditch this half-assed plan, and go home. I told myself to run on the count of three. *One. Two. Three.*

I bolted from my hiding place.

I'd only gone a few steps when I slowed, then stopped. I clenched my jaw against another surge of terror as I realized I couldn't go to the car. Not without Collith. He might have ordered me to wait for him there, but when had I ever listened to an order?

I was about to turn when a sound shattered the stillness. It was brief, soft, but the silence was so absolute that it felt like a gunshot.

Time stopped.

My chest heaved as I spun to confront the Beast. It squatted on the roof of the barn, every detail and feature shrouded in darkness. There was only the shape of its ominous wings and the feel of its gaze on me. The sound I'd heard must've been its landing.

Where was Collith? I tried to search the Beast's hands for any sign of blood, but the moon had retreated and I could barely see anything.

The creature didn't move. I was still frozen in terror, but when seconds ticked past and nothing happened, other thoughts began to trickle in. Did this thing even recognize me, or was it as mindless as it seemed? Judging from the state of the crime scenes, the Beast was more animal than anything else.

Thinking about those bodies made my breathing falter. Was it possible for the pulse to speed up and slow down at the same time?

Gritting my teeth, I tipped my head back and glared straight into the Beast's face, or where I thought it was. My fists clenched so hard that fresh pinpricks of pain flared up—nails. The pain cleared my head a little. I put my arm behind me, trying to keep every movement furtive as I reached for the gun in the waistband of my jeans. I had to keep the Beast's attention away from it, somehow.

"I'm not afraid of you," I whispered. A sliver of pride went through me when there was no trembling in the statement, no obvious underlying falsehood.

The Beast still didn't react. My breathing was uneven as I tried to work up the courage to wrap my fingers around the gun. That hulking shape just sat there. Suddenly I felt a strange, inexplicable rush of irritation. Why didn't it *do* something? Attack, leave, anything?

Fuck this. I tensed, finally about to raise the gun.

Then the frozen air shattered when the Beast murmured back, "I don't want you to be afraid of me."

CHAPTER SIX

*H*earts didn't do things like crack or break. I knew that. It was just a figure of speech, and people said it to express unimaginable pain.

But in that moment, I swore I felt my heart break all over again. I stared up at that hulking silhouette, trying to reconcile the voice of my best friend coming out of it. The boy I'd built sandcastles with and taught to swim, now a thing that could fly, tear, and kill.

"Ollie?" I whispered.

I'd barely uttered his name when he shifted and jumped from the roof. I'd expected him to land forcefully, like thunder shaking the ground. But Oliver used his wings as if he'd had them his entire life, flapping them to temper his weight.

As his feet struck the earth, his movements were startlingly graceful. Every time I'd imagined Oliver's monstrous form, or pictured him murdering those people, he'd moved like the stuff of nightmares. Blurred, abrupt, unnatural. The fact that Oliver seemed so at ease in this body, so right, made my stomach churn.

Then he stepped into the faint light, and every coherent thought left my head.

I'd seen his beastly form once before, when Oliver had broken free of the dreamscape, but my mind had been dim with shock. Numbed by horror. Now I stared at every detail of the monster I had created so many years ago. He truly was the stuff of nightmares. A creature that only a child's mind could create at its most imaginative ... or its most frightened.

The only clothing Oliver wore was a pair of dark, faded jeans. Moonlight gleamed on his bare skin, forcing me to notice how the lines of his body were different than before. His limbs were sharper than they used to be, the lines harder. The golden cast to his skin was mostly gone, too, as if he hadn't spent a moment in the sun since he'd left the small world we once shared.

His wings weren't reminiscent of angels or fairy tales. They were dark, almost a deep emerald at certain angles. Some parts looked like thin, stretched leather. Similar to a bat's wings, if bats had feathers, I thought distantly, shifting my focus to the rest of him. Oliver stood there without a word, enduring my examination. Long claws grew where his fingernails should have been. Black veins still crisscrossed his skin wherever I could see it—his wrists, his throat, his jaw. The only unchanged parts of Oliver were the general shape of his face and that bright hair.

Well, those weren't the only parts, I thought faintly. There was one other feature, one aspect about this creature that was completely, utterly, and wholly Ollie. A pang of uncertainty went through me, and I reached up without thinking, my hand trembling.

In the barest of touches, my fingers brushed over Oliver's freckles.

In an instant, the same moment I made contact, the monstrous features melted away. As if there had been a spell tucked beneath my fingertips, or magic that only worked when we were together. Within seconds, he was my Ollie again. The black veins melted away, the claws retreated, and his body shifted into the familiar shape I'd known in the dreamscape. Into the person I'd fallen in love with so very, very long ago.

I stepped back, and my hand fell limply to my side. Both of us were silent while we waited for the other to speak. As Oliver looked at me with his sad blue eyes, I told myself to stay focused on what he'd done. I commanded myself to hold onto my hatred, and remember the vow I'd made. Oliver would pay for what he had taken from me. He was a rabid dog that needed to be put down.

But I'd been telling myself these things for months. Standing in front of Oliver now, all I could feel was the pain. And then I heard myself whisper, "Was any of it real?"

I didn't even try to pretend that I didn't care. With anyone else, I would've donned the mask of the Unseelie Queen, or built such thick walls around myself that nothing could've breached them. Oliver was different. He'd always been different, and Collith had known that. *I* had known that. It was why I'd been doubting myself all these months. Fearing that when this moment came, I would succumb to these exact feelings. So I did what I'd told myself to do, and I remembered the moment Finn had died in my arms.

Slowly, hardly daring to breathe, I bent my wrist and began to tug out the holy knife hidden beneath my sleeve. I hadn't counted on facing Oliver at this proximity, and stabbing him in the heart would be far more effective than shooting him with a bullet. Whatever the Beast was, he'd been formed of Fallen magic, and our kind responded to traditional weapons the most.

Oliver searched my expression, his eyebrows knit together. His voice was hoarse when he finally answered, "Yes. God, yes, it was real. Fortuna, you have no idea how badly I want—"

"Ask me if I care what you want," I spat, my grip curling around the knife's hilt. Before Oliver could speak, I barked a laugh and shook my head. "No, wait. If I have to hear the sound of your voice, then I just want to know why. Why are you slaughtering innocent people? And why was Lucifer torturing you?"

A muscle worked in Oliver's jaw. "I've come here to—"

"Fortuna!"

I jumped at the sound of my name. *Shit*. We were already out of time. Collith had sounded far away, but he could still sift. He'd probably be here any second. I kept my eyes on Oliver as I shouted back, "I'm here! I'm okay."

Oliver didn't look away, either. Those achingly familiar eyes flicked between mine. "Do you love him?" he asked quietly.

"Yes." I didn't hesitate, and I saw how much this pained Oliver. Off in the distance, Collith called for me again. He'd abandoned all caution, apparently. It was sinister how my name echoed through the darkness. I turned back to Oliver, knowing I had to act *now*. But once again, it felt like my mouth had a mind of its own as I added, "If you're still here when he arrives, he'll tear you apart."

"I'm not scared of your faeries," Oliver said in a voice I'd never heard him use before. Cold. Deadly. The Beast's voice.

We sounded eerily similar when I answered, "You should be. And you should be scared of me, too."

Oliver knew we were out of time, too. He bent his head, his hands forming into fists. He didn't look up as he spoke, and every word sounded like it caused him pain. "I came back to ask for your help, okay? I'm . . . I'm bound to him."

"Bound to him?" I echoed, frowning. "What do you mean?"

When he jerked his head back up, his teeth were bared. They were sharper than before. Teeth meant for tearing through skin and tendon. "I mean, from the moment Lucifer and I laid eyes on each other, I've been powerless," Oliver snarled.

I stared at him as what he was saying sank in. My mind flashed to every crime scene, seeing them in an entirely new light. "You mean . . . all those people . . . all those families you killed . . ."

I trailed off, swallowing. Could Oliver really be telling the truth? Had Lucifer forced him to do everything? God, if it was true, the guilt must've been eating him alive . . .

It didn't change anything, though. I shook my head slowly, tightening my grip on the holy blade I was still holding. "Lucifer didn't make you lie about what happened to my parents, Oliver. He didn't make you kill Finn. I could've forgiven you for so much, but not that. Not Finn."

My voice dropped when I said his name. I tipped my head back and searched Oliver's expression for the remorse I wanted. It was there, shining amongst the pain. But it wasn't enough.

So I flicked the blade open, lifted my hand, and finally stabbed Oliver in the heart.

I stared into his eyes, expecting to see them cloud with betrayal. Instead, Oliver barely reacted. A muscle flexed in his cheek. He wrapped his fingers around the knife hilt, and his gaze never left mine as he pulled it out of his chest. The entire length of the blade was wet with his blood. Oliver tossed it down, and the knife made a dull sound against the grass.

"I am made of fear," he said. "Fear isn't killed so easily, Fortuna."

Before I could respond, Oliver flapped his wings and shot into the air. He became a shape against the night sky again, and as I arched my head back, I remembered what he'd wished for when Lucifer had been torturing him. Oliver had wanted to fly amongst the clouds.

My mind chose that moment to remember something else. Something Collith had said to me, once. *I thought Nightmares were creatures of pain and darkness. Why, then, are you constantly seeking freedom and light?*

I listened to the sound of Oliver's wingbeats fade, and a breath later, Collith himself was there.

"Are you hurt?" he asked. Blue light streamed from between his clenched fingers, and his features were more pronounced. Otherworldly.

I managed to shake my head. "No. He didn't touch me."

It was the truth. Collith must've heard it, because the heavenly fire in his palms faded and his breathing gradually quieted. We both stared in the direction Oliver had gone.

"I stabbed him with a holy knife, Collith," I murmured. "Right in the heart. It didn't even slow him down."

Collith was silent. The night crowded close again. The crickets resumed their song, and even the breeze felt like a relieved sigh.

"I'm moving back in," Collith said finally.

He didn't say anything else. He was probably waiting for me to argue, or counter with a mocking rejection.

"Okay," I said.

On Friday night, my Shadow Court gathered for family dinner.

Normally it was Emma who brought us all together, but to everyone's surprise, Danny was the one who suggested it. The low sound of "Moon River" filled the corners of the loft. The lyrics floated through all the light and the warmth, heading for an open window at the end of the hall, where evening smells and breezes came through. Fresh-cut grass. Rain. Cold. I felt my nostrils flare as I inhaled, enjoying the contrasts between those scents and the food being made behind me.

Tonight I stood at the counter, slicing a loaf of bread while I watched my family. Hello twined between my ankles and demanded attention in her high, nasal voice. A pan of red sauce bubbled on the stovetop, and Emma had taken out all the soup pots we owned to boil the noodles, since we were cooking for ten. But she'd abandoned her post the second Collith had held out his hand and asked her to dance. Ariel had followed Collith's lead and led Cyrus onto the impromptu dance floor, and now the four of them were swaying to Andy Williams, light from the fire casting their shadows across the rug. Collith laughed at something Emma said, his white teeth flashing, and Cyrus looked down at Ariel with a soft light in his eyes that I'd never seen before.

Danny and Damon sat on the floor nearby with Matthew tucked between them. My nephew held building blocks in his small hands, and he grinned when Collith bent Emma into a gallant dip, then pretended to almost drop her. Emma shrieked and snatched at his shoulders, swatting Collith the second he pulled her upright. Stanley barked and ran up to them with obvious concern, his tail thwacking Collith's leg.

Adding to the chaos, Seth and Gil sat on the barstools across from me, having a spirited debate about the British Parliament, strangely enough. Their voices rose and fell, but their stances were relaxed. Easy. The two of them had grown close these past few weeks, especially since Seth's lease had ended and he'd moved in with Adam and Gil. Vampires didn't seem to have the instinctive dislike for goblins that they had toward werewolves—far the only issue they'd had was whether or not to hire a housekeeper, since Gil was a slob, no surprise there.

The second I had the thought, a face filled my mind. And despite the low heat of happiness within me, I couldn't help but think about the people missing at this family dinner. *Finn.* I pictured his golden eyes and remembered how his fur had felt between my fingers. If he'd been here, my werewolf would've been in front of the fire, no doubt. Lyari was absent, too, and she hadn't responded to my invitation or the update I'd sent about Oliver.

Oliver. Another reaction sliced through me, this one harder. Sharper.

It had been three days since I'd seen him. Three days since Collith had come to the loft with a duffel bag and had started sleeping on the couch just a few feet away from my bedroom door. Three days since I'd found out Lucifer was controlling the creature I had created.

For the millionth time since that night, I wondered how the two of them were connected. Was it simply because Oliver had come from a dream, and dreams were Lucifer's element? But didn't that mean I should've had equal power over Oliver?

When I'd reached into his mind, all I saw was darkness. Lucifer's darkness.

"Pasta is ready," Emma declared, startling me. "Everyone get your wine glasses and sit down."

We all moved to comply. Damon and Cyrus helped Emma drain the pots, and I carried an enormous bowl of garlic bread to the table. Wood creaked as my family settled in their chairs. Collith slid into the spot beside me, and I glanced sidelong at him as I offered one of the wine bottles. He accepted it, his fingers brushing mine. Slowly, Collith reached over and filled my glass before he poured the wine into his, every movement deft and graceful. I followed the length of his long arm, all the way to his beautiful face, and found Collith's hazel eyes already staring back at me. Another startled jolt went through my frame. For a moment, we just looked at each other.

". . . stretched pretty thin. The sheriff has increased our patrol numbers, since we can barely keep up with the calls."

With effort, I refocused on what Danny was saying. Seth must've asked a question, because Danny was looking at him while he talked about increasing crime in Granby. His fork glinted as he twisted it mindlessly in the spaghetti, a frown hovering at the corners of his mouth.

When I glanced around the table and saw my family's sober expressions, I knew they were all thinking the same thing. *Lucifer.* Was his presence here influencing the humans? Or was something even worse going on? I thought of the demon I'd almost hit on the road, and how there were probably more like it out there.

Danny eventually fell silent, and for a few seconds, no one else spoke. Music still played from the speaker on the counter—the bluesy tones felt at odds with the fear I sensed in the air now. But I didn't reach for it, or allow myself to touch any of the bonds that would reveal what, exactly, the people I loved were afraid of. I kept my hands in my lap, tightly clenched. I stared at one of the pots on the table, the one directly in front of me, and fought back the memories that always returned whenever I was tempted to use my power. A bloody corpse mounted on an earthen wall. A bright doorway. Finn's body on the floor.

Then Gil made a joke, and everyone laughed. The tension dissipated. The bread bowl went round again, followed by a newly opened bottle of wine, and the conversation drifted to easier topics. The rigidness left my shoulders, little by little, until I was laughing, too, absorbed in a story Seth told us about a hacking job he'd done for a gang of goblins in New York, but instead of changing police records, he'd taken the gang's money and created a digital trail for the police to follow right back to them.

"Why didn't you tell me that little story when you were selling your usefulness?" I demanded, laughing.

Seth's forehead wrinkled. "Oh. I didn't even think of that."

I started to respond when another hush fell over the table. This time, it was because Danny had stood up. Everyone watched as he stepped back from his chair, giving himself enough room to kneel. Then he gazed up at Damon with so much love in his eyes that it almost felt intrusive to watch them. There was a small box in his hand that I hadn't even noticed him take out. With his other hand, Danny reached out and grasped Damon's fingers. My brother held onto him tightly, as if he were proving to himself this wasn't a dream.

"Damon Sworn," Danny began shakily, "I asked your family to gather tonight because they're important to you, and I knew you'd want them to be part of this moment. You are the love of my life. You and Matthew make me happier than I've ever been. I know the risks of being part of your world, and I don't care. A short life with you is better than a long one without you. For as long as there is breath in my body, I will do my best to protect you, and fight with you, and love you. Will you do me the greatest honor . . . will you marry me?"

We all waited in spellbound silence. For as long as I lived,

I would never forget the look on Damon's face, and in that moment, it was worth it—all the pain, all the fear, every terrible thing we had been through to get us to the here and now. I would do it again if it meant seeing my brother this happy.

"Yes," he said.

Sounds of excitement and congratulations filled the room. Stanley lifted his head in the corner, his dark eyes brightening with curiosity. Danny rose from the floor, grinning from ear to ear, and he and Damon kissed. I watched the grooms briefly press their foreheads together before each of them turned away. Damon's arms wound around me, and I held him close, my eyes squeezing shut as my chin rested on his shoulder. "Congratulations, little brother," I whispered.

Damon kissed my temple and pulled back. He gave me a familiar, crooked smile that instantly made me think of our father. "Thank you, Tuna Fish."

Something about the way Damon spoke made it clear he was thanking me for more than this. I blinked rapidly and stepped away to let others get their chance to hug him. Once the chaos had died down, I picked up my glass and raised it in the air.

"To Damon and Danny," I said.

Echoing my words back, everyone around the table smiled and held up their drinks. I committed every detail to memory, hoping that maybe I'd get a chance to tell Finn about it someday. I imagined him again, in his wolf form, curled on the rug as he so often had been. I held onto the image as I tipped my glass back, and the rest of my family followed suit. Gil clapped Damon on the shoulder and Seth hugged Danny, grinning from ear to ear.

Emma started asking questions about the wedding while the sound of knocking floated through the loft. I left the table at the same moment Gil mentioned bachelor parties. I was still smiling as I opened the door. But when I saw who stood on the other side, my smile faded.

Laurie's expression was grim. I'd seen it enough times this

summer that I instantly knew what it meant, and my grip tightened on the doorknob. If he was coming to tell us in person, it had to be bad. "We should go downstairs," I said.

Laurie nodded, and I followed him into the stairwell. He walked through the garage and pulled the door open, stepping out into the night. I followed, stopping on the driveway, holding my arms tightly against my middle. Laurie turned to face me. His face was pale and solemn, his lips pressed together into a hard line.

"How many?" was all I said.

As I waited for the answer, tension coiling inside me, a cool presence came up from behind. A moment later, Collith's scent wafted past. Laurie's eyes flicked to him, but his expression didn't change. "My little bird couldn't give me a number," he replied. "She said there were too many . . . pieces."

My stomach clenched. Images threatened to break through my defenses—I caught a flash of an upturned hand on a bloodstained rug, fingers curled—but I focused so hard on Laurie that he became all I saw. His defined jaw, the straight slope of his nose, the shadows darkening the perfect planes of his face. And it occurred to me, just then, at the worst possible moment, how deeply in love with him I was.

"Thank you for telling us," I said.

Laurie must've heard the distance in my voice, because there was a subtle shift in his jaw, as if he'd started to clench it. "Let me know if you find anything," he replied.

Then I blinked, and he was gone.

"Should we say goodbye to your brother?" Collith asked, keeping his voice low. Even down here, we could be overheard.

I glanced up at the window above us. A smattering of laughter floated through the night, carried on the wind like dandelion seeds. That warm glow of light felt so far away. I clung to the mental snapshot I'd taken earlier, and I realized I couldn't stand the idea of ruining it.

"No. Let them celebrate," I said. I knew my family would want to know about the latest crime scene and where I was going. For now, I'd send a vague message to the group text. I wanted to give them tonight. Just one night.

As I turned away, there was an ache in my chest. It felt like something inside me was dying. *Hope*, I thought. The hope that I could actually be free again. That I could have the life I'd always wanted. We moved toward the woods, and the cold sank into my bones. I could feel Collith looking at me, but I didn't meet his gaze.

A few steps later, the trees swallowed us whole.

CHAPTER SEVEN

This time, there weren't any flashing lights, empty ambulances, or crime scene tape.

There was only darkness and silence.

There were no neighbors, either. We were on a rural patch of land in western Canada, and the house was at the edge of a sunflower field. The crops were in full bloom, and it should've been a beautiful sight. Cheerful. But the moon and stars were blocked by thick clouds, making the flowers' dark centers look like round, eerie faces. It felt like they were watching as Collith and I crossed the yard. Even the birds and crickets seemed subdued, as if they sensed that something terrible had happened.

As if they knew that evil had been here.

Collith and I walked up the porch steps, and even now, neither of us spoke. We'd been silent all the way from Granby. To my surprise, the wood creaked beneath his weight, distracting me. Faeries moved soundlessly, and Collith was better than most. The few times I'd heard his footsteps had been because he hadn't wanted to catch me by surprise.

Faeries were light on their feet . . . but goblins weren't.

The thought made my gut tighten. Until now, I hadn't seen

many signs of deterioration, but I'd been a little distracted. Collith and I hadn't talked about it since that night at the motel. Did he plan to make the full transition? Or was he hoping to bond himself to one of the faerie Courts again?

We reached the top of the stairs, and I glanced at Collith's face, wondering if he'd noticed the change in his tread. Before I could see his expression, he sifted. Collith reappeared seconds later, his hand around the doorknob. He opened it without hesitation, which meant he'd confirmed there was no one else in the house. No one alive, at least. The thought made my jaw clench, and I imagined all my emotions emptying out of me like water down a drain.

As Collith's hand fell away, the door hinges moaned. Within seconds, a dark hallway loomed before us. All my worry about goblins was snuffed out like a candle. Collith stepped inside, his mouth tight and grim. But I hesitated on the threshold.

I could already smell the blood.

Dread blazed through me, leaving a single truth in its smoking wake. *I don't want to see this.* I didn't want to walk past more people that my best friend had murdered, or relive my parents' deaths for the millionth time. I also didn't want to feel that gut-churning guilt. To look down at those torn, broken bodies and know that none of them would be dead if it weren't for me.

Which was exactly why I needed to.

I would look at every single victim in this house, and I would acknowledge the part I'd played here, just as I had at all the other gruesome sites.

With this thought at the front of my mind, I pressed my lips into a thin line, clenched my hands into fists, and forced myself to move down the hallway. My soft footsteps were loud in the bleak silence, Collith's even more so. It felt like shouting in a graveyard.

The house was in shambles. Through the wide doorways on either side, I could see into each room as we passed. A single lamp had survived the destruction, casting soft-edged yellow light. The few pictures that did remain on the wall were crooked. The floor was covered in broken glass and shattered furniture. This family had put up a fight, I thought as I stepped over an upturned table. There were streaks and splatters of blood on the wooden floor.

But there were no bodies. Not yet.

Collith went up a set of carpeted stairs, and I followed him silently, studying more pictures that had survived the destruction. My stomach clenched when I saw three children, each of them appearing so often that it was obvious they lived here. There was a framed photograph of a couple who had to be their parents, and there were also images of an older couple, their hair white as an angel's wings.

I was so absorbed in the pictures that I didn't notice Collith had halted at the top of the staircase until I nearly collided with his back. Something about the way he stood made the hairs on my arms stand on end. My dread got louder. It buzzed in my ears as if we'd ventured too close to a hornets' nest. I stopped beside Collith and looked over at him, trying to prepare myself. But that stubborn lock of hair had fallen into his eyes, hiding his reaction. I swallowed and turned to see what had made him go so still.

Blood soaked the carpet. It was concentrated in such a way that made it obvious someone, or multiple people, more likely, had been dragged away. Collith and I followed the dark streaks slowly, and they led us toward the master bedroom. Just like last time, I kept putting one foot in front of the other until we reached the doorway, where I knew we'd find what was left of this family. All my instincts shrieked to *look down, look away*. Instead, I raised my gaze to memorize every detail.

The bodies were in the same condition we'd found the others. Laurie's comment about there being too many pieces made sense now. If I'd had to guess, I'd have said there were two victims. They were probably the parents I'd seen in the pictures, but after what had been done to them, it was difficult to tell. The man was tied to a chair, his head bent, and the woman was on the floor. They seemed to be human, judging from the color of the blood. There was so much of it that the floorboards looked like they'd been painted. It was everywhere else, too—on the legs of the furniture and sprayed over walls. Along with bits of bone, skin, and other things I didn't want to identify.

I stopped a short distance away. I may not have had any forensic training, but it was obvious these people had been tortured. The man was missing fingernails, and the woman's fingers had been cut off. It looked like her eyes had been gouged out, as well. Did that mean the other victims had been tortured, too? Was it for sport, or did Oliver actually want something from these people? I studied the grisly scene in search of answers, breathing through my mouth and ignoring how the room had started to tilt.

"He made him watch," I said quietly. I saw Collith's head turn in the corner of my eye, but I didn't look away from Oliver's victims. I could see what had happened clearly now, almost like a movie in my head. My stomach rolled as I went on, "The Beast tied the man to that chair so he had to watch his wife die."

Collith didn't respond. He'd stayed near the doorway, and his mouth was a thin, dark slash. At least there was no sign of the children, I thought faintly. But what would we find in the other rooms?

"He was here," Collith said finally.

There was something in his voice, like a serrated edge, and I knew instantly who he meant. I stared at Collith in disbelief, my pulse quickening. Lucifer and Oliver really were working together? Did that mean he'd been telling the truth about being controlled, too?

It took me a few seconds to respond, because I was still trying not to puke all over the floor. *My fault. This is all my fault.* "You've never picked up on his scent before," I managed. "What was different about this family?"

Collith just shook his head. All these houses, all these bodies, and we still had no answers.

I tried to scrape my thoughts together. I told myself I could fall apart later. Right now, I had to commit every detail around us to memory, because I sure as hell wasn't taking pictures of this with my phone. We were looking for a pattern, some way to predict where Oliver—and apparently Lucifer—might go next. So we could actually save people, instead of staring down at what was left of them.

My gaze went back to the man in the chair. I shouldn't have been so surprised Lucifer was involved. He was the one with a taste for torture, and only a twisted mind like his would think to murder a man's wife in front of him for information.

"Fortuna," Collith said. I turned at the sound of his voice, and he inclined his head. "There's more."

More. The word echoed through me as if I were a hollow shell. I just nodded and followed him out of the room. We went back down the upstairs hallway, through a door at the opposite end, and up another flight of stairs. This one was much darker and narrower than the former. The boards creaked underfoot as we climbed.

Seconds later, we arrived in an attic study. I turned my head slowly, taking it all in. On a normal day, I would have called it cozy, with all the thick rugs, the walls of bookshelves, and the big, arched window. Today was not a normal day.

When I confirmed there were no children in the room, I felt a horrible twinge of relief. But there had been a third adult in the house, and I recognized the white-haired man from the pictures. He sat behind a desk and wore an old, pressed suit. It was immediately obvious Oliver hadn't killed this one.

Because he'd shot himself.

"Collith," I said, noticing the blood splatter on the window.

"I see it."

Unlike the couple downstairs, the person in the chair hadn't been human. The stains on the glass behind him were blue.

"We should look in the desk drawers," I said. Before Collith could say anything, I circled the desk and drew close to the body, tugging my sleeve down so I wouldn't leave any fingerprints. Just as I reached for the drawer, I noticed something white in the male's limp, dangling hand.

He was holding a piece of paper, I realized in a rush.

Collith had come up behind me. He saw the paper, too, and moved in a blur, taking it out of the guy's fingers before I could. But he didn't read it—he just handed it to me without a word.

I took it slowly, knowing Collith had gotten the note so I wouldn't have to. He was trying to spare me whatever horrors he could, no matter how small. My gaze lingered on him for an extra beat, my heart aching. Then I forced myself to look down at the trembling paper.

There were only three sentences, but they hadn't been written in haste. The handwriting was neat and clear. I read the male's last words once, then twice.

I have heard about the others. I am the last.
He will come for me soon.

He seeks the grave of Olorel.

Collith swore under his breath as he reached the same conclusion as me. There *had* been a purpose behind all this, a connection between the victims. These people hadn't been hunted and eaten—they'd been killed for information. For whatever reason, Lucifer thought they knew something about Olorel's grave.

That was why he was doing this to all these people. Every time Lucifer got a lead, he sent Oliver. And judging from the fact that they'd slaughtered so many families, the devil still hadn't found it.

Why was a long-dead original angel's grave so important? How did Thuridan tie into all this? Or the mark?

Once again, I reviewed what I knew about about Jassin's

adopted son, and the faerie that my best friend had fallen in love with, for some unfathomable reason. Well, maybe not so unfathomable now that I'd been inside his head. Thuridan had been kind once. He'd been the sort of person who protected his gentle brother and befriended a lonely, isolated Lyari, who'd been spurned by all their peers.

Then he'd become a Guardian of the Unseelie Court. He'd cut off his brother and Lyari like they'd meant nothing to him, and years later had marched into my Court to accuse me of murder.

He was also afraid of werewolves. Deeply, deathly afraid.

None of this was relevant, though. No matter how many details I came up with, I couldn't piece together a reason why on earth the devil would want him. Or why Oliver was doing such terrible things to innocent people, I thought, looking down at the spatter of blood near my shoe.

It was beginning to feel like I was trapped in purgatory. I was going around and around—obsessing over Lucifer, Thuridan, Oliver—and drifting through all these bloody houses, but nothing was changing.

No, that's wrong. I raised my gaze, a frown hovering at the corners of my mouth. I looked at the body in the chair again. Even if I couldn't figure it out, I knew at least one detail had changed. These victims, this house, was different from the others, somehow. I didn't know why, but the mere fact that Lucifer had deigned to make an appearance was proof of it. Before tonight, only Oliver's scent had been at the scenes. Was the Dark Prince closer to finding this mysterious grave, or had he actually learned where it was? And what did that mean for us?

The ominous message also explained the wreckage downstairs, and the fact the children were gone. This family had known the devil was coming. They must've sent their kids away, then waited here for Lucifer to show up. But why? Was it just to keep his attention on them, or had they actually thought they might survive if they fought back?

Even if they could've beaten Lucifer, they'd never have stood a chance against Oliver.

The paper crumpled in my hand, startling me. I held it up again, frowning as I glanced between the white-haired male and his final words.

"Something isn't adding up. The note, or the timeline, maybe," I muttered. I went over it in my head, thinking out loud. "So he hears the Beast killing the two downstairs, then shoots himself. The Beast comes up and sees the body, but just ... leaves? And how did this guy know his killer wouldn't find the note?"

We were still standing close to the desk, near enough that the distinct smell of decay was getting to me. Lost in thought, I turned away and instinctively started walking toward the stairs. Unless the dead guy had a message in his other hand, there was nothing else to learn here. I was desperate to be back in the fresh air, far away from the stench.

"He didn't just leave."

Collith's voice was soft, but it stood out in the heavy stillness. I paused near the top of the stairs and looked back at him. "What?" I said.

Collith's expression was strange. His gaze dropped to the piece of paper I was still holding. "The Beast. He didn't just leave."

"How do you ..." I trailed off as the answer came to me. I looked down at the note and thought, *Of course*.

Oliver's scent.

"He found the note and read it," Collith said, confirming my suspicions. "Then he put it back."

The implications of what he was saying sank in. I pursed my lips to hide my reaction, but I knew Collith could hear it. I stared at the floorboards, my heart racing.

Just as the white-haired male had known the devil was coming, Oliver had known that, eventually, I would come here, too. He'd tucked the note back in those curled fingers and kept its existence from Lucifer. It meant that he truly did have some humanity left. It meant that he wasn't loyal to the Dark Prince.

It meant that he was trying to help us.

I lifted my head and refocused on Collith. He'd gone back to appraising the body, his dark brows knit together. I probably should've been doing the same, but all I needed to do was close my eyes and I could see every detail. I'd had enough death and horror. Now I only looked at Collith. There was a faint sensation in my chest, and it was one I'd felt before. A gentle tugging, as if there were a string around my heart and the other end was tied to his. He could've kept this from me, the fact that Oliver had defied Lucifer and left us a clue.

I wasn't sure it was a truth I'd even wanted to know, but when Collith and I had been together—if we could even call it that—lies had been our undoing. If I'd wanted proof that he had changed, and things between us were different, here it was. The invisible string tugged again, and I wasn't sure whether it was fear or love. Maybe both. For me, the two always seemed to go hand in hand.

I waited until Collith met my gaze, and then I said, "Let's go home."

Something in his expression shifted. Something that made me feel a little better in this awful place. Nodding, Collith crossed the room and followed me down the stairs. We made our way back through the house, and when I saw that open doorway at the end of the hall, it took everything inside me not to run toward it.

Seconds later, we were beneath the stars, breathing fresh air. Our rental car was parked right out front, since the house was so rural there was no chance of witnesses. Collith opened the door for me, and I lowered myself into the passenger seat, fighting a sense of déjà vu. He circled the hood, got in on the other side, and pressed the start button. Gravel crunched under the wheels as he navigated down the driveway and back onto the paved road.

"The Order will hear about this, if they haven't already," Collith said.

Pressure bloomed behind my ribs. I mentally added it to our growing list of problems. "And then they'll be even more motivated to find him. Dracula will get involved, if he hasn't already."

Collith didn't respond, but I could see the signs of worry he didn't know I'd learned to recognize. The subtle tightness in his jaw. The distant look in his eyes. Neither of us spoke again as we returned the rental car and then ordered a ride to our next destination, the address of the closest Door. Within minutes, a car stopped next to the curb where we stood. The driver was a middle-aged human with a kind face. Collith waited for me to get in first and folded his long body in next to me. He sat close enough that every time our driver turned, Collith's hip brushed against mine.

Neither of us moved away.

Once we'd arrived, the driver pressed on the brakes and bent his neck to peer upward. His tone was dubious as he said, "Are you sure this address is right? Pretty sure it's a slaughterhouse."

"It's right," Collith and I answered in unison. Then we got out and closed our doors at the exact same moment.

"We've been spending too much time together," I told Collith, walking toward the looming building. Behind us, the driver hadn't moved. I could feel him staring in our direction, but Collith and I both ignored him.

Collith shrugged. "As the humans say . . . jinx."

"You can't say it *now*." My lips quirked. "You have to say it right after the jinx happens."

"Says who?" Collith countered. We reached the door and he opened this one for me, too.

I touched the corner of my mouth, feeling the soft rise of a smile. It seemed impossible after everything we'd just seen. I walked past Collith, and when he moved to follow, his hand pressed against the small of my back. The brief pressure felt like he was saying it again, those words he'd murmured to me at the last house. *I've got you, sweetheart.*

And as I stepped into the darkness, feeling the familiar *whoosh* of magic, I believed him.

My nephew was dreaming about elephants.

I stood beside his crib, staring down at Matthew's sleeping face. The images from his mind were brief, almost hesitant. I saw a long nose spouting water. A baby elephant pressing against its mother. A herd of them playing in a sunny lake, surrounded by birds and tall grass.

When the images had first started coming to me, I'd been softly startled. I almost dismissed them as my own random thoughts, like changing the channel on an old, flickering television. But then they kept coming. The mental pictures felt like they were floating from a certain direction. I'd followed them ... and looked down at Matthew.

That was when it clicked.

His deep, steady breaths were the only sound in the moon-tinted room. His eyelashes fanned against his cheeks in dark fringes, and for the thousandth time, I was struck by how much Matthew looked like my brother. I looked down at his small hand, which rested on his chest, fingers splayed. I resisted the urge to reach down and touch that downy skin.

Another elephant soared through the stillness, releasing its strange, high call.

I didn't know what it meant, that I was seeing Matthew's dreams. It seemed my abilities were constantly growing and evolving, and right when I became convinced I had a handle on them, they changed again. Maybe that was just the nature of magic and its unpredictability.

Or maybe Matthew was a Nightmare, and this was the beginning of his own power manifesting.

Whatever the reason, I liked that my nephew had good dreams, in spite of everything he'd been through.

Leaving Matthew with his elephants, I eased backward and reached for the door. He didn't stir as I gently closed it behind me. The tension left my shoulders, and I let out a long, low exhale.

Collith lifted his head from where he stood in the kitchen. There was a silent question in his eyes.

"Fast asleep," I said, smiling. I started toward him.

"Good." Collith finished pouring a second glass of wine and set it on the other side of the counter, directly across from him. The one by his hand was untouched.

It had been a week since our trip to Canada, and Damon had asked us to babysit tonight. His request was more out of desperation than trust. Emma was in Denver for the weekend, and Cyrus had been working more shifts at the bar lately, so my brother didn't have a lot of options. I couldn't exactly blame Damon for his reluctance to ask, since trouble did seem to follow me.

But I was determined to prove to him, and to myself, too, maybe, that I could do this. Be a normal aunt. Do normal things, like babysit.

As I slid onto the barstool, I considered telling Collith about the elephants in Matthew's dreams. But something stopped me. There were certain memories, certain thoughts that belonged to the quiet moments. To be tucked away and pulled out only when you needed a little joy, or to be reminded of the good. So I smiled my thanks at Collith and raised the glass to my lips, taking a long drink. Collith gripped the stem of his wine glass with his fingertips and picked it up, swirling the glass and the wine inside, and then did the same, his throat shifting as he swallowed.

A companionable silence swelled between us. Music played from the Bluetooth speaker, and I'd lived long enough with Collith to recognize one of his playlists. It wasn't that hard, since he preferred classical. Listening to it always put Collith in a good mood, and I needed him to be in a good mood when he heard what I had to say. If I'd been waiting for the perfect time, this was it.

Without preamble I said, "I'm going to meet with Lucifer."

"Forgive the pun, but why the hell would you want to do that?"

I jumped at the sound of Laurie's voice. The Seelie King leaned against the counter, his arms folded, legs crossed at the ankles. I hadn't seen him since the family dinner, and for a moment I just drank in the sight of him. I didn't dare ask why he was here, because I worried it would make him leave sooner. And I wanted as much time with Laurie as I could get.

When I spoke again, my gaze moved between the two faeries, addressing both of them. "I bet Lucifer knows. He was fascinated by the Beast, even before they met. Apparently there's some kind of weird connection between them, and it's how Lucifer is using him to do his dirty work. But the devil doesn't use anyone without doing his homework first. He doesn't make decisions without weighing every outcome, every weakness. Which means he probably knows the Beast's," I added.

"How do you know that?" Laurie asked, tilting his head.

I blinked at him. "What?"

"How do you know there's a connection between the Dark Prince and the Beast?" he asked. His eyes glittered, and I could feel Collith watching me now, too.

Fuck, I thought. I knew, even before I opened my mouth to answer, that they were *not* going to like what I was about to say. "I spoke to Oliver," I admitted.

"When?"

This was from Collith. I glanced at him, hesitating. He wouldn't like the next part, either. I twisted my wine glass and watched the red liquid cling to the sides. "The night we found him at that barn," I said.

Silence. When I lifted my head, I caught Collith and Laurie looking at each other. A wordless communication passed between them. Normally I'd have been annoyed by it, but I didn't have much ground to stand on right now. I wasn't sure why I hadn't told them about the conversation with Oliver. I'd had plenty of time, and they deserved to know the truth about Lucifer and the creature I had created.

But every time I started to do it—tell Collith when he handed me a cup of coffee, or scroll to Laurie's name when I unlocked my phone—I stopped. I wasn't sure why, exactly. Whatever the reason, it was the same thing stopping me now.

So I said nothing while Collith and Laurie processed my revelation together. After a few seconds, Collith refocused on me and leaned his elbows on the counter. Tension coiled in my stomach; I knew he was about to ask what else Oliver and I had talked about.

"Any ideas on how we're going to find the Dark Prince?"

I hid my surprise. Collith gazed back patiently, still holding his wine glass in a light grip. *We*, he'd said. I hesitated again. "Collith, if you're there, his guard will be up. I need to see Lucifer alone."

"I'm going, Fortuna." His tone was matter-of-fact. "I can remain out of sight, as a compromise. But anywhere you go, I go."

"Collith—"

"Anywhere you go, I go." He repeated it firmly.

I fell silent and studied him. There was a hardness in Collith's eyes that reminded me of something Laurie had once said. *I believe that, sometimes, you mistake us for men, Fortuna. You forget what we truly are.* Most days, Collith was level-headed and reasonable . . . but I didn't see any of that reason now. I reminded myself that I was picking and choosing my battles, and I had a feeling this was one I would lose, anyway.

Laurie moved, drawing my attention back to him. "You haven't answered the question. Do you have a way to contact the devil that we don't know about?" he asked.

"No, but I know how to contact one of his spies." I paused, gathering the courage to confess yet another secret to them. "Lyari Paynore."

Neither of them said anything. There was no trace of surprise in their expressions.

"You knew," I said. It wasn't a question. Again, neither of them spoke. I let out a breath and realized that I was too tired to be annoyed. "Fine, well, since you two know so much, tell me how I can get Lyari to have a conversation. She's so ashamed that she won't even look at me."

Laurie grinned. "Have I taught you nothing? If she won't talk to you, make her. Never underestimate the power of annoying the shit out of someone."

"You should get that engraved on your throne," Collith muttered.

"Or his headstone," I put in.

Before Laurie could answer, the baby monitor on the counter crackled—Matthew was shifting in his crib. We all fell silent, waiting to see if he'd truly woken up. A few seconds ticked by, music floating through the stillness. The small lights on the monitor stayed dark.

Suddenly Laurie's nose wrinkled. "Good God, can that smell really be *normal*?"

The corners of my mouth deepened, and there was an amused gleam in Collith's eyes as he turned to me and said, "Where does your brother keep the diapers?"

Laurie made a distressed sound and said nothing to either of us before vanishing. I pressed my lips together to hold back another smile. "If the bottom drawer of the changing table is empty, there should be an unopened pack in the closet," I told Collith.

He nodded and strode toward Damon's room. Hoping to air the smell out, I walked to the window at the end of the hall and pushed it open. Movement on the other side of the glass caught my attention. I found myself looking down at Laurie, who stood on the lawn, still visibly gagging. My lips twitched yet again, and I drew back from the glass before he could catch me staring. I went back down the hall, moving more quietly once I drew close to the open door.

I grasped the knob with cautious fingers and pushed it a little more, making the crack just wide enough for me to peer inside.

Collith sat in the chair beside the window, holding Matthew against his chest. My nephew was curled on his side, his head tucked in the curve between Collith's jaw and throat.

Seeing him with a child in his arms caused a reaction deep inside me, like sparks or a combustion of chemicals, and for the millionth time, I thought of the vision Mercy Wardwell had once shown me. The feeling was followed by a whisper of frustration as I remembered my conversation with Collith at the motel. *Until this is all over, I think there should be some boundaries.*

I turned away, getting another faceful of the smell that still clung to the room. I winced and decided Laurie had the right idea with fresh air. I went over to the door, jammed my feet into my sneakers, and made my way down and through the barn. I strode across the driveway to join Laurie in the yard. I waited for him to make some kind of joke or suggestive remark, but he stood there and gazed up at the barn. There was a set to his mouth that told me he wasn't really looking at it, though.

"You never said why you were here," I ventured.

Laurie gave me a sidelong glance. "Do I need a reason?"

I cupped my elbows and held my arms against me. "Typical faerie. Answering a question with a question. Too bad I'm wise to your tricks now."

The Seelie King didn't smile as I'd expected him to. We stood there together, and the silence around us was similar to the one I'd just shared with Collith—safe. Easy. A bird sent its voice into the night as if it was calling out, not in search of another, but simply because it could.

Then Laurie said, "You're going to meet with the Dark Prince no matter what we say, aren't you?"

"Yes," I replied, matching his bluntness. I knew it would've been easier to lie ... I just didn't want to. I met Laurie's gaze and waited for the argument to begin. He just looked back at me calmly, his silver eyes bright in the dimming world around us. I raised my brows. "You're not going to rant at me or try to talk me out of it?"

"I prefer to use my mouth for productive reasons," Laurie answered. I watched those beautiful eyes fall to my lips and linger there.

Of its own volition, my mind went back to the nights I'd experienced just how *productive* that mouth could be. Knowing Laurie would detect any change in my scent, I averted my gaze. But looking at the barn made me think of Collith, and the frustration I'd felt in the bedroom doorway came rushing back. I shifted so the loft was out of sight and leaned against the tree, pressing my palms into the bark. My gaze returned to Laurie. The storm inside me caused a streak of recklessness, like a flash of lightning.

"If I asked you to kiss me, what would you say?" I asked abruptly.

Laurie's expression didn't change. He searched my face as if it were a map and he knew exactly how to read every line and landmark. "Did Collith reject you, darling?" he said.

He was too perceptive for his own good. Embarrassment flooded me, and I quickly turned away. "Never mind. Forget I asked."

Laurie's hand slid around my waist and tugged me back. Softly startled, I put my hands over his and tipped my head to meet his gaze. The corners of Laurie's mouth tilted up in a faint smirk. "He's never been the brightest bulb, that one. If you asked *me* to kiss you, Firecracker, I wouldn't say anything. Because I'd just do this."

He bent and claimed my mouth, which had parted open in surprise. In an instant, I was lost in the taste of him, in the way his tongue moved so perfectly against mine. I'd forgotten how *good* it felt with Laurie, and how good he was at waking this part of me. He pulled me into him, his springtime scent teasing my senses as I pressed closer, harder, burying my fingers in his hair.

Then I remembered where we were. I turned my head away, breaking the kiss, and willed myself to step back. But I lingered in the circle of Laurie's arms, reluctant to leave his warmth. I looked at him again, trying to commit this moment to memory.

There must've still been some surprise in my eyes, because Laurie flashed a dark, crooked smile and said, "Did you expect me to be noble? I've told you before, I have no interest in nobility."

"What are you interested in, then?" I asked quietly, aware that Collith could come out any second. I wasn't worried about how he'd react . . . I was afraid of what else might happen. I'd slept with them both when I'd thought I might be going to Hell forever. I wasn't ready for whatever it might mean if we did it again.

Laurie's mouth softened. He ran the ball of his thumb down the edge of my jaw. "I could show you."

There was a promise in his voice, but it wasn't entirely seduction. There was the faintest note of sincerity, too. I studied the Seelie King's features for the thousandth time, thinking how I always seemed to notice something new whenever I looked at him. Like the arch to his eyebrows, or the straight slope of his nose, or the shape of his lips' Cupid's bow.

He was like a creature from a fairy tale, and part of me longed to run off with him into the woods, never to be heard from again.

"Good night, Laurie," I said.

Once again, his expression revealed nothing. The barn door opened just as Laurie replied, "Good night, Lady Sworn."

"He fell asleep again. I'll be back soon." Collith came over to us and kissed my forehead, pressing the baby monitor into my hand. Then, with Laurie at his side, he turned away.

"Wait, you're leaving, too?" I asked his retreating back.

Collith paused at the tree line and winked. A moment later,

he sifted. Laurie lingered a bit longer, his face the picture of innocence. "It's only an appointment at the barbershop, dear," he told me.

"At eight o'clock at night?" I countered.

Laurie vanished without answering.

I went back upstairs. Once I'd reached the loft, I closed the door and rested my forehead against it, heaving a sigh that moved through my entire body. "What the hell am I doing?" I muttered.

A slight sound made me turn. Nym had emerged from his room, and I watched him drift over to a bowl of fruit on the counter. Although he wore my brother's clothes now, and Emma had managed to give Nym a haircut, it was still obvious there was something . . . not-human about him. It was how he moved, and the way his fingers danced over the orange he'd chosen. Even now, I couldn't quite put my finger on it.

"When the bird of the heart begins to sing, too often will reason stop up her ears," Nym told me sagely.

My hands fell from the door, and I joined Nym at the kitchen island. For a few seconds, I just observed as he peeled the orange. I knew I would find most of it somewhere in Nym's room tomorrow during my daily check, which had become necessary after the food he'd taken in there began to stink up the entire loft.

"What is that from? A poem?" I asked finally.

I didn't expect him to answer, but then Nym said, "Hans Christian Andersen."

"How refreshing. Collith and Laurie are always quoting obscure old shit at me. Have you been here all night, Nym?"

The faerie's brow crinkled, and it was a look I recognized—he was trying to remember where he was. *When* he was. Traveling through time so much had jumbled Nym's mind, and the damage seemed to be permanent. I thought he'd been doing better since he had moved in with us, but there were still days and moments we lost him. *Like now,* I thought with a stab of sorrow, watching the struggle in his expression.

"Tick tock," Nym said, frowning deeply. Hoping to ground him, I reached across the counter to put my hand on his sleeve, but Nym didn't even notice. He was staring at something else now, his gaze directed downward. "There's something in your pocket. Tick tock."

"Oh, okay. Let me check." I hadn't put anything in my pockets, but I humored Nym anyway and reached into the center of my hoodie. To my surprise, my fingers collided with a long, thin object. I pulled it out and looked down at the soft thing in my hand. The thing Laurie must've slipped in while we'd been standing next to that tree. His voice echoed from the past like a caress. *Its darkness only makes the rose more beautiful, wouldn't you agree?*

The flower's subtle fragrance permeated the air as I reached for Nym's hand again. I tucked the stem in his palm and curled his long fingers around it, giving my friend an encouraging smile. "It's beautiful, isn't it?" I said.

Nym stared at me for a moment, and little by little, I watched as his young and ancient face smoothed into a calm expression. The Time Walker nodded at me, not in gratitude, but resolve. As if we'd decided something together.

In the next breath, he was gone.

I blinked at the place Nym had been standing. He'd taken the rose, and there was nothing else left of him but the orange on the counter, peeled and torn apart. After a moment, I went to the cupboard and got a bowl, placing the pieces inside. Then I picked it up and crept into Damon and Matthew's room, easing into the chair by the window.

As I ate the fruit, its sweetness clinging to my tongue and making my fingers sticky, I listened to my nephew's soft breathing and the cries of young elephants.

CHAPTER EIGHT

Another week passed. There were no more dreams or crime scenes, not a single development that would help us find Oliver. I became more determined than ever to arrange a meeting with Lucifer. But when I still didn't hear back from Lyari, I decided to take Laurie's advice.

On Saturday morning, I sent her another text and went to Adam's. I found him, Gil, and Seth in the bay. Adam sat on the couch, his arms resting on the cushions behind him. Gil and Seth sparred on the mat, both of them only wearing basketball shorts, their torsos gleaming with sweat. They circled each other, and Adam's usual rock music played from an ancient radio on the shelf. Seth was bouncing on his feet, and as I set my bag down next to the couch, I bit my lip to hide a smile.

"Hey, Adam," I said, raising my chin at the vampire. I glanced around his empty shop. "You know, I've been curious about something. Do you ever, like, have any actual customers?"

"I don't know, Fortuna. Do you ever get anyone's order right at the bar?" Adam deadpanned, never taking his gaze off the fighters in front of him.

Gil and Seth hooted. My eyes narrowed at Adam, but my

lips twitched. "Pissing off the person who handles your coffee every day. I thought vampires were supposed to be smart. You know, considering the fact you've literally had a thousand years to evolve."

"Less talking, more cutting," Gil drawled, his dyed hair glinting in the light. "Or do you not care about learning how to defend yourself anymore, doll face?"

Seth walked off the mat, his bare feet slapping on the concrete. He took a towel off the couch and slung it around his neck. While I removed my jacket and shoes, stripping down to the absorbent tank top I was wearing and a dark pair of yoga pants—black was best whenever I trained at Adam's, since it hid the bloodstains from any humans who walked in—the two of them talked about areas Seth needed improvement. Which was, unfortunately, all of them.

Despite his supernatural speed and strength, Seth was no fighter. That didn't stop him from trying, and it didn't stop us from teaching him. A storm was coming, and we all knew it. Seth was one of our own now. The thought of him not being able to protect himself was unacceptable. Even Adam had taken to treating him like a little brother.

Once I'd set my shoes off to the side and done a few warm-ups, I took my sword from the weapons rack. I'd been keeping it here since I came so often. As I lowered the blade and adjusted my grip, I noticed how it seemed lighter. I was getting stronger.

The thought sent a surge of pride through me, and fresh resolve. I grabbed a second sword before turning to Gil and joining him on the mat, all the bright lights of the shop shining down on us. I handed it to him without a word. A whisper of apprehension went through me, but I kept it from my expression as I lifted my chin and got into position, readying myself.

Sparring with Gil was different to sparring with Adam. Months ago, I'd asked Gil to teach me more about my Nightmare abilities. He had held true to that agreement with far more enthusiasm than I liked. When we fought, he didn't just go for my jugular—

Gil went for my heart, too. Once or twice, he might have taken it too far. He'd brought up the day I'd killed Collith, and all the people I had killed at the black market. Those were memories I tried not to think about, or at least, I'd used to. Gil didn't exactly give me much choice in the matter. To teach me control, he told me, he had to bring me to the brink of losing it.

As our eyes met across the mat, I gathered a quiet breath and released it slowly through my nose. I searched for the place inside myself that no one else could access. A hideaway full of glittering water and birdsong. A scene with open skies and a swaying, creaking fishing boat.

So when Gil asked, "How's your hunt for the Beast going?" I gave him no response.

And when he came for me, I reacted entirely on instinct.

"Make sure there's a bend in your elbow," Adam instructed from the couch. He watched us for another moment before adding, "You're developing a habit of withdrawing your arm to prepare for the thrust. Fortuna, you're not focused. This is beginner shit."

"Sorry," I muttered, correcting my stance.

Gil smirked. "How embarrassing."

My eyes narrowed at him. Without warning, I swung my sword. Gil blocked the assault, but it was close, and he knew it—surprise flashed in his expression. My chest heaved as I said, "Remember when I asked for your opinion? Oh, wait, that didn't happen."

In an expert movement, he swung his arm around, using so much strength that I was forced to follow it. Our blades separated with a hard, hollow sound. Gil stepped away and began to circle me. "Still ruled by your emotions, I see," he remarked.

I gave him a cold smile. "Am I?"

In an instant, I rolled down his blade in an anti-clockwise direction, raising my own to shorten its reach. As I came out of the spin, the tip of my sword scraped across Gil's chest. I didn't give him a chance to recover before I spun again. The vampire rushed to block my second assault, and his features sharpened with concentration. We both knew I could've done far more damage if I'd wanted.

Gil didn't taunt me again. We kept going, one minute stretching into two. Every once in a while, Adam called out a correction, but Gil's attention only shifted from our fight when someone behind me said, "My lady? Are you all right?"

I lowered my sword, breathing hard, and looked over my shoulder at Lyari. "Oh, good. You're here."

"I need more caffeine," Adam said abruptly. He finally got up from the couch and headed for the door, muttering as he passed, "Better get some from Bea's while it's still safe to drink."

"We'll come with you," Gil declared. He took my weapon without comment and strolled off the mat. He hung up our swords, then slung his arm over Seth's narrow shoulders. "I've a hankering for some greasy food. Did Gretchen add fish and chips to the menu yet? She promised she would."

Seth murmured something back, and the door hinges squealed as they left. I watched Lyari scan the room, searching for an immediate threat.

"He really loves the sound of his own voice, doesn't he?" I asked dryly. Still trying to come down from training, I went over to the couch and rummaged through my bag. I said over my shoulder, "I have an update. Multiple updates, actually. We found out that Oliver is being controlled, and he has been this whole time. I'll give you three guesses who's doing it. All of the victims are connected, like we thought—the Dark Prince has been looking for something, Lyari. Olorel's grave."

My fingers closed around the water bottle I'd been looking for. As I took a drink, I faced the faerie and saw that her nostrils were flaring. She pulled her phone out of her pocket and unlocked the screen, then showed it to me. "'Danger,'" she said flatly. "'Life or death.' *That's* what your message said."

I raised my eyebrows, twisting the cap back on the water bottle. "Isn't it?"

Lyari let out a long breath through her nose. "I don't have time for this, Your Majesty."

"Why not?" I challenged as she turned away. I tossed the bottle onto the couch and hurried after her, my voice slicing through the music that was still playing. "Are you back at the Unseelie Court—is that it? Or maybe you're running errands for *him* again."

Lyari stopped. She swung back around and closed the distance between us, then shoved her face in mine. *"Never,"* she hissed.

Satisfaction blazed through me, and suddenly I knew exactly how Laurie had felt so long ago, when he'd goaded Collith at the Unseelie Court by proposing to me. The words he'd said that day echoed through my memory. "There you are," I said.

"What do you want from me?" Lyari demanded, pulling back. "Do you not understand how terrible it is to be here? I am no longer *fit* to be your Right Hand!"

She tried to hide her pain, but some of it slipped into her voice. I felt an answering ache in my own chest. This wasn't just about her transition. I knew that she blamed herself for Finn's death, just as I did. For the first time, I looked at Lyari and realized why I'd always been drawn to her. From the very beginning, even after she'd struck me, she had stood out from others. We were different in so many ways, and yet, the one thing we shared made those differences insignificant.

We were afraid.

We both hid it well, me behind my bravado or my hate, and Lyari behind her uniform or her honor. Each of us terrified that we were broken or lacking in some way. Love terrified us most of all. But without it, we'd get lost in the dark. We'd become the very things we feared.

"I want you to come home," I told Lyari firmly. "If not for your sake, then for mine. Emma has been asking where you are incessantly. She misses you."

"She does?"

I smiled at her, softening. "Of *course* she does. We all do."

"I . . . miss all of you, as well." Lyari's posture was stiff as she said it. For a second, I thought about hugging her, but I quickly dismissed the idea. I reached for a towel instead.

"There was another reason I reached out," I said as I began to dry myself off. I forced myself to meet Lyari's gaze again. "I was hoping you still have a connection to him, or a way to contact his people."

"Why?" she asked instantly. Just as I had an Unseelie Queen mask, Lyari had a Guardian face, and she wore it now. She didn't ask who I was talking about—the two of us had never played stupid games like that. It was one of the reasons I liked her so much.

It was also why I didn't hide the truth from her now. "I want a meeting," I said.

"To save the Beast?" Lyari's eyebrows knit together, her tone lilting with disbelief. She knew about my history with Oliver, of course, and the vow I'd made.

"To save *everyone*. The devil will keep killing until he gets what he wants, and there'll be consequences whenever he does find that grave." I paused, allowing her to see the unease in my eyes. "Something tells me all of this is only the beginning, Ly. I have to do whatever I can to stop him."

The corners of her mouth deepened. "Even if I did agree to such a reckless request, I don't have any connections to him left, my lady. I swear to you on the ashes of my bloodline."

Lyari fell silent, probably waiting for me to argue. Unfortunately, I believed her. *Shit*, I thought. Of course this couldn't just be easy. Out loud I said, "It's okay. I'll figure something else out."

I couldn't quite hide the strange note in my voice as I realized what this meant. Without Lyari, my only other connection to the devil was . . . Oliver.

I felt my friend's sharp eyes assessing me. Had she guessed

what I was thinking? Just as I had with Emma when she'd been too perceptive, I allowed my exhaustion to shine through, hoping Lyari would blame that for whatever she'd seen. Relief caught in my chest when she said, "Get some rest, Your Majesty. You look terrible."

"That's so sweet of you," I said. She started to turn away again, but my voice stopped her. "Hey, Ly? Think about what I said, okay?"

She stood there for a moment, one hand on her hip, the other resting on the hilt of her sword. I couldn't see her face, but something in the line of her shoulders emanated . . . consideration. "Okay," she said at last.

Before I could say anything else, she sifted.

I was slightly disappointed as I moved to get my things. I'd been hoping our conversation would end with her sitting in the passenger seat and returning with me. As usual, I had been too fast, too ambitious. Some things moved more slowly, and I needed to be patient. Today was a start, at least. I remembered the look on Lyari's face when I'd asked her to come back.

A good start, I thought.

As my car keys jangled in my hand, I realized that it was probably for the best Lyari hadn't accepted my invitation. It might've just put her in harm's way, like Finn. Tonight, I needed to be alone.

Tonight, I was going to summon Oliver.

For once, fate was on my side. When I got back to the loft, I found it empty.

With how many people lived here, and also people who didn't live here coming and going, too, there was always someone around. Making noise, living, talking. I liked the chaos, but it could make sleep a challenge. Especially when one of your roommates was a baby. As I set my keys down, I looked around the still, shadowed room and knew exactly what I'd do with this opportunity. There was cleaning to do—since Matthew had come into our lives, there *always* seemed to be cleaning to do—and there were some things of my own I'd been wanting to do. Things that were unrelated to Oliver and Lucifer, who consumed my every waking moment and most of my sleeping ones, too.

But cleaning and to-do lists would have to come later.

Instead, I went right to the couch and lay down. There was a blanket draped on the armrest, which I shook open and draped over myself. The scent clinging to the blanket hit me. It smelled like Collith. All the tension left my body and I released a long, low sigh. My eyes fluttered shut, and within seconds, I was falling into darkness. Just before I plummeted to the depths, I had a single thought.

Oliver.

Summoning him was even easier than I'd thought it would be. I could feel his familiar essence on the other side of consciousness, lurking like a shark beneath the water. The moment our minds connected, I felt a burst of doubt. Maybe this was a terrible idea. Maybe I should've found another way to contact Lucifer. What if Oliver used my power again? What if he hurt someone else I loved when I woke up?

It was too late to stop now. I'd already jumped. Terror ripped through me, and I opened my eyes expecting to find myself in one of Oliver's dreams, which could only be rife with blood and death.

Grass rustled all around me.

Stunned confusion clouded my mind as I turned in a circle. I'd thought I would never see this place again. With Oliver free and the fact that we hadn't been here since the night Finn died, I had believed it was destroyed, or at the very least lost in the dark recesses of my mind.

The dreamscape wasn't destroyed, but it was changed.

The sky roiled with gray clouds. A few rays of light managed to break through and touch the ground, but there was nothing whimsical about the picture. Wind howled over the grass, whipping the long strands in every direction, making our peaceful meadow a violent sea.

Tonight I wore a white dress. It flattened against my breasts and thighs as I scanned the horizon, searching for him. A moment later, it felt like my heart stumbled in my chest.

Oliver stood in the distance, a dark shape against the dying light.

Slowly, we began walking toward each other. The wind seemed to come from every direction, as if it couldn't decide whether to urge me toward Oliver or push me away from him. Once we were within earshot of each other, we stopped. The wind tousled Oliver's golden hair, and I longed to reach up and fix it as I had a thousand times before. My fingers curled into fists. There was a beat of tense, tangled silence between us.

"Is this real?" I asked tightly.

As soon as the question left my mouth, I thought of Finn. I felt the gentle sway of the fishing boat beneath us as he told me, *Depends on your definition of real.*

It felt like I was going around in circles, asking the same questions and making the same mistakes.

Oliver was silent. I lifted my chin to face him, and he gazed back at me with sadness in his eyes. I knew I needed to ask about Olorel's grave, but the responding ache in my chest made it difficult to think about anything except Oliver, and us, and how we'd gotten here.

"Why is this the first time we've been back?" I gestured to the hills around us. "Why haven't I seen the dreamscape since you . . . since . . ."

I stopped, my throat filling, and Oliver's shoulders hunched against the wind as if he was cold. It was that night, I thought as

I watched his jaw tighten. He didn't want to talk about it, either. Well, that was too damn bad.

"You guard your mind with a door. Until tonight, it's been closed to me," Oliver said.

The sound of his voice made the ache worse. I swallowed and turned my head, looking toward the horizon. In the short time since we'd been standing there, the clouds had gotten darker. The sky that had once been such a bright, endless blue was bleak and churning, as if the dreamscape itself was mourning what we had lost.

I turned back to Oliver reluctantly, knowing we didn't have much time. Any second now, someone in my family would return home and probably wake me. I'd come here for a reason. The wind blew a lock of hair into Oliver's eyes, and he sounded so much like the boy I'd always known as he asked, "How are you?"

My heart was throbbing now. I wanted to respond with something cruel, but all I could bring myself to say was, "Not great."

"Same," Oliver murmured. His gaze bored into mine, so piercing and blue. I looked back and forced myself to remember the last house. The freshest memory of what Oliver was. *Torn limbs. Exposed ribs. Red walls.*

"I saw your latest," I said abruptly. There was another heartbeat of thick, tense silence. Then Oliver was the one to look away, his jaw clenching again. So he did feel shame for what he'd done, I thought, watching the tics and tells in his profile. Even from the side, I could read him better than any map or book. I was still watching Oliver when I finally told him, "I found the note, too. What does Lucifer want with Olorel's grave?"

Oliver's voice was flat. "I don't know. He doesn't trust me. He gives the orders, and I have to follow them."

My eyebrows rose. "If his control over you is so absolute, how were you able to put the note back? Why did I dream about him torturing you? You're not a dog, Oliver. You're not his pet."

My words made him withdraw even further, and the wind became ferocious now. It whipped more strands of Oliver's sun-touched hair around his face as he growled, "I don't want your pity."

"I don't pity you. You made every choice that got us to this point. The only reason I opened the door tonight is because . . . because I need you to arrange a meeting with him." My heart raced as the words left my mouth.

But Oliver was already shaking his head. "No. He won't tolerate any more delays, Fortuna. He's merciless. If you do something to interfere, he'll kill you. Regardless of whatever you think exists between you."

There was no reproach in his tone, but I still bristled with guilt and shame. Above us, the sky continued to dim. "If you won't help me, why did you even come?" I snapped.

"I'm here because I miss you."

Oliver said it so simply, and his bluntness disarmed me. Grief burned through my veins, and for an instant, I swore I could taste ash in my mouth. I glared at him through a sheen of bright, furious tears.

"All these years," I said bitterly. "You watched me grieve them. You held me every time I cried. You stayed silent every time I wondered who was responsible. You had so many chances to tell the truth. So many fucking chances. I can't decide what makes you more monstrous—the fact that you killed them or the fact that you've been keeping it from me ever since."

I expected Oliver to flinch again, but instead, he just looked tired. His shoulders fell in a barely perceptible movement. "You're not the only one who's been tormented, Fortuna. I'm not the monster you think I am. I'm just the monster you wanted me to be."

"What the fuck does *that* mean?" I demanded, my hands still fisted at my sides. It had started to rain now, just light pinpricks of cold on my cheeks.

Oliver met my gaze, and though his eyes were full of pain, they were bitter, too. "It's as I said the night I cleaned your wounds—you created me. I am a thing born of fear and violence. When I became reality, that was all I knew. The moment you regained consciousness, I was forced back inside. That's where I was able to learn and grow. Most of it alongside you, remember?"

I didn't answer. The storm was gaining strength, and I could feel one gathering inside me, too. I needed to run, to get away and *think*.

I'd squeezed my eyes shut, and before I could say anything to Oliver, I felt his hands cup my cheeks. Mine immediately rose to grip his wrists. "Don't touch me," I whispered.

In an instant, his warmth fell away. I still hadn't opened my eyes, and every sound felt enhanced as he asked, "Is that really what you want?"

Doubt fluttered in my chest like some small-winged thing. I frowned and shook my head, then finally opened my eyes and looked at Oliver again. "I don't know."

Thunder made the ground tremble. He glanced up at the sky, a frown hovering in the lines around his mouth. I searched his face for any sign of the Beast, almost desperate for it, but all I could see was Ollie. Confusion and turmoil swirled through me.

When he lowered his head again, his features had hardened, as if he'd decided something. "I love you, Fortuna. And I know you love me, too," Oliver said.

"Do you know what loving you feels like?" I cried, flattening my hand against my chest as if I could protect the heart aching within. But it was far too late for that. I swallowed, my eyes wide as I stared at Oliver and continued raggedly, "Loving you is like holding onto a rope that's constantly pulling me into the darkness. Even as my hands tear and bleed, I hold on. It would be so much better if I let go, but I just keep—"

"And you think it's any easier for me?" Oliver countered, his jaw feathering as he glared back. His eyes were overly bright, betraying his pain. "I was a prisoner, forced to watch you come and go. Forced to stand by and listen as other lovers brought you pleasure. Forced to stay even when you didn't want me anymore. I *was* hardly more than a dog begging for scraps!"

My voice was cold now. "Then let's finally be done with this, and let each other go."

"Fine. You first," Oliver challenged.

"Fine." I whirled and walked away, shivering in the biting wind. There was something wilder about this place now, as though all our pain had changed it. The light sheet of rain had given way to a thickening torrent.

Oliver's long-legged strides caught up with mine in no time. "If you really wanted to leave, you wouldn't still be here," his low voice said by my ear.

"That's not—" I started just before he pulled me back in a way that was entirely unlike the Oliver I'd always known. I instinctively wrenched my arm, and my heel slipped from the movement. We both went tumbling.

Oliver tried to break my fall, twisting so that he took the brunt of it. I landed on top of him, my palms sliding through the dirt, which had turned into mud thanks to the rain. I came to a stop with my mouth a breath above Oliver's. I looked into his eyes, panting. He was panting, too. With every breath, I felt his body brush against mine. Thunder rumbled around us, my hair streaming over my shoulders. Oliver's fingers tightened against my sides. His gaze dropped to my mouth, and slowly, his erection hardened between my legs.

That was all it took. Like a match to an open flame, we exploded into movement. Oliver sat up, his hands sliding up my back as we kissed, our mouths and tongues moving hard and fast. We consumed each other while Oliver guided me onto my back, and he only eased away to remove my underwear, then his pants. I propped myself up on my elbows, battling impatience and need. At first, I watched the muscles in Oliver's stomach tighten and flex. Then my gaze slowly rose, stopping on the freckles over the bridge of his nose.

As he returned, I felt him pushing my dress up around my hips. Moments later, Oliver loomed over me and his head lowered, nipping and kissing my neck. My fingers splayed along his hard triceps. I tipped my head back, heedless of the mud and the rain—I barely felt it. This was wrong, I thought. God, I knew it was wrong. The walls were coming down on every side and neither of us cared. I drew my legs back, skimming them along Oliver's body, and then opened wide for him. I clawed at his back, trying to urge him forward, and he folded over me for another heavy kiss before positioning himself square with my opening. Anticipation pooled inside me. Lightning streaked across the sky, barely more than a distracting flash as I lost myself in Oliver's taste again, his smell, the way his hands felt on my bare skin.

But when I felt the tip of Oliver's cock brush against my folds, reason returned in a rush.

"Wait. Stop," I gasped.

Oliver yanked away. I tugged my dress down and scooted back, too. We were both still breathing hard, and I knew that if I didn't leave now, I might give in to the desire still roaring through me. "Tell Lucifer that I want a meeting. Tomorrow morning at Adam's shop. You *owe* me, Oliver," I added raggedly.

His face twitched like I had stabbed him again. He got to his feet, and he watched as I did the same, keeping a healthy distance between us now. "Fine," Oliver said.

Surprise made me pause. I'd been ready for him to put up a fight. "Fine?"

He nodded and began to turn away, as if he was going to leave. But then Oliver paused. He angled his body in my direction again, not quite facing me, his eyes lowered. The wind almost snatched his voice away as he said quietly, "I may pull you into the darkness, but you pull me into the light. Beautiful, blinding light. However this ends, just know that."

I swallowed. We kept staring at each other through the storm, and every beat of my heart felt like a raw throb. "We can't ever—" I started.

Oliver's attention shifted, and just like that, he was the Beast again. Those black veins spread beneath his skin like tree roots, his eyes going completely black. I twisted around to see what had made Oliver change so quickly. When I saw the figure coming toward us through the rain, my eyes widened, and it felt like the ground fell out from beneath me.

"Collith? How did you . . ."

He stopped on the path, and those familiar hazel eyes moved down my body, probably checking for injuries. Strangely, Collith wore the clothes he'd been in when we'd met for the first time, and the collar of his gray coat stirred in the gathering storm. "I couldn't wake you, and there's a situation that needs your attention," he said.

"Situation?" I repeated, my pulse picking up speed. "What do you mean?"

Instead of answering, Collith's nostrils flared, and I realized there were probably still traces of my fear in the air. And maybe something else, too. Heat rushed into my cheeks, but Collith wasn't looking at me—all of his focus had gone to Oliver.

"So you're him," he said.

"And you're him," Oliver replied. His voice was like gravel, probably due to how his teeth had elongated. I glanced down and noted his claws, which were black as a starless night.

As the faerie and the Beast sized each other up, I was completely at a loss for what to say. It felt like my two worlds were meeting in a crash collision. Even though we'd been hunting Oliver for months, I had never imagined him and Collith together. It was so surreal that it took me an extra moment to remember why he had come.

"You said there was a situation?" I managed, focusing on Collith.

He didn't respond. He was still studying Oliver, and something in his features had gone predatory, as well. It was a look I'd never seen Collith give anyone before. In that moment, I knew he was considering whether or not to kill the Beast. Ironically, I couldn't let him do that, not until Oliver had arranged my meeting with Lucifer. I turned and closed the small distance between me and Collith.

"Hey. Let's go home," I said. When he gave no indication that he'd heard, I put my hand on his chest. "Collith."

He put his hand over mine, and his gaze finally returned to me. The dangerous glint hadn't completely faded, but he sounded more like himself as he replied, "Yes. We should go."

I didn't dare look in Oliver's direction again. Collith knew me too well, and my expression might have given something away. So without another word to either of them, I closed my eyes and thought, *I want to wake up.* I imagined the warm loft I'd left behind. I pictured the soft lights and the high ceilings. I heard the patter of Hello's small feet and Matthew's happy babbling. A breath filled my chest, and I released it slowly, all the tension easing from my body.

When I opened my eyes again, I was home.

I sat upright, and the blanket that had been draped over me fell to the floor. Collith knelt beside the couch. Once he saw that I was conscious, he stood. I took his hand and let him help me up, too.

"Okay, now what's the big emergency?" I asked. My voice felt too casual for what had just happened, but I didn't know how else to act.

Collith just inclined his dark head and said, "It's downstairs."

It? I would've been alarmed, but Collith's demeanor was calm. Intrigued now, I followed him down the stairwell, trailing my fingers along the wall to steady myself.

The moment I reached the bottom step, I scanned the barn. At first, everything seemed normal. Then I sensed movement nearby, and my gaze snapped toward the training room. I stiffened.

"Easy," Collith murmured. "I don't think it intends us any harm."

Just as I started to demand answers, there was a soft sound that reminded me of the click of Stanley's claws. Seconds later, a huge, scaled creature crawled timidly into the light.

For a moment, I stared with disbelief, and I wondered if I hadn't left the dreamscape after all. A slow, delighted grin stretched across my face.

"Narfu?"

CHAPTER NINE

As morning crept over the horizon, I sat on the bench in front of Adam's shop and tried not to fidget.

Gray clouds roiled in the sky. They brought wind with them, and change, along with white dandelion seeds riding the air. While I waited for the devil himself to show up, I kept glancing over at the office door to reassure myself that no one was inside. It was Sunday, and the shop was closed. The guys had all gone across the street to Bea's, just as I'd known they would. I hadn't told any of them I was coming. Not even Collith knew, since I'd left in my running clothes. I had taken Emma's car, which Collith undoubtedly heard, but it wasn't unusual for me to try a new trail somewhere nearby. If I'd told him the truth, he would have demanded to be present for this meeting, which I had never agreed to so my conscious was clear. Mostly.

Although Laurie wasn't here, either, I knew what he'd say about that. I could picture his smirk as he drawled, *Well, well, look who's thinking like a faerie.*

I'd chosen our meeting place carefully. I didn't want Lucifer anywhere near the homestead, and I didn't want him in a public place, either. But I was still close enough to the bar that I could call for backup.

If Lucifer did show—I didn't exactly have a way of confirming with Oliver that he'd passed on my message—this would be my second reunion in the past twenty-four hours. But I knew it wouldn't be nearly as joyful as the first. The corners of my lips quirked as I thought about Narfu.

The demon had been so careful when he'd embraced me, the tips of his large claws lightly grazing my shoulders. Narfu was back at home now, situated comfortably in the barn. He had refused to come upstairs, which was probably for the best, since I didn't fully trust him around Matthew. Emma ignored my warnings and brought Narfu a pile of blankets and pillows. When I'd left the demon, he had been sitting on his new makeshift bed, his long neck arched back to peer up at the window. Some of the terror that had been clinging to him was gone.

I already knew what Laurie was going to say when he heard about our latest arrival. *Another stray, Fortuna?*

I wasn't clear on the logistics of having a giant lizard for a roommate, but we'd figure it out. It was a good thing the house was fairly isolated.

Suddenly the mental image of Narfu vanished, and my skin prickled with awareness. I wasn't sure what made me turn—there was no sound, no shadow. One moment, I was alone, and the next Lucifer stood there in all his golden glory. A surprised breath caught in my throat.

"Hello, Fortuna." He wore a black suit, and it was similar to others I'd seen him in. Even in direct light, the defined features of his face were smooth and flawless, as if they'd been chiseled from stone by God. Not for the first time, I resented Lucifer's beauty. I hated that I noticed it. I tore my gaze away from him and searched for Oliver, but the devil seemed to have come alone.

"It's good to see you," Lucifer said. He studied me, and his smile faded. "You haven't been sleeping."

"The last time we saw each other, you shoved a fence post through my stomach," I reminded him coldly. "I don't think you really care about whether I'm sleeping well or not."

"To what do I owe this pleasure, then?" Lucifer asked. Startling me, he bent and settled on the bench. He sat on the other end, but I could still smell him. Just like that, I was back in Hell, in Lucifer's bed, that enticing scent all around me as I completely lost myself in him.

"The killing needs to end," I said, meeting Lucifer's gaze without flinching. My voice was steel. "And you're going to release whatever hold you have over Oliver."

His expression didn't change—he'd been expecting this, probably. Lucifer turned his head, the bright daybreak catching strands of gold and making them glitter. He scanned the horizon, his full lips deepened at the corners. At last he replied, his voice as neutral as ever, "The Beast has proven himself useful in my purpose here."

Resentment surged through me, and I felt my fists begin to clench. I forced my fingers open again and schooled my features back into a cool mask. It wasn't a no, I reminded myself. Lucifer wasn't the only one who knew what to expect. He might've been the Dark Prince, but he was still Fallen. He liked bargains and ploys just as much as a faerie. This was the part where I offered him something in exchange for Oliver's freedom. I opened my mouth to ask Lucifer what he wanted . . . but I couldn't do it.

"And what is your purpose here?" I asked instead.

"That is the question, isn't it?" Lucifer squinted at the sun. "Perhaps one day I'll have a chance to ask the Maker again."

A blatant dodge. He wasn't going to tell me anything. I'd known it wouldn't be that easy, but I still had to try. Because Laurie was right about one thing—Lucifer hadn't clawed his way to this world just to play human or get out of Hell. And if he didn't want me knowing the truth, it meant I probably wouldn't like it.

Frustration threatened to overcome me again. How could I

stop him if I didn't even know what he was doing? Judging from the demon Lyari had killed, and the fact that Narfu was in my barn right now, Lucifer's plan was already at work. He'd never tell me anything . . . but that didn't mean I couldn't get information out of him. He obviously wanted to talk.

"A couple weeks ago, something ran me off the road," I said impulsively. "It had long limbs and its skin was white. I remembered seeing a similar creature during my time in Hell. You wouldn't happen to know anything about that, would you?"

"Sounds like a yar demon," Lucifer remarked, leaning against the backrest of the bench. He propped his elbow on it and his forearm dangled between us. "Their magic is incredibly useful. For the most part, it involves shielding and blocking. Their presence can even affect technology."

"Why is it here?" I asked. This time, silence met me. No surprise there. I changed tactics and said, blurting the questions rapid-fire, "How did you know what Oliver was? What he'd done?"

Lucifer's shoulders moved in a slight shrug. "It's here because I've been . . . experimenting. Regarding the Beast, I simply put two and two together, my lady. As you've become aware, Nightmares can manifest dreams or fantasies into reality. It was immediately obvious that your Oliver wasn't just a dream, and I'd already deduced that you consider him your childhood friend. The fact his creation coincided with your parents' deaths couldn't be coincidence."

For a moment, I sat in stunned silence. So it had taken Lucifer seconds to see what it took decades for me to figure out. The realization definitely smarted. And if Lucifer was able to do that, he probably knew how to kill Oliver, too. Just like I told Collith and Laurie.

I also wanted to ask about these experiments, but if I had any hope of getting answers from Lucifer, I needed to rattle him. Throw him off his game. The devil was always ten steps ahead of us, and there was only one way to even the playing field—emotion.

I looked at Lucifer again, and the wind played with a strand of my hair as I asked, "Did Persephone ever manifest anything?"

Lucifer stood up from the bench in one smooth motion. His expression was neutral, but there was a stiffness in the way he held himself that made satisfaction curl inside me. "Like it or not, Lady Sworn, you are a creature of dreams, just like me. You are capable of so much more if you open your mind to the possibilities. I can show you, if you'll let me," Lucifer added.

He held his hand out. I looked at it, then up at him, my lips pressed together in thought. I didn't miss that Lucifer hadn't answered my question about Persephone, either. But I had finally learned my lesson when it came to bastards and bargains, and this time, I decided to settle for good, old-fashioned violence.

I got to my feet, too, and tipped my head back to meet the devil's gaze. "If you don't stop killing people, or using Oliver for your dirty work, I'll end you. I don't know how yet, but I'll find a way. I *always* find a way."

"So full of fire, aren't you?" he murmured. A small smile flickered at the corner of Lucifer's lips and flared bright in his eyes. He ran his finger along the edge of my jaw, exactly where Laurie had touched me the last time I'd seen him. "It's going to be glorious watching you burn."

I shoved his hand away. "Never again," I hissed.

"*Never* doesn't exist for an immortal." Lucifer's voice dropped, the heat of it trying to penetrate the wall of ice around my heart. "It wasn't all a lie, Fortuna. We can still have what we shared in Hell."

"Never again," I repeated, quietly this time. But I had never been more certain of anything. I held Lucifer's gaze without flinching.

His mouth tightened, and he stepped away. It felt like the temperature fell around us. "I forget, sometimes, that you were raised amongst humans."

Lucifer said this like it was an insult or a shortcoming. I just looked back at him silently, wondering how I'd been so blind. How I had ever thought I'd actually loved someone with such a black heart. I comforted myself with the knowledge that, someday, he would be dead.

He must've seen the hatred in my eyes, the dark promise, because Lucifer turned and walked away without another word. Birdsong filled the air as he strolled toward a thin line of trees, his hands in his pockets. A moment later, he faded like a mirage.

I let out a long, tense breath. My meeting with Lucifer had accomplished nothing—I still didn't know why he was here or how to kill Oliver. But I had to talk to Collith about it, no matter how much I didn't want to. There could be consequences for what I'd just done, and we needed to be prepared. With slow reluctance, I started toward Emma's car. My movement startled a pair of crows, and one of them took flight, letting out an angry cry. There were others nearby fighting over a scrap of bread, but I noticed the crow that remained was eerily still. It watched me with its head cocked, as if it had asked a question. I frowned and shook myself, reaching for the door handle. I got in and started the engine, then headed for home.

I swore I felt the crow's eyes on me all the way until I turned the corner and disappeared from sight.

That night, I tried to summon Oliver again.

I lay in bed and waited for sleep to come, but every time the darkness crept near, my thoughts drove it away again. Collith was furious with me. He hadn't shouted or even said much since I'd told him about my meeting with Lucifer, but it was obvious. After our conversation, he had started working on a project downstairs and I'd gone for a long run. When I got back, he was still at it, sawdust flying through the air. He hadn't even come up for dinner.

Around 2:00 a.m., I finally gave up and slipped out of bed. I didn't know what I'd say to Collith, but I couldn't leave it like this for another second. I crept from my room and circled the couch expecting to see him sleeping in his usual place. I faltered when I discovered it was empty. All the blankets were folded and neatly stacked. A whisper of anxiety went through me. Had he gone to stay somewhere else for the night? Was he coming back?

Tomorrow, I promised myself. I'd talk to him tomorrow. Everything would be fine. Collith and I had survived far worse than this, and it was normal for him to take some space.

Once again, I removed a blanket from the pile and stretched out in Collith's spot, surrounding myself with his scent. Sleep claimed me within minutes. I tried to think of Oliver, as I had last time.

Instead, I dreamed of Laurie.

The vantage point of this dream was strange. Instead of seeing the world through his eyes, or as if I were standing next to him, I was peering down at the Seelie King like I was a bird tucked amongst the treetops. His bright hair shone like a star. He stood in a dense forest, the leaves all around him a dark, deep green, the tree trunks thick with moss, massive roots winding through the soil. It must've rained recently in this dream, because mist hovered over the ground and dampness clung to the air like invisible skin.

Laurie's clothes were simple, for once—he wore a thin, dark shirt with long sleeves and jeans. He was standing differently than he usually did, too. There was none of the languid nonchalance or casual, devil-may-care arrogance Laurie typically used to piss off everyone around him. Tonight he was preternaturally still, his arms crossed as his silver eyes roamed the darkness. It was obvious the Seelie King was waiting for someone.

Moments after I'd had the thought, I felt a shift in the air.

Laurie spoke without turning his head. "I was beginning to think you'd stood me up. So Fortuna arranged a meeting with good ol' Luci, eh?"

"Yes," the reply came. "But their conversation didn't go well."

A moment later, Collith appeared through the trees. He rested his palm against a low branch as he ducked beneath it, entering the small clearing. It was almost like he'd dressed for a battle. He wore a black T-shirt and dark tactical pants, and I would have put money on the fact that he'd hidden knives beneath those clothes.

Laurie watched Collith approach with an unreadable expression. "I figured. She has about as much tact as a lumberjack swinging an ax in a china shop," he remarked.

Collith smiled. It was a look he often got when he was looking at me. "A very endearing lumberjack."

Laurie just kept studying him, and he made no effort to hide the admiration in his eyes. Collith didn't acknowledge it, but he didn't move when Laurie lifted his hand and brushed that stubborn lock of hair out of Collith's eyes. They stared at each other silently, their faces a breath apart. Then Laurie turned away, saying over his shoulder, "You had to pick this place, didn't you?"

"I was feeling nostalgic," Collith answered. He stayed where he was, but from this strange vantage point, Laurie was out of sight.

The Seelie King's voice floated through the night. "And where is our lady right now?"

"I just checked on her. She's sleeping."

Laurie reappeared, returning to the spot he'd been standing in before. "You're not going to ask why I summoned you here?"

"I already know why," Collith said.

Laurie's gaze ran over him slowly. "Yes, I suppose you do. You came prepared. I'm surprised—no objections? No tedious arguments or speeches about morality?"

Collith looked back at Laurie with an expression that sent a chill through me. It was the face of the Unseelie King. Cold. Calculating. "Not tonight," he said.

What's so significant about tonight? I wondered.

"Do you trust me?" Laurie asked.

"Not really."

"Good. One of us needs to be the voice of reason here." Laurie took his phone out. The glow of the screen lit up his hard expression, and when I saw that, another whisper of apprehension went through me. Laurie held the phone out to Collith. "An hour ago, one of my people found something. I know where the Beast is."

Silence swelled between them. After a few seconds, Collith handed the phone back. His eyes looked black in the night-darkened forest. "She'll never forgive us," was all he said.

"Oh, sure she will. She just might stab us a few times before she does. Shall we?" As Laurie pocketed his phone again, raising his brows expectantly, Collith didn't move. Some of the lightness left Laurie's expression, and his voice was lower when he said, "She will *never* kill him, Coll. That's not who Fortuna is. She may be angry—some of her hatred might be real, even—but she protects the people she loves. Even when they don't deserve it. *Especially* when they don't deserve it."

She will never kill him. After those words came out of Laurie's mouth, I barely heard the rest. I could only focus on the realization searing through me. This was no dream, and Collith and Laurie planned to go after Oliver. Tonight.

And just as Collith had feared, I *was* furious with them. Furious they hadn't told me, that they'd taken this choice from me. They were also going to get themselves killed!

Completely oblivious to my silent fuming, Laurie began to move out of view. His voice floated back. "Okay, let's go."

"Wait." Collith stayed where he was. His brow furrowed, and the corners of his mouth deepened. "We can't do this."

Laurie groaned. "I knew it. I *knew* you'd lose your nerve."

"I love her, Laurelis. Don't you?"

Laurie opened his mouth to respond, but something made him pause. His jaw clenched and he stared toward the trees. "Yes," he said.

The admission sent a blend of strange emotions through my veins. Resentment. Jealousy. I felt myself begin to frown in bewilderment, but then, in a burst of horror, I realized the reaction wasn't mine. Those feelings didn't belong to me. Once I figured that out, I understood what was actually happening.

This wasn't a dream, or some bond to Collith and Laurie allowing me to see their conversation.

It was my connection to Oliver.

The bizarre angle. The odd vantage point. I *had* summoned Oliver. I was seeing everything through his eyes, which meant this was real . . . and he was hiding right above the spot where Collith and Laurie stood. I had to warn them! A soundless scream tore through me and I imagined myself beating at a wall between us. *Look up!*

Neither of them reacted.

My panic made it difficult to hear what Collith was saying, but as I mentally writhed, he continued his conversation with Laurie as if there weren't a massive, deadly creature lurking over their heads. ". . . haven't mentioned how you plan to put this thing down. All we know is that it isn't susceptible to holy blades or bullets," he said.

Collith, move! I screamed at him.

Once again, the faeries didn't hear me . . . but Oliver did. He must've made a noise, because both faeries went still. In that moment, I swore even the stars held their breath. Slowly, Laurie tipped his head back.

As his cold, metallic eyes met Oliver's, the faerie king's expression didn't change. His voice was calm as ever as he said, "I thought we'd try cutting off its head first. And if that doesn't work, then we'll just burn the fucker."

He means with heavenly fire, I thought at the same instant everything exploded.

They moved with the speed of Fallen. Oliver dropped from the tree and it felt like *I* was doing it, like it was *my* heart pumping with adrenaline and *my* threatening growl that rent the air. Laurie's hand was a pale blur as he reached back. A moment later, his sword flashed. Collith's arms flew out, his hands, wrists, and arms beginning to crackle and glow. He gathered his power while Laurie and I fought.

Stop! I screamed at them. *I'm here!*

They moved so fast that even inside Oliver's head, it was hard to track. It was dark, too, and all I saw was the glint of a blade or the flash of a claw in the moonlight. I tried to slice Laurie open while the silver-haired faerie swung at my neck, my wings, my arms, anything to gain the advantage. Again and again, we just barely missed each other. Laurie had a cut on his cheek and his bicep. My thigh burned from a slice courtesy of Laurie's sword.

The Seelie King was the best fighter I knew, other than Lucifer, and Oliver wasn't just holding his own—he was winning. But there was one thing Laurie had that Oliver didn't.

Collith.

His heavenly fire crackled in our direction, and Laurie sifted just in time to avoid it. I reacted quickly, as well, but Collith must've anticipated that the Beast would evade his first assault, because his other arm shot out a split second after I moved, separating the inferno into two.

The second blaze hit me square in the chest and I soared backward.

Oliver roared in pain, and I screamed with him. My spine slammed into a tree trunk just before I crumpled. Then I rolled, again and again, and Collith's fire followed me the entire way. The smell of burned flesh filled the air. At the exact moment the lightning finally abated, Laurie was there, swinging his sword toward my neck.

At the last possible moment, my wing shot up and slammed into Laurie, throwing him off balance. The tip of his sword entered my shoulder instead. But I barely reacted, and my palm slammed into Laurie's chest.

Time seemed to slow. Laurie's body folded, his feet lifting off the ground as he flew backward. I swung away, holding one hand against the spot where the lightning had struck me while my shoulder bled freely. I took a running leap, but my movements were weak and clumsy. No, *Oliver's* movements were weak and slow. Still trapped inside his head, I frantically tried to figure out how badly he'd been wounded. Everything hurt. Oliver beat his wings, and the force of the gust knocked Laurie and Collith back again. It bought Oliver precious time to reach the treetops, where he plunged into the shadows.

Silence descended upon the night.

Oliver breathed heavily, but he fought to control it. Collith and Laurie didn't make a sound, which couldn't mean anything good. I knew as well as Oliver did that he probably had seconds before Collith lit this place up, and him with it.

Oliver bit back a groan and pushed himself off the tree. His wings snapped open, and at the same instant Collith blasted his fire, Oliver flapped. He shot into the air, just above the stream of deadly blue heat, then flapped again. Oliver gritted his teeth and kept doing it, until he was back in the night sky, safe from my protective lovers.

Oliver, I sobbed. *Ollie, are you all right?*

He didn't answer, but I felt his pain. It was nearly as bad as the handful of seconds he'd been consumed by the heavenly fire. Every movement sent a rush of agony through his entire body. But Oliver didn't make a sound. He focused on flapping his wings, and getting as far away from Collith and Laurie as he could before his injuries won out.

I'm coming, I told him. *You're not alone. Just get somewhere safe, and I'll find you. I promise.*

Oliver lifted his head and spotted something in the distance—another barn, strangely similar to the first one we'd found him at. He gritted his teeth and kept going. I felt the cost of every wingbeat, every second he stayed in the air. But Oliver knew just as well as I did that stopping wasn't an option, not until he'd reached some kind of shelter and put distance between himself and the faerie kings. His vision started to blur.

Then he fell from the sky like a piece of lead.

Ollie! I screamed. He spun and tumbled, wings and feathers streaming. Within seconds, the ground hurtled up to meet him.

At the same moment Oliver plummeted through the roof of the barn, my eyes snapped open.

CHAPTER TEN

I flew upright on the couch.

My eyes were wide, and a layer of perspiration clung to my skin. His name was a whisper in my heart. With every frantic beat I heard it. *Oliver, Oliver, Oliver.* He was wounded—I'd felt it like every flame and stab had gone through both of us.

I hurried into my room and pulled on the first clothes I could find in my closet and shoved my wild hair into a baseball cap. My entire body was trembling, but even in my panic, I moved carefully and silently through the loft. Beside the door, I jammed my feet into my tennis shoes and grabbed one of the jackets hanging on the hooks. Then I was gone, plunging into the shadowy stairwell.

The second I stepped outside, the cool night pressing in all around me, I was running. I started down the path that had formed from all our comings and goings, my shoes pounding on the forest floor. I didn't need names or maps; I knew exactly where to find Oliver.

When I threw myself into the darkness, my only thought was of him.

On the other side, I found myself in more trees, but a blast of wind hit me—it was about to storm, wherever I was. This seemed to be a common occurrence whenever Oliver was near. Rain pattered against my face. I put the jacket on and ducked my head down, pressing on without hesitation.

Luckily, Oliver had taken shelter near the Door. I'd only gone a few miles when a barn appeared through the trees. It was the same one I'd seen through Oliver's eyes just before he passed out. I breathed hard as I finally slowed, arching my head back to instinctively take in the details of this place. It was obvious that it had been abandoned for a long time. There were two gaping holes in the roof, and the entire structure was sagging like the walls were moments from collapse.

I pulled the door open cautiously, and the handle clacked as I let it go. I slipped inside, still struggling to get my breathing back to normal. My shoes squished with rainwater on the dirt floor. I scanned the barn, reaching up to lower my hood. My heart drummed in my ears. The space was full of broken stalls and old hay. And there, in the corner . . .

"Ollie." I rushed toward him. Oliver's wings drooped on either side of his limp body, and I stepped over one carefully before I knelt at his side. He was tucked in a pocket of darkness, but the holes in the roof let in just enough light from the night sky that I could make out faint details. Oliver must've been directly beneath a leak, because rain sluiced down his naked torso, leaving streaks through the blood. Why couldn't I find any injuries? I began running my hands over him, trying to remember what I'd seen. Collith's blast of fire had hit him, I was sure of it. "Are you okay? Here, let me—"

"I'm fine," Oliver said, his hands catching hold of my wrists.

It was true. I pulled one hand free and ran my fingertips down the skin where I was certain I'd seen Laurie's sword go in. It was smooth, and all that remained of the wound was a smear of blue. The only visible damage was on Oliver's wings. The bones were still rebuilding, the skin and feathers regrowing. It was a miracle he'd been able to fly.

Now that I had confirmed Oliver was all right, it felt like

something came loose in my chest. I let out a shuddering breath and looked up. "Do you . . ."

Whatever I'd been about to say faded as my gaze locked with Oliver's. Slowly, the adrenaline coursing through me shifted, becoming something else. My hand fell, and in the next breath I was pulling away. I stood up and took several steps back. Oliver got to his feet, too. Heat and awareness swelled between us. I stared at him, remembering what it had felt like when I'd thought he was dying. When I'd thought I had lost him.

Oliver was having similar thoughts—I could see it in the darkness of his eyes, sense it in the tension radiating off his coiled, hard body as he drew closer and closer. His arm rose, and he ran his fingertips down the side of my face. He didn't speak. I didn't break the silence, either. The choice trembled between us. Temptation spread through my core, low and hot.

I knew it was wrong, and twisted, and fucked up in too many ways to count. The thought of touching him should've made me shudder. I should've been glad at the sight of his blood, my fingers itching to finish the job.

But what I felt most was just . . . relief. It sighed through my veins and slipped out of my mouth in the faintest of sounds.

As soon as he heard it, Oliver bent his head to kiss me.

Just like last time, our mouths met in a desperate frenzy. I felt my hat fall off, but I didn't care. All I could think was that Collith had been right. Again. His voice echoed through my head as heat flooded the rest of my body. *You love him, Fortuna. You may not want to admit it, but if you're going to survive this, you need to.*

It felt like my heart was throbbing in time to the pulse between my legs. I wrapped my arms around Oliver's neck and kissed him harder, hungrier. Without breaking away, he lifted me into his arms and walked across the room, setting me on top of a barrel. A wooden post pressed against my back. It was surprisingly solid, and it held my weight while Oliver pulled my jacket off, along with my shirt, and I unbuttoned his jeans. The stillness filled with the sound of our panting, and rain dripping down, and the whisper of a zipper.

Then Oliver pressed his hardness between my legs. Suddenly the yoga pants I'd put on felt very, very thin, and too thick all at once. Of its own volition, one of my hands stole down and wrapped around Oliver's length. It was as well-sized as I remembered, and hard as a rock in my grip. I bit my lip and closed my eyes. *Wrong, wrong, this is wrong.*

But why did it also feel so terribly right?

I was still wavering when I felt Oliver's arm shift. My hand shot back up, and I held onto his shoulder as Oliver's fingertips crept beneath my waistband. A moment later, he put his finger inside me. I bit my lip and arched my back, pushing myself into him. Oliver made a deep, satisfied sound.

"I love how wet you are," he said against my ear.

My teeth clamped down on my lip harder. At the same moment Oliver dipped his head and sucked teasingly at my neck, he added a finger, and a helpless sound slipped out of me. I flattened my palms against his chest and willed myself to push him away, but it felt like something was crying out inside me, begging to give in, to satiate the hot need rising higher and higher.

Then, slowly, my grip unfurled. Barely touching him now, I skimmed my palms over Oliver's broad shoulders, down the firm planes of his back, and over the curve of his firm ass. I raised my head and found our mouths a breath apart. Oliver stared into my eyes as he used his other hand to tug my pants down. It felt like every touch left a trail of sparks behind. I barely registered the cool air whispering over my bared skin.

"Tell me you don't want this," Oliver said quietly. "Say the words, and I'll let you go."

I didn't move. I didn't speak. A war raged inside me. The cold urge to throw the words in his face, and make the choice that I knew was right . . . and the hot, roaring desire that didn't give a fuck about any of it beyond this, the crackling power between us and the low, tingling heat of need. Rain splattered onto my face, and I hardly felt that, either.

I met Oliver's gaze again, and I didn't look away as I used my hold on his backside to urge him inside me. He answered with a single plunge, filling me completely, and I released another involuntary, breathy moan.

Oliver caught the sound in his mouth. He went still again, pressing his forehead to mine, his hard length buried to the hilt. I clenched around him, impatient.

"*Fuck*, Fortuna . . ." Oliver whispered my name as he worshipped me with his mouth and his hands. I worshipped him right back. It felt so *good*, finally being able to touch him in a way I'd been resisting all this time. I wanted more.

Once I was throbbing so urgently I was on the verge of begging him to keep going, Oliver's hips began to thrust in a sensuous rhythm, moving in a deep, torturous, taunting escalation. Every brush sent ripples through the rest of my body, building heat and urgency—until Oliver was fucking me hard and fast, still holding me in his arms as if I weighed nothing. I reached over my head, fumbling for a handhold. My other hand was tangled in Oliver's hair, almost fisting it. He filled me up, again and again, just barely scraping against the most sensitive part of my body.

Past the pleasure and the blinding bursts of heat, some part of me knew there would be consequences to this. As we consumed each other, I heard Oliver's voice in my head, echoes from a memory of two people who no longer existed. *Over the years, I've wondered why any species bothers to love the stars. They burn so briefly, then fade so permanently. Is the bliss and the beauty worth the absence and the sorrow?*

Once, I didn't think it was worth it. All the agony of loss, just for a moment of happiness. But as I reached the peak of my pleasure, I knew that had changed. Now I couldn't deny that I was willing to endure the greatest pain for this fleeting moment of ecstasy. With him. With Oliver.

We would both pay, and it was worth it.

Oliver reached his climax moments after mine. I was just returning to Earth while his cock twitched inside of me, and Oliver released a deep groan. His muscles flexed and strained as the sound drew out of him.

Once we'd both gone still, both of us momentarily spent, Oliver's forehead lowered to my shoulder. I was still sitting on the barrel, and now that I wasn't completely distracted by him, I noticed how precarious the lid was.

Oliver must've noticed at the same time or picked up on my discomfort, somehow. He finally pulled his cock out of me and scooped me up into his arms. He lowered himself back to the ground and set me between his legs, my back resting against his chest. Then he rested his chin on the top of my head, as if he'd just arrived home after a long, long journey. My entire body rose and fell as I heaved a soul-weary sigh.

"What are you thinking?" Oliver murmured.

I was thinking that the body I had given him was warm. Solid. Mortal. Which meant the body I'd given Lucifer was the same. But what if he was a different kind of monster than Oliver? What if I had completely restored the Dark Prince, as he once was, and brought him back as an original angel?

If that was the case, I didn't think he could be killed in the sense that he'd be obliterated from existence—if anything, slitting his throat in this dimension would probably just send him back to his own—but even banishment would be better than doing nothing . . .

My thoughts cut short when Oliver's body jerked. I twisted around to give him a sharp look. "What's wrong?"

"He's summoning me." Oliver refocused on my face, and his features seemed sharper, suddenly. His eyes were strange, the sea-glass blue giving way to something else. "Olorel."

Adrenaline was a dull roar in my ears. I turned, kneeling in front of him, and held onto Oliver so tight my fingers dug into his skin. "Wait, what about Olorel?"

Oliver spoke haltingly, as if there were a hand wrapped tightly around his throat. "That's when . . . he's making his next move."

My heart sank. As I desperately tried to think of how to stop Lucifer, something else occurred to me. Wild hope flared. "Wait. Lucifer has no way to find the grave now! The only person who knew is dead, right? In one of the houses, there was a faerie who shot himself. He left a note. The one you put back in his hand, because you knew I'd find it. 'I have heard about the others. I am the last. He will come for me soon.'"

"He . . . has a backup plan . . . another way to find it," Oliver gasped. Perspiration gleamed at his brow and he'd started trembling. "I d-didn't tell him, Fortuna. When he had . . . had me on that table, I didn't . . ."

Before I could ask any more questions, Oliver wrenched himself free. He pulled his clothes on with rough, abrupt movements, and then swung toward the doors. I scrambled up and rushed after him without hesitation, extending a hand to touch him. "Ollie—"

"Don't, Fortuna!" he rasped, jerking away.

Too late. I'd seen the color of his eyes. The bright, violent red. The hunger of the Beast, and the guilt of the man. As Oliver yanked the barn doors open, I reached for him again, fighting a rush of pity. This . . . creature, this being, was like me. Dark. Apart. Strange. I'd created him, just like he said, and apparently Oliver had inherited my demons. The eternal inner battle between my power and my humanity. The urge to bury my face into fear like it was a bloody carcass and *feast*, and the small voice telling me to resist.

"You *can* fight it," I told him, my fingers curling around his arms. As if I could hold Oliver together, keep him here, with just the warm press of my fingers. "I do. A lot of the time, I fucking win, Ollie."

He turned his head, not quite looking at me. His voice was a rumble as he asked, "And when you don't?"

Unbidden, I thought of Belanor. Of the last time I'd seen him, and what I'd done to him. Lucifer may have handed me the knife, but he'd only coaxed out what had already been inside me. When I didn't win against those dark urges, I became the Beast, too. I was no better than Oliver.

Before I could say anything else, his body quaked, and he doubled over in pain. When Oliver peered up at me, long teeth gleamed against his bottom lip.

"Olorel," he repeated, those dark veins creeping into his face. They looked like thin, dead tree branches. "You have until then to stop him."

"Or *you* could stop him," I said, my voice soft. I kept my hands at my sides, fighting the urge to touch him again. Oliver had claws now; he was losing control.

"He still needs . . ." A thin line of blood slid out of Oliver's nose. His lips moved as he fought to keep speaking.

Panic sluiced through me. I abandoned caution completely, rushing forward to slide my hands along his jaw. His skin was so hot that it hurt. "Ollie, stop. It's okay, I can figure it out."

But Oliver didn't look at me. He frowned at the ground, his brow furrowed. I knew that look in his eye. Oliver had my demons, which meant he had my stubbornness, too. He held onto the edge of the door, a vein bulging at his temple. Then his body gave a violent wrench, and I heard a terrible cracking sound, as if every bone in his body had broken. Oliver gave a pained shout, his face twisting. "He wants—"

He cut off with a cry, bending over. As I watched fully formed wings sprout from his back, then explode into the air so hard that black feathers rained down, I knew Oliver would pay for this, too. Lucifer would find out what he'd told me, if he hadn't already. I'd seen what the devil did to the ones who disobeyed him or betrayed his trust. As I watched Oliver retreat into the rain, I remembered.

Bloody tools on a table. The pale glint of exposed bone. The ragged edge of an agonized scream. Wide, glazed eyes. The memories cut through me like the knife I'd used through Belanor's flesh.

My heart lurched, and I ran after him, blurting, "Don't go back, Ollie. We'll figure this out, you don't have to—"

He flapped his wings, and the gust knocked me back, just like it had Collith and Laurie. I went flying as Oliver rose into the air. I recovered just in time to see him disappear into the dark sky. Within seconds, the sound of his wingbeats faded.

I stayed where I was, my mind dull with helpless shock. The rain hit my upturned face again. It had calmed now, the deafening torrent slowed down to a silvery drizzle. A black feather floated toward me, flitting through the weak moonlight. I held out my palm, and I barely felt anything as it settled against my skin. I closed my fingers around the wispy strands.

I stood there for another minute, maybe longer. Eventually I retrieved my things from the floor of the barn and made my way back home in a slow, detached state. I got to the Door without incident, and no one stopped me as I stepped out on the other side. Leaves rustled beneath my shoes with every step.

Minutes later, I stood in the bathroom of the loft, staring at myself in the mirror. There was no sign of Collith or Laurie, and my family was exactly how I'd left them, as if everything had been a dream. But it wasn't a dream, I knew that. I still had the proof in my fist, in the water that dripped from the ends of my hair, in the soreness between my legs. My mind went back and replayed everything that had happened tonight. The fight between the three males I loved, and what I'd just done in that barn. I gazed at my pale reflection, holding the feather in one hand and a sleeping pill in the other.

Weak, I thought, watching the eyes in the glass darken. I couldn't be trusted to make the right choices anymore.

I put the pill in my mouth and swallowed it.

CHAPTER ELEVEN

Furious whispers drifted through the stillness.

There were other sounds, too. I could hear the steady drone of Cyrus's lawn mower outside, and the gurgling of the coffee maker. My eyes cracked open and reacted to the sunlight streaming through the windows. I couldn't remember the last time I'd slept this late. I sat up slowly, squinting, and waited for my vision to adjust.

I'd fallen asleep on the couch again. Collith and Laurie were in the kitchen, still speaking in low, tense voices. Both of them had changed and showered since last night, their hair and skin gleaming in the morning light. I waited for the faeries to notice I was awake. Within seconds, Collith's dark head turned, and our eyes met. Their conversation was cut short. Collith left the counter and strode into the living room.

He set a steaming mug on the coffee table beside me. "Good morning."

"Good morning." I reached for the mug while he settled on the other couch. "Are Emma and Damon gone for the day?"

Collith nodded, watching me take my first, cautious sip. As

Laurie came into view he said, "There's something we need to tell you, Fortuna."

"I'm connected to Oliver, you idiots. I saw the whole thing go down," I said with a neutral expression. I couldn't exactly be mad at them for keeping their kill-the-Beast plan from me when I had secrets of my own. Laurie sank onto the cushion next to mine, and to hide my rush of guilt, I leaned forward to set the coffee back onto the table.

As I moved, Laurie's eyes latched onto me, but he wasn't looking at my face. I followed his gaze downward, and in an instant, I spotted the bruise peeking out from beneath my ratty T-shirt. *Shit*. I pulled the hem down quickly, covering it, but of course it was too late. Now Laurie knew something was up.

Before those sleeping pills had kicked in, I'd showered last night, so I knew they couldn't smell Oliver or what had happened between us. What I had allowed to happen. The thought of telling Collith and Laurie made my stomach tighten. How could I explain it to them when I didn't even understand why? Oliver had killed one of my closest friends. He'd killed my *parents*. He'd also left a string of bodies across the entire fucking country. It was disgusting that I had even let him touch me.

I kept all these thoughts from my face, though.

Neither of them asked the question. After all, we weren't together. Any of us. They didn't have the right to wonder where I'd been the night before, or whether I'd been with someone. But we were still *something*, no matter how much I'd fought it. A connection that bound the three of us together in a way that felt as irrevocable as breathing. It was that connection causing the shame in my throat, blocking any attempt I might've made at confessing the truth.

Collith finally broke the silence. His voice was tight. "Are you all right?"

I considered the question. Physically, I was fine. In every other way, I was as far from all right as someone could get. But they needed to know what Oliver had said about Olorel, which also meant admitting where I'd been just a few hours ago. Another rush of hot shame filled my throat, making it difficult to speak. "Last night—"

One of the windows shattered.

In an instant, I was off the couch, Collith and Laurie standing on either side of me. We watched as Katashi and Yaeko climbed through the empty window frame like spiders. The image was only strengthened by their black clothing. Both of them held katanas, and they moved with silent, lethal intent. How had the kitsunes gotten past Savannah's protection spells? Why were they here?

A second after I asked the question, I knew the answer—this had something to do with the Order's search for the Beast. Nan had warned us her people would still be looking, too.

Katashi confirmed this a moment later when he said, "You've failed to kill the Beast, Nightmare, so now we're going to do this our way. Your presence is required at Raas. We have some more questions we'd like to ask you."

"And I thought *I* was dramatic," Laurie remarked. "An invitation would've sufficed."

"I'm afraid you're not invited to this meeting," Yaeko crooned. "In fact, you and Collith Sylvyre have been removed from proceedings."

It felt like I was falling. My mind raced. Why did the Order want me, specifically? Why were they going to the effort of keeping Laurie and Collith away? Maybe they knew the truth about my connection to Oliver, somehow. Or maybe they just wanted to separate the three of us because we'd be easier to execute that way.

As if he'd reached the same conclusion, Laurie's smile cooled. His eyes hardened into gleaming metal. "It's cute that you think Lady Sworn is going anywhere without us."

On my other side, Collith tilted his head. Though he spoke as calmly as ever, his gaze was unnaturally bright. "The codex states that it's illegal to conduct a meeting without every representative in attendance," he said.

"Every representative *will* be in attendance," Katashi countered, flipping his katana.

Laurie rested his hand casually on his sword hilt. Yaeko noted the gesture, and her expression went cold. "It would be treason to resist. This is a direct command from the Order."

Even as she spoke, it was obvious to everyone that Collith and Laurie didn't give a shit about commands. To protect me, they would defy the Order and kill these kitsunes—I could see it in their eyes. I could sense the tension coiling in their bodies. Usually, the two of them were so calculating. If they'd been thinking clearly, Collith and Laurie would've realized that Laurie could lose his throne again, or they might get seriously hurt if Yaeko was as good as Laurie said.

If they did fight, there was a good chance Collith and Laurie would win. I knew how powerful they were. I'd witnessed it.

But I wasn't willing to take that risk.

"I'll go," I said. Collith and Laurie turned toward me at the same time. I didn't let them see my fear, and my voice was hard as I told them, "It's fine. I'll be fine. There are other people in the Order who have my back, remember?"

"Don't waste your breath, darling," Laurie said dismissively, shifting his gaze back to the kitsunes. "We're going with you, end of story."

I hesitated, painfully aware of the people watching us. My first instinct was to resort to force and use my powers. Shoot first, ask questions later. That was my old way of doing things. So I held the image of a lake in my mind, the hum of cicadas all around while a boat beneath me swayed. I focused on Katashi, because out of the two of them, he seemed the most likely to listen. "Can we have a minute?" I asked.

The fox's demeanor was hard as granite. "Afraid not, Nightmare. How do I know you won't try to escape?"

"Let's be clear," I said curtly, "if I wanted to escape, I could. There is no 'try' about it. If I wanted to, I could end your life right now. But you're still standing there because I allow it. So, rest assured, I will come find you when I'm done. Not to mention I need to put on some fucking pants."

Silence met my hard words. A second ticked past. Two. Three. I held Katashi's gaze without flinching. Then he said, "We'll be downstairs."

Yaeko shot him a look of disbelief and outrage, but the other kitsune just inclined his head. A muscle tightened in Yaeko's cheek as she stormed toward the window. Katashi followed at a slower pace, and they both dropped out of sight. I suppressed a shudder—there was something so creepy about how they climbed the side of the barn like that.

Once they were gone, I took a low, steadying breath. It felt like pressure was closing in from every direction, and there was a small voice at the back of my head, reminding me how much was riding on how I handled these next few moments. But the kitsunes were waiting, and we didn't have much time. I stepped forward and turned, facing the faeries that had come to mean so much to me.

"I'm asking both of you to stand down. One of the reasons I've been so afraid to make a commitment . . . to choose . . ." I faltered. I looked down, but I could feel Collith's and Laurie's eyes on me as I struggled, and they waited patiently. After a moment, I raised my head and told them, "I won't be in a relationship where my choices are taken from me. Where my voice doesn't matter. Prove to me, right now, that my fears are unfounded. Let me go."

"And what if you don't come back?" Laurie countered.

"Better one of us than all three of us," I said quietly. My softness disarmed him, and for once, Laurie didn't have an immediate answer. I took advantage of his silence and moved closer, reaching up to cup his cheek. The Seelie King put his hand over mine, and his eyes slid shut. They opened again when I told him, "The Beast was my mistake, Laurie. It's about time I faced the consequences of my actions."

He still didn't respond. My eyes lingered on his for another moment, silently pleading for him to understand. To respect my wishes. Slowly, I turned away and looked at Collith next. With him, I knew I didn't need to say as much. I stood on tiptoe and kissed him on the cheek, then whispered in his ear, "If you follow me, I'll know, and I will never forget."

As I pulled back, he gave me a faint, resigned smile. "It's nice to see you again."

His response made me pause. I pursed my lips, blinking hard. Then I nodded, allowing Collith and Laurie to glimpse the feeling in my eyes. It was the best goodbye I could manage without revealing any fear. After that, I padded into my room and got a fresh pair of jeans from the closet. I pulled them on, walked silently past Collith and Laurie, and headed for the stairs, hoping that I'd done enough to convince them. And I prayed, as I strode through the barn and out into the bright afternoon, that I'd live to see them again.

The kitsunes were waiting by the woods. Neither of them spoke while I closed the distance between us. I stopped in the shadow of a tree and said, "Let's go, then."

Yaeko sneered. "If you're as dangerous as you say, it wouldn't be very smart of us not to take precautions."

I frowned. But before I could utter another word, she lifted her arm and swung the butt of her katana at my head.

I awoke in Raas with a pounding headache.

While I didn't recognize the room I was in, I recognized everything else instantly. The glass walls, the dark water beyond.

Wincing, I sat up from the daybed I'd been lying unconscious on and took in my surroundings with a single glance. Honey was here. She stood with her back to me, and the stillness was broken by the sound of clinking silverware.

The envoy must've heard me stirring, because she turned her head slightly and spoke over her shoulder. "Well met, Lady Sworn. I made some tea in case you woke up with some discomfort."

"Thanks." I stood slowly, making sure that my legs were working properly before I put my full weight on them. Honey crossed the little room holding a small, white cup. As I accepted it, I couldn't bring myself to tell her that I wasn't a fan of tea. I kept my expression neutral while I took a brief sip. The taste was even more bitter than I'd anticipated, and I felt my facial muscles twitch. "Wow. This is *so* great. Thanks again."

"Of course, my lady. Please take all the time you need. When you're ready, I believe the others are waiting for you." Honey gave me a kind smile. I mustered a weak one in return, and took another drink of her disgusting tea.

"I'm ready now," I said. I just wanted to get this over with. I went to the side table where Honey had made my tea. Despite its taste, I was reluctant to set the cup down. There was something comforting about the warmth seeping into my fingers. But I forced myself to do it anyway, because I might need my hands free to defend myself.

Honey turned and walked to the door, touching a panel on the wall beside it. The door slid open, and I followed her into the room with the bar. Voices floated through the stillness as we approached that far room. Our footsteps sounded overly loud. I held my head high and donned the mask of the Unseelie Queen once again. Something told me I was about to need her strength, her ruthlessness.

Everyone else was already here, I saw as we stopped in the doorway. Well, almost everyone. Wichonne and Mercy hadn't arrived. My gaze shifted from their empty chairs to Alexander

Nørgård and a water nymph I didn't recognize—his cousin's replacement, apparently, since Laurie had so generously removed his head. Dracula sat beside them, alone, just as he had been last time. Anna and her beta were here, the massive werewolf standing behind her chair like a sentry. Nan and the two kitsunes occupied the same spots as before, as well. And there, sitting in the last two chairs . . .

Oh, fuck, I thought, trying not to let any panic show on my face.

Mab sat in the chair representing the Seelie Court.

Micah sat in the chair for the Unseelie Court.

"Lady Fortuna Sworn," Honey announced, bending into a brief, graceful bow before she backed away, leaving me there. I fought to control my heartbeat, knowing it would give me away in this room full of creatures who could hear a pin drop. But with Mab and Micah here, I had a feeling this meeting was *not* going to go well.

Shit. I should've let Collith and Laurie kick the kitsunes' asses back at the loft.

As Alexander stood from his chair and began to round the table, I realized how vital it was that I didn't let them pick up on any hint of fear. People were only afraid when they had something to hide. So I watched the water nymph king approach with a look close to boredom. "Hello, again," he said.

I was a little surprised he was being so courteous, considering I'd played a small role in his cousin's death. I gave Alexander a bemused look and replied, "Hello."

He extended the crook of his arm. I only hesitated for the span of a heartbeat before I took it. Alexander might be a besotted idiot, but as I faced Mab and Micah, who were both slightly turned in their chairs to watch me, he felt like a lifeline in a sea full of sharks.

He'd noticed the faeries' intent stares, too. "As representatives of the fae courts, I assume you've met Queen Fortuna?" Alexander asked.

"Oh, you're a queen again?" Micah said with raised brows. He looked around the room with exaggerated confusion. "And where is your throne?"

I gave him a derisive smile. "Where is yours? Oh, right, you're a Shadi. Your bloodline wasn't even in the running."

If Collith had been there, he would've sighed. He also probably would have pinched the bridge of his nose, which was something he only did when I'd really, really fucked up.

Like right now. Micah's eyes narrowed, and the look he gave me was familiar. I knew when I'd made a new enemy. Micah had never been a fan of mine, but now, it was personal. I swallowed a sigh of my own and inwardly kicked myself. I'd have to be smarter than this if I wanted to leave Raas alive.

Alexander must've agreed, because he propelled me into motion without warning. Nan's voice floated through the shimmering room as we walked toward the open chairs on the other side of the table.

"As you can see, King Laurelis and Queen Viessa have been replaced for these proceedings, per our vote," she said. "Wichonne Babdock has recused herself, so she will not be in attendance, either. Shall we begin?"

As Alexander pulled out a chair for me—thankfully, the spots on either side of it belonged to him and the werewolf alpha—Collith's warning whispered through my memory. *If these creatures find out you're not only the creator of this Beast, but that you're capable of making more things like him, they'll see you as a threat.*

Trepidation crept down my spine as if someone had exhaled an icy breath behind me. I met Micah's gaze and lifted my chin in a wordless challenge. I could take this sniveling, pampered faerie.

I couldn't say the same for Mab, though.

I still had a couple friends at the table, I reassured myself. There was Alexander, apparently, and the Shapeshifter Queen also seemed invested in me. My situation wasn't completely dire, right?

Then everyone looked at Nan, and she said, "It's been brought to our attention that you have a connection to the Beast, Lady Sworn."

It felt like the air in my lungs froze. Somehow I kept my breathing steady, even as my mind raced. How could they possibly know that? Only my family knew, and the members of my Court, and Collith and Laurie. None of them would've betrayed my secret.

Doesn't matter, I thought. I'd have to worry about that part later. Right now, I was on trial, and a table full of Fallen kings and queens were waiting for my answer. I couldn't utter a single lie, but if I told them the entire truth, they'd probably kill me on the spot. The Order didn't know what kind of connection I had with Oliver—if they did, I got the sense Nan would have phrased her opening line differently.

I fought the instinct to fix my gaze downward. Instead, I spoke to my allies in the room, meeting their eyes without flinching.

"It's true. That creature used to be a person, once. I knew him . . . and I loved him. But then he killed Finn." I forced myself to say his name, because I knew they would hear the pain. Hear how real it was. I paused for a moment, waiting for the burst of grief to pass. Then I looked at the Shapeshifter Queen again, who I had saved for last. "The Beast has to die for that, and I have to be the one to do it. The only challenge has been *how*. I put a holy blade in the Beast's heart and it did nothing. But last night, Collith struck him with heavenly fire, and that seemed to be more effective. We plan to keep trying until we're successful. Those are the facts, and anything else is none of your business . . . Your Majesty."

I added her title with a respectful nod. My answer wasn't intended to insult anyone, and I didn't want to make more enemies. I just wanted to *survive*. Nan pinned me down with that shrewd gaze of hers, and no one spoke. Silence hovered over the table like a pent-up breath.

Beyond the glass walls of this room, the water continued to shift and darken. I must've been unconscious far longer than I'd realized. Night had fallen, and it felt like we were at the bottom of the world, where moonlight and humanity couldn't reach. I looked around at the members of the Order one by one, hoping to find some in their eyes.

Then Mab's voice rang into the stillness. "I disagree," she said.

All the moisture in my mouth turned to ash. *Here we go,* I thought.

Nan's head tilted with an air of polite interest. "How so, Queen Mother? Let us open the discussion. I believe Lady Sworn has said her piece."

Mab addressed the others around the table. "It's quite simple, actually. This Beast is causing an uproar. For so many years we have known peace and safety, and in a matter of weeks, a creature connected to *this* female"—her darting glance pierced me like a bug to a board—"threatens to destroy it. If the secret of Fallenkind is at risk of exposure, and Fortuna Sworn played a part, every detail very fucking well *is* our business."

Mab talked about me without looking in my direction. I fought the urge to hold my armrests in a death grip and kept my hands loose in my lap. I breathed slowly and deeply, maintaining tight control over my heartbeat.

"What are we even suggesting here?" Alexander asked slowly, leaning forward to rest his elbows on the table. "That Lady Sworn is . . . responsible for this animal, somehow? I know Nightmares are rare, Queen Mab, but I don't think their abilities involve command over a psychotic shapeshifter."

Mab gave the water nymph king a cool, speculative look, and there was another beat of silence in the room. Then, dismissing Alexander completely, she turned her head toward Nan and said, "Your Majesty, I feel I should point out that I'm here to ensure the Order's neutrality in today's proceedings. One of my colleagues has informed me that Lady Sworn was inadvertently responsible for a water nymph's death at the last meeting of the Order. How can his cousin possibly offer an unbiased perspective?"

Nan's expression was smooth and composed. She appraised Mab with an acuity that was at odds with her young face, and I wondered how I hadn't seen it at the black market the day we'd met. After another moment, the Shapeshifter Queen turned toward me. Nothing in her features had changed, but something made my stomach sink just before she said, "King Alexander and Lady Sworn, please step out of the room."

Mab, one. Fortuna, zero, I thought grimly. Now I was the one who refused to look in her direction. I pushed my chair back and began to walk around the table, remembering my last conversation with the Wolf Queen. That hadn't just been a warning—it had been her *final* warning. Since I hadn't pushed Laurie away, not completely, Mab had obviously decided to take care of me herself.

And with just a few words, Laurie's mother had taken out one of my allies. I might not have known Alexander would even *be* an ally, going into this, but now he was off the board. Panic fluttered in my throat. Would she keep picking them off one by one?

I stopped in the doorway, facing the table of powerful figures. As I tried to think of something I could say, Honey appeared. She put her hand on my elbow, and I jumped, startled by the contact. The skin of her palm pressed against the bare skin of my arm. In an instant, I realized it had been on purpose. Honey was afraid for me, and she wanted me to know it.

"Allow me, my lady," the envoy murmured. There was a warning in her kind, lined eyes.

I didn't know this person, but something made me trust her. I let Honey lead me away, and Alexander fell into step on my other side. Honey released my arm quickly, as if she knew of my aversion to being touched. She accompanied us back to the room I'd woken up in, stepping aside so Alexander and I could enter before her.

Just as she began to follow us, Honey went still. A frown hovered at the corners of her mouth. I'd seen that look on every supernatural creature's face before—Honey had heard something. She bent into another swift bow and said, "Please excuse me."

She stepped back, and the door closed with a hissing sound. I went over to the wall to examine the panel more closely. The screen was completely dark. It didn't react even when I tapped it.

"How does this open?" I asked Alexander.

Instead of looking at the panel, he watched me with a fascinated expression. "It reads your handprint," the water nymph said. "Well, my handprint, and Honey's, and the rest of the Order members. Guests aren't given security access like that."

So I couldn't leave this room without his help, I thought, ice forming in my veins. I really was a prisoner. The Order must've known, or at least suspected, that I was responsible for Oliver. They wouldn't be treating me like this otherwise.

What would I do if the Order decided I was a liar, or too much of a liability?

"You'll wear out the rug," Alexander said from the daybed, startling me. I spun toward him again.

"What's the worst-case scenario here?" I demanded. "What are they deciding right now?"

He opened his mouth to reply, but a commotion down the hall distracted both of us. Our heads turned toward the door. Alexander was frowning. "This room is soundproofed, but I swear I just heard—"

The door opened. Strange sounds echoed through the connected rooms as Alexander and I froze, uncertain what to do.

Then Lucifer appeared on the threshold.

Shock rocked through me. For an instant, I wondered if this was a dream. The devil strolled in like he'd been invited, and the door closed automatically, cutting off the noise coming from behind him. Lucifer halted before us. He wore a two-piece black suit that looked like Armani, and his skin was vibrant and golden, as if he'd spent his afternoon sunning on a yacht. His bright, lion's mane hair spilled over a crisp white shirt collar.

When our gazes met, Lucifer's eyes crinkled at the corners, as if he was genuinely happy to see me. "Lady Sworn," he said.

"Asshole," I snarled. "What the fuck are you doing here? Where's Honey?"

Lucifer made an amused sound. "I know you're not fond of expressing gratitude, but regardless, you're welcome."

"*Gratitude?*" I repeated with an incredulous, sharp-edged laugh. "For what?"

The devil tilted his head. "Did you truly think that meeting was going to end in your favor?"

My nostrils flared. "It's *your* fault I'm even in this situation!"

"Fortuna."

Once again, the sound of Alexander's voice made me blink. "Um, yes?"

He waited until my gaze darted over to him before he asked, his voice carefully bland, "Who is this?"

I had to give it to him, no one would guess how scared the water nymph king was. The only reason I knew was because I could taste it, a subtle flavor that I couldn't define. I didn't blame Alexander for being terrified—anyone, Fallen or human, would instantly fear the beautiful figure standing in the room with us, even if they didn't know who he was. The power coming off him was so strong, so crushing that it almost felt like gravity.

"This is Lucifer," I told Alexander.

He made a sound, but all my focus was on the devil. I watched a shadow pass over his golden features. "You know that's not my name, Fortuna. Why won't you say it?" he murmured.

I looked him in the eye and said, "Because Heilel is dead to me."

"Just a moment. Let me see if I'm understanding this correctly," Alexander interjected. "You . . . were with *him*?"

I kept staring at Lucifer, who gazed calmly back. My voice was flat as I answered, "We broke up. Religious differences. He thought he was God, and I didn't."

Alexander was silent for a second. "Wow. I *really* didn't stand a chance, did I?"

Lucifer's focus finally shifted away from me. He looked at the water nymph as if he were an insect and he was thinking about stepping on him. I hurried to say, "I don't need you to rescue me, Lucifer. If you want to impress me, then do what we discussed. Simple as that."

"Say my name."

I frowned, my eyebrows drawing together. "What?"

Lucifer moved closer, slowing when he saw me tense. Alexander put a hand on the hilt of his sword. But I didn't move, and Alexander didn't draw his weapon. Lucifer dared to edge even closer, until his familiar scent drifted past my senses. Once, it would have intoxicated me. Now I just tipped my head back and glared up at the devil, wishing I had my knives or my gun.

"Say my name, and perhaps I'll consider it," he challenged quietly, his hand rising toward my face. His fingers skimmed my jawline.

I imagined jamming a holy blade into his gut. "Get your hand off me," I growled.

"You've said my name a thousand times," Lucifer murmured, searching my gaze. "What is it that stops you now? Are you afraid?"

Before I could respond, a sword appeared between us. The glassy tip pressed into Lucifer's lapel.

"I may not have a chance with her, but that's never stopped me from trying before," Alexander said. "Lady Sworn told you to remove your hand."

Annoyance flashed in Lucifer's eyes. "Do you think she'll find it charming, your insistence on playing the white knight? A creature of her power, her caliber? You are a minnow and she is the kraken."

My opinion of Alexander Nørgård went up a notch when he stood his ground. Lucifer's power filled every corner of the room now, crackling, teeth-grinding energy that was familiar and alien all at once. Alexander must've felt it, but his hand didn't waver. He raised the hilt of his sword, poising the blade against the hollow of Lucifer's throat.

"I won't tell you again," the water nymph king said.

Lucifer went still. He studied Alexander for another beat, and I was so terrified that I didn't dare intervene. I had visions of Lucifer striking like a snake and Alexander's head flying. But I took advantage of his attention being elsewhere, cautiously reaching for his mind. Maybe I could solve all our problems by killing him right here, right now.

But Lucifer's mind was a fortress. Just as I'd known it would be. It was guarded by walls, and thorns, and something that snarled. The darkness inside him was only broken apart by flashes of red, just like the skies of Hell.

I withdrew from Lucifer's psyche at the same moment he began to retreat, finally ending the standoff between him and Alexander. The door behind Lucifer opened as if it was responding to a silent command. He looked at me, but he didn't say another word before he took another step and the door slid shut between us. I stared at it in disbelief.

"He backed down. When you pulled a sword on Lucifer, he backed down," I said, replaying the whole scene through in my mind.

"You say that like it's so baffling." Alexander sounded vaguely insulted.

"Lucifer could've beaten you with his hands tied behind his back," I replied distractedly, only half-hearing the annoyed noise Alexander made. I was still mulling over those last moments of the confrontation. It felt like I'd missed something important. Why had Lucifer given up so easily?

The devil never did anything without a reason. Every word, every decision was calculated. It was a step closer to his endgame. And what was his endgame? I asked myself.

That one was easy. Above all else, he wanted Olorel's grave. But the last update I'd gotten on Lucifer's search for the grave didn't connect to this. Oliver's voice echoed through my memory, and I remembered the agony in his eyes. *He has another way.*

Say the two things were connected, I thought, still staring at the door. Why break in to the Order's headquarters? Was it really to save me, or did coming here align with this mysterious new tactic to find the grave?

Bright, searing realization flared in my mind. It was immediately followed by a hot rush of horror.

"Open the door," I said hoarsely. Alexander looked at me, and when he didn't move, panic roared through my entire body. *"Open the door."*

Whatever he saw in my face made Alexander leap to action, and he slammed his palm onto the wall panel. I was already over the threshold before the door had finished its whooshing sound. I darted into the other room, and when I saw the carnage, my heart rammed up in my throat. I spun and raced past the bar, heading for that third room. I'd left the Order sitting at the table—

I skidded to a stop. My eyes darted around, registering every detail with a familiar numbness. The silence rang in my ears.

They weren't sitting at the table anymore.

Now they were dead. All of them.

No, not all, I thought faintly. It was difficult to tell from this vantage point, because there were demons and Fallen alike scattered everywhere, but I was pretty sure there were fewer council members than there had been at the start of the meeting. I forced myself to move deeper into the room and look at every face. The scene reminded me of all the houses Collith and I had been to, once Lucifer and the Beast were done with them. I sensed Alexander appearing in the doorway. He made another sound, this one quiet and stunned, but I kept going. It was impossible to avoid walking through the gore. My shoes squelched with every step.

One of the demons, I noted, was the same species as the one that had attacked me on the road. *This* was why Lucifer was getting them through. To do his dirty work. They were his lackeys, here to be muscle and nothing more. How many could he possibly have if they were this expendable to him?

During my search, I didn't see Nan, or Dracula, or Mab. Unless they were amongst the corpses near the elevator, they must've escaped somehow. I felt a surge of sorrow when I found the werewolf alpha, along with her beta. The kitsunes were also amongst the dead. I hadn't liked them, but I certainly hadn't wished them dead.

When I found Micah's body, however, I couldn't bring myself to feel the same regret. Numb from the shock of seeing their ruined bodies, I raised my gaze toward the place where the Horn was mounted.

The wall was empty, just as I'd known it would be.

Lucifer hadn't been here for me. He'd just bided his time in the other room while Oliver and the demons had taken care of the Order. The Beast was even more powerful than I'd thought, if he was able to overpower these council members. I looked around at the carnage again, wondering if this was all just a bad dream. It looked like my other dreams. Blood covered the floor, the walls, the ceiling.

As my gaze fell on a severed hand resting at my feet, I remembered those strange sounds Alexander and I had heard. Now that I'd seen this, I knew exactly what they'd been—tearing flesh, breaking bones, and anguished screams cut short. It had all happened so quickly the Order had barely been able to make a sound, much less defend themselves.

Another piece clicked into place. *This* was why Lucifer had never bothered to cover his tracks with all the killings. Clever, clever devil. Those messy crime scenes had carried out two purposes. The first was to find that damn grave. The second was get the Order's attention. He'd *wanted* them to intervene. To meet.

He hadn't been after the members, not if some of them had managed to escape. It had to have been because he'd wanted to find Raas itself, and consequently, the Horn he must've known was here. But why hadn't Lucifer come the first time I'd attended a meeting?

I turned my back on the bloody room, unable to stomach the sight anymore. Alexander stood in the doorway, his eyes wide as he looked at all his dead comrades. I walked toward him, my voice strained as I said, "Can we go? Please?"

Alexander caught up with me and didn't protest as we headed for the elevator. But when we reached the hallway, I slowed at the sight of a small figure lying across the path, face down.

"My lady, don't—" Alexander started.

I approached Honey's body. Or what was left of it. I studied the keeper first, then the gruesome scene around her. My mind worked through the details, and a scenario began to form. Earlier, when Honey had heard that sound, it must've been the elevator moving. She'd gone to investigate, and Oliver had come out. He'd shoved her, sending her into one of the beams between the glass panels. That explained why it was bent.

But whatever Honey had been, she'd given the Beast a run for his money. Every other body within sight was a demon, and they were in even worse shape than Honey.

I rolled the keeper onto her back as gently as I could, because it felt wrong to leave her like that. Then I pushed myself up and kept walking toward the elevator. Once again, Alexander followed me wordlessly. He didn't speak as we got on. He put his hand on the panel, and the doors slid shut, blocking out the sight. Once we started moving, Alexander's voice floated through the horrible stillness.

"You know more than you told the Order, Fortuna Sworn."

I kept my eyes on the doors, my thoughts returning to Lucifer. I couldn't stop ruminating on his timing. Why hadn't he come to Raas sooner? Why tonight?

My mind went back to the day of the first meeting. My heart quickened when I remembered that I'd had a dream about Oliver that night. A dream full of grimy glass walls and indescribable pain. Lucifer had been asking him one question over and over again. *Where is it?*

Oliver had refused to tell him. He'd tried fighting back, tried fighting Lucifer's control. The agonizing pain I'd felt in the dream had only been a moment, a tiny fraction of the horrors he must've endured. But Oliver hadn't given in. *That's* what he'd been trying to tell me at the barn. So Lucifer must've just followed me this time instead of trying to use his beloved Beast.

I frowned and shook my head, clearing it. I was focusing on the wrong part of the puzzle.

Why the Horn? Laurie had said it was useless to our kind. Unless . . . unless Lucifer wasn't our kind. My stomach sank, and suddenly I felt like I was going to be sick.

All this time, I had been wondering what I'd created when I brought the devil into this world. The fact he thought he could blow the Horn told me everything I needed to know.

Lucifer was an original angel again.

The elevator stopped, and Alexander and I got off quickly, both of us eager to put this place behind us. We walked silently up the stone steps. When we finally reached the narrow opening in the rocks and slipped into the open night air, I breathed deeply, trying to get the smell of blood and death out of my nostrils. Beside me, I could hear Alexander doing the same. We still didn't speak as we started down the beach.

We'd only gotten a few steps when, a few yards ahead of us, something emerged from the water. It was too small to cause worry, but I still reached for a weapon that wasn't there—I hadn't even tried hiding one when the kitsunes came for me at the loft.

Something had told me they would've known. Now I wish I'd tried anyway. I began to gather my power around me, and the air prickled as if a storm were coming.

"My lady," Alexander said in a low, urgent tone. "Wait."

As we drew closer, and I got a better look at the creature, tension seeped out of my shoulders.

It was an otter.

Once it got to dry sand, the animal paused. Its body began to snap and crack. I immediately recognized the signs of a shapeshifter, and in that same instant, I knew who the otter was. Relief unfurled in my chest. Alexander and I stopped, waiting patiently for Nan to finish changing forms. The small otter continued to contort, pieces of skin and fur plopping wetly to the sand.

Less than a minute later, a familiar brown-haired girl knelt in front of me. She was naked, and I saw her skin pebble in the biting wind, but otherwise she didn't seem affected by the cold. Nan pushed herself up, strands of her long hair draping across her pale body.

"I'm glad you survived," I said, guilt piercing my heart like a hundred tiny needles.

"I almost didn't. I've never seen anything like that creature. The speed of it . . ." She shook her head, and the look in her eyes was a blend of wonder and horror. "At first, I thought it had come for you. But after I dove into the water, I hid and watched it take the Horn. What possible use could a creature like that have for a weapon meant for angels?"

The genuine bafflement in her voice made the needles inside me burrow deeper. My jaw clenched, and I turned my head away, scanning the dark horizon as I worked up the courage to tell Nan and Alexander about Lucifer. They deserved the truth, or some of it, at least, not only because he had just slaughtered most of the Order, but so they could warn their people. Now that Lucifer had the Horn, he could move to the next phase of his plan, whatever that was. I just knew it wasn't anything good.

"The Dark Prince is here. In our world. He's the one who wants the Horn, and he's the one who controls the Beast," I said. I still couldn't bring myself to look at them. I was afraid they'd see the shame in my eyes.

Alexander was silent, but I could feel the force of Nan's attention intensify. "How do you know this?" she asked.

"Because I've met him. He likes useful things, and the prince considers Nightmares incredibly useful." Bitterness swelled in my throat. Lights appeared on the other side of the water as a car made its way down a winding road. "He sent the Beast to fetch the Horn while he spoke to me and Alexander."

Nan looked to Alexander, her eyebrows raised in a silent question. He nodded. "It's true."

"What does he intend to do with it?" she asked.

This, I knew, was meant for me. I finally turned back to her. The dim moonlight touched the smooth planes of her young-looking face, which went cold as I said, "I have no idea."

The Shapeshifter Queen's fear whispered over my tongue—dandelions. She looked at me with her brows knit, as if I'd disappointed her. "This would have been good information to know much, much sooner, Fortuna Sworn."

"Telling you about him would've led to more questions," I said. Nan's frown only grew. Time to change the subject. I turned to Alexander, who had remained curiously subdued throughout our conversation. "Is the Order gone, then?"

"We are never gone. There are contingencies in place for an event like this. Well," he amended, "maybe not quite like this."

"Oh, so you didn't expect the Dark Prince to show up in this world and steal an ancient artifact off the wall of your super-secret headquarters?" I asked dully, remembering the sight of Anna Tombs's ruined body. One of the demons could've killed her, maybe, but the marks on her ribs told me otherwise. I'd seen enough of the Beast's victims to recognize the work of its claws.

Oliver had taken out a werewolf alpha like she was nothing.

Alexander didn't answer, and the three of us fell silent. It was still surreal that, not far below our feet, a massacre was suspended in the water. People I had known.

"We should get to safety. It's foolish to be in the open like this," Nan said. Something in her countenance tightened. "I will send someone to retrieve the remains and notify their families."

She didn't say anything about the reason the Order had met tonight in the first place, and I decided not to remind her. Nan's body began to snap and crack again. As she grew wings and launched into the air, I expected her to transform into an owl, like she had the first time I'd seen her shift.

Instead, she changed into a small, black bird.

A crow.

CHAPTER TWELVE

Colors and lights burst in the dim sky.

Awed *oooh*s and *ahhh*s sounded from the nearby campfire. I sat a short distance away, on the ground, my arms wrapped around my knees. Like everyone else, I'd tipped my head back to watch the fireworks.

Twilight clung to the horizon, and the smell of hamburgers still lingered on the warm air. I sat apart from my family, close enough to listen to their scattered conversations, but far enough that I wouldn't poison their happiness. Even now, beneath all the pretty lights, I was consumed by Lucifer. Wondering where he was. Worrying about what he was doing. Had he used the Horn? Was the apocalypse about to begin?

Or maybe it already had.

My mood darkened even more at the thought. I held my knees harder as the sky exploded with glitter and stars, and a delayed *boom* shook the air. Matthew squealed and reached his small arms upward, as if he could catch one of the falling lights. I watched him and thought about how much I had to lose if Lucifer pulled off whatever he was planning.

"The alcohol and general merriment is that way," a familiar voice said from behind me. "Why are you over here?"

I tried to think of a sarcastic response, but nothing came to me. There was only the painful truth, lodged somewhere under my heart like a splinter.

"It feels wrong," I admitted, keeping my eyes on the sky.

Laurie didn't ask what I meant. I sensed him settle on the ground beside me, and I hid a faint pulse of surprise—I didn't need to look to know he was wearing nice pants. Usually Laurie would rather die than ruin an outfit. He stretched one leg out and bent the other, propping his wrist on top of it. A drink rested in the grass between us. He must've set it down without my noticing.

"Is your town aware that it's August?" Laurie asked, arching his head back to watch the show.

I made an amused sound. "The fireworks are part of the Carnation Festival. It's nearby."

Laurie was silent for a moment. I rested my cheek on my knee and studied him. More fireworks burst in the sky, and the flares lit up his beautiful face like stage lights. His expression was softer than usual, not quite sorrowful, but just on the edge of it. "I won't give you some tedious, sentimental speech about how the werewolf would've wanted you to be happy," Laurie said. "What I will say is that I barely spent any time with the mutt, and even I know that if he were here, he'd be giving you those annoying puppy-dog eyes."

I knew he was right, but I didn't move. "What are you doing here?" I asked eventually.

Laurie tilted his head and gave me a sidelong glance. "Oh, just making sure you're not about to lose your grip on reality, is all."

"I'm not crazy. The voices tell me I am entirely sane," I countered. It was a weak joke, but Laurie still grinned. I couldn't bring myself to smile back. My voice was soft as I said, "You never responded to my text."

His throat moved as if he was swallowing a sigh. The second I saw that, I knew Laurie hadn't come with good news.

"That's why I'm here, actually. I've been looking into it. Well, more accurately, the people on my payroll have been looking into it." Laurie's voice was low, and he spoke quickly. His eyes were on Matthew, who had ventured closer as he followed a firefly. Danny wasn't far behind.

I waited until the pair were out of earshot again before I turned back to Laurie. My stomach was heavy with dread. "We both know there's only one reason he wanted that Horn. Angels would definitely know where to find Olorel's grave, right?"

"Amongst many other things, yes. But the Dark Prince could have something else in mind. My mother has a very, very long memory. She told me, once, that angel blood is rumored to lend power to anyone who consumes it. Knowledge." Laurie tossed the rest of his drink back. "The last people to guzzle angel blood were Adam and Eve, and we all know how that turned out, of course."

I frowned. "Wait. Adam and Eve? They killed an angel?"

Laurie frowned back, as if he was confused by the question. "Yes. What do you—Oh. Most mortals believe the nonsense about fruit. Much prettier story, I'll give you that. The truth is those insipid humans wanted to know what was outside the Garden, so they killed an original to find out. This occurred after the Fall, of course. My mother claims there was a rumor amongst the angels that Lucifer was the one who told Eve the secret. They say he went to her in a dream, appearing as a snake."

Lucifer. I hadn't managed to forget him, not for one second, but hearing his name out loud brought all my fear back. It brought the guilt back, too. I turned from Laurie and looked up at the sky again. I'd stopped seeing the fireworks, though. Now I just saw the devil's face, and I heard his voice as he said, *It's going to be glorious watching you burn.*

Laurie's voice was soft. "We don't blame you. None of us do."

I began to ask which part they didn't blame me for, since there were so many. But then I just shook my head, rejecting the relief he was trying to offer. "It was my choice to love him," I said.

Another cluster of lights scattered across the horizon, but Laurie didn't look away from me. I turned and searched his eyes for any trace of judgment or disgust. Instead, his hand rose, and he cupped my cheek. The base of his thumb skimmed the edge of my jaw in a whisper of movement. "The devil made you dependent on him," Laurie murmured. "He made certain that he was the center of your universe. That isn't love, Fortuna."

A faint, bitter smile curved my lips. "No wonder he tricked me so easily. What do I know about love?"

I said it flippantly, but the words were heavy with memories and thick with the past. When Laurie looked back at me, I saw all those moments in his eyes, too. All the pain we'd caused each other. The missed chances, the misunderstandings, the bad timing.

"You know a lot more than you think," Laurie said.

Something hovered between us. A question. It was one he'd asked before, and I was afraid that if I rejected Laurie this time, I would never see him again. The thought was unbearable.

Then I remembered another question.

How long do you intend to torment my son?

My grip tightened on my knees. I forced myself to shake my head. "Very recent events would indicate otherwise."

Now it felt like Oliver hovered between us, along with everything else keeping us apart.

Laurie didn't pull away, though. His brows were slightly drawn together, as if he knew I was hiding something. His voice was soft as he said, "I'm not asking for much, Fortuna. I don't need a conventional life with you . . . I just want you to be in it."

It felt like he'd opened his chest and bared his heart to me.

I stared at Laurie and tried to hide the struggle from my eyes. It would be so easy to give in. To keep him, forever, because I couldn't imagine being without him. But I knew what the right choice was. After how many selfish ones I'd made, I couldn't keep repeating the same mistakes. I needed to say no, when all I wanted was to tell him yes.

"It wouldn't be fair to you," I said.

Laurie frowned. "Why? Why wouldn't it be fair to me?"

Just as I started to answer, Mab's voice whispered to me again. *When will enough be enough?*

Pain streaked through my chest like a lightning bolt. Searching for the right words to give to Laurie, and a way to end the conversation without shattering us, I looked over at my family. Night had fallen without my noticing, and I could only see the parts of their faces lit up by the fire and the sky.

That wasn't all I'd missed—Collith had arrived at some point, too. He sat with Danny and Damon, bouncing Matthew on his lap, listening closely to my brother as he talked about nursing school.

I looked at Collith, and suddenly I knew exactly what to say. Exactly what I could tell Laurie that would make him give up.

When I finally turned back to the Seelie King, I didn't try to hide how much it hurt.

"Because I love him more." Tears stung my eyes. I gave a helpless shrug. "I love him in a way that I can't even describe. The sort of love that defies reason. It's just . . . it's part of my body now, mixed with the marrow of my bones, and there's no ignoring or escaping it. You would only ever get part of my heart, Laurie, and that's just not—"

"I would be utterly content with any portion of your heart, Fortuna."

Another lightning bolt struck me. I put on the mask of the queen, and I willed myself to have her coldness, too. "You may be fine with it, but I'm not," I said.

It wasn't completely a lie, what I was saying to him. It just wasn't completely the truth, either. But Laurie must've heard a note of sincerity in my voice, because his hand finally fell. My skin cooled where his fingertips had been.

"Very well," he said, his eyes shuttered. "I shan't beg, don't worry."

I pursed my lips and fought the urge to swallow. There was the barest hint of strain in my voice as I said, "Will you—"

A noise cut me off, and I froze. Everyone else went still, too, their eyes full of confusion as they searched the air. It was the strangest, most chilling sound I'd ever heard. It echoed through the sky and went on for several seconds before it faded away like a death knell.

"What *was* that?" I breathed.

Collith's head turned as he looked for me. Damon had taken Matthew from him, and my brother huddled with his son and fiancé. Collith stood over them as if he was protecting them. I had never seen him so pale.

"That," he said, "was the Horn."

The words had no sooner left Collith's mouth than the sky lit up with a brief, white flare. It looked like a falling star. As I tracked its progress, I remembered what Laurie had told me back in Raas. *The Horn is one of the three holy items in this world, and it's supposed to summon the Host of Heaven.*

"We need to find it," Laurie said now, his voice terse. "Wherever the Host is, you can bet the Dark Prince and his lapdog will be, too. Two birds, one stone. We kill the Beast and stop Lucifer from using the Host."

I glanced at him, but Laurie was already on his phone, typing so fast that his fingers were difficult to track.

"How do you know the Host goes straight to the one who blows the Horn?" I asked, frowning.

"I don't. But if Lucifer isn't with the Host, he's looking for it. Good, Sorcha's already working on a location."

"Did you just say *Sorcha*?" I demanded. "As in, Sorcha Cralynn?"

Laurie answered without looking at me, still typing on his phone. "She is my Whisperer, Fortuna. Who do you think has been supplying me with information all summer?"

"We'll have to use the Door," Collith muttered as we all watched the flare fade into nothing, leaving only a dark, smoking sky. Wherever the Host had landed, it wasn't anywhere close to Colorado. I wondered how many people had seen the light.

My family was coming this way now—they'd heard Collith's reply about the Horn. The arrangements happened quickly. Cyrus and Ariel would stay behind to protect Emma, Danny, Damon, and Matthew. Gil and Seth went to town to watch over the locals, including Bea and Gretchen. Savannah had warned us that if Lucifer blew the Horn, we should prepare for a potential reaction of biblical proportions. Not to mention we had no idea what Lucifer's plans were if he got to the grave. It just seemed like a good idea not to leave anyone we cared about unguarded.

I waited in the driveway with Collith and Laurie. Everyone was ready, but we still didn't have a location. The Seelie King held his phone in his long fingers, keeping the screen where he could see it.

My skin was starting to crawl with agitation when his phone brightened with a new text. This time, he read it out loud. "The Anza-Borrego Desert."

My mind worked quickly. "Damn it. We'll have to wait until morning. Unless Sorcha can give us specific coordinates, Laur, we'll have to search the entire desert. That's a lot of ground to cover, even if we're looking for a crater, or however it is that all-powerful angels land on Earth. The fastest way to find them will be from the sky, and unless you've got a helicopter I don't know about, we'll have to ask for help from the dragons. And dragons—"

"—have shit nighttime vision," Laurie finished, his jaw hardening. He lifted his phone again, and the screen cast a gentle glow over his features as he searched for something. "Sunrise isn't for another ten hours."

"The Dark Prince will have the same problem," Collith said.

"The Dark Prince has demons and witches at his disposal," I said grimly. "But we'd just be sitting ducks out there. We might as well meet back here in a few hours. I'll go talk to Cyrus. See you soon, Laurie."

I met his gaze and nodded, remembering the dark note we'd left things on. *I shan't beg, don't worry.* Laurie's expression was unreadable, but he nodded back. I turned away, fighting the instinct to run. There was nothing we could do until tomorrow, I reminded myself. Even if I asked Savannah to do a location spell, I already knew she wouldn't have the ingredients she needed. We didn't have anything that belonged to the Host. I walked the rest of the way with slow and controlled steps, trying to lay out the hours ahead.

It felt like the rest of the night went by in pulses. Knocking on Cyrus's door. Stepping inside. Telling them about Sorcha's findings, and the change of plan. After that I returned to the loft, where I sat with Narfu for a while. I explained to him what was happening, too, even if I wasn't entirely certain how much the demon understood. He stayed curled in his nest of blankets, and the sound of my voice seemed to lull him to sleep. At least one of us got some rest. When I rejoined everyone else upstairs, I found them just as unsettled as I was. The memory of that sound haunted all of us, and the threat of the unknown hovered over our heads. Collith hadn't returned, but Nym was here, and he was more troubled than usual. He stared at the collection of clocks on the mantle and kept muttering under his breath, "Tick tock, tick tock."

Eventually we drifted off, one by one. Emma squeezed my shoulder before she went to bed. Damon and Danny told me to wake them if there were any updates. I stayed on the couch, once again wrapped in the blanket that still smelled like Collith—apparently it was getting to be a habit. But this time, it didn't help me sleep. I stared at the window and waited anxiously for the light to return.

Hours later, I found myself standing at the edge of the desert.

Cyrus and Tabitha were small, dark specks in the sky. It was almost six in the morning, and the world was just waking up. Under normal circumstances, the sight of the sun rising over the dunes would've been beautiful. Right now, I was too restless to take much notice. Laurie leaned against the driver's side door of an ATV, and Collith sat on the ground nearby, his knee drawn against his chest.

We'd gotten the rental and driven out as far as we could. I hadn't realized how big this place would be. I'd looked it up on Google Maps last night, of course, but seeing it on a screen was vastly different than looking out at it. The wind made my shirt flap against me, and I stared out at the rolling hills. "This could take . . ."

I trailed off, because it felt disloyal to Cyrus, somehow. He was out there, at the crack of dawn, scanning miles and miles of land for any sign of movement. He was actually *doing* something, while I stood here twiddling my thumbs. A burst of impatience went off inside me, and it was all I could do not to run toward that barren waste.

"Easy, Firecracker," Laurie said quietly. "Tabby is the best assistant I've ever had. She'll find those dusty angels in no time."

And then what? I wondered. How did this end? If we did get to the Host first, was it as easy as warning them about Lucifer and watching the angels go right back to where they'd come from?

"Do you think he's out there somewhere?" I muttered, squinting at the horizon. There were still only two shapes against the sun, getting smaller and smaller with every passing moment.

"Without a doubt." Collith's voice was grim.

I knew he was right—it was why we'd come armed to the teeth. Each of us bore a sword, and I'd also brought a stash of holy weapons. There were several knives hidden beneath my clothes, along with one gun. There were several more in the rental. Not that any of them would do much good against any of the things we were about to face, but at least we wouldn't be completely defenseless . . . only mostly defenseless. The thought made my throat tighten.

None of us spoke again until Laurie said, "They've found something."

My heart leaped when I saw that Cyrus and Tabitha were coming back. The three of us piled into the ATV and launched into the desert again, following the dragons farther and farther out. The engine roared in my ears, and I held tightly onto the handle over my head as the vehicle bumped and lurched. I kept one eye on the clock and one on the desert, constantly scanning the sand.

Laurie must've seen something I couldn't, because he came to a slow halt. I glanced up at the sky, noting that Cyrus and Tabitha had begun to land, as well. As the dust around us settled, I followed Laurie's gaze through the windshield. My heart lurched.

There was a lone figure off in the distance.

The three of us got out again, and Laurie and Collith took their protective stances on either side of me. We approached the naked, brown-skinned male, but even though he must've heard the engine and our slamming doors, he didn't move from the rock he was sitting on.

Once we were close enough, the three of us stopped. Silence descended again, and I couldn't hide my awe as I felt the true depth of this creature's power. Laurie had been wrong about one thing, I thought dazedly, watching the figure finally turn toward us. The Horn hadn't summoned an entire host of angels.

It had only summoned one.

"Well met, Fallen," the angel said solemnly. He scanned each of us before his golden eyes landed on me, and stayed there. "I am Michael."

CHAPTER THIRTEEN

The force of the angel's presence was ancient. Terrifying.

Standing before him, even though I was a short distance away, I felt young and small. I had no idea what to say or where to start. Collith and Laurie were also silent, as if they'd been overwhelmed by his power, too.

Michael got to his feet, wincing. I frowned and searched for any visible injuries. Had he been hurt during his descent?

"We cannot stay here," the angel warned, shifting his stance. "My brother is searching for me. He is in this desert, but I cannot determine his location."

He meant Lucifer. Fear darted through me.

"Wait!" I blurted, taking a step forward. Michael paused. Without thinking I said, "Does He know?"

I wasn't just talking about the devil, but I wasn't sure why I couldn't say the rest. Somehow, Michael still understood the question perfectly. "The Maker knows all, Lady Sworn," he told me.

That's what I was afraid of. Pain and fury ripped into my heart like rabid dogs. My voice shook as I said, "If the big guy knows everything, and He's aware of all the awful shit that happens here, why not *do* something about it?"

"That is not the Maker's place. When They gave you free will, They relented the ability to control the outcome of your choices."

A vile insult rose in my throat, but I swallowed it. Like he'd said, we didn't have any time to waste. "Where is the grave?" I asked Michael bluntly.

The angel shook his head, but those ancient eyes were devoid of any remorse. "That would be interfering, my lady."

Frustration erupted in my chest, and the heat of it melted away my fear. "Interfering?" I repeated in disbelief.

"There are rules that cannot be broken. Laws and equations that hold the worlds together. The Maker does not interfere because even They must adhere to them. So They help in whatever ways They can. Nudges. Whispers. The sort of interferences that still leave the choice up to you. That leave your free will untouched."

"Nudges? Are you saying . . . you're saying this was all God's plan?" I made an abrupt gesture toward the desert. "Meeting Gwyn, Dracula, the Rat King, all the rest—you're trying to tell me we were just telling a story that was written for us?"

This time, Michael didn't respond. I knew he was about to leave again, and I should let him, if Lucifer really was somewhere nearby. Desperation made my heart quicken. We *had* to know where the grave was. Lucifer would get to it, one way or another, and he needed to find it empty when he did.

"Who is Thuridan? You can at least tell me that. Why was he so important to Jassin? Why did Lucifer take him?" I shot the questions at Michael like bullets, relentless, reckless.

Collith shifted beside me, as if he was stopping himself from intervening. I glanced over at him, and then Laurie, but the Seelie King was focused on Michael, his silver eyes shuttered and calculating. I turned back to the angel, still frantically hopeful that he would give us answers.

Michael's features shifted slightly, as if he'd reached a decision. "As you know," he said, "Jassin served the Dark Prince, who spoke to him in his dreams. My brother bid Jassin to protect the boy."

"And why did Thuridan need to be protected?" I asked, hardly daring to breathe. We were actually getting somewhere, and part of me was terrified Michael would clam up any second.

He searched the horizon, and I watched the rising sun paint his skin red. If I didn't know any better, I'd say Michael swallowed a resigned sigh just before he said, "Because his true name is Thuridan of bloodline Olorel. On the day of the Fall, the boy snuck into the Battle of Red Pearls and followed his father through the tear. He inherited Olorel's abilities at a tender age, and Olorel had the foresight to fake his son's death before he sacrificed his own. He knew the Dark Prince might seek to use that power for his own gain.

"But Heilel watched everything through his dreams and mirrors—he knew the truth, not only that Thuridan was alive, but what the boy could do. Once Olorel was gone, Heilel selected Jassin as the child's guardian. He had a witch alter the boy's appearance so the other elders wouldn't recognize him."

Michael paused again, and I was so afraid it would end there. After months of fruitless searching and wondering, we finally had a chance to learn the truth. We could finally gain the upper hand on Lucifer, or at least feel less like fools stumbling around in the dark. "You still haven't answered the question," I pressed. "How does Thuridan fit into Lucifer's plans? Why does the devil need to find Olorel's grave?"

As I spoke, I tried to hide the extent of my eagerness, as if it might stop Michael from answering. I didn't miss that Collith and Laurie still hadn't made a sound, either. The angel's gaze returned to me, deeply penetrating, as if he were evaluating my very soul. More seconds ticked past. I bit my tongue, sensing that it was important I remain silent this time.

It was the right call. At last Michael said, "The remains of an angel never decay. That is why the fae burn their dead, even if they do not remember the origin of the custom. Power lingers in places and bones. Why do you think witches use them for their spells? I imagine if you combine Olorel's remains with Thuridan's significant power, it might be enough to create more than a tear."

"He wants to open a Door," I whispered, my eyes wide with horror. "A Door between worlds."

Michael's expression didn't change, but his eyes looked darker, somehow. "Not a Door. A Gate."

We had to stop it. If the creatures of Hell poured into this world, humanity wouldn't survive. For a gut-wrenching, terrible moment, I pictured it. An army of those things that had attacked me on the rooftop of Lucifer's tower, killing and raping their way through every city, every continent. Earth would burn, and everything good would be replaced by darkness.

I didn't let panic get its claws into me.

This was the reason, I thought, frowning at the ground. *This* was why I'd ended up in Hell. I knew how Lucifer operated now, and I could use that knowledge to beat him, once and for all. I put myself in the devil's shoes and that twisted, dark mind of his.

When Lucifer couldn't succeed with seduction, he used magic.

Magic, I thought. The mark. Thuridan. The grave. He was gathering *ingredients*. Lucifer was working another spell, just as he had for his crossroads deals. Why else would he wait until a specific day to make his next move? It was the anniversary of Olorel's death. Another ingredient, a specification necessary for the success of such complex magic. That's how he planned to open the Gate.

More often than not, the solution was simple. What prevented a spell from working? Not having all the ingredients. If Lucifer didn't have Thuridan, he wouldn't be able to let his army in. His entire plan collapsed into dust.

I spun back to Michael. The angel had been standing there

silently. I was surprised he'd stayed at all, considering what we were up against. Another wave of fear crashed over me, bigger and harder than the last one. I met Michael's gaze, and my voice was sharper than I'd meant it to be as I asked, "Will you be here? If that Gate opens and the armies of Hell come out?"

I already knew his answer, even if his wistful smile didn't already say everything. "That would be considered a very large interference, I'm afraid."

"So I get free will, and you don't?" I challenged.

"Fortuna . . ." Collith murmured, stepping forward. I shot him a sidelong glance and saw the wary look he gave Michael.

But the angel didn't take offense at my question. "They didn't make the rules. Those rules have always been in place, in order for any of this to exist. Even me," he said simply.

"How about a riddle, then? Come on, I know you probably love those," I wheedled. But Michael's body began to lighten, as if he were blowing away on the wind, and my words seemed to fall on deaf ears. I knew he was leaving, going back to that world behind the pearl-crusted gates. I raised my voice, and it had lost its playful edge, becoming something sharp and serrated instead. "You started all this when you slit Persephone's throat. Now it's time to finish it."

"I think you forgot to grab your sense of self-preservation when we left the house, dear," Laurie murmured beside me.

I didn't answer, because Michael's body had begun to solidify again. He gave me a long, hard look. Maybe the angel wasn't as detached as he'd seemed, I thought, knowing he could probably hear every word going through my head. But it was the truth. If Michael was actually about to be helpful in some way, then he must've felt some regret about what had happened at the Battle of Red Pearls.

"We don't need to play games," Michael said. "I have already proven that if you ask a question I can answer, I will."

Frustration surged through me. But he wouldn't tell me

where the grave was, and it was the thing we needed to know most. It was our one shot at beating Lucifer—we could burn Olorel's bones or use them as leverage.

I was about to turn to Collith and Laurie when another thought slipped into my mind. Suddenly I knew what I wanted to ask. As I faced Michael again, hot shame slid through my veins. But it wasn't enough to stop me.

For him, I would get down on my hands and knees if I had to.

My voice was tight as I said, "Can he be saved? Ollie?"

Even now, there was no surprise in Michael's eyes. But there was . . . something. If I didn't know any better, I would say it was pity. "Can a wolf change its nature?" he asked.

Pain filled my throat. "By that logic, I can't be saved, either," I said tightly.

The angel's gaze was steady, and his eyebrows rose in a nearly imperceptible movement. "You are not a wolf, Lady Sworn."

I frowned. Tears blurred my vision, and I blinked them away, praying no one had seen them. "What am I, then?"

Michael turned, as if he'd heard something I hadn't. Collith and Laurie were looking in the same direction. A moment later, I felt it—power. Teeth-grinding, tingling power that was as visceral as a charge in the air. I recognized it instantly, and dread gripped my bones as I followed that pull.

Lucifer stood nearby.

And Oliver stood behind him.

We'd waited too long, I thought with a jolt of terror. *I'd* waited too long. In the auburn glow of dawn, the devil looked even more like something that had come from another world. He stood with his back to the horizon, sunlight and red desert air streaming all around him. My gaze fell to the sword he held loosely at his side, and apprehension gathered in my throat, blocking out anything I might've said.

Lucifer hadn't come for me, anyway. He smiled at Michael and said, "Hello, brother."

I glanced over at the angel, unsure what to do. His expression hadn't just reverted to its earlier glacial state—looking at him made my insides quake. I was reminded, as though I could ever forget, just what he was. Michael might have been wounded and earthbound, but he had as much power as Lucifer, maybe more. He was a true immortal, and the way he looked at Lucifer made my own power rise instinctively. I imagined gathering it around me like a shield.

"Hello, Lucifer," Michael said.

As if he'd been given a silent command, Oliver moved. Collith and Laurie reacted, readying to launch into action, but Oliver was only dumping out the contents of a bag. Pieces of something fell to the ground between all of us. I stared at them for a beat, then realized what I was looking at. It was the Horn, broken in half. Practically crumbled. The thought sent a chill through me, because I realized exactly what Lucifer was saying with this little message of his.

It meant the devil only had one shot.

"That's right. I'm back at my full strength, brother," Lucifer said, holding out his arms. "Now, shall we do this the easy way, or the hard way?"

The taunt confirmed what I already knew—that I'd made Lucifer into an original angel again. He was basically as unstoppable as God.

I felt a flood of terror and guilt, and my fingers twitched as I longed to reach for the gun at my hip. But I'd only brought it in case we ran into a Fallen creature that was actually susceptible to holy bullets. They wouldn't even slow Lucifer and Oliver down.

Michael raised his arm in a wordless response to his brother, and a sword materialized in his hand, beautiful and deadly looking with its bright edges and considerable size. The fact that he didn't speak to Lucifer, and yet he'd just been talking to me, sent a message to all six of us standing there. There was no contempt in the angel's expression, but it hung in the air, somehow.

"The hard way it is, then," Lucifer sighed.

There was another breath of stillness, like the hush that fell just before something terrible happened. Then the brothers flew at each other.

Both of them moved faster than any creature I'd ever seen. Collith pulled me back as dust shot up everywhere, clouding around the battling angels. Watching Lucifer and Michael fight, I realized I would've been zero help. I tried to track their blocks and blows, but they were practically blurs. At first, they seemed evenly matched.

But Michael was wounded, and Lucifer was desperate.

I didn't see what actually happened—one moment, the angels were battling, and the next Michael stumbled back, a ray of light bursting from his gut. He didn't make a sound as he fell to one knee, a hand going to his wound. Lucifer approached him at a leisurely pace now, and he lifted his sword to run his tongue along the blade. A repulsed shudder went through me. I expected Lucifer to vanish, since he had what he wanted, didn't he? He'd just needed Michael's blood.

All of us waited, and the air thrummed with silent, breathless tension. Michael's head turned, and his gaze found me again.

They are connected, his voice whispered in my head. *What happens to one happens to both*.

I stared at him in confusion. Did he mean Lucifer and Oliver? Why tell me this now?

"Goodbye, brother," Lucifer purred.

When he lifted his arm, I finally realized what he was about to do. Too late, I rammed against the devil's mental defenses, hoping to catch him unawares. But I bounced right off, and his sword finished its sweeping motion. Michael's head toppled from his body. He died in an explosion of blinding, howling light.

And I was standing closest to the blast.

The second it hit me, it felt like my body came apart. As I cried out in agony, I saw the alarmed look in Collith's eyes. I saw

Laurie's mouth form my name. The world tilted, and I lost any sense of where I was or what else was happening. There was only the pain. A bright, blazing excruciation the likes of which I'd never known before.

And then there was nothing.

I flew upright, as I had the countless other nights I'd woken from a bad dream.

But this wasn't a dream. I wasn't sure how I knew, I just did. It didn't have the feel of one. Even though, in some ways, this place certainly did remind me of the dreamscape. I searched the vast spread of hills around me, my brow furrowed with bewilderment. I definitely wasn't in the desert anymore, and there was no sign of Michael, Lucifer, Collith, or Laurie. Where was everyone? How had I gotten here?

I was too dazed to panic. My mind continued to work slowly. The last thing I remembered was getting hit by that blast of screaming power, and a level of pain I had never experienced before. It was what I imagined getting burned alive would feel like. In those final moments, I'd been convinced I was about to die. I looked down at myself to search for injuries. I frowned when I discovered only smooth skin and whole, unbroken limbs. But I felt . . . different. Off-kilter. Desperate for answers, I turned my head to search for the others again.

My eyes stopped on a figure kneeling nearby, and a whisper of shock went through me.

Olorel had never been real to me—not really. I'd seen him briefly in Lucifer's memories, during the Battle of Red Pearls, but even then, he had seemed like nothing more than a character from a story. A legend. A figure from the past.

Now he was actually a person. As Olorel drew something on the ground, I studied the angel that was still celebrated by his descendants thousands of years later. He wore what I suspected were animal skins, and he looked younger than I'd thought he would. His hair hung past his shoulders, longer than Laurie's, and part of it was tied back with a piece of leather. His beard was thick but trimmed, his body hard and corded. I watched the muscles in his arm flex as he finished whatever he was drawing in the dirt.

Without looking up from his task, Olorel called out, "Why are you here?"

I would've panicked, but I knew the fallen angel wasn't talking to me. Because this was a memory, I realized in a rush. *Michael's* memory. I could feel him now, all around me, his thoughts and his essence cool and subtle, like the flow of water. I was still me, but I was also Michael, too. His words were mine as he said, "I could ask you the same thing."

"Ulesse went for a walk." Olorel still didn't look up from the shape at his knees.

Ulesse, I repeated to myself. The name stirred a memory. Then I remembered—Nym's bloodline. The Time Walkers.

"And what did he see?" Michael asked. Both of them were speaking in Enochian, but I still understood as if they were speaking clear, perfect English.

Olorel straightened and tipped his head back. "He saw death. And pain. And fire. It has already begun, Michael. Some of our brothers and sisters have slipped through the tear she made."

I mentally froze on those words. *The tear she made.*

Because I was sharing a mind with Michael, I knew that Olorel meant Persephone, and the brothers and sisters he was referring to were demons. My thoughts raced so fast that I almost missed it when Olorel replied, "Which is why I must close it."

Close it?

Michael was calm as ever, but from my hiding place, I felt a rush of adrenaline. I remembered a conversation I'd had with Lucifer during my time in the underworld. He'd told me the story of Persephone. How they had met and fallen in love. How they had been separated and then, years later, had found their way back to each other.

Persephone did it? She actually got to Hell? I'd asked Lucifer.

She survived for three days.

Holy shit, I thought. If I'd had my own heart, it would've been thundering in my chest. A Nightmare had created an opening to another dimension, allowing demons to come through. And if a Nightmare could open a Door, it stood to reason that I could close one, too.

Lucifer himself had given me the key. He'd told me how it could be done after I'd brought him into my world. *If a Nightmare is powerful enough, she can bring her dreams to life. She just has to believe it can be done, or feel something strongly enough that a part of her believes.*

"You shouldn't interfere," Michael warned, his voice cutting through my own memories. "The imbalance will right itself, and the cost—"

"The cost will be my life," Olorel said calmly. He got to his feet, his fingers smeared with dirt. He did nothing to wipe it off.

Michael was silent for a moment, and I felt the struggle in him. He cared for Olorel, but he also cared about the law. He had always followed it to the letter, even as his favorite siblings rebelled and fought and broke every rule like insolent children. He looked down at what Olorel had drawn. I didn't recognize it, but Michael did—it was an Enochian symbol meant to repair, or undo.

"Even with the aid of the Word, your power will not be enough," Michael said finally.

Olorel gazed back at him, his features still curiously blank. "No, it will not."

Another shock went through me as I realized what was happening, what this memory was.

All of Fallenkind believed Olorel had sacrificed himself to create the Unseelie Court. But that must've been a lie. A cover-up.

Olorel was about to die trying to fix what Persephone had done.

Just as Michael began to answer, something made the angel pause. He looked over his shoulder, but Olorel didn't move. He waited calmly. When Michael turned again, whatever he'd seen had made him go pale. His voice was low and urgent as he said, "Don't do this, Olorel."

Olorel gave the angel a small, hollow smile. In that moment, he looked so much like Thuridan it sent a startled jolt through me. "Careful, brother," he murmured. "It almost seems as if you're tempted to interfere."

I would never know what Michael said, or what he'd been so afraid of, because the memory began to fade. In the space of a blink, the angels were gone. The sky went after them, its vibrant colors going from bronze and pink to white and gray. No! I needed to know how Olorel had done it! It wasn't just my family's lives that depended on it—it was *everyone's*. I tried to bring the memory back by picturing the vibrant sunset that had surrounded Olorel and Michael while they spoke.

It didn't work. The grass started to go next.

"No! Please!" I dropped to my knees and envisioned the lush, golden hills, trying to imagine it between my fingers as I buried them in the dry earth. It was no use, though. The grass had already vanished, and so had the clouds. I leaned back, trying to hold back the sob rising in my throat. *Damn it, damn it, damn it!*

"Fortuna."

I whirled at the sound of his voice, confusion tearing through me. My best friend stood there, amongst all the gray and empty air. He was my Oliver again, without any of the veins or wings or claws. He was even wearing his old white T-shirt.

"Ollie?" I whispered, my heart so full of hope that it ached. "How are you here? This isn't my memory."

"I'm using our connection to reach you. I saw you get hit by the blast. It's time to wake up." Oliver paused, his expression inscrutable. "Come on, Fortuna. The Dark Prince knows where the grave is. And . . . your faeries are worried."

He meant Collith and Laurie, no doubt. Everyone else would be worried, too. But I didn't move. I stared out at the dimming horizon, which was also disappearing. My hands were limp in my lap. *So close,* I thought. I had been so close to finding out how to save them. The Horn was broken now, which meant it would be impossible to summon another angel. The knowledge of how to shut the Gate had died with Michael. I'd failed.

It would have been so easy to pretend this actually was a dream. So easy to make myself believe Oliver and I were back in our secret place, with the sea glittering on the horizon, the old oak tree casting its shadow nearby, and the cottage off in the distance. I thought of all those afternoons we'd spent there, me in front of the fire, Oliver at his easel. I used to find so much comfort in watching him.

"Do you still paint?" I asked faintly.

If Oliver found the question strange, he didn't show it. "No. Not anymore."

"Why?" I asked.

Oliver paused again. "Because it hurts too much."

I looked at him, then. I met my best friend's gaze and remembered who we used to be. Such young, silly creatures with carefree dreams and impossible hopes. I'd never imagined it could turn out like this. I'd never dreamed that sweet, freckled boy would become a Beast, or that sad, lonely girl would grow up to kill him.

"Tell me how to save you, Ollie," I whispered.

"You can't," he answered, his eyes bright with pain and all the days we wouldn't get to have. Then he said, his voice hardening, "Wake up, Fortuna. Wake up."

"Oliver, wait," I began to say, my own voice tinged with desperation. But it was too late.

Every dream had to end, and I was already gone.

CHAPTER FOURTEEN

*T*his time, I woke up in a bed that smelled like Laurie. His scent was so familiar that it had become as recognizable as coffee or freshly mown grass. One of those commonplace, everyday scents. As soon as it hit me, the spark of panic in my mind went dim. I sat upright and looked around. Light shone from a crack beneath a nearby door, casting a subtle glow over the room. I recognized it instantly.

I was back at the Seelie Court.

As soon as I had the thought, everything from last night came rushing back. The fireworks, the conversation with Laurie, the Horn. My heart pounded harder. I remembered finding Michael in the desert and confronting him. The battle with Lucifer. I remembered what Michael had said to me, mind to mind, when he'd realized he was going to die. *What happens to one happens to both.*

I remembered the memory Michael had given me as his body came apart. What I'd seen after I was caught in that blast of white light.

Your power will not be enough.

No, it will not.

Don't do this, Olorel.

Why had Michael looked at the other angel with such horror? What had he seen right at the end?

Since I'd experienced the memory through him, I had felt Michael's physical reaction. Like he was being torn in two. I knew that feeling well. Maybe angels and my kind weren't so different after all. Maybe we hadn't fallen as far as we believed.

Piano music floated through the stillness, cutting my thoughts short. I pushed the luxurious covers aside and stood, noting that someone had taken my clothes off. Probably Laurie. Wearing only my bra and some lacy underwear, I spotted my cell phone on the nightstand and went over to pick it up. It was almost 11:00 a.m. I'd been out for five hours.

I took my phone with me and crossed the huge room. I opened the door and slipped through, then quickly went into the elegant bathroom I'd used last time. Within seconds, I discovered that Laurie had kept my toothbrush from that day. There was also a dress in my size, with buttons down its flowered length . . . along with matching lingerie, of course, because it was Laurie.

Ten minutes later, my hair wet, my skin scrubbed clean of all that dust, I opened the bathroom door and followed the sound of the piano music. My bare feet moved soundlessly against the shining, tiled floor. I'd examined every inch of myself in the shower, and other than some soreness, I seemed to be completely fine. There were no scrapes or bruises from hitting the ground. Even the bruises from my training sessions with Adam and Gil were gone.

Healed, I thought as I walked toward another familiar doorway. But how? Had Zara been here . . . or was it Michael's power?

They were questions I'd have to ask Laurie. I stopped on the threshold and crossed my arms, taking advantage of this rare opportunity to observe the Seelie King. He sat at the piano, wearing what looked like designer sweatpants and nothing else. The hard lines of his body shone in a shaft of morning light pouring in through the curtains. His hair hung free, still slightly damp from his own shower. His long lashes cast a shadow over his cheek as he gazed down at the keys. The song drifting through the quiet, sun-dappled air was . . . hesitant. Afraid, maybe. Pleading.

I'd only been standing there a few seconds when Laurie's gaze rose to mine. There was no hint of surprise in his expression. He finished the final, lingering notes of the piece without looking away from me.

"I've never heard that one before. It's beautiful," I said softly.

Laurie's fingers danced over some random, trilling notes. "Thank you. I call it 'Fortuna.'"

I paused, searching Laurie's expression. A strange little throb went through my heart. "You wrote that? And you named it after me?"

He gave me a pitying look and played some of the piece's chords again. "Of course not. I named it after another Fortuna I know. Goodness, this is awkward now."

My lips twisted as I kept watching him. Sometimes I forgot how kind Laurie could be. So much had happened since we'd met, and we had both made terrible mistakes, but he was still the person who'd left me a chair in that cold, empty room beneath the Unseelie Court.

While Laurie's clever fingers moved into another melody, I inevitably started thinking about the day ahead. I needed to tell Collith and Laurie everything I'd learned from Michael. But . . . I found myself reluctant to face it all yet. Right now, I wanted nothing more than to admire the sight of Laurie in the light streaming through the window, and listen to his beautiful music.

"Is this always how you start your day?" I asked him. "You play?"

Laurie tilted his head as he considered my question. "No. *This* is always how I start my day."

The tune cut short as Laurie shifted his attention to the top of the instrument—it was littered with composition pages and crumpled balls of paper—and swept a careless arm over it. Everything tumbled to the floor. A marble bounced and rolled. Laurie cocked his head again and looked at me, the picture of sensuality and mischief.

An automatic denial rose to my lips, but I couldn't seem to actually say the words. Seconds passed, and I felt my eyes widen when they still wouldn't come out. Dear God, was I actually tempted to say yes?

My face must've given something away, or Laurie could smell my arousal, because he rose from the piano bench. Suddenly all the teasing was gone from his expression, and I recognized the intent way he looked at me. *Fuck,* I thought, instantly fighting the urge to back away. The hunt would only excite Laurie more.

He was a faerie, after all.

He stopped in front of me. His fingers trailed up the length of my arm and across my collarbone. Then he skimmed them along the side of my neck. His voice was thick with promise as he said, "I miss this. And this. And this."

"We need to talk," I said, willing myself to push him away. I put my hands on his chest to do exactly that.

Laurie's hand slipped beneath my dress, and he ran a single fingertip along the skin just above my underwear. "I think talking is the last thing we should be doing right now."

"Laurie . . ."

A floorboard squeaked. Laurie didn't even react, but I did, and something inside me lurched in panic when I turned my head and saw Collith. He leaned against the doorjamb, his face shrouded in shadow. For a quiet, shivering moment, none of us moved.

Desperate for someone to speak, I stepped back from Laurie and looked between the two of them again. There was a forced note of nonchalance in my voice as I asked, "Can someone fill in the blanks, please? The last thing I remember is being in the desert and watching Lucifer and Michael fight to the death."

"You were hit with Michael's power," Laurie said, turning

away. He walked over to a side table, where there was a teapot with steam rising from its spout. "Would anyone else like a cup?"

"No, thank you," I said slowly, watching him pour the hot tea. "What does that mean, exactly?"

"We don't know. I'm afraid knowledge of the original angels has faded over time," Collith said, pushing off the door frame to draw closer. He nodded at Laurie. "I'll have some. Lemon, please."

I watched them with a distracted frown. Collith poured his tea, then stirred it with subtle, graceful flicks of his wrist. He said something to Laurie, but my mind had gone back to the memory Michael had shown me. Back to his last conversation with Olorel. And I knew, even though it was still my first instinct not to trust anyone, that I couldn't keep this to myself.

"We need to talk," I repeated.

My gaze rose and met Laurie's. This time, he saw something that made him fall silent. Without a word, Laurie walked over to the settee and sat, stretching out his legs as he brought the delicate cup to his lips. Collith looked at me and nodded as if to say, *We're listening*.

So I took a deep breath, and I told them everything, starting with what Michael had whispered to me just before he'd died.

When I was done, silence filled the room like a winter night. At some point while I was talking, I'd wrapped my hand around the edge of the piano. I stared down at my hand now, thinking how just a few hours ago, my knuckles had been covered in bruises. If Michael's power did that, what else had it done to me? While Collith and Laurie absorbed the revelation that their entire fae history was a lie, I relived that final moment with Michael again.

"'What happens to one happens to both,'" I repeated, frowning at the memory. "That's what Michael said to me just before he died. He meant Oliver and Lucifer, right? He must've. So we only need to kill one of them!"

My gaze shot up, but their expressions made my excitement dim. "I would agree," Collith said.

"What is it? This is a good thing, right?"

"The Dark Prince is an angel," Laurie reminded me. "If the Beast's life is tied to his, then they're both pretty damn near indestructible."

He was right. No wonder they both looked so grim. And right now, there was nothing we could do with this newfound knowledge, anyway. Lucifer knew where the grave was.

I also didn't miss that Collith and Laurie weren't bringing up the biggest revelation of all—that I might be capable of closing the Gate. The part of the story I had considered leaving out, but in the end had decided to trust them with. Because the toxic, broken pattern between us could only end if someone took the first step toward changing it. I knew Olorel's reply haunted all three of us.

The cost will be my life.

All at once, the monumental reality of it hit me. The truth about what I'd learned, and what I might have to do. Feeling overwhelmed and hungry for some normality, I exhaled loudly and glanced at a clock on the wall. "I should go. I have a closing shift at the bar tonight. Thanks for the dress, Laur."

I shot a parting smile up at him and turned for the door. I knew I'd see Collith later. If he wasn't waiting for me in the parking lot at Bea's, he usually stayed up until I got back to the loft. Ever since I'd been attacked by that yar demon, he hadn't been taking any chances.

"You can't go home," Laurie called after me.

"No, don't—" I heard Collith say at the same moment I halted.

I turned, raising my eyebrows. "I beg your pardon?"

Collith shot Laurie a look that said, *Now you've done it*. I scowled at him. I was about to remind Collith that I wasn't a child when he said, "Home is the first place Lucifer will look for you. The Dark Prince has probably had a spy posted there for months, giving regular reports on us. He'll know the second you step foot on the property."

I shrugged. "Okay . . . and why am I hiding from Lucifer? He's known where I am for months."

"He saw you get hit by the blast," Laurie put in. "He actually *does* know what that means. He might want to kill you, or he might have some other terrible use for you. Collith put you onto Cyrus's back a split second after it happened and brought you straight here. One of the Dark Prince's creatures tried to follow, but we beat it to the Door."

"No. I'm not going in to hiding. Not again."

"We've considered every outcome, Fortuna, and going home is a bad idea."

Frustration blazed in my veins. Fighting for control, I raked my hair back and let out another breath. I knew they were trying to help me, I knew that. They thought they were just being protective. But . . . it didn't feel right. It was like the bars of a cage were closing in around me.

"Could we not fight, for once? Please?" I asked. A faint note of pleading slipped into my voice.

I expected Collith to answer, and a jolt of surprise went through my frame when Laurie said, "This isn't a fight, Firecracker. It's a discussion."

"What makes you think either of you get a say in what I do?" I countered. Even as the words came out of my mouth, I knew how unfair they were. I let out a breath and closed my eyes for a moment, clenching one of my hands into a fist. "I'm sorry. I don't . . . I don't know how to do this."

"Do what?" Collith asked softly.

I opened my eyes and looked at him. Both of them. Collith's expression was patient, his gaze gentle. Laurie's expression revealed nothing, and he'd gone still. It was his stillness that betrayed him, though. Betrayed how much he cared about my answer, as if taking just a single breath would frighten me into silence. I swallowed, and my insides quaked. Why did it feel like we were standing at the very edge of something? Like whatever I said next had the potential to change everything between us?

The room was so quiet that I could hear the birds outside. I looked at Collith and Laurie again, knowing they deserved the truth, no matter how much it terrified me. "I—"

An image filled my head, a vivid slam of lines and colors that struck without warning. I bowled over, crying out as pain crackled through my body. I clutched my skull so hard that I felt the bite of my own fingernails. Collith and Laurie were both saying something, and one of them had grasped my waist to steady me. Their voices were like humming power lines. I could only focus on the pictures, the agony, the way my teeth ground together. It should've hurt, but it was nothing compared to what was happening in my mind. I heard voices that weren't Collith or Laurie's. I saw a hand pointing at a faded piece of paper. I saw shapes in ink. I moaned and leaned against the warm body holding me upright. *Make it stop, make it stop . . .*

All at once, the pressure building inside me eased, and the claws tearing through my brain retreated. I started breathing again, in short bursts at first, then slower and deeper. After a few seconds, I relaxed against Laurie. I knew it was him now because of that distinct springtime scent.

As I rested in the circle of his arms, I waited for the Seelie King to make a joke or give a rousing speech, but he was silent. Once again, stillness hovered through the suite. It reminded me of the forest in deep winter—the sort of silence that only happened when the entire world, even the trees, had gone to sleep. The image, along with Laurie's scent, made me think of that night in the snow, when he'd held me just as he was holding me now. It felt like years ago.

Eventually, I felt normal enough to open my eyes. The walls of Laurie's room looked back at me. I glanced around, noting that we were alone again. Collith had probably left to get Savannah.

The only way to fight magic was with magic, and she was the most powerful witch we knew. What the hell *was* that? Some residual effect of Michael's power? Would it happen again?

Laurie's voice rumbled against my ear. "What does my fear taste like, Fortuna?"

At first, I frowned in confusion. He knew I couldn't get past his mental barriers. Laurie was too strong, even for—

I could sense it, I realized in a rush. It was faint and distant. I held myself completely still, absorbing the flavor of Laurelis Dondarte's fear. "Like rain, I think," I whispered. "It tastes like rain."

There wasn't much that frightened Laurelis Dondarte, but the sound of my screams was one of them.

I finally sat upright, and put my hand on Laurie's shoulder for balance as I shifted, putting my knees on either side of him. His eyebrows rose. "What are you—" he started.

Then I bent my head and kissed him.

Laurie responded instantly, his hands pressing to the small of my back. He pulled me so close that our chests smashed together. He tasted as good as I remembered. My tongue moved with his as if we'd done this a thousand times before, but it wasn't enough, it never was with Laurie. Our breathing became ragged and his fingers were tangled in my hair now, touching me with that hint of roughness I liked so much, as if he was claiming me. As if this was the last chance we'd ever get, and he intended to make the most of it.

But eventually, I pulled back. I sighed through my nose, my entire body moving with the breath. My mouth felt deliciously swollen. "Collith . . ."

"It's okay. He knows, and it's okay," Laurie murmured, arching his head back. One of his rings flashed as he tucked my hair behind my shoulder.

I gave him a bemused look. "Good to know, but I meant that we should tell him I'm okay."

"Already done." Laurie held up his phone as proof. But

Collith could still come back any second, and I wasn't sure I was ready for—

Laurie's palms skimmed up my bare thighs, pushing up the dress. While his erection pressed against the thin material of my thong, he reached up and undid my buttons. His tongue and lips teased and explored the skin he exposed, little by little, as he pulled the front of the dress open. Open air whispered over my breasts. Laurie cupped one of them, thumbing my nipple through the thin lace of the bra he'd given me, while his other hand slipped downward. I bit my lip and held his shoulders tighter.

"I need to be inside you," Laurie breathed against my chest. A moment later, I felt his fingers slide along the wet folds of my labia. "Let me be inside you, Fortuna."

A helpless sound escaped me. I wanted to say yes. I wanted to ride Laurie in a way I hadn't done for so long. I wanted to watch the ecstasy fill his eyes while I brought him to the brink, then back again in a torturous rhythm, just like he'd done to me.

Laurie must've smelled my arousal, or maybe my thoughts were shining nakedly from my eyes. The look he gave me made liquid pool between my legs. "Dirty little Nightmare," he said huskily.

And I knew, then, that I was about to give in. But just as Laurie was on the verge of slipping his fingers inside me, my eyes shot open. In a jolting rush, my arousal was replaced by panic. By an inexplicable urge that didn't feel entirely like my own.

"Paper," I said urgently, getting off Laurie. I hurried to fix my underwear and fasten my dress. "I need paper!"

"Do you really need that right *now*?" he asked, his voice strained.

"Yes." I hurried over to the piano, where everything Laurie had pushed onto the floor still lay scattered. I snatched up the pen I'd spotted when it had fallen. I whirled around, about to search the entire suite, and I drew up short with a startled sound. Standing right in front of me, Laurie wordlessly held out a sketchpad.

"Thank you." I didn't spare him a glance as I flipped it open. I set it down on the piano, clicked the pen, and began to draw.

"What's going on?"

Collith had returned. I still didn't look up, and Laurie's voice floated across the room, followed by the clink of a spoon against china. "Fortuna has been struck with the all-consuming need to do an impression of Picasso, evidently."

Soft footsteps rippled through the stillness, and then Collith's enticing scent teased my senses. He didn't say anything, but I felt his silent concern. The scratch of my pen filled the air between us.

"I think when Michael died, I didn't just get his memories. I got a message from him," I muttered as I drew, my movements abrupt and frantic. The images in my head were already fading. Soon they'd be completely gone.

It wasn't a map, exactly, but that was the closest thing I could think of. There were no notes on it. No keys or discernible reason it should hold significance for us. Just a bunch of lines and shapes, some of which weren't even connected. But I knew, I just knew in my gut that these images meant something. It hadn't been an accident, me getting Michael's memories. In his final moments, the angel had been trying to help us. He'd *interfered*.

"What is that?" Collith asked. Laurie came over to the piano, holding his teacup, and peered down at the sketchpad. A frown pulled at his pouty mouth and there was no recognition in his eyes. Apparently they were just as lost as I was. I felt my heart sink at the realization. Part of me had hoped something would make sense to them.

"I don't know," I said finally. I kept staring down at the lines of ink.

After a few seconds, it clicked—there was something missing. A slight difference from one of the images in my head to what I'd put on paper. This one was more vivid than the rest, and maybe it was because I'd been there before. As a kid, with my parents, on the last road trip we'd ever taken together.

Yet another coincidence? Or had it been another one of those "nudges" Michael had mentioned?

Leaning forward again, I drew the last shape on the map. It was a place. A landmark called Teter Rock. I still had the picture of my family standing in front of it. I'd looked at that rock countless times over the years.

Once I was finished drawing it, I leaned back and smiled at Collith and Laurie. "I better get that shift covered. Lucifer may have the location of the grave now, but he's not the only one," I said.

Laurie's eyebrows rose. "You mean . . ."

I nodded. Triumph raced through my veins, headier than any drug, and it made my heart pound so hard I knew they could hear it. "I know where they are."

CHAPTER FIFTEEN

The tents seemed to go on for miles.

We'd waited for the cover of night to make our journey to the Flint Hills, and it was all too easy to find Lucifer and his army. The devil wasn't hiding, I thought as I gazed out at the endless campfires and torches. There had to be hundreds, if not thousands. The darkened hills almost looked like a sky full of strange, flickering stars.

"So many," I muttered, trying not to let any fear show in my face.

"Mercy says he's been garnering followers since the Fall," Savannah said beside me. She made no effort to hide her dread, and I knew she was thinking of Matthew. I was thinking about him, too, and all the other people I needed to protect from this horde.

There were three of us hidden on the hill, lying flat on our stomachs high above the devil's gathering forces. We'd kept our rescue party small, since the entire plan depended on stealth. I'd still brought weapons, though, in the likely event that something went wrong. I had four knives hidden beneath my clothes and one small gun, which was loaded with holy bullets, of course. We now knew that holy weapons were useless against demons, but having it made me feel braver.

And right now, I needed all the bravery I could get.

Savannah seemed to think this eerie gathering was made up of Fallen. But even from here, I could see things moving amongst the tents that were unmistakably demonkind. I thought of Narfu, and the creature that I'd almost run down on the road. A yar demon, Lucifer had called it.

I remembered Laurie's theory when I'd told him about it. *Now we know what snake boy has been doing in West Bengal. He must be getting them through somehow.*

When I'd met with Lucifer, the morning we sat on the bench outside Adam's, he had practically confirmed it. *I've been . . . experimenting,* he'd said.

His experiments must not have been entirely successful, if he was still determined to open the Gate. I scanned the sea of tents again and suppressed a shudder. If this was what failure looked like, I was terrified to consider what Lucifer would consider a triumph.

I must've shifted or let out a brief tremor, because Lyari's face turned slightly, her hard eyes darting over at me. When I'd texted her about our plan to rescue Thuridan, she had responded instantly, and she hadn't hesitated when I'd asked her to come tonight. As her silent question floated between us, I shook my head as if to say, *Nothing, I'm fine.* I knew that if I tried to say the words out loud, Lyari would hear the lie.

The truth was, I wasn't fine. I still didn't feel normal after the encounter with Michael. I was on edge, yes, but I'd been on edge my entire life. This was different. Ever since I'd been hit with that blast, I could feel something inside me, lurking beneath my skin, running through my veins. The need to be in constant motion had worsened. Even during quiet moments—especially in quiet moments—I fought the urge to fidget.

"How long do you think it'll take?" I muttered, trying to

ignore the anxious flutters in my stomach while I continued to stare down at all the lights.

"The kings are fast, but with this much ground to cover . . ." Lyari's expression was grim, and I knew it wasn't just because of the daunting numbers spread out before us. She wanted to be down there, too. Looking for Thuridan and actively doing something to help him. But the faeries had decided to split up so one could stay with me. We'd left Seth and Gil in the woods, far from here, in case we needed backup. Seth had proven to be an advantage with tech, and when it came to Lucifer, it was best to prepare for anything.

Savannah shifted, and I looked over at her again. Her fingers were curled into the dirt and she'd closed her eyes.

"What's wrong?" I asked.

"There's a spell on the land," she murmured, her brows furrowed in concentration. "I can't quite . . ."

Once again, there was movement in the corner of my eye, and I turned the other way. Laurie knelt next to Lyari. The edges of his dark hood fluttered in the wind, and I caught a glimpse of the tense lines around his mouth as he said, "I found him. Let's go."

As we stood, I looked around for any sign of our fifth member. "Did you text Collith?"

Laurie shook his head. "No. My phone died."

I pulled my own phone out, but the screen was dark. I frowned and held down on the button again. Nothing happened. "Mine, too," I muttered.

"He didn't respond to my summons," Laurie said.

Something fluttered at the back of my mind. The sense that I was missing something. I turned to Lyari with a distracted twist to my lips. "Will you text Collith?"

"I will send a message, but there's no time to wait for him," she said curtly, pulling her phone out. A moment later, she frowned and showed me the screen. Dead.

I shifted toward Savannah, but the necromancer was already

giving me an apologetic look. "I left mine with Seth and Gil. I didn't want to risk losing it," she told me.

Shit. There was no way to tell Collith that Laurie had found Thuridan. It was the first hole in our plan, and there were probably more, I thought grimly. My adrenaline kicked up a notch. Lyari was right, we couldn't wait. Besides the fact that we needed to stop Lucifer, I'd also seen what he did to his prisoners.

Of course, there was a small possibility he was treating Thuridan like a king. Maybe Thuridan wouldn't even want to come with us, like Damon hadn't wanted to leave Jassin.

But we couldn't take that chance.

Savannah stayed behind, as planned. We stole down the hill, and at the bottom, I tried to calm my heartbeat. When we reached the outskirts of the camp, I realized it hadn't all been tents I'd seen from above—there were buildings, too. These soldiers had been here long enough to erect small structures. A smell stung my nostrils, and I grimaced. The latrines must've been nearby.

A few steps beyond the reach of that smell, we encountered the first demon.

I froze, a lightning bolt of terror striking my chest. Laurie was concealing us from sight, I reminded myself, trying to get my feet to budge. Only the thought of Lyari and Laurie seeing me standing there, frightened as a child, helped me find the strength to keep moving.

The demon walked on two legs, and it towered over us as it passed. The creature's skin looked like crusted earth, as if its body had been encased in volcanic rock. But the scaly texture ended at its neck, where it just began to look like charred flesh over a hairless skull. The demon had no nose, only two slits, and its jaw was elongated. Fangs jutted beneath an overbite. Its milky eyes roamed the rows of tents, as if it could sense us.

I averted my gaze and hurried after Laurie and Lyari, trying to move as quietly as possible.

The next few minutes were hell. Laurie led us through the

maze of rows of tents, stopping every now and then to look or listen. Sometimes we had to wait for a creature to pass. The deeper we got into camp, the louder it became.

I searched for any glimpse of Collith, but there were only more demons, more Fallen creatures that were loyal to Lucifer. At one point we passed a werewolf, and not even Laurie's illusion could fool its sharp nose. The second we saw the creature go still, its ears perked with interest, fear exploded in the air. The three of us stopped breathing, and I cursed my own heartbeat again, knowing it was about to give us away.

But the wolf's head jerked in the opposite direction and it took off running, howling at the top of its lungs. The sound made the hairs on my arms stand on end. I shot a glance at Laurie but he just smirked and led us away again, moving so quickly that I almost tripped over a clump of earth. We weaved through the shadows again, and adrenaline pulsed in my ears. Eventually Laurie stopped and gave us another signal.

"There," he said under his breath.

Finally. Relief blended with the adrenaline. I leaned over and followed Laurie's gaze. Beyond the two tents we were hiding between, there was another torch-lined row. One of the tents was obviously bigger than the rest, and two demons stood guard. Torches crackled on either side of them. The guards looked like boars, but their arms were humanoid, the biceps bulging beneath pale, smooth skin as they stood there with gleaming weapons that looked like glass axes.

"We'll lead them away," Laurie said, glancing at me.

I nodded. In the next breath, I grabbed his arm to stop him. "If Lucifer chose that species to guard Thuridan, there's a reason," I warned.

Laurie pressed a hard kiss against my surprised lips, and then he sifted. He reappeared across the path, directly behind one of the demons. Lyari cursed and stepped into the open, as if to follow him. The boars reacted to them instantly—they could see through Laurie's illusion, I realized with horror. They were also wearing thick armor, so Laurie and Lyari didn't waste time trying to fight. They just ran, and the boars instantly charged after them, their excited squeals echoing through the night.

Seeing my chance, I ran across the path and slipped through the unguarded tent flaps.

And there was Thuridan. He was alone, his arms tied in front of him around a wooden pole in the center of the room. It was obvious he'd been beaten, and recently, since his healing capabilities hadn't kicked in yet. His eye was so swollen that it had fused shut, and it looked like a small plum. His lip was split open, and while the bleeding seemed to have stopped, blue stains had crusted to Thuridan's chin and throat.

Hearing the whisper of the tent flap, Thuridan's good eye cracked open. It seemed to take him a moment to register who was standing in front of him. "Never thought I would be glad to see you," he growled.

I kept my voice down as I tilted my head and asked sweetly, "Oh, are you finally getting tired of being everyone's little bitch?"

Even with one eye, Thuridan managed to glare at me. "It is my honor to serve the Unseelie throne, but I'm not eager to die for some ancient asshole trying to claw his way out of Hell."

"Not eager to die?" I repeated distractedly, kneeling to examine the ropes securing Thuridan to the pole. A second later, I swallowed a curse—the knots themselves didn't seem all that complex, but the skin on Thuridan's wrists and forearms was red and blistering. His guards may have only used rope, but they'd drenched them in holy water.

This was going to *hurt*.

"The spell for the Gate will require my life," Thuridan said as I got down on my knees and pulled the pocketknife out of my boot.

I made an unamused sound. "Lucifer and his spells."

Thuridan didn't answer. His eyes were on my hands, which hovered just above the rope. I knew that every moment I hesitated,

I was putting the others in danger. Our entire plan was to get in and get out as fast as we could. *Well, here goes nothing,* I thought.

And then I began cutting the rope.

The pain was immediate. It was like touching acid. My skin began to heat, and within seconds, it was unbearable. I gritted my teeth and reminded myself I'd heal, or we could contact Zara when this was done. But the ropes were thick, and sawing at them with a small pocketknife was going to take time. A shriek lodged in my throat. Distraction. I needed a distraction.

"How do you know all this? About the Gate, and the spell?" I asked Thuridan through my teeth. "The Dark Jackass isn't the type to just . . . just volunteer information."

My hands dropped and I bit back another scream. My arms trembled. *Keep going,* I told myself. People I loved were out there buying me time. Every second counted. Without letting myself think about it, I raised my hands back up and started cutting again.

"I saw it in a Telling," Thuridan said abruptly. He had been silent for so long I'd assumed he wasn't going to answer. My fingertips began to turn red again as he continued, "I'd been feeling anxious about the grand escape Peeks and I had planned, and I also didn't want to leave Lyari. I thought a glimpse of the future would absolve my fear. Instead, I saw my death. I saw my blood spread across the grass, and I felt my soul depart from the broken flesh. The witch performing the Telling said that a great power would find me and take my life. It would be a creature of darkness, she said. And from the moment I first spoke to you, I believed I'd finally met that creature."

"Gee, thanks," I muttered. To my surprise, I felt a pang of sympathy for the asshole in front of me. He'd been used and lied to his entire life, only for the terrible fate of watching his life-blood pour into a bowl.

Good thing we were here to change that.

A moment later, I was forced to drop my hands again. Pain

screamed through my fingers. *Distraction,* I thought again. I looked down at my red, shaking hands and said, "Peeks was in the vision, wasn't he?"

I lifted my head in time to see Thuridan's face muscles twitch with surprise. He nodded, the movement abrupt and jerky, as if the admission hurt him. When he started talking, I found the strength to begin again on the ropes. A hissing noise accompanied the waves of agony moving through my arms. It sounded like water hitting a hot pan.

"I saw his death before mine. He was kneeling beside me, looking defiant and terrified all at once. It was the same look he gave our father or the bullies who tormented us so. Stubborn little fool," Thuridan added. A soft, reluctant smile touched his lips. The sight of Thuridan smiling was so strange that I caught myself staring at him. I quickly refocused on the cutting.

"You th-thought that by distancing yourself from him, you could separate your fates. Prevent his d-death," I said. Thin tendrils of smoke had started rising from my raw fingers, as if I was moments away from catching fire.

Thuridan nodded, his gray eyes inscrutable as he watched me. "I asked Father to use whatever influence he had to get me stationed far away. As far as I could get from a Door or any chance of Peeks bridging the distance between us."

The pain was unbearable. My brain short-circuited, desperate for me to stop. "Why werewolves?" I blurted.

Thuridan blinked. "What?"

"Why are you . . . why are you so afraid of werewolves?"

"I'm not—" Thuridan stopped, tight-lipped, his eyes flashing. "Because of my father."

"Which one?" I asked through my teeth.

I could feel Thuridan's gaze intensify. "You know?"

"I know." One of the ropes finally broke apart, and I almost let out a sob of relief. I leaned back, my hands falling limply to my lap. I almost sobbed again when I realized I still had his other wrist to do. But once again, I didn't give myself a chance to think about it. Steeling myself, I reached for the second rope—

A hand rested hesitantly on my wrist. "Let me," Thuridan said.

I pulled away, relenting the knife to him. Thuridan started cutting, and in spite of his wounds, he moved with the speed of a faerie. His ruined fingers clenched the pocketknife so hard that even the burned skin turned white.

As he cut, he spoke. "As I reached maturity, Jassin began to suspect my powers had gone dormant. I hadn't used them since Olorel died, not even when the other children beat the shit out of me. One night Father took me to the surface, and we ventured deep into the forest. He held out a single knife and said that we were in werewolf territory, then sifted back to Court. It was a full moon."

Thuridan ended there. He kept working, apparently finished with his dark story. Or finished sharing it with me, at least. But considering that he'd still enlisted with the Guardians, even after Jassin's little experiment, I could guess how it ended. I studied the faerie's stormy expression and wondered what caused Thuridan Sarwraek more pain—the memory of his father's cruelty, or touching a rope drenched in holy water.

My mind went back to our first meeting. I'd been queen then. In spite of what Jassin had done to him, Thuridan returned to the Unseelie Court to avenge his death. I wanted to ask how he could be loyal to someone so monstrous, but I already knew the answer. It was the same weakness everyone shared, whether you were human, angel, or Fallen.

Thinking of the evil creature that Thuridan had loved made me think of the other people he loved, as well.

"Peeks talked about you," I said, surprising both of us. "I spent some time with him while I was being held at the Seelie Court, and he told me his side of the story. Maybe you should go see him before . . . before Olorel. It might be the last chance you get."

Thuridan finished sawing at the frayed strands, and the

remaining rope fell away. But he was looking at me, a puzzled frown hovering at the corners of his mouth. "You are an odd creature," Thuridan declared.

"You're welcome," I said as he got to his feet. The faerie returned my knife and avoided touching anything else with his useless hands. I tucked it back in my boot, straightened, and said, "Come on, we need to find the others."

"Why are you doing this?" Thuridan asked.

I'd started toward the tent flaps, but the question made me pause. "You know why."

I didn't say her name, but it floated between us. I saw something in Thuridan's eyes soften, and he looked toward the tent flaps. He spoke as I turned again, his voice hesitant. "Is she—"

There was a cracking sound, and I spun around just in time to see Thuridan crumple at Oliver's feet. His neck was bent at an unnatural angle. Just as panic began to blaze through me, I reminded myself that Thuridan was a faerie. He would heal.

A moment later, Oliver lifted his head and saw me. His eyes went wide with horror. "Fortuna? What are you doing here?"

"Stopping Lucifer," I said. Desperation and urgency roared through my veins. "Help me, Ollie. Help us."

He opened his mouth to speak, but nothing came out. I watched Oliver's features twist in agony just before he bent over in a blur of motion. He held his middle and released a sound so guttural, so terrifying, that I knew the monster was overcoming him. He wrenched left and right, crashing to his knees. There were more cracking sounds, as if all of his ribs were breaking one by one.

As I watched Oliver's body tear itself apart, I saw how vulnerable he was. Awareness made my heart quicken. Now was the time to end this, I thought. I should attack Oliver while he couldn't defend himself or heal as quickly. Maybe it would actually take this time, if I truly believed it would. I'd brought Lucifer and Oliver into this world because they'd felt so real to me. Why shouldn't I be able to use my power to undo them, too?

It occurred to me that someone had probably heard Oliver, and any second now, more demons could come streaming into the tent. My brief window of opportunity was closing. I knelt and plucked the pocketknife out of my boot again. Oliver was still on his hands and knees. I closed the space between us and stood over him, clutching it in my sweaty fist. Oliver didn't even notice. He shouted again as black veins began to spread through his entire back like cursed ivy. I imagined bringing the knife down and plunging it into him.

I couldn't do it. I just . . . couldn't.

Feeling exploded my chest, but there was no time to think about it. A furious cry lodged in my throat as I spun away from Oliver and took a step toward Thuridan's prone form, intending to drag him out of the tent while Oliver was still transforming.

But once again, I had waited too long.

Oliver's shadow stood out starkly against the doors of the tent. I watched it stand upright, and this silhouette was bigger than my Ollie. Much bigger. I froze, remembering the horror in Nan's voice after he'd attacked the Order. *I've never seen anything like that creature. The speed of it.*

The dark shape spread its wings wide again. Dark feathers spread like fans on either side of the creature's massive frame. I felt a breath on the back of my neck. A tremor wracked me, and I could barely breathe past the terror. This was Oliver, I told myself. Somewhere inside that hulking thing, there was still the boy I'd built sandcastles with. Slowly, careful not to make any fast or threatening movements, I turned.

And then I was looking into the face of the Beast.

"Ollie," I whispered. "You can—"

A rumbling sound vibrated through him, and his arm flew up. Claws clamped around my throat so tightly that I choked. The Beast turned, and then I was flying backward, my hair flying past my face. My spine slammed into the wooden pole that Thuridan had been tied to, and I hit it so hard the air whooshed from my lungs. A moment later, Oliver loomed over me. There was no recognition in his eyes as he bent and took hold of my throat again.

"Ollie," I rasped, putting my hands over his.

That was all I could get out before his grip on my neck tightened.

Wheezing, I caught sight of a figure standing behind the creature. The one that must've done something to force Oliver's violent shift. My gaze met Lucifer's, and he looked back without any expression. He stood there so casually, with his hands shoved in his pockets. Why wasn't he *saying* anything? Was I really such an insignificant threat to him?

My vision began to darken, and I knew I was moments away from losing consciousness.

Enough, I thought, reaching for my power. It responded instantly, and there was so much magic that my head swam. There was no time to wonder at this—I imbued my veins with it and slammed against Oliver's psyche. It was a weak assault, but he was so startled that he opened his claws and dropped me.

I fell to my knees, coughing, and my power continued to gather around me like a storm. I managed to push myself up, and I was about to release it in a maelstrom of terror and chaos when something came toward me in my peripheral vision. I turned just in time to see a female close in, her hands outstretched. She had black lips and slitted pupils. Her ears were pointed, like a faerie's.

Before I could react, she cupped my face and kissed me. The second her lips made contact, a hot, blinding pain rushed through my entire body. I heard myself gasp. Just as the ground rose up, strong arms caught me. A familiar scent assailed my senses.

I couldn't open my eyes, but moments before oblivion claimed me, I had enough strength left to whisper, "Let me go."

"Never," the devil murmured back.

CHAPTER SIXTEEN

Wind made the walls of the tent flap.

I recognized the sound as soon as I regained consciousness. Despite the pain that made my temples throb, I had enough sense to keep pretending I was still knocked out. It wasn't a total lie—whatever that demon had done to me with her kiss made my thoughts scattered and slow. I struggled to think of a plan beyond playing possum. I reached for my powers, but the place where I usually found my magic was thick and dark, as if it had turned to mud. The only reason I didn't panic was because my reactions were muted. Buried beneath the demon's lingering influence. As soon as I realized what was happening, Dad's lessons kicked in.

Examine your environment, I told myself. That was the first step. I stopped trying to touch my magic and focused on my physical senses instead, keeping my breathing deep and even.

There didn't seem to be anyone else in the tent with me. Beyond the wind, I could hear brief snatches of sound, and they weren't comforting. Something *roared*, and the creature I imagined was much, much bigger than a lion or a bear. I was still in Lucifer's camp, then. I didn't seem to be injured beyond the effects of that demonic magic, but I was so thirsty that my tongue felt like cotton. I tried to swallow, and the action caused another burst of pain down my dry throat. I couldn't hold back a wince. Maybe I'd been passed out longer than I thought.

A moment later, something touched my mouth. I was so startled that I jerked away, my eyes flying open.

"Easy," a familiar voice said.

It took another second or two for my vision to clear, and when it did, I saw that Lucifer knelt in front of me holding the end of a ladle. Water dripped off it. My focus zeroed in on those drops clinging to the curved bottom, then followed them down to the grass. I thought about spitting in the devil's face, but God, I was thirsty. If he was going to bespell or poison me, he would've done it by now.

So when Lucifer brought the ladle back to my lips, I drank.

And as the cool water slid down my parched throat, I heard Laurie's voice in my head, echoing back from that quiet conversation on the night of the fireworks. *The devil made you dependent on him. He made certain that he was the center of your universe. That isn't love, Fortuna.*

"You can have more in a few minutes," Lucifer said once I'd emptied the ladle. "You may be Fallen, but you'll still vomit if you drink too much."

He stood and walked away, presumably to put the ladle back. Now that my eyes were open, I looked around quickly. Everything was hazy, and it felt like I was peering at the world through a dirty microscope.

Lucifer and I were alone, but we were no longer in the tent where I'd found Thuridan. This one was massive, and far more elegant, with three wooden posts throughout that held the ceiling high. The space had the same touches as Lucifer's tower—dark wooden furniture, thick rugs, an enormous bed, and a round table where the devil undoubtedly held his war councils. There was even a sleek bar. It was nighttime outside, and the space was lit with what looked like antique oil lamps, along with a low fire a few yards away. I was handcuffed with my arms behind me, and they were wrapped around one of the wooden beams.

"What . . . what did that bitch do to me?" I mumbled. Forming words was still difficult.

Lucifer stood with his back to me. "That was a galbraith demon. Her kiss takes your power. Or, if you're not Fallen, your life. The violence of it always sends her prey into shock," he added.

"Oh, great," I rasped.

His arm shifted, and I heard the sound of glass clinking. "She really liked you, though. Said you tasted like heaven."

Taking advantage of Lucifer's distraction, I wrenched at the handcuffs to test their strength. The movement was weak; I needed more time. I needed to get Lucifer worked up. He was never sloppy, but he did feel, I knew he did, and emotions made people lose focus. Emotions could lead to mistakes.

I lifted my head to look at Lucifer. I didn't need to think about what to say—there was a lot I wanted to say to him. And there was still too much we didn't know. My voice was hoarse as I said, "So I guess this is the part where you tell me your endgame. What's your big, bad, evil plan, Luci? Are you really such a cliché that your motive behind everything is to rule the universe?"

Lucifer turned around, and this time, he held a drink in his hand. He leaned against the bar, crossing his legs at the ankles, and put the glass to his lips. I watched his throat shift as he swallowed. Then he lowered the drink and said, "I don't intend to rule it, my lady. I intend to end it."

I wasn't surprised by his response, since I'd known the second I'd seen his army. But hearing the truth out loud still made my stomach clench, and it took me an extra moment to speak. "Why?" I asked.

The devil's features hardened. "Because the Maker loves them. His precious humans. And He needs to be punished."

I knew how violent Lucifer's punishments could be. I felt cold, suddenly, but I kept the wariness out of my voice as I said, "Punished for what?"

"For turning us away at the gates. For what He did to her," Lucifer murmured. His eyes shone with hatred.

The way the Dark Prince spoke of his creator was so different from how Michael had. Lucifer's view seemed to be so much more ... personal. As if he really was a son rebelling against his father. Silence fell between us, filling the tent like darkness. At the same time, the wind began to strengthen, and the walls of the tent flapped harder. Something outside began to howl. Goosebumps raced down my arms, making every hair stand on end. I fought to control my heartbeat, and focusing on the flutter in my chest helped me control the urge to yank frantically on the handcuffs.

After a few seconds, Lucifer seemed to return to himself. His gaze cleared and found me again. "Would you like more water?" he asked.

"No. I want you to let me, Oliver, and Thuridan go," I answered curtly. I talked as he came closer. "You made your choices, Lucifer. If you're reckless enough to break the rules, you need to be ready for the consequences."

"Spoken like someone who has broken a rule herself, once or twice." Lucifer knelt, and as the words left him in a low murmur, fondness shining in his eyes, he skimmed his finger down my cheek just like he used to. Something glinted at his throat and caught my eye. At this proximity, I could make out the edge of a shape beneath his collar ... a key?

A moment later, I jerked my head away to get as far from his touch as I could. Lucifer's hand fell, and he got up. His expression was unreadable as he added, "I figured if I couldn't bend Heaven, why not raise a little Hell?"

"How long have you been practicing that cute line?" I mocked. My gaze went to the chain around his neck again. That *had* to be the key to my handcuffs.

Lucifer didn't respond. It felt like the galbraith demon's poison was starting to wear off, but I still needed more time. I had to keep him talking.

"There's one thing I don't get. Well," I amended, "there are a *lot* of things I don't get about you. Why does Hell acknowledge Olorel? I saw Michael's last memory of him. He didn't sacrifice himself to create the Unseelie Court. He did it to—"

"—close the Door that Persephone opened," Lucifer finished, looking unsurprised. "Yes, I am aware. I suppose I might've left some things out when I told you our story."

"You 'left it out' because you didn't want me to know I could close the Gate," I countered, giving him a look of pure loathing. I tugged at the cuffs to test their strength.

A muscle in Lucifer's jaw flexed. "Yes," he said bluntly. "But not for the reason you think. When she created the tear, Persephone didn't know how much energy it would take. The price such powerful magic would extract."

He stopped, and I knew it was because he'd already told me the ending to this story. Those words echoed through my memory.

She survived for three days.

My gaze flicked to the tattoo on Lucifer's wrist, and I knew his grief wasn't feigned. Once, I would've felt pity for him. Seeing the gleam of pain in his eyes would have weakened my defenses. But tonight, I looked at the devil and only felt loathing. "So Olorel drained his entire life force to stop you from coming through," I said flatly.

Lucifer made a low, bitter sound and took another drink. "Even with all that power, Olorel couldn't end someone else's spell or destroy the Door. He could only close it. The Unseelie Court was a cover story, a way to explain his death. It was decided amongst the Order that no one could ever know there was an opening to Hell. They buried the secret so deeply that even I didn't know where to find it. And that, my lady, is why Hell acknowledges him—Olorel is the reason we've been locked out for so long."

He gave me a humorless smile and tossed his drink back, finishing it this time. I fell silent. Once again, I thought back to the other conversation we'd had about Olorel. When I'd discovered that Hell acknowledged the day just as the fae did, I questioned Lucifer about it.

It holds a different meaning for us, but yes, we celebrate it. To an extent, he'd told me then.

What meaning does it hold for you? I asked.

It's a promise.

"A promise," I echoed now, remembering.

Lucifer's expression hardened. "*My* promise. I will kill Olorel's son, and then I'll use the dust from my brother's bones to undo what he sacrificed himself to accomplish."

Lucifer retrieved something on the desk chair. A sword belt, I saw as he secured it around his hips. A ripple of unease went through me. Where was he going? Where were Collith and Laurie? The demon's magic prevented me from using my own to find them, or at least attempt to. I wrenched at my wrists in a burst of frustration, and when the devil turned, I felt my lip curl. "I'm not letting you open that Gate, Lucifer."

"I figured as much. Which is why I wanted to speak with you tonight." He rested his hand on the hilt of the sword and tilted his head as he regarded me. "I have an offer for you, my lady. I will free your friend and let the rest of your loved ones live . . . if you remain in this camp. Lay down your grand plans and your weapons. Do nothing when I go into those hills on Olorel, and I swear that no harm will come to those you hold dear. Including the Beast."

My only response was to spit at his feet. The corner of Lucifer's mouth tilted up in a sad smile.

"You took longer than I thought you would," he said without looking away from me. At first, I frowned in confusion. Then my senses prickled, and my head snapped to the side.

Laurie stood in the middle of the tent.

The sight of him sent a jolt through me. Laurie held a heart in each hand, his skin coated in blood all the way to his wrists. The three of us were completely silent as Laurie opened his fingers and let the hearts fall. They made fleshy, wet sounds as they hit the ground.

"You might want to post an ad on Indeed, because you're short two employees," the Seelie King drawled.

Lucifer didn't react to Laurie's sudden appearance or the hearts that had rolled to a stop near his boots. He glanced down at them, and his tone was polite as he raised his gaze and said, "Laurelis Dondarte. I've wanted to meet you for a long time."

Laurie grinned, and I had never been more terrified for him. "Well, here I am," he replied. "Although I should warn you, there's something the humans say that seems pertinent to this moment."

Lucifer sighed as if we were all boring him, but he'd play along. "And what's that?" he asked.

"Never meet your heroes," Laurie said. Then he unsheathed his sword and launched at the devil.

Just as it had been with the angels, they fought too quickly for my eyes to track. But this battle was considerably shorter than the one I'd witnessed in the desert—despite Laurie's considerable skill, he was no match against a creature who had been alive when this planet was hardly more than a garden. In the space of a blink, Laurie was on his knees, Lucifer standing over him with the tip of his sword pointed to his throat.

When I registered what was happening, I stopped breathing. I reached for my powers instinctively, desperate to intervene, but they were still muffled beneath the galbraith demon's influence. My voice sounded strangled as I said, "Lucifer. Lucifer, please. Let him go. We can talk about a deal, all right?"

"Don't offer him a goddamn thing, Fortuna," Laurie growled, never taking his eyes off the male in front of him.

"I confess to some disappointment," the Dark Prince replied blandly. "I never imagined the infamous Seelie King would be so . . . predictable."

"I doubt you were expecting this," someone else said. It wasn't Laurie.

A sword burst through Lucifer's chest. Shock lurched through me again, but I hardly felt the handcuffs bite into my wrists. I watched with wide eyes as Lucifer dropped his sword, his hand gone limp. The second that lethal blade was no longer pointed at his throat, Laurie sifted out of sight.

"Good to see you again, old friend," the devil rasped, blood spraying from his mouth.

Collith's face appeared over Lucifer's shoulder. His eyes were darker than I'd ever seen them. "Go back to Hell, *old friend*."

He wrenched the sword out of Lucifer's body, and light shone from the wound in a single, ethereal beam. Under any other circumstances, I'd have called it beautiful. In the next breath, I saw Collith's arms rise. Lightning scalded my eyes and the tent caught fire like a tinderbox. I could already feel the heat whispering against my skin. At the same moment my eyes met Lucifer's, Collith turned the heavenly fire on him. Lucifer bellowed in pain as it consumed his entire body.

Realizing this was my chance to finally escape, I steeled myself to wrench at the handcuffs with all my strength. Before I could, I felt someone's fingers brush against my wrists. Then Laurie appeared, filling my vision as the walls around us burned.

"I can't get the cuffs off," he said.

Knowing Lucifer, they were probably fortified with a spell. My eyes flitted to the devil's black, burning body. "There's a key. It's around his neck."

Laurie swore and moved with preternatural speed. In a blink, the Seelie King was standing beside Collith and speaking in his ear. Collith's crackling power relented, and he lowered his arms, his chest heaving. Laurie became a blur again, and I saw the gleam of the chain Lucifer wore as it moved. Then Laurie was back, his hands brushing against my wrists as he put the key in the lock. The handcuffs fell away, landing in the dirt with a hollow sound. I pulled my arms away from the pole and pushed myself up. An instant later, my legs gave out from beneath me. Laurie caught me effortlessly, his springtime scent briefly blocking out the awful stench of burning flesh.

"I don't think I can walk on my own yet," I admitted, my arm wrapped tightly around his neck. I'd have to explain about the galbraith demon later. From the corner of my eye, I saw Laurie's jaw clench.

"Lean on me, Firecracker," was all he said. For once, I didn't argue. I forced my shaky legs to obey me and started walking toward freedom. The smoke was so intense now it stung my throat and my eyes. Collith was right behind us.

"Wait. I'm not leaving without Thuridan," I said as we neared the tent flaps.

Collith pulled one open and stepped aside. "He's outside with Lyari."

Relief bloomed inside my chest. My protests faded and we hurried back into the night, leaving the intense heat and thick smoke behind.

Just as Collith had promised, Thuridan stood there, whole and unharmed. Lyari waited beside him, standing so close that their arms touched. The ground around them was littered with corpses, and Lyari's sword dripped with ichor.

"Did you kill him?" she asked flatly, her eyes on the tent, as if she was considering whether to go in. The frames collapsed a moment later, sending sparks up like a beacon.

"I doubt it," Collith muttered.

The words had barely left his mouth when something flew at us, letting out a noise that sounded halfway between the cry of an eagle and the snarl of a great cat. Lyari's sword flashed, and the winged creature hit the ground in two pieces, its warning call abruptly cut off. But I knew any other demons nearby must've heard it.

"This is the part where we *run*," Laurie hissed.

The five of us launched into motion. We darted between the tents and plunged back into the cover of darkness. Hopefully any demons coming in this direction would be preoccupied with the fire and getting their master out—it was definitely one hell of a diversion. As we fled, I could feel Laurie's power trembling around us, hiding us from sight, but we still encountered creatures that could sense us or see through his illusion. Collith, Lyari, and Thuridan fought them off together, since Laurie couldn't do much with me as a dead weight. Our progress was slow and terrifying. Desperate hope pumped through my veins, but even I could see that we were fucked. We'd made too much of a racket and been spotted too many times. With my powers out of commission, the odds that we'd get out of this camp alive were low. But we kept going, and no one said a word.

Our small band had just gotten past another cluster of guards when something made Collith pause again. I cast a wary glance around us, but there were no demons in sight.

"We don't have time for this," Laurie said tersely. I frowned at Collith in a silent question.

Before he could respond, someone behind us called, "Lady Sworn."

I faltered, startled by the sound of Thuridan's voice. He'd never said my name before. I twisted in Laurie's grasp, and I heard him swear in my ear. Thuridan and Lyari had stopped. My friend wore an expression I'd never seen on her face before. *Devastation,* I thought, my brows drawing together in another surge of confusion. What was going on? Laurie was right, we didn't have time for this.

I was about to urge them onward when Thuridan's eyes met mine. They shone with grim resignation, and the words died in my throat. "He couldn't close it," Thuridan said quietly. "So he put it somewhere useful. My father—"

The ground exploded around Thuridan. I caught a fleeting glimpse of something, a creature with long legs and a dozen beady eyes like a scorpion, before it grabbed the faerie and they both slammed back into the earth, vanishing from sight.

"*Thuridan!*" Lyari screamed. She raised her sword and started to bend down as if she intended to dig, but Collith yanked her back with all his strength.

"Stop!" he snarled, pinning her arms down. "Look!"

I'd just spotted what he and Laurie must've seen, because the Seelie King released me and moved to stand slightly in front of me, his shining blade at the ready. Thankfully, I didn't need his help anymore, since a fresh rush of adrenaline had hit me.

"Oh, fuck," I breathed.

Demons swarmed through the openings between the tents like angry hornets, coming right for us. They'd surrounded us. I caught glimpses of species I'd never seen before, creatures that Lucifer must've been careful to hide from me during my time in Hell. Things with the body of a man and the head of a bull, all of them holding spiked maces aloft in their meaty fists.

Just as Laurie began cutting the first wave of demons down, I jumped in to help Collith. We dragged Lyari away while Laurie slaughtered anything that came near us. Lyari struggled against our hold, fierce as a lion. Bellowing. Roaring Thuridan's name over and over. She knew what it meant, leaving him here.

The snarls, shouts, and roars rose into the night. Even though we were running, we were still moving too slowly. Lyari continued to fight us, yanking and wrenching at our hold on her. Any second now, the demons would overwhelm our small band. Collith and Laurie could sift, but I knew better than to tell them to go on without us. I swore and reached for Lyari's sword, which she was still clutching in her hand—

Just like he'd once done with Finn, Laurie moved in a blur. Lyari's head snapped, and there was a terrible cracking sound. As she sagged, I jerked back around, my jaw so tight that the ache matched the pain in my chest. Rage blazed in my veins as if my blood had turned to fire.

"We can fight about it later," Laurie snapped. "Coll, do you mind?"

He thrust Lyari at Collith like she was a rag doll. Collith took her and ran. I did, too, sprinting as fast as I could now. We reached the edge of camp and didn't hesitate to begin our ascent. The hill was so dark that I prayed I didn't roll my ankle on a rock as I scrambled up, and up, and up. Even with Lyari's weight, I knew Collith was slowing down for me. I didn't let myself look back. I just focused on the top of the hill and pushed through the pain blazing through my sides. All the snarls, growling, and screeches seemed distant now, but that didn't mean we were safe. I arched my head back, peering toward the dark sky in search of any silhouettes, listening for the sound of wingbeats.

Laurie's voice cut through the haze of concentration around me. "Look."

A fresh jolt of adrenaline surged through my veins. I followed his gaze and turned back toward the camp. But there were no more demons chasing us . . . because they'd all stopped.

They stood in a perfectly straight line, as if there was an invisible wall at the base of the hill. There was a flash of gold amongst the demons, and though we were too far away to make out details, I recognized Lucifer. He seemed completely healed. Terror struck my heart like a bullet. Had he just . . . let us go? Was he really so invincible? Or was I just that small of a threat?

Well, if that was what Lucifer thought, he was right. We'd come here for Thuridan, and he was somewhere in the ground now. I searched the crowd of eerie faces for him, just in case, but there was no sign of the faerie that Lyari loved.

As the weight of failure settled on my shoulders, I remembered Thuridan's last words. *He put it somewhere useful.*

What the hell did that mean?

"Let's go," I muttered. I wouldn't be getting any answers tonight, and there was nothing more we could do. Staying here any longer was just tempting fate. I turned and walked away, a lingering sense of unsteadiness whispering through my legs. Collith adjusted his hold on Lyari and followed, along with the rest of our small rescue party.

As we returned to the hills, I heard that small voice again. A cruel taunt at the back of my head, whispering one thing over and over.

Your fault. Your fault. Your fault.

CHAPTER SEVENTEEN

A branch hit the tree beside me with such force that it shattered, splintering in every direction.

Collith shifted, casually blocking most of my body. For once, I let him. I wasn't interested in dying with a stick in my chest, or losing an eye to flying debris.

Moonlight shone down on the clearing where we had finally stopped. My sides still ached from how far we had run, but it didn't feel like far enough. We couldn't have put more than a few miles between us and Lucifer's camp. The car was nearby, and if I'd had any say, we would've been getting in it right now. It hadn't been my choice to stop.

It was Lyari's.

While she continued her rampage, I took stock of the others, making sure they were all right. Laurie stood behind a tree nearby, his lips turned down in a thoughtful frown. Savannah and Seth were also tucked in the shadows, positioned where they could avoid the destruction. Only Gil stood in the open, his back pressed against one of the trees. Despite the danger, his eyes stayed fixed to the ground, a cigarette burning between his fingers.

The road was close, and they'd been in the car, just as we planned. But they'd both come running when Lyari started.

Reassured that no one had gotten hurt, I turned my attention back to the figure in the center of the clearing. *Well, no one is hurt physically, at least,* I thought with a wince.

My friend was almost unrecognizable in her grief.

When she'd begun to regain consciousness, we had paused for a brief rest . . . and to prepare for whatever was coming. It didn't take long. The second Lyari was coherent, she had tried to go back. Collith got in her way and said something I couldn't hear, his voice low and solemn. He'd blocked Lyari from sight so none of us could see her face. Whatever he said had made her go still.

Then, with an enraged cry, she'd bent and grabbed the first thing she could find—a rock the size of a cantaloupe. It had soared through the air and hit the ground so hard that grass and soil sprayed. Lyari bent to find something else, then threw that, too. She'd done it again, and again, and again.

Now the ground was littered with divots and rubble. The trees around us had been torn or broken. Every strike and enraged cry echoed through the night.

"She's going to bring the entire horde down on our heads," Laurie muttered.

I didn't think Lucifer's army would be coming after us, but I also didn't want to take the chance. Laurie was right. So I inhaled through my nose and released the breath slowly, then edged out from behind Collith. A clump of dirt sailed past me, followed by another rock. I flinched but kept going. When I was almost struck by a heavy piece of bark, Laurie cursed and sifted out of sight.

He reappeared beside Lyari and grabbed her wrist in a vise-like grip. Unlike Collith, he didn't speak. But Lyari froze as if he had, and for a long moment, she just looked at him. Laurie looked back at her, and after a few tense seconds, he slowly retreated. Lyari stayed in the center of the clearing, her chest heaving. Tears shone in her yellow eyes, bright as diamonds.

I couldn't bear it. I closed the distance between us and stopped in front of her, hesitantly reaching for Lyari's arm. She jerked away as if my touch had burned her.

"He didn't deserve this," she spat. "He was *good*, he was. You didn't see, you didn't believe, but I knew."

"You need to let me make you part of the Shadow Court," I said quietly. It wasn't normal, this kind of display from Lyari, no matter how brokenhearted she was.

But she acted like I hadn't spoken. She covered her face, and her voice was muffled as she cried, "You said we'd save him!"

"I know I did, and—"

Lyari dropped her hands to glare at me, and I went silent. There were . . . ridges above her eyebrows. No, they were thorns. Small, fleshy thorns sprouting from her forehead. I stared at them, and the truth hit me in the gut like a fist.

Lyari was a goblin. A fully fledged, completely transitioned goblin.

Whatever she saw in my expression made Lyari go cold. She bent to snatch her sword off the ground.

"Lyari—" I started, but she shouldered past me and stormed into the darkness. She must've expended too much energy healing to sift, or maybe she couldn't anymore now that she'd made the transition. I stopped at the edge of the trees, my hands clenching as I considered whether or not to follow. But Lyari wasn't destructive like I was. She didn't succumb to her impulses.

That was before, a small voice reminded me.

"She'll come back when she's ready," Gil said. "She always does, right?"

I swallowed. "This is different. She's not . . ."

"Not what?" Seth asked. His expression was calm, and he looked back at me steadily. But I felt the silent challenge. The dare to finish my sentence.

He was right to challenge me. Whatever I was feeling was just old prejudice. Lyari was a goblin now, but she wasn't gone. She'd just changed, like all of us did. Like we were meant to.

"We should go," I said finally. "It's not safe here."

The others moved in silent agreement. We started walking again, heading in the direction of the car.

An hour later, we emerged from the woods at the edge of the homestead. The barn came into view, bright and welcoming, and the sight of it made something in me loosen. Emma had left the lights on for us. We followed the gentle glow, silent as we climbed the stairs single file.

As soon as I entered the loft, I went over to the refrigerator and took out a pitcher of water. Everyone trickled into the kitchen while I moved to the cupboard where we kept the glasses. I returned to the island and poured from the pitcher, then took a long drink. My swallow was audible in the silent room.

"What happened?" Gil asked finally. He knew we'd failed to rescue Thuridan, of course, but there hadn't been time to tell him and Seth where everything had gone wrong.

Collith's eyes darkened. "He was expecting us."

"Are you going back again?" Seth ventured. "Will you try another way?"

"There's something else," Savannah said. She stood with her arms crossed over her body, and her jaw was clenched with tension. "If we do go back, this will be important information to have."

I sighed. "Do I want to know?"

"It's about the spell I sensed. It took me a while to figure out—I've never encountered anything like it before. The magic was strange, similar to hearing a new language. But on the way home, I noticed this." Savannah pulled a smartwatch out of her pocket and held up the darkened screen. "I know the same thing happened to your phones. The Dark Prince's camp is surrounded by a powerful boundary. I don't know the exact parameters of the spell, since only the witches that cast it can tell you that, but it obviously keeps out anything modern or advanced."

That word triggered a memory. I thought back to my secret meeting with Lucifer outside of Adam's shop. When I'd asked him about the demon on the road, he'd told me, *Their magic is incredibly useful. For the most part, it involves shielding and blocking. Their presence can even affect technology.*

Lucifer must've used the yar demon for his spell. It was probably another reason why he was creating tears like the one in West Bengal. Which meant that even if we did go back with reinforcements, we could only use swords or magic to fight. Guns and bombs would've evened the playing field, but of course Lucifer had thought of everything.

"Is the boundary spell why they stopped like that? All in a straight line?" I asked Savannah.

"The boundary spell probably answers to the Dark Prince's wishes," she said, nodding. "He's keeping the demons contained, and everything else out. But for whatever reason, he allowed us into his camp tonight."

My grip on my water glass tightened. I stared at the counter as I murmured, "I think . . . I think he just wanted to see me. He knew I'd come for Thuridan. He let us waltz inside just so he could offer me a deal."

"What deal?" Laurie asked.

My gaze rose. "He said he'd set Oliver free and let the rest of you live if I stayed with him."

Laurie made a low, humorless sound. "I hope you told him where he could shove that offer."

"Actually, I just spit at him."

At this, Laurie gave me a slow, secret smile that made my stomach flutter. "That's my girl."

"So we can't get back in, and we can't nuke the camp." Gil hesitated. "I guess that means the Gate is opening, then."

The enormity of what I'd done crashed over me. By bringing Lucifer into the world, I had single-handedly brought on the apocalypse. "We failed. It's over," I said.

There was a pause, and then Collith replied, "Not if we're there when he opens the Gate. We'll stop whatever comes out of it."

I made a soft sound of hopelessness and shook my head. My limbs felt heavy with defeat, and I forced myself to move. I didn't want the others to see the depth of my despair or try to comfort me. I found myself at the end of the dining table, staring down at the meaningless shapes and symbols that Michael had left behind in my brain. I'd left the drawing here in hopes that the more I looked at it, the more it would make sense. So far, no such luck.

"You've never seen the seven cities," I said, tracing one of the lines with my fingertip. "You have no idea what we'd be up against. We would need an army. And I don't know about you, but I don't have any of those lying around."

"I can arrange meetings. And I'm sure Laurelis—"

Collith stopped, and my attention shifted, too. We all looked toward the other end of the table. At some point while we'd been talking, Nym must've emerged from his room and started setting pieces of paper down. Slowly. Deliberately. The faerie's gaze was downcast, his expression strangely serene. As if he was fulfilling some purpose, or doing something he'd done a thousand times before. I drew closer to see the pages. They were the sketches he'd had on his walls. Then I looked closer, and I went still with shock.

Each one was a puzzle piece. All of the lines connected, spanning dozens of pages, creating a single, final image. I'd looked at Nym's drawings so many times, but I had never *seen* them. The completed picture was undeniably from the battle we were about to fight. Some of the details we'd seen before in the smaller works, like the armor I wore and the rolling hills behind me.

But some details were new.

Before, I'd been surrounded by vague depictions of Fallen. Werewolves. Dragons. Now the warriors around me were familiar and vivid. Collith. Laurie. Cora. Dracula. The Wild Hunt. Even the Rat King. And at the center of it all, I sat atop a horse.

No, I thought, staring at the thin, harsh lines of the creature's body. *A kelpie.*

My focus shifted back to the other figures in the image. Judging from this, there were at least four armies. We'd attack Lucifer from every direction, surrounding him and the demon horde like the eye of a storm. As I touched one of the drawings, marveling at how it had all come together so perfectly, Gil's comment drifted back to me.

It makes me wonder if I was wrong about Him, after all, and maybe He does take an interest in us. Manipulate us. Because I refuse to believe my luck is this shitty.

I remembered my amusement. *You really think God instrumented it so we'd meet the Rat King?*

Now the idea didn't seem so ludicrous.

Maybe the Maker had seen the threat Their angel posed to humankind. Maybe Michael hadn't been completely full of shit, and even his master couldn't break the rules that created balance. Maybe this was the only way They could offer help. How had Michael put it? Nudges. Gentle nudges. Subtle opportunities. Small moments. Every step had led me down this path, to this night, when humans needed saving the most.

Stranger things have happened, I thought, tapping my finger against the image of my face. My mind worked quickly.

"Olorel is just over a month away," I said. "Which means we have that long to convince these people to not only form an alliance, but fight side-by-side on a battlefield where they may very well die. Nym, are these drawings a certainty? Or are they just possible outcomes?"

"Tick tock," he said, his eyes troubled. "Tick tock."

Guess we weren't getting any more help from Nym, then. I continued to stare down at his drawings, my chest filling with hope. Hope was dangerous, I knew that. Hope got you hurt.

'But sometimes . . . sometimes it was exactly what you needed.

In a burst of resolve, I got up from the table and went back into the kitchen. "What are you doing?" Collith asked.

"I'm making a fresh pot of coffee."

"Why?" Gil sounded wary.

I opened the cupboard where we kept the grounds and smiled over my shoulder. They were all watching me with concern in their eyes. "Because we're going to make a plan. Lucifer may think he has this in the bag, but he doesn't get to win. Not this time."

"She's got that look in her eye," Laurie said to Collith in a conspiratorial tone. But he was smiling, too.

As the coffee brewed, I watched my small family begin to form a strategy. My gaze went back to Nym's drawings. There weren't many of us now, but more would come. And like Collith had said, when that Gate opened, we would be there. While the others held back the tide, I'd use my power to close it.

Even if it was the last thing I ever did.

The countdown began.

During the day, my life bore some semblance of normalcy. Well, as normal as a Nightmare's life could be when she lived in a loft full of other supernatural creatures, and she was literally trying to stop the devil from unleashing Hell on Earth. I worked my shifts at the bar, because Gate or no Gate, there were still bills to pay. I spent time with my family. I trained at Adam's shop. Now more than ever, my skill with the sword was vital.

It was during one of those training sessions that I discovered something—Michael had given me something else when he'd died. Thanks to his blast of power, I was faster. Stronger. The changes were subtle until I started fighting, and then it was unmistakable. I would've realized it sooner, but the galbraith demon's poisonous kiss had muffled everything.

We all discovered it at the exact same moment. Adam had just brought up his arm in what should've been a killing blow—during a training session, at least. I'd left myself vulnerable for a split second, and for a vampire, a second was all they needed. I should've been a goner.

But I moved instinctively. Before I could even blink, I had moved. Adam's practice sword struck mine and I felt the vibration through my entire body. Adam and I stared at each other through our crossed weapons. I couldn't decide who was more shocked.

"Holy shit," I heard one of the guys say. I could barely hear it over the thrum of magic in my veins.

Then I felt my lips curve into a slow, wondering smile.

Within a matter of days, I got so good that I even started beating Adam.

If the boys weren't around, I trained at home with the new equipment Collith had bought. Until now, we'd been using the first floor of the barn mostly for storage, but with Narfu living there and our ever-expanding household—not to mention Collith's need for a project—it was transformed. Now the space was brighter with newly installed lights, the floor was sealed concrete, and Collith had added several walls. Every time I opened the barn, that new-house smell whooshed in to greet me.

In the moments I wasn't working or training, I was reading.

I had no shortage of material to get through since Viessa had started sending over everything she could find amongst the fae. I'd kept her up to date on everything that was happening, especially after we'd failed to save Thuridan, and her response had been the shipments. They arrived every few days in old, heavy trunks, carried by stoic-faced Guardians who silently took the trunks of everything I had finished and left as silently as they'd come.

Despite the amount of research I'd already done over the past year, I hadn't seen any of these new books or papers before—all of it was from bloodlines we'd never had access to, back when Lyari and Collith had been trying to help with my search. The Unseelie Queen knew how much was riding on getting that Gate shut, too, and she had commanded her entire Court to cooperate with me. The result was overwhelming, to say the least. Sometimes my family tried to help, but more often than not, it was me at that dining room table. I stooped over the books for such long stretches of time that my neck began to hurt.

Those were the daylight hours ... but night was a different story.

Night was when the Fallen emerged.

Once again, Collith and I used the Door to journey to other places in the world. Once again, Sorcha and Laurie provided us with leads or locations. But now, instead of looking for Oliver, we were looking for allies.

Looking ... and failing.

The morning after I was denied an audience with the Rat King, I drove to Adam's shop in a foul mood. My mood worsened when I discovered the door was locked. They were probably just at Bea's. I went back to the car, glancing across the street as I considered whether or not to stop by. But I needed to hit something, or run so hard that I couldn't think. So I drove back home and blasted music the entire way. By the time I walked back into the barn, I was practically vibrating with pent-up energy.

For once, the new-house smell did nothing to lighten my mood. I closed the door harder than necessary and took off my jacket, immediately starting toward the training room. I'd only gone a few steps when Collith appeared in one of the doorways, holding a screwdriver. There was sawdust on his button-up shirt and his hair was wilder than usual.

"Back so soon?" he said.

"Shop was closed," I muttered, reaching down to take off my shirt. I wore a sports bra underneath, and the air conditioning whispered over my skin as I tossed my shirt and bag onto the new couch near the mats. I glanced at the enormous reptilian creature across the room. He was tucked in the shadows, nestled in blankets I'd brought down for him since he seemed to prefer the floor. "Hey, Narfu."

The demon chirped. I began stretching, thinking I'd just take my frustration out on the punching bag. But when I turned, Collith had put his screwdriver down and also removed his shirt. Now he only wore the dark jeans he'd been working in, and his naked torso gleamed in the light. He still had a tan from the summer sun, and the lines of his abdomen flexed when he tossed his shirt next to mine.

"You've been so focused on the sword lately, why don't we brush up on your hand-to-hand?" Collith suggested, raising his eyebrows at me.

"Sounds good." I swallowed and turned away quickly, knowing he'd sense any arousal. I bent to take off my shoes and socks, and Collith did the same.

A moment later, we stepped onto the mat together. I positioned myself into a ready stance. Left foot forward, feet shoulder-width apart, fists at my waist. Collith mirrored me, the lights shining down on his perfect fae features. Narfu watched us from his corner, sitting so still that he looked like a statue. His strange black eyes were bright, but I couldn't tell if it was concern or excitement.

It was a reminder that I needed to get a grip on my own feelings. In the past, my bursts of power—and most of the mistakes I'd made—were because of those unchecked emotions. Anger, fear, pain. Now, as I faced Collith, my entire body tensing in readiness, I imagined Finn's lake again. I waited for the lapping water and creaking boat sounds to lull me into calm.

But tonight, it didn't work. Collith waited patiently while I stood there, breathing deeply and trying to find another place, another grounding method.

Then the dreamscape popped into my head.

Since the night I'd freed Oliver, I had stopped using our place as an anchor. What had once been happy memories had turned to pain and dust the second I'd found out what Oliver was. What he'd done. But now I thought about the hills of golden grass and that big, rustling tree. I heard the distant roar of the sea. The roiling anxiety within me slowly quieted, until my mind contained only blue skies and the cry of a seagull.

A moment later, I opened my eyes and launched at Collith.

He slipped and parried my first strike instantly, then went on the offense, forcing me to back away. A stationary target was easy to hit, so I kept moving, trying to stay off his line of attack. But Collith came at me like a hammer, giving me no chance to think, only react. I used my elbows against his strikes and ducked beneath his arms. Even with Michael's power, sweat was already dripping down the small of my back. Adam was fast, but Collith was faster. I remembered that he'd trained with an original angel, and Sylvyre had not been gentle or patient.

"What are you feeling right now?" Collith asked as we circled each other. His expression was as calm as ever, and something about his composure got under my skin. Guess I hadn't anchored myself as well as I'd thought.

"Pissed," I snapped. I attempted a spinning kick to his torso, which Collith artfully dodged. Narfu chirped from his corner, and there was definitely tension in the sound. But I couldn't spare him a glance or a soothing word. Collith and I went back to circling, and I watched his every movement sharply, trying to anticipate him.

"Okay. What else?" Collith countered, that stubborn lock of hair hanging over his eye.

"Pretty sure I'm just pissed." Hoping to catch him off guard, I lunged forward, going for a palm-heel strike. But Collith took advantage of the vulnerable position I'd put myself in—before I could check myself, he spun as if we were dancing and bear hugged me from behind, using his preternatural strength to keep me from breaking free. His smell assailed my senses, dark and earthy and alluring.

"Anger? Pretty sure that's fear I'm tasting," Collith murmured. His lips brushed against the tender shell of my ear as he leaned even closer and asked, "What are you afraid of, Fortuna?"

I gritted my teeth and dropped into a crouch. In the same breath, I shifted my hip and wrenched one of my arms back to elbow Collith in the testicles. He saw it coming and was forced to release his hold—human or faerie, no male liked getting hit in the balls. I swung around so quickly that, for an instant, it almost felt as though I'd sifted. Collith recovered in time to block me, and we went at each other so fast, so hard that I barely felt the jarring pain that shuddered through my bones with every strike.

Neither of us was able to flatten the other, and I was tiring. Collith must've been struggling, as well, because he eventually relented, backing away from me until he reached the edge of the mat. I leaned over and braced my hands on my knees, breathing hard. A drop of sweat slid down my temple. I watched it fall and splatter on the plastic, but my thoughts had returned to the war. Collith's question echoed through me.

What are you afraid of, Fortuna?

I stared at that round, dark spot as I said, "No one is coming, Collith, and we both know it. I can't convince any of them. I failed."

Even Cora had denied me. The memory burned through my mind for the hundredth time since that night, and I gritted my teeth again, wondering yet again if there was anything I could've done differently.

Moonlight shone down on the clearing. The young werewolf alpha stood in front of me, her chin held high. Her fear tasted like apples, but none of it showed in her expression or the way she stood. If I hadn't been so desperate, I would've been proud. Cora had come a long way from the timid female I'd met last year.

"Since when does a wolf back down from a fight?" I demanded, ignoring Collith's gentle touch on my arm. For all of these meetings, he'd been the diplomat, the good cop. Usually his cool presence could temper my flares of frustration, but not tonight. Maybe it was being back in these woods, where we'd faced Astrid, the old werewolf alpha. Being here made me think of Finn.

And I knew that if we couldn't convince Cora to help us, or any of the others, I would lose more people I loved.

"If what you're saying is true and the world is about to be overtaken by demons, what good would it do to fight them? My pack would only get torn apart," Cora told me. Behind us, her people made sounds of agreement. The sounds rose into the night and were swallowed by distant, aloof stars.

Silence fell as they all waited for my response. For a moment, I just stood there, wishing I was the kind of person who could make eloquent speeches. I wished I could pawn this conversation, this task, onto Collith or Laurie. But they weren't the ones who had caused all this; they weren't the reason we were in danger. I'd brought Lucifer into our world, and according to Nym, it would be me who kicked him out of it.

But I couldn't do it by myself. We needed everyone—the faeries, the wolves, the rats. To defeat the Dark Prince, Fallenkind would have to unite for the first time since we'd tumbled from the skies. We had to put aside old prejudices and ancient grudges, and we couldn't let fear send us running into the dark, as we'd been doing for centuries. It was time for change.

The taste of apples was still in my mouth. I knew that if I exposed it, Cora would look weak in front of the pack. So I stepped closer to her, ignoring her beta's warning growl, and my voice was low as I said, "What good would it do surviving if you hate yourself afterward, Cora?"

There was another beat of silence as she looked back at me, her eyebrows knitted together, as if she was reconsidering. The trees rustled in a brief gust of wind, and my ponytail tugged to the side. I kept my eyes on her. Waiting. Hoping. Praying.

My heart had just started to lift when the alpha shook her head again. "I'm sorry, Fortuna," she said.

My heart sank right back down, and then it kept going. It felt like there was a heavy stone in my chest and a dozen knots in my stomach. Once again, the pack waited for me to answer. My reputation must've proceeded me, because there were more flavors on my tongue now. Apparently even the werewolves were afraid of my famous temper. The truth was, I probably could've forced them to do what I wanted.

But that would make me no better than Lucifer.

In the end, all I said was, "I'm sorry, too."

I nodded at Cora and the werewolf standing next to her, and Collith murmured a polite farewell. Together, we went back the way we'd come and walked through the crowd, who parted to form a path. But then I stopped at the edge of the trees. Knowing that every werewolf in the clearing could hear me, I looked at Cora and called, "If you change your mind, the Dark Prince plans to open the Gate on Olorel. We'll be gathered in the Flint Hills at dusk."

This time, the alpha said nothing. She stood there, exactly where Astrid had once stood, her eyes dark with regret. Regret, but not uncertainty. When I saw that, I knew there was nothing I could say to change her mind.

With Collith at my side, I turned and walked into the dark forest.

The memory had just begun to fade when Collith sifted and reappeared in front of me. I reacted immediately, backing away to defend myself against his fists, but this time, my heart wasn't in it. My mind went back further, thinking of the other meetings we'd had.

First, we'd visited the kitsunes. They didn't trust me, not just because of who I was but because of what had happened to Katashi and Yaeko. After that, we went to the witches. While Wichonne Babdock had received me warmly, and she'd agreed to send word out to her people, the Mother of Witches hadn't made any promises.

I'd tried to find the Queen of the Shapeshifters next. But Nan, of course, was nowhere to be found.

The only one who had actually committed to fighting was Dracula. He'd also volunteered the use of some C-4 he could get his hands on, which I accepted. It wouldn't do much against the armies of Hell, especially with the spell barrier, but it was something.

I was so distracted that I wasn't ready when Collith moved in a blur, landing a front kick that knocked me entirely off my feet. I hit the mat hard enough to make the air leave my lungs. I wheezed, my vision blurring. Distantly, I heard Narfu make a sound that normally would've sent a quake of fear through me, but I was having a little trouble breathing at the moment.

"Easy, boy," Collith said.

When I could drag in a breath again, I lifted my head to make sure the demon wasn't ripping him to shreds. Narfu was still on his nest of blankets, but he peered at Collith with an intentness that made me remember something Lucifer had said when I'd tried to get him to remove the collar around my friend's neck. *Narfu comes from a violent species, and the collar keeps his impulses in check.*

It was a good thing Narfu was on our side . . . but there were probably hundreds of his kind about to come through that Gate, and they wouldn't be fighting those "impulses."

"Again," I rasped at Collith.

I was still lying on my back, and he held his hand out to me. The corners of his mouth had deepened and there was a telltale line between his eyebrows. "Fortuna, you need to rest."

I shoved his hand aside and got to my feet, breathing raggedly. "Again," I repeated.

Collith didn't look happy about it, but he nodded. I returned to the starting stance, my body already aching, and I pushed through the twinges of pain as we continued.

During our next round, other members of my Court began to trickle in. Gil and Seth, holding coffee cups that said *Bea's* on the side. Cyrus and Stanley, who must've heard us when they'd got back from their morning walk. They all settled on the couches to observe me and Collith, and part of me was aware of their conversations, bits and pieces floating over like small feathers.

But I was entirely focused on Collith. As our sparring went on, and on, and on, I began to see a faint light of surprise in his eyes. Before I'd gotten some of Michael's abilities, I never would've been able to fight this long or hold my own against a faerie. And Collith knew it—his blows began to land harder and faster.

"You've been holding out on me," I panted as I stopped another strike with an outer forearm block.

His eyes gleamed. "Not anymore."

In the next breath, Collith tried to position himself behind me, probably going for a chokehold. I grabbed his forearm and pushed his elbow upward, rotating my body away. Gil made a low comment that I couldn't hear.

Unlike my other training sessions at Adam's shop, there was nothing light in the air today. No one made any bets, there was no trash talk or shouts. They could probably sense the tension radiating from me, or feel it in the bond between us. I knew my control was slipping. The image of the dreamscape was far away, along with all the strength it had brought me. I began to get sloppy and slow.

The next time Collith knocked me on my ass, I didn't get back up.

I stared up at the ceiling, thinking about the sheer magnitude of what we were about to face. A hundred Narfus, maybe even thousands, and a thousand more deadly species that we knew nothing about. And who knew what other spells and dark magic Lucifer was conjuring behind the safety of his invisible wall? Despair caught hold of me and burrowed its claws deep beneath my skin.

"It's going to be a slaughter," I said quietly, knowing everyone in the room was listening. We were so still that I could hear air coming out of the vents. I swallowed and continued, "The fae will follow me into those hills, and none of them will come out. An entire species wiped out because of my mistakes, and probably far, far more."

For a few seconds, no one said anything. Then Cyrus's quiet voice penetrated the stillness. "The fae won't be your only ally on that battlefield."

I sat up instantly, already shaking my head. "No, Cy. That's not happening."

His expression didn't change, but there was something in his voice as he replied, "Are you saying I'm not capable of making my own decisions?"

"No, that's not at all—" I stopped. Because it had been exactly what I was saying. Cyrus knew the risks, and he deserved to make his own choices, as everyone else did.

The thought of him being on that battlefield, even as a huge fire-breathing dragon, sent a burst of fear to my heart. I knew Cyrus was in the drawing, but I didn't want my family anywhere near that Gate. It would be a liability, a distraction, because I'd be focused on protecting them instead of the fight.

Just as I opened my mouth to reason with Cyrus again, Emma's gentle voice drifted through me. *Being surrounded by people you love isn't a weakness, Fortuna—it's a strength.*

I finally stood up and got off the mat. I should've been sore, every part of me aching from the bout with Collith. All I felt was a twinge or two as I went to the couch and flopped down beside Gil.

"Chin up, love," he said, bumping his shoulder against mine. "The world has to end sometime. At least this way we can die together."

"You always know just what to say," I responded wryly. I slumped against the back cushion and let out a long sigh. "I don't *get* it. I expected it to be easy, persuading them to fight with us. Nym drew all those pictures because he saw it happening with his own eyes . . . right?"

Collith hesitated. He squatted in front of us, his elbows propped on his knees. "Nym had already sustained damage from his travels when I met him, Fortuna. He is loyal to those he considers a friend, but I'm not sure how much we can trust his word," he admitted.

The doubt that had taken root inside me only grew bigger, twining through my chest like a vine. Nym's mind was broken. Maybe he'd only been drawing his dreams, instead of what he had actually seen during his time traveling.

And if that picture was just from a dream, what else could Nym have gotten wrong?

Once again, Cyrus's quiet voice floated through the bleak stillness. "I could go with you next time. In my other form," he added.

I looked over at him again. I had to admit, for a moment, I was tempted. I imagined it, showing up with a huge fucking dragon behind me. The fear would be so heady . . . another small, resigned sigh slipped between my lips.

"Thanks, Cy, but for once in my life, I don't want to use fear. Joining this fight needs to be of their free will, just like it's yours. Has anyone seen him, by the way?" I added. Everyone looked at me and I clarified, "Nym, I mean. Every time I look in his room, he isn't there."

Before anyone could answer, Cyrus lifted his head sharply. I glanced at the others, noting that they wore similar expressions of alertness.

"What is it?" I asked, following everyone's gazes, which seemed to be laser-focused on the door. I strained to hear something. I could only detect the soft sound of the air conditioning and Narfu's claws scraping against the hard floor when he shifted. There must've been something outside, though, because no one moved.

I stood from the couch and crossed the room to retrieve my socks and shoes. I pulled them both on, then put my shirt on, too. As I left the room, I felt a whisper of air, and suddenly Collith was beside me. He didn't say a word, but his arm brushed mine, the backs of our hands skimming. His silent support quieted my unease. In the next moment, I opened the door ... but no one stood on the other side. I frowned and glanced at Collith.

"They're in the yard," he murmured. "Do you feel it?"

The second he said it, I felt a familiar tingle—magic. I stepped outside and immediately spotted a figure standing on the grass. She was bent over a wooden bowl, a bag on the ground next to her feet. Surprise made me falter.

It was Mercy Wardwell.

"Glad to see you're alive. What are you doing?" I called over to her, unable to hide a hint of wariness in my voice.

"Protecting myself," the witch called back. She finished whatever she was doing and straightened. Her gray eyes looked like steel. "Death clings to you, Fortuna. It gets bigger every time we meet, and it affects the ones around you, too."

A rush of irritation pushed out my exhaustion. I was *really* getting tired of Mercy Wardwell and her thinly veiled judgment. As I walked toward the witch, my shoes crunching over gravel, I tried to remember what Gil had taught me. I reminded myself that I didn't kill people anymore ... especially ones that were related to my nephew.

"Why does Savannah get the benefit of the doubt and I don't?" I demanded. "I may struggle with the dark, but at least I'm fucking struggling. I still try to do good and learn from my mistakes."

Mercy closed the rest of the distance between us. I expected her to stop and say something, so I wasn't prepared when she reached for me and, without warning, plucked a hair right out of my scalp.

"Ouch!" My hand flew to my head and I glared at her. "What the *fuck*, Mercy?"

Without a word, the witch returned to her spot. There was

a line in the grass I hadn't noticed before—her protection spell, no doubt. I wondered what would happen if I tried to cross it. Best not to risk it, I decided quickly, imagining myself getting an electric shock or growing a donkey tail. I'd never been able to get a full read on Mercy Wardwell, but I had always been a little scared of her. So I just stood there and watched as she put my hair in the wooden bowl that reminded me of the Tongue's, back at the Unseelie Court. Mercy produced a lighter and tipped her wrist, setting the small flame against a candlewick peeking over the edge of the bowl. The moment I saw that, I finally realized what was happening.

She was about to do another Telling.

She'd done one for me before, but in the world of magic, that didn't mean much. Mercy had only caught a brief glimpse of one possible future. Would she be able to find a future at all now? My heart quickened at the thought.

Mercy sat on the grass and crossed her legs, then adjusted her long skirt and rested her hands on her knees. The lines of her body were loose and relaxed. However annoyed I was, I knew better than to interrupt a witch in the middle of a spell. Collith and I observed silently as Mercy inhaled the smoke coiling up from the bowl. A full minute passed.

When the witch spoke again, her voice was softer. Distant. "Four times, there will be a knock at the door. Four times, you must be here to open it."

"Pretty sure you have your wires crossed," I muttered. "These sorts of things come in threes, didn't you know?"

Mercy just opened her eyes and gave me a calm, enigmatic smile. "I wish you luck, Fortuna."

I swallowed my instinctive sharp retort and watched her regather the supplies and ingredients. "That's it? You're not going to help us?" I asked.

"What do you think this is?" the witch countered, quirking

a brow at me. She straightened again, holding the handle of her bag in both hands.

Fine, I thought, biting back another sharp response. "Okay, well, do you have any idea when I can expect those knocks?"

Mercy cast a glance toward the sky. "On the full moon. That's always when these things tend to happen," she said.

"And where will you be on the full moon?" I couldn't stop myself from asking.

The witch's eyes flashed. "I'm not the only one who casts judgment, you know. I cannot always be at your beck and call, Fortuna Sworn. We all have a role to play, and mine is not at your side. Clean up your own mess. And don't get my niece killed while you do it."

Mercy left it there. She began walking toward the trees and I watched her go, fighting the urge to sling a final insult at her departing back. However much it stung, I knew she was right. Her voice echoed through my head. *Four knocks.*

As far as Tellings went, that was pretty damn vague. I'd like to think it meant four potential allies were coming, the four armies Nym had drawn, but what if the meaning was more sinister? Should I send my family away again?

"You've changed," Collith said.

I turned to him. The morning light tinted his skin gold and brightened his eyes, making the irises look green. As I studied them, I could've sworn the look in those eyes was pride. "What do you mean?" I said.

Collith inclined his head toward the barn. "What you said to Cyrus earlier, and the control you've been showing every day—not just when we're meeting with the monarchs."

I gave him a weak smile and turned from the yard. "Well, let's hope I've changed enough to get us through this."

We were both quiet as we went back inside. Collith must've been more tired than he let on, because he drifted back into the room where he'd been working earlier. As for me, I walked over to the wall in the training room where Collith had mounted all of our weapons. My sword hung in a place of honor, right at the center. I wrapped my fingers around the hilt and took it down, reveling in how weightless it felt now. Then I went to the mat and turned, my gaze meeting Gil's.

He sighed. "Don't say it."

I raised the sword and said, "Again."

CHAPTER EIGHTEEN

Rain pattered against the roof as I stared down at Michael's message for the thousandth time.

I'd been looking at it so long that the lines had started to blur, the shapes becoming even more meaningless, if that was possible. The sounds of the storm didn't help. Every time the thunder rumbled, it felt like a giant voice trying to warn me, to rush me. *He's coming. Hurry.* Hurry.

I was about to start a fresh pot of coffee when the door to the loft opened, and Emma came inside. She was wearing a pink raincoat, and she'd recently permed her hair and dyed it yellow. As Emma hung her glistening umbrella on the hook, the image she made felt like a page from a children's book. Despite my exhaustion, I felt a smile tug at the corners of my mouth.

My amusement faded when Emma turned and I saw the expression on her face. "What's wrong?" I asked instantly.

"You better get down there." Emma gestured to the stairwell, her eyebrows furrowed with worry. I nodded and rose from my chair, hurrying to the hook where my coat hung.

Less than ten seconds later, I shoved the downstairs door open and walked outside. Laurie and Damon were in the yard, both of them holding swords. A small, strange crowd had gathered around them, watching whatever was happening between the Seelie King and my brother.

I did a swift assessment of who was here. Seth sat on the porch steps, and Gil stood slightly above him, resting his weight on the railing. They must've just driven over, since Seth's car was now parked behind mine. Cyrus rested against the side of his truck, his hands shoved in his pockets. The tense line to his shoulders belied the casual stance, and told me that Emma hadn't been exaggerating—something was wrong. Ariel stood beside Cyrus, her arms crossed. She was frowning, too. I went over to them, darting glances at what appeared to be a training session.

"What's going on?" I asked Ariel, assessing the situation. At least Laurie and Damon were using practice swords. The blades were metal, but the edges were dull.

"Your brother asked for some pointers," Ariel said, but I barely heard her. All I could focus on was my brother now. A cut bled on his shoulder, and one of his eyes was swollen. Without another word to Ariel, I rushed toward the fighters.

I was still several yards away when Laurie knocked my brother down.

The sound of Damon's body hitting the hard ground made me see red. I got to them just in time to hear Laurie say, "You aren't fit for the battlefield, Nightmare."

Damon glared up at him. "I didn't ask for your opinion. I asked you—"

"You asked me to prepare you," Laurie countered. "Part of that is evaluating your skill. And my conclusion is that no amount of training will prepare you for what we'll face on Olorel."

My brother's cheeks were red with humiliation. I stood beside Laurie now, but the Seelie King didn't acknowledge my presence. I was about to reach for Damon when Laurie spoke again, and his tone made me pause.

"You are not weak, Damon Sworn. I met Jassin Sarwraek. For you to have survived him for so long, and create a new life after him, must take a very impressive individual." Laurie stepped closer, and he offered his hand. "So don't be weak now."

After a brief hesitation, Damon took it and allowed Laurie to help him up. As he rose from the ground, Laurie pulled Damon close and murmured something. They parted and turned to me at the same time. I glared at Laurie, my nostrils flaring. "I'll deal with you later," I muttered.

Laurie quirked a brow. "Promise?"

A blaze of temper went through me. I disregarded the Seelie King and examined my brother, holding his face toward the weak daylight. He'd definitely have a black eye, but the damage didn't look too extensive. Laurie must've pulled his punches. Damon was still breathing hard, and there was a gleam of perspiration near his temple. Even that slow scrimmage had tired him.

However much I didn't want to admit it, Laurie was right—if Damon stepped onto that battlefield, he would die. Or get the rest of us killed by taking our focus off the fight while we were trying to protect him.

But that didn't mean Laurie was off the hook, I thought, looking hard at the cut on Damon's shoulder. Something inside me turned to stone.

No one embarrassed my little brother but me.

I grasped the hilt of the practice sword Damon still held, my fingers lacing between his. He gave me a questioning look as he released it. I responded with a quick, reassuring smile before I turned again. My smile faded when I fixed my attention on Laurie, and I pictured him delivering the blow that had left Damon bleeding.

"Since you have so generously taken it upon yourself to teach my brother a lesson, I'd like to do the same for you," I told him.

The Seelie King had been examining his nails. He looked up when I started speaking, and his eyebrows rose at my words.

"Darling, I know you've been training with your vampires, but I'm in a different league than a couple of corpses," he warned.

"Oi!" Gil called indignantly. "I think I'm offended!"

"Get in line," Laurie called back, never taking his eyes off me.

I shrugged. "Prove it. Let's see."

Laurie's lips curved. "Very well. Shall we make this more—"

"No bargains, Laurie," I cut in flatly. "Just you and me. Right here, right now."

"I live to serve, my lady," the Seelie King said with an elegant bow. That little smile hovered around his mouth as he backed away, swinging his sword upright. I felt a prickle of anticipation, knowing I was about to make it vanish. I got into position, and by now I'd done it so many times that my sword felt like an extension of myself, just as Adam had promised.

Laurie hadn't been here for any of our training. He hadn't seen what I was capable of . . . and that was exactly what I was counting on. If I'd learned anything during my time amongst the Fallen, there were two things that could take down a power player—stupidity or arrogance. Laurie was no idiot, but he had the latter in spades.

To his credit, Laurie figured out pretty quickly that he'd made a mistake. I moved faster than he anticipated, spinning past his defenses to cut his shoulder in the same place he'd cut Damon. By the time Laurie tried to swipe at me, I had already danced out of his reach. He blinked, and his gaze met mine. Just as I'd predicted, Laurie wasn't smiling anymore.

The clash of our swords echoed through the yard. Our bodies were blurs of motion as Laurie tested me again and again, trying to find weaknesses in my defense. There were none. I allowed myself to be guided by my instincts, and the remnants of the ancient angel that still lived in my veins. My movements were swift and precise. When Laurie showed his first sign of tiring, I switched my sword to my left hand and gave his weapon a hard shove that forced him to take a step. At the same moment he sank his weight into it, I lifted my leg to meet his momentum.

And then I knocked Laurelis Dondarte, King of the Seelie Court, right on his ass.

The sound his body made as it hit the ground sent a surge of satisfaction through me. Gil whistled, and I heard someone else mutter, "Holy shit."

"Were you planning to tell me that Fortuna has Michael's power?" Laurie muttered as Collith hauled him upright. I hadn't even noticed his arrival.

"It's my power now," I put in, giving Laurie a hard look. "I appreciate what you were trying to show my brother, but if you *ever* hurt him again, I won't come at you with a training sword."

Laurie gave me an inscrutable look. "Noted."

Everyone else had already started to disperse, probably to give us space. The tension wasn't exactly subtle. It had eased now, since I'd said what I needed to say to Laurie. But even though our fight was over, I was glad the others had made themselves scarce—there was someone else I needed to talk to.

"Come on, little brother," I said, wrapping my arm around Damon's shoulder. I was careful not to touch his cut. "Let's get out of this rain."

Damon's mouth was tight, as if he knew what was coming, but he nodded. I steered us toward Cyrus's porch, which was always dry. I ascended the short flight of stairs and sat on the top step. Damon settled next to me, leaning his elbows on his knees. He didn't give me a chance to start the speech I'd been practicing in my head.

"I'm not staying behind, Fortuna," he said firmly. "Not this time."

The careful speech dissipated, and all the reasonable words on my tongue faded. For a moment, I considered it again. I wanted to give my brother the choice as I had with Cyrus, and Gil, and all the others I loved who were coming with me to face Lucifer. But then I pictured it—Damon trying to fight not only one demon, but thousands of them, swinging his sword just as clumsily as he had a few minutes ago—and the image almost made me shudder.

When I refocused on him, I didn't try to hide how scared I was. My voice was harsh as I said, "You'll be a target on that field, Damon. You're my weakness, and everyone knows it."

After I'd spoken, he was silent for a moment. I could tell from the shadow in his eyes that he wanted to argue, because recognizing the truth didn't make it easier to bear. My brother's jaw clenched so hard it looked painful, and he turned his head away, probably to hide the pain in his expression. His voice floated to me through the soft, pattering rain and the cool damp. "I can't stand by and let my family fight while I'm safe at home."

Now it was my turn to go quiet. I would have felt the same way if our roles had been reversed, and I wasn't sure there was anything Damon could've said to convince me to stay behind. But he *had* to stay behind. I wouldn't survive losing my brother. If I didn't find a way to persuade him, I'd have to handcuff him to the porch.

While the words formed in my head, Gil and Seth came into view. Both of them waved, and Damon and I waved back. Gil was holding the keys this time, but as far as I knew, he hadn't gotten a driver's license in the U.S. yet. The headlights flashed as he unlocked the vehicle, and they got in quickly to escape the rain. Gil reversed down the driveway while Seth looked nervous in the passenger seat. When they reached the road, the vampire peeled away with an obnoxious squeal of his tires, and I rolled my eyes as the sound echoed.

Damon was still waiting for me to say something. I kept staring out at the yard, wondering what our parents would have done if they'd been there. Mom always had some ancient legend or story to tell, and Dad was so eloquent. For the millionth time, I wished we'd gotten more time with them. There had still been so much to learn. All I could rely on now were my memories.

"Do you remember when we were kids, and we used to catch raindrops with our tongues?" I asked suddenly, turning to look at Damon.

He smiled. "My favorite was the time Dad started to tell us how rainwater can carry parasites and viruses, and Mom got so annoyed that she brought us all outside and we danced in the yard. The neighbors probably thought we were nuts."

Something in my chest tightened, as if pain and love were trying to coexist in a place that was too small. "I'm surprised you remember that. You were so little," I remarked.

"I remember a lot of things." Damon's voice was soft.

Talking about our parents was exactly what I needed, because suddenly I knew what to say. I angled my body toward Damon and reached for his hands. The gesture made him blink, but I felt his fingers curl around mine as I said, my voice edged with sincerity and pleading, "If something happens to me, I need you to live, Damon. Think about your son. What if Matt does turn out to be a Nightmare? There won't be anyone to help him, or show him how to control his power."

"What about Gil? Or Collith?" Damon reminded me.

I pursed my lips and looked away. "They'll be at the battle."

I didn't say it, but I didn't need to. We both knew the truth, which was that a lot of us wouldn't be coming back from the Flint Hills. And if things went very badly, there might not be anyone coming back.

Terrible images danced before my eyes. I tried to blink them away, and I found myself staring at the yard again. I looked at the indents in the grass and remembered the moment Laurie had whispered something in my brother's ear. "What did he say to you?" I asked.

Damon didn't ask who I meant. He peered out at the yard, too, his jaw still working. "He said, 'Are you really going to make her lose you again?'"

As soon as he told me, I could picture the moment perfectly. I heard the purr of Laurie's voice and imagined that familiar gleam in his eyes, which most people took for ferocity or cruelty. Only a lucky few knew it for what it truly was. I made a soft sound of exasperation and felt my animosity toward Laurie begin to fade. "He's such an asshole sometimes."

"Yeah," Damon agreed. "But he's a smart asshole."

"That is why they gave him a throne, I suppose," I said with a sigh. Of their own volition, my eyes went to the window above us. I didn't see a silhouette or hear any laughter, but I knew, somewhere deep inside where the soul must be, that they were up there. Both of them.

Damon followed my gaze again. "Are you together?" he asked suddenly. "The three of you?"

I tore my gaze from the window, startled. No one had asked me that before. Hearing the question come from Damon was disorienting, maybe even a little jarring, like waking up from a dream and finding out someone else had caught a glimpse of it. I didn't know how to answer, and all I could think to say was, "Would it weird you out if I said we were?"

My little brother smiled faintly, and he shook his head. "Not at all. I think it works, actually. Collith steadies you and Laurie—I've seen it. And Laurie makes you both laugh, especially when you're at each other's throats, or during those moments you need someone to pull you out of your own head. And all the while, the two of them keep you safe every time you manage to piss someone off or take on the most powerful, evil fucker you can find. Can't exactly be upset about that, since my sister is a little prone to chaos."

Damon nudged my shoulder with his, and I tried to smile back. Thinking about my situation with Collith and Laurie brought all the uncertainty back, and right now, I had much bigger things to focus on. I needed to be steady.

"We're not together," I said finally. I left it there.

Neither of us moved, and I realized that it could be the last time Damon and I were here, just the two of us, alive and well. "Will you do one more thing for me?" I ventured.

"Anything." Damon said it quietly, but there was no hesitation. I couldn't help thinking about how we'd started. The brother sitting beside me was such a far cry from the one I'd found at the Unseelie Court that, for a moment, I couldn't speak. I looked at him again and felt the sting of gratitude in my eyes. I'd made so many mistakes and done so much to regret, but Damon was the one thing I had gotten right.

"Just . . . don't give up," I told him. "Please. No matter what happens on Olorel, no matter who does or doesn't come back . . . promise me that you'll live, Damon. That's all I've wanted for you. That's all I've *ever* wanted."

When my voice broke, Damon leaned over and pressed his temple against mine. After a moment, the tension eased from my shoulders and I gently pressed back, remembering that I wasn't someone who avoided being touched anymore. I was safe, and I was no longer alone. I breathed in my little brother's scent, and even though it had changed since we were kids, it still made me think of home. Of our parents. Of a time before Lucifer, or pain, or fear. My mind filled with the memory of that storm again, and I heard echoes of my mother's laughter as she twirled and spun, holding onto us so tightly that it never occurred to me to be afraid.

I wanted that for Mattie. I needed to know there could still be good for him, in spite of the world he'd been born into. As silence and rain surrounded us, I couldn't help glancing toward the loft window and imagining it—a future for that beautiful little boy upstairs. The images flew through my head, so full of light and possibility that I ached with longing.

And suddenly I knew how to convince Damon to stay behind.

I straightened and turned to him. Just as I had for Finn, I showed my brother what I saw. It was as effortless as breathing. The bond between us flared, and we watched as Matthew grew from a laughing baby to a gangly, grinning boy. One that looked more and more like the grandfather he'd been named after with every passing day ... of which there were many. Soccer games, Christmases, school dances, and all the things that came with life and living. The sweet-faced boy went to college and became a kind man. And all the while Damon was there, happy and graying, eventually holding his own grandchildren. Enjoying countless more Sundays and years with Danny.

"I promise," Damon said, answering me at last.

Hearing those words made the tightness in my lungs dissipate, just a little, and it felt like I could breathe for the first time in weeks. Damon wouldn't be at the battle. He'd be here, safe, while I led the rest of our family onto a field of fire and blood.

Now we just had to win.

I exhaled and looked out at the yard once more. This time, I thought about our father. I remembered what he'd always told us after one of us had made a promise. "Nightmares may be lies," I recited softly.

The corner of Damon's mouth tilted up in another ghost of a smile. "But we don't have to be liars."

I found myself staring toward those distant trees at the edge of the property. The trees that had become the divide between the life I wanted and the life I couldn't seem to escape. I kept my eyes on the churning leaves as I said, "Since you're not a liar, Damon, I need you to tell me the truth about something. Why am I failing at this? Why can't I get anyone else to fight with us?"

Damon's posture remained loose, his fingers laced between his knees, but he studied me for a long moment. As if he was considering. I didn't rush him. Instead, I committed this moment to memory, since we probably didn't have many left. Fine mist clung to Damon's skin, and the pronounced curve of his throat shifted as he said, "Since Finn died, you've been different. You've forgotten something really important, and I think it's why you haven't been able to get your allies."

I tilted my head to meet Damon's gaze, my eyebrows raised. "What did I forget?"

He nudged my shoulder with his again and said, "You're Fortuna Sworn, sis. You're not a wolf, you're a fucking *lion*."

I tried to laugh, but there was sadness in the sound. "If you say something about roaring, I'm getting off this porch," I warned.

Damon just watched me with a shadow in his eyes, as if he was wishing things were different, too. "You'll find a way to save us, Fortuna. You always do."

Not this time, I wanted to say. I swallowed the words, because they wouldn't do either of us any good. Another silence hovered around the porch. There was nothing else to say, at least for now, but I wasn't ready to leave yet. I didn't want to go back upstairs and stare at Michael's message for hours on end.

"Want to just sit here for a while? Until the rain passes?" I asked Damon.

He peered out at it, the damp still glistening on his skin. "Yeah. Sure."

More rumbles of thunder shook the ground. This time, I didn't hear an ominous voice or feel a rush of urgency. It was only music. They were only raindrops. We were only two people sitting on a porch, enjoying each other's company. Just Fortuna and Damon. I rested my head on his shoulder and enjoyed the scents of the storm, watching it wash everything away. The past was behind us, and the future didn't matter. There was only right now, and now, and now.

And that was more than enough.

Sunlight made the Cape Fear River glitter.

Seagulls circled the air high above the water, their gray wings spread wide. Waves lapped at the shore, created by a blue-sided boat moving past. I stared out the window, my chin resting in the hollow of my hand. To anyone else in the cafe, it might seem like I was looking at the view. But I was focused only on one thing.

The leaves.

They were brown now. Falling to the ground like the weary final gasp of a quiet death. It was a glaring reminder of the passage of time—Olorel was inching closer and closer. I'd been trying to ignore that fact, because every time I thought about the shrinking number of days between now and then, terror threatened to find a way through the wall of focus I'd built around myself. Terror that we'd fail, and we wouldn't get that Gate shut or win against Lucifer's demonic horde.

Because even though my Court wouldn't be going to those hills alone, it still felt like we were marching toward the end. Not just the end of our lives, but life as we knew it. If the seven cities of Hell came to Earth, those demons would torture and kill every living creature here. Including my family.

I couldn't let that happen.

I'd been training harder than I ever had before. Every night, I slept six or seven hours, and then I was up at dawn. Hacking at that goddamn bespelled wooden man Viessa had sent me after I'd told her about Michael's power, and how my comrades were struggling to match my tenacity. I pictured Lucifer's face with every strike. When I wasn't doing that, I did push-ups and lifted weights—carrying a sword and wearing armor wasn't as easy as it looked in the movies, and I wasn't about to die in battle because I hadn't prepared.

On the rare occasions I wasn't at Adam's, Bea's, or the loft, I was somewhere far, far away from Granby, still meeting every Fallen dignitary or monarch Collith and Laurie could find. I spoke with the werelions of Bulgaria. The hyenas in Kenya. I'd even tried to convince a commune of goblins to help us.

At first, every single group either turned me down or gave noncommittal answers. Only a handful had come forward since then to say they'd help, but it wasn't enough. It wasn't nearly enough.

Which was how I now found myself in a small cafe in Wilmington.

It was midday, so the surrounding tables were completely empty, save for one man in the corner wearing headphones. It seemed risky talking about the war in such a public place, but I didn't fully trust that the water nymph king wouldn't try to steal me away if we met on his turf. I'd still taken note of all the exits and escape routes, just in case.

"You came without your fae guard dogs. I'm impressed."

At the sound of that smooth, familiar voice, I tore my focus away from the dying leaves outside and looked up at Alexander Nørgård. By all appearances, he'd come alone, too. As he smiled and waved at the server, I said mildly, "They know I can defend myself just fine."

What I really wanted to say was a little more vicious, but I was here to convince the water nymphs to fight with us, and probably die in the process. That would be harder to do if I told Nørgård that Collith and Laurie hadn't come because they didn't even see him as a threat. In fact, they'd been watching a football game when I'd left. Cyrus had invited them, along with Adam, Gil, Seth, Damon, and Danny, and all the guys had decided the TV was better at the loft. They'd been in the living room while I was getting ready, the sound of shouting and referee whistles drifting through my bedroom door.

"Have fun fishing, honey," was all Laurie had said as I'd walked out. I had shot him the finger in response.

As I watched the water nymph king pull out the chair across from me, I wisely kept this information to myself. Nørgård sat down and said, "I don't doubt it. I've done extensive research since we met, my lady, and I firmly believe that I'm looking at the most powerful creature on the planet. I would be a fool to insult your capabilities."

"So you're openly stalking me now?" I asked, ignoring the rest.

Just as the water nymph started to respond, a figure appeared next to the table. The human's blinding smile made me think of Ariel. "Hi, there!" she chirped.

Nørgård tipped his head back and gave her another charming grin. "Hello! I'd like a Coca-Cola, please."

She nodded. "Absolutely. One soda, coming right up. Is there anything else I can get you?"

"Whatever the lady would like." The water nymph raised his eyebrows at me. I started to shake my head, then reconsidered. Keeping my hands preoccupied would stop me from fidgeting.

"I'll have a small coffee, please," I said. The human smiled again and took our menus. The moment she walked away, all the politeness dropped from my expression. "This isn't a social visit, Mr. Nørgård."

He leaned back in the chair, propping his elbow on the backrest. "Call me Alexander."

"You must know why I'm here," I insisted.

"I've heard things in the currents. My contacts on land have also had disturbing things to report," Alexander said, some of the light leaving his eyes.

I wasn't sure I wanted to know the details of those reports. I held the water nymph's gaze, and my voice was hard as I said, "Then you also know that he has to be stopped."

The humor was completely gone from his expression now, and his attention shifted toward the window beside us. Sunlight shone on the smooth, solemn planes of his face. "What I know is that war isn't as glorious as legend makes it out to be. It only brings pain and death," he answered.

He'd come here to reject me, I could hear it in his voice. But instead of getting frustrated, I studied Alexander and remembered Damon's words to me the other night. *You're a lion.*

Lions didn't hesitate. Lions used their teeth and their claws when they went in for the kill. I leaned forward, gazing at Alexander intently. My voice was low and intimate as I told him, "There's a saying, you may have heard it before. The enemy of my enemy is my friend."

The water nymph went still at my proximity, and he wasn't staring out the window anymore. He didn't even react when our server returned and set down our drinks. I'd seen that look a thousand times, on a thousand others, and I knew it better than the lines of my own palm or a photograph of my parents. Alexander Nørgård was caught in my thrall. For a brief moment, I felt a flare of triumph, thinking I'd won.

Then the nymph's eyes shifted away, and the intensity between us eased. Alexander's demeanor became brisk as he ripped the paper off a straw and dropped it into his soda. I clenched my jaw and fought a wave of frustration, sitting back against my chair.

"My loyalty cannot be bought," Alexander said, lifting his cup to take a sip. Then he swallowed and added, "However, it can be rented."

I made a sound of disbelief. "You expect someone to pay you for fighting on the Fallen's side? *Your* side?"

Alexander rested his elbows on the table and moved closer, just as I had. Once again, this was a look I knew well—desire. "Marry me," he said.

"Pass," I said flatly. I didn't even pretend to think about it. "What else do you want?"

Alexander spread his hands helplessly. "I have everything I could possibly want."

Now I really was frustrated. I fell silent and struggled to control my expression. Our server hurried past again, and the sunlight bounced off two water glasses in her hands, making the sword beside Alexander flash, too. Something about the play of light triggered a memory. I saw that moment in my mind again, when Alexander had pressed the edge of his blade against Lucifer's throat.

It looked so much like Lyari's sword, I thought with a frown. Too bad she'd never gotten to use it on Lucifer, since he'd released Lyari from her contract ... right before he had practically fled from their duel. I remembered the swiftness of his departure when Alexander had stepped up to defend me, as well.

I'd never made the connection before, but it couldn't be a coincidence, could it?

"Where do you get your weapons?" I asked suddenly. My heart was beating so hard I could feel it in the hollow of my throat. I didn't know why, exactly. I just had that feeling like ... like I was onto something. Something big.

The water nymph quirked an eyebrow, obviously thrown by the abrupt topic change, but he answered easily enough. "We have a trade agreement with the Unseelie Court, who mine the materials themselves."

"Do you know what it looks like?" I asked. I'd never seen any such operation during my time at Court, but then again, I hadn't exactly been as involved as I could have been. Seeing Alexander's confused look, I clarified, "Whatever they're mining?"

"They looked like rocks." He shrugged, still bemused by my intensity. He could probably hear my pulse. "Small, gray rocks."

Small gray rocks. My heart was going wild now. When I'd first awoken in Hell, I'd found myself in a warehouse full of stones exactly like that. Another coincidence? Or was Lucifer mining ... demon glass? But how could an identical mineral be on two completely different planets?

Unless ... unless it wasn't. What if it was only in *one* place? But if the Unseelie Court wasn't on Earth, that meant ...

In a rush of memory, I heard Thuridan's last words to me. *He couldn't close it. So he put it somewhere useful.*

"Oh my God," I breathed. Somehow, Olorel must've known what Lucifer's vulnerability was—the demon glass. Which was mined in Hell. Those words went around again. *He couldn't close it.* If you couldn't destroy something, what did you do?

You hid it.

It turned out that Lucifer didn't know everything. In a way, Olorel *had* created the Unseelie Court. It wasn't just to give his people a safe haven or to protect the secret of an opening to Hell. It was because of *where* the Court was located.

Spurred by a rush of adrenaline, I shoved my chair back from the table. Alexander blinked in surprise. "What just happened?"

"He didn't close the Door. He *moved* it," I said urgently. My mind kept racing. "He put it somewhere *useful*. I have no idea how Thuridan knew, since Olorel died before he could tell anyone. Maybe Michael said something. But it doesn't matter. It's the fucking truth, I can feel it."

This explained why the Unseelie Court was underground. Why it was always so cold. Why there was no electricity. Those tunnels ran through the bedrock of Hell, where no beast or demon had found them for millennia. Olorel had buried the Door as deeply as he could so his brother would never discover the truth—all this time, Lucifer could've come into our world any time he wanted.

"What of our negotiations, Lady Sworn?" Alexander asked, watching me pull my jacket on.

"Here's what you can do with your negotiations." I flashed him my middle finger and took my purse off the back of the chair. As I started rummaging through it, I spoke without looking up. "If you want to be a coward and stay in the water while the rest of us die, then you'll have to live with that for the rest of your miserable life. I can tell you one thing, though—that life won't be very long. Not even the deepest parts of the ocean will be safe from him."

I dropped some money beside my coffee cup, which was still full, and turned away without another word to the water nymph king. His voice stopped me just as I took my first step.

"Wait."

I paused. When the scent of salt burst on my tongue, I figured out the real reason Alexander kept dodging me.

He was afraid.

But none of that fear showed on his face, I saw as I turned back. Alexander stood next to the table, his arms hanging loosely at his sides. "What do you need?" he asked.

I hid my surprise and answered, "Fighters. A lot of them."

He nodded. "Anything else?"

"Information," I said instantly. "Do you know where the fae mine those swords at Court?"

Alexander raised his eyebrows. "Why not ask one of your pretty lovers, or the Unseelie Queen?"

"Because they're not here, and I want to know right now," I said bluntly. Following an impulse, I returned to Alexander and pulled Michael's final message out of my purse. I unrolled the worn paper, then flattened it on the table. Thank God I'd taken to bringing it with me everywhere. I placed the salt and paper shakers on two corners, ketchup and mustard on the others. I pointed at each symbol as I said, "As far as we can tell, this is supposed to represent the Flint Hills. Until now, we had no idea what the other two were supposed to be. But now I think . . . this could be the Unseelie Court."

Alexander shot me an incredulous look. "What makes you believe *I* have any idea where the pointy ears get their precious material?"

I gave him a look back that told him I wasn't buying it. "You're a king, and you're ancient. There's no way you made a deal with faeries without knowing all the facts."

Alexander relented with a sigh, bending closer to examine my scribbles. "From what I can recall, the mines are almost directly below the tunnel entrance. Here."

The water nymph put his finger on the map. I stared down at it, chewing my lower lip in contemplation. Following another impulse, I dug a pen out of my purse and drew circles around all three of the symbols. When I was finished, I straightened with wide eyes. *Holy shit*.

Because of how I'd originally laid the shapes out on the paper, and how they were positioned, my circles formed the Olorel bloodline crest. Maybe it didn't represent three moons, and it never had ... maybe it was always meant to be a message. Every circle was a location. The first was the Flint Hills, where Olorel had moved the Door and created the Unseelie Court. His bones were there. The second was the Unseelie Court and the demon glass mine, which apparently had been in Hell all along. Olorel hadn't even been alive to make a family crest, so who had done this? Michael? Nym? Lyari's mother? That part didn't matter, not really, I told myself, still staring down at the map.

The bones. The demon glass. But what about the last circle? I stared at that final, mysterious symbol, which now peered up mockingly from the third circle's center.

"Someday I'm going to marry you, Fortuna Sworn," Alexander said, bringing my attention back to him.

Truth be told, I'd half-forgotten he was there. In a burst of urgency, I pushed the shakers and condiments away, freeing the drawing, and quickly rolled it up. "You don't want to marry me. I'd probably end up killing you," I replied shortly.

Watching me, the water nymph let out the smallest of sighs. "But what a blissful life it would be until then."

"I'll see you on Olorel, Alexander. You have my number if you need to talk logistics." I paused, realizing he could interpret this as an invitation. "But that's *all* you can use it for."

His eyes twinkled. "No promises, my lady."

I made an impatient sound and turned away. By the time I reached the door, I'd already forgotten the water nymph again, my mind consumed with the world-altering revelation Alexander had inadvertently given me. I rushed into the evening air, barely registering the smell of the river or the shriek of a nearby seagull.

I started in the direction of the closest Door, which was tucked away at the back of a local church.

Fortuna Sworn.

The voice slithered through my head like an eel, accompanied by a small whisper of pain. I frowned, scanning the street and the sidewalks for anyone standing still or peering in my direction. But the humans in sight weren't paying me any mind. Slowly, I began walking again.

Fortuna Sworn. Look to the water.

As the voice whispered through my mind a second time, it had a slimy feel to it. Goosebumps rose along my arms, and I turned toward the Cape Fear River, which was directly to my left. The beach was practically empty.

The water wasn't, though. There was something out there, and my heart quickened at the eerie sight. As I watched, it rose higher, and higher, a dark shape against the dim horizon. Then its body came out, rivulets streaming down the creature's sides, and I realized what I was looking at.

"It's you," I said. My power swelled instinctively, ready to tear through this thing's psyche if it tried to lure me in. Kelpies were no joke, not even to the deadliest of Fallen.

Before I could ask why it had come, its voice slid through my head again. *I will ride with you to face the Dark Prince,* the creature said.

I'd been afraid it was going to say that. I'd memorized all of Nym's drawings, and the kelpie had been one of the missing pieces. I licked my lips, stalling for time while my mind raced. "Why?" I asked.

I spoke with the Time Walker, the kelpie replied. It said nothing more.

Another rush of realization hit me. All of Nym's mysterious disappearances. The fact that some of my new allies had changed their minds. He must've been visiting them, one by one, accomplishing what I couldn't. Convincing them to lay down their lives for this fight.

The horse in front of me shifted, forcing my attention back to the offer floating between us. I regarded the creature with the wary respect it deserved, considering every angle if I were to accept.

Only an idiot would get on the back of a kelpie, considering they liked to drown their prey. But then I thought of Nym's drawings again. I held an automatic denial back and truly considered it. A kelpie could sift, like a faerie, and they were fast. Incredibly, unbelievably fast. A single bite from their pointed teeth could tear flesh like paper. A mount like that could actually stand a chance against an army of demons.

The second I heard myself think it, I knew I was going to say yes.

"How do I know you won't drag me to the bottom of a lake the second I get on?" I asked.

The creature huffed through its nose and stomped its foot. *Foolish child. A kelpie has not accepted a rider in centuries. Recognize the honor of my offer before I rescind it.*

Wariness prickled over my skin at the display of temper. But I stayed where I was, staring at the kelpie silently as I acknowledged the risks. This creature could betray me, or try to eat me. The heart of a Nightmare was still highly coveted. There was one huge advantage that might make it worth the risk, though. Not only could kelpies shift . . . they could take their riders with them. In a battle, an ability like that could be what saved my life, or helped me take out some truly fucking lethal demons.

My palms were damp as I said, "I accept your offer."

The kelpie didn't roll its eyes, but I swore I could hear it in the creature's voice. *Of course you do.*

"The Flint Hills," I replied, ignoring this. "That's where we'll face him. It's happening on Olorel, at sunset."

I stood there for another moment, uncertain how to proceed, since we couldn't exactly shake on it. Then the kelpie shifted again, making mud squelch beneath its lethal hooves. *I am Sarod*, it said, bending its long neck into a bow.

This creature already knew my name, but it seemed rude not to respond. I bowed back and said, "I'm Fortuna Sworn. It's nice to finally meet you, Sarod."

Part of me expected the kelpie to respond with a wise comment or some pretty sentiment. Instead, it just turned its huge body back to the water and returned to the deep.

Until Olorel, that eerie voice said in my head. A moment later, the kelpie was gone, with not even a ripple to prove I hadn't imagined the entire thing. I stood there for an extra beat, processing what had just happened. What I'd agreed to.

After another moment, I shook myself and whirled away. There was so much to do. It was fortunate I was already heading for a Door, because my first stop after the meeting with Alexander was the Unseelie Court. Viessa had no idea that she was sitting on our possible salvation, or that a planet of demons existed above her. After that, my Court also needed to know everything I'd just learned . . . and about the allies I had finally procured us.

I couldn't *wait* to see the look on Collith's face when I told him what I would be riding into battle. My mouth curved at the thought.

He was going to shit a brick.

CHAPTER NINETEEN

"Mercy Wardwell is full of *shit*."

I glared up at the moon. It peered back at me serenely, round and bright against its dark backdrop. The full moon, Mercy had said. Well, the moon was as full as it was going to fucking get. Midnight had come and gone, and half of the people in the room behind me were asleep. I was pretty sure I'd seen Damon drooling earlier when I was pacing in front of him.

Collith appeared beside me. "Fortuna, not even Mercy Wardwell can have total control over magic. A Telling is just like any other spell. It's—"

"—unpredictable," I finished on an exhale. "I know. She just sounded so certain . . . and we need this, Collith. We *really* need this."

Toward the end, my voice dropped to a strained whisper. I kept staring up at that faraway moon as if it could hear my silent pleas. Gently, Collith gripped the curve between my neck and shoulder, giving it a soft squeeze as he pressed his cheek against my temple. When his scent reached me, it felt like another spell, all the tension seeping out of me like a fading winter frost. A sigh filled my throat, and my chest sank as I leaned into Collith.

I'd been on edge all day. Not even a shift at Bea's could take my mind off the full moon and all it might bring, according to Mercy. I'd practically ripped a customer's head off when he wouldn't stop gawking at me. Normally that sort of shit rolled off me, but not today. There was too much at stake.

We waited in the training room. There wasn't enough seating, and there was no TV down here to entertain the boys, but I hadn't wanted to risk missing the sound of a knock. Damon was slumped on the couch, his head tipped forward at an angle that looked incredibly uncomfortable. Danny was working the night shift, so Gil and Seth filled the space beside my brother, talking quietly. Ariel sat cross-legged on the floor, teaching Cyrus how to crochet. In the corner, Narfu had nestled so deeply in his pile of blankets that all we could see of him was his long, drooping tail. Savannah and Emma were here, as well, but both of them were upstairs with Mattie. They'd asked that one of us bring news whenever something happened.

But so far, nothing had happened. Absolutely nothing.

At the same moment I felt the tension return to my shoulders, Ariel's soft voice reached me. "The nymph king agreed to help us, didn't he?" she asked.

I shot her a grateful look, recognizing her attempt to offer some encouragement. Even now, at our darkest hour, Ariel's sunshine hadn't dimmed. "Yes," I sighed. "But his reasons aren't exactly reassuring. Alexander Nørgård is . . . well, he's a little . . ."

"Fortuna has a fan," Gil whispered loudly, waking my brother. As Damon blinked and sat up, Gil continued, "Clearly the chap has never shared a bathroom with her. That would sort his feelings right out."

My gaze narrowed at him. "What are you saying?"

Gil's eyes twinkled, and when I saw that, I couldn't even pretend to be annoyed. He'd been doing so much better since I'd used our bond to ease his cravings. "I only meant—"

A knock echoed through the loft.

We all looked at each other, and I saw my shock mirrored in everyone else's eyes. It felt like my stomach had dropped out of my body. A moment later, I recovered and rushed to the weapons rack. First, I snatched one of the sheaths hanging there and slung it around my waist. The second I had the notch in place, I reached for my sword. Collith was already doing the same, our movements in perfect sync. The two of us strode from the room together. My heart was hammering hard enough to send vibrations through the rest of my body.

When the door came into view, I stopped and stood there for a moment, just staring at it. My chest had swelled with so much hope that it felt like I might burst if I opened that door and there wasn't an ally standing on the other side. I didn't think I could stand it.

We really need this, I thought again, moving forward. If we could make our army bigger, even just a little, maybe we'd all have a fighting chance of getting out of this alive.

But first, I had to open the door.

Collith stood at my side. He didn't say anything—didn't question my hesitation, didn't rush my uncertainty—and his quiet strength steadied me. I took an extra moment to make sure my mental guards were in place, since we didn't know what was standing on the other side of the door, and then I forced myself to reach for the knob. It opened slowly, emitting a low, long whine that floated through the stillness.

Gwyn of the Wild Hunt smirked at me.

I felt my jaw loosen, and for the first time since I could remember, I was completely speechless.

"I heard a rumor that you were trying to gather an army," the huntress remarked. "And I thought, *You know, it's been millennia since I've been in a good fight.*"

Moving with the speed Michael had given me, I unsheathed my sword and pointed it at the hollow of Gwyn's throat. In the seconds that followed, I sensed my Court gathering behind me, but I kept my focus on the faerie in the doorway as I refortified my mental walls. Her power, while not nearly as substantial as Michael's, still made my skin prickle.

Gwyn's eyes gleamed. "I see there have been some developments while I was away."

"Where the *fuck* have you been?" I snarled.

"As usual, you're asking the wrong questions," Gwyn told me, annoyingly unperturbed, even as her throat moved against the point of my blade. Her gaze was steady. "The one you should be asking is not where I've been, but how I could've resisted your call. I am bound to you, after all. Such a thing should've been impossible. Unless, perhaps, I didn't hear you."

My brow furrowed, and I searched Gwyn's expression. I *had* asked myself that question, and I'd also considered the possibility that my summons weren't reaching her. Frustration heated my veins and I shook my head, reaching the same conclusion as every other time I had tried to explain Gwyn's resistance to our bond. "There's no place you could go that I wouldn't be able to . . ."

The faerie's eyebrows rose. "Funny thing about magic. Sometimes it has a little trouble in the pockets between worlds."

The pockets between worlds. My heart quickened. So every time I'd tried to contact her these past few months, Gwyn hadn't been on Earth. She hadn't been in this world at all . . . and I had a feeling I knew exactly which dimension she'd gone to. My arm was beginning to tire, but I didn't lower it. If anything, my distrust had only grown. "How? Why?" I demanded.

Something ancient and feral crept into Gwyn's expression. "To understand the Hunt, you must become part of the Hunt. Do you consent?" she asked.

"No," I said instantly, shaking my head again, recognizing the trap. She'd barely put any effort into it, but even now, the huntress couldn't resist trying to add me to her ranks. "So the Hunt can travel between worlds. Got it. No questions here."

The corners of Gwyn's luscious mouth tilted in amusement, and the sight sent an icy breath down the back of my neck. After all the horrors I'd experienced, I had forgotten to be afraid of the fae . . . but facing this creature again was a jarring reminder of how dangerous they could be. And how careful I needed to be. The last time I'd gone head-to-head with Gwyn, I'd gotten the upper hand on her. Fallen, especially faeries, held deep grudges and long memories.

When I didn't say anything else, she raised her eyebrows. "Are you going to invite me inside, or shall I take my news elsewhere?" Gwyn questioned.

News? I hid a scowl, realizing that I was about to step aside for the faerie who had cost Laurie his throne and drowned me in a dirty, frozen creek. From the moment we'd met, Gwyn and I had been moving pieces on a board, and now, in our silent little chess game, she'd outmaneuvered me.

I finally lowered my sword and scanned the area behind her. There was no sign of the Wild Hunt, but that didn't mean anything. This could still be a trap or some kind of attempt to wriggle her way free. I just had to trust the bond would prevent Gwyn from harming anyone. I opened the door wider and inclined my head, sounding anything but welcoming as I said, "Come in, then."

A small, satisfied smile hovered around the huntress's lips as she brushed past me. I didn't think the way her shoulder brushed my chest was accidental, and from the way Collith's eyes narrowed, he didn't seem to think so, either. I closed the door and moved to rejoin my Court, facing Gwyn with all of them still standing at my back. Collith stayed at my side, and he was so close I could feel the coolness emanating from his skin.

Gwyn stood a yard away from us. Her ancient, calculating eyes took stock of every person in the barn, ending with me. Her expression revealed nothing. She inclined her head and began, "Several months ago, I received an intriguing summons. A small creature from another world. At first, I ignored its calls. Crossing dimensions isn't easy, and every journey takes a toll on my people. But the little thing was relentless. It said my name again and again. It interrupted my sleeping. My hunting. My fucking. So eventually I gave in, more out of annoyance than any real curiosity.

"But what I found was intriguing. The wee beastie led us to a place full of stones. At first, I didn't understand what it was trying to tell us. Truth be told, I considered killing it, just to shut the damn thing up."

My heart had quickened at the mention of those stones, and I knew Gwyn could hear it. "Did you?" I asked.

"No," she answered, her expression still unreadable. "The creature kept putting those damn rocks by us, and finally, one of my hunters decided to break one open. When he touched what was inside, he nearly lost his hand. I knew, then, what we'd stumbled upon. So we pushed ourselves to the limit, again and again, to bring back as much as we could."

I stared at Gwyn, certain I'd misunderstood. "Wait ... you brought the stones *back*? To this world?"

"And forged them," she answered matter-of-factly.

Without waiting for my response, Gwyn turned and strode to the door, her powerful legs crossing the distance in just a few steps. When she opened it, several of her hunters stood on the other side. I tensed, and I sensed the members of my Court doing the same. Gwyn grasped a sword that one of her people held and turned again, flipping it upside down.

"Weapons fit for an army facing an onslaught of demons from Hell," she declared, coming back over to me. She presented the sword for my inspection. The pommel was covered in strange, beautiful symbols. "There's more where this came from. Much more."

I'd recognize that glassy material anywhere. It was exactly like the weapons the Guardians carried. I raised my gaze back to the hunters, taking in what else they'd brought as they all entered the barn. Axes, maces, spears, more swords . . . one of them even had a flail. I stared in wonder. *Holy shit*.

Gwyn had stolen from the devil.

"You are a fucking *badass*." The second the words left my mouth, I regretted them. I'd just showed my entire hand and given Gwyn the ultimate bargaining chip. Wariness shot through me, and I inwardly cursed myself as I added, "Let me guess. You want something in exchange for them."

Her lips curved in a small, satisfied smile. "A mere trifle. Just my freedom."

I didn't smile back. I looked at the huntress coldly, thinking about it from every angle. "We need you on Olorel, Gwyn. We need every fighter we can get."

"The Wild Hunt will still join the battle against the Dark Prince. You have my word," Gwyn said.

Despite all the lores and legends, I knew now that faeries could lie. They lied as easily as they killed, and fucked, and drank. My lip curled at Gwyn. "Am I supposed to rely on a pinkie promise? And how do I know you won't kill me the second you're not under my control anymore?"

"You don't," she said, just as I'd known she would.

I fell silent again as I considered all the angles a second time, and then a third. I swallowed down a curse and a rush of frustration. *Goddamn it*. We needed Gwyn and her hunters, desperately, yet those weapons could change everything. Our holy blades only harmed demons when they were inside a host, and the creatures coming through that Gate would be different. We had the stores from the Unseelie Court, sure, but most of that had gone to Viessa's Guardians and the water nymphs. Our other allies would need demon glass, as well.

In the midst of my silent struggle, I remembered that Gwyn was in Nym's drawing. The Time Walker had depicted her at my side, standing amongst the rest of the Fallen who were there to fight.

An anxious sigh lodged in my chest. It was a gamble, but I was betting on my friend. He believed, so I would, too.

My insides trembled as I met Gwyn's gaze. "You have a deal."

The second the words left my mouth, both of us felt it—the connection between us dissipating. The bond melting away into nothing. Gwyn belonged to herself again, and she was once again the sole commander of the Wild Hunt. The faerie's eyes slid shut for a moment, and a small sound left her. The look on her face was one of such pure relief that I was almost glad about the decision I'd made. The risk I'd taken.

I glanced at Collith, wondering what he thought of what I had done. He wore that royal mask of indifference, but I could still sense the tension rolling off him. He didn't trust the huntress, and for good reason. I hid another flutter of apprehension and returned my focus to Gwyn. Her hunters had taken the liberty of fully entering the barn, and they stood behind her now. I didn't like having them in here, so close to all the people I cared about. But if we were going to fight together, we had to trust each other.

I just hoped I didn't regret it.

"How many—" I began, but the sound of knocking cut me off.

That makes two, I thought dazedly. Maybe Mercy hadn't been full of shit after all. I walked over to the door again, and opened it slowly.

This time, Cora stood on the other side. She'd brought her entire pack, too.

I grinned at the sight of her, and a weight I hadn't known I'd been carrying began to fall away. "You came," was all I said.

In her usual solemn way, Cora offered her hand. "You were right. This isn't just your battle to fight—it's all of ours. I'm sorry I was such a coward."

I wrapped my fingers around hers firmly, without hesitation, and looked her in the eye as I replied, "A coward wouldn't have shown up. Thank you."

Her beta came forward to greet me, the tall female I'd met the night Collith and I had gone to see their pack. I gave her a warm greeting in return and invited them inside. Cora made a signal to the other wolves that had accompanied her, and they came through the door warily. My Court moved to acknowledge them. Their kind smiles set our visitors at ease, and I felt a swell of pride as I watched them. I glanced toward the Wild Hunt, and after a moment of hesitation, I began to make introductions between them and Cora's pack.

We'd just started discussing the details of the battle when there was another knock at the door.

I swung the door open to a massive shape on the other side, the light against his back. But then his tail flicked into sight over his shoulder, and I knew instantly who it was.

"Luther?" I blurted, too startled to disguise my disbelief. Behind me, the room went utterly silent.

The Rat King ducked his head and stepped over the threshold. He was just as big and pale as I remembered, and as I instinctively retreated, I scanned the driveway and the trees. The shapeshifter seemed to have journeyed here alone. I was on the verge of thinking he'd come in peace when Luther straightened and flashed his yellowed teeth in a terrifying grin.

I hadn't seen the Rat King of Munich since escaping Belanor. Down in those dank tunnels beneath the city, I'd used his childhood trauma against him and kicked his ass in front of his subjects. Truth be told, I was lucky Luther had only turned me away when I'd gone to see him.

My voice was neutral as I said, "What are you doing here?"

"I have come at my queen's request," the wererat informed me. "I swore to her that I would give the Nightmare an audience."

He must've meant Nan, I thought. I had mixed feelings about the fact that she'd convinced Luther to fight. When his people denied me at the sewers, I'd been frustrated, yes, but part of me had been relieved, too. But for the sake of my family and all of fucking humanity, I needed to swallow my dislike and play nice with this asshole.

I met his gaze and said evenly, "Thank you for coming."

"I'm not here for you, *Hure*."

My eyes narrowed. I didn't need to speak German to know what he'd just called me. My voice was sickly sweet when I replied, "Being a dick won't make yours any bigger, you know."

From somewhere behind me, I heard the familiar sound of Collith's sigh. The Rat King's lip curled, and his eyes held a dangerous glint. I had a feeling that if I took a peek inside his head, I wouldn't like what I saw. Collith must've agreed, because he shifted, his arm brushing mine.

"I still look forward to the day I can beat that attitude out of you," the wererat rumbled.

For a moment, I was tempted to fill his mind with the bombs that had taken Luther's mother and his childhood. To remind him what I was capable of. But I had already humiliated this creature several times over. Everyone had a limit, and I didn't want to find out where Luther's was. So I stepped closer and lowered my voice, saying for his ears alone, "Don't forget . . . I know what you're afraid of, Luther. I still remember the delicious, smoky taste of your fear."

The Rat King was silent. My words sent the exact flavor I'd just described creeping over my tongue. I turned away from him and surveyed the strange gathering that had filled the barn. My heart began to pound harder as I scanned their faces. The faeries. The rats. The werewolves. The Wild Hunt. Everything Nym drew had come to pass.

And it still wouldn't be enough. I knew that, and they did, too. But they'd still come.

I nodded at them and said, "Thank you for standing against Lucifer. The world may not remember us or the sacrifices we'll make, but you don't know what you're living for until you know what you would die for. The people in this room may not share much in common, but we do have that."

Cora smiled at me, and Gwyn just watched me with those sharp eyes of hers. The Rat King sneered. It would have to do.

After that, I offered to feed everyone, but they declined. One by one, our new allies left, disappearing back into the night. As the Wild Hunt took their leave, Gwyn and I made swift arrangements for our weapon exchange. Eventually, it was just me and my Shadow Court again. Once we were alone, I tucked my hands in the crook of Collith's arm—I felt a small jolt of surprise go through him—and rested my head on his shoulder.

"Mercy was still wrong, you know," I murmured. "She said there would be four knocks. But there were only three. Just like I told her."

Collith didn't answer. I tipped my head back to see his face, and something in his expression made me turn. I looked toward the other side of the barn, where the doorways to the other rooms were.

Lyari stepped into the light.

Her yellow eyes were bright with trepidation, and I saw her fingers twitch, as if she'd been about to raise her hand. Despite the changes in her appearance, I still knew her. I knew she wanted to hide the thorns above her brow.

"I guess that makes four," I said with a smile. I paused for a beat before I gave in to the urge to cross the room and hug her. Lyari froze for a moment, clearly taken off guard. Then her arms slowly rose, and I felt the light press of her fingers against my back. I didn't make her stay like that for long before I stepped away. I couldn't stop smiling.

"I'm really glad you're here, Ly. So glad."

Her throat shifted in a barely perceptible movement. "So am I."

I clapped one hand on her shoulder and faced the others. "I guess that's it, then."

"It wasn't four."

For most of the night, Seth had been a quiet presence. At the sound of his voice, I turned to him in surprise. "What, Seth?"

"That wasn't four knocks," he clarified. "It was only three. Lyari didn't use the door."

I frowned. "Mercy—"

A polite, firm knock floated through the barn. My frown deepened as a ripple of unease went through me. But a witch had foretold this. She'd said I would have four visitors. This was just part of the plan, right? Still, I hefted the sword that Gwyn had left with me, readying myself as I headed for the door again.

When I opened it, my eyes widened in terror, and I almost slammed the door in the newcomer's face. His thin lips curved into the smile that I still saw in my dreams.

"Well met, Nightmare," he said.

Prince Samael, ruler of the Fourth City of Hell.

The demon prince stood in the doorway so casually. As he waited for me to speak, it was all I could do not to recoil. The only outward indication of my reaction to Samael's presence in this world—*my* world—was a slight, barely perceptible tightening of my hand on the edge of the door. I tried to say something, but I couldn't move. I knew that if I did, I might give in to the panic breathing down my neck.

"Fortuna, who is this?" Collith asked.

I was so startled by the question that I glanced back at him. They didn't know, I realized, seeing Collith's frown. They had no idea who was standing in front of us and what he'd done to me. Or tried to do.

For a moment, I considered staying silent, because that was what my kind had been taught. Stay silent, stay hidden, stay safe.

But I was no longer interested in being silent.

I met the demon's gaze with steel in my own and said, "This is Prince Samael, ruler of the Fourth City of Hell. He's also the guy who tried to sacrifice me on a slab of stone one time."

From the corner of my eye, I noted the glint of Laurie's hair as he tilted his head and regarded Samael. His tone was full of mild interest as he mused, "It just occurred to me that it's been far too long since I've ripped someone's spine up their throat."

Samael smiled, and the sight was chilling. The demon prince had fangs. Long, retractable fangs. "I'd like to see you try, flea," he said.

A deadly light shone in Laurie's eyes as he smiled back. At the same moment the Seelie King opened his mouth to reply, I interjected, "If you came here to finish what you started in Hell, I'd think again. You don't have the element of surprise this time, and I won't lose a moment's sleep if I have to kill you."

Samael's nostrils flared at my tone, and I felt a vicious stab of triumph. The mask of civility *was* just an act. I stood rigidly and mentally reached for my power, waiting for any excuse to use it. And yet, despite his flash of irritation, the prince's voice remained neutral when he replied, "I've come to form an alliance with you, Nightmare."

"Not interested." I started to close the door, and Samael's palm hit the wood with such force that it creaked. Laurie and Collith tensed at the same time, but I held my free hand up toward them, keeping my gaze on the demon prince. My voice rang with command as I warned, "Step back."

"A third of my brother's armies are loyal to me," Samael said, ignoring this. "A third, Nightmare. The Dark Prince doesn't know it, of course, but they await my orders for which side we should fight with in the battle that is to come. I could tell them to stay hidden, and continue killing alongside my brother's forces . . . or I could tell them to join yours."

I hid a scowl. Samael had my attention, and we both knew it. Damn demons and their deals.

"You want your brother dead." I didn't say it like a question, because it was obvious where this was going. But Samael's eyes darkened as if I'd insulted him.

"I want to rule the seven cities," the demon prince corrected me. "If there were another way, I would take it, and believe me, I have agonized over it for centuries. That time has cost my people. For too long, my brother has allowed his attention to wander. Too long he has kept his eyes on the horizon while our world continues to weaken. What you and I want isn't so different, Nightmare. I simply want to protect what I love."

Laurie made a faint sound of disdain. Although I didn't answer right away, I wasn't buying it, either. A good guy wouldn't have done what Samael had done to me. But instead of his pathetic lies, I kept hearing those other words in my head—*a third*. I kept my desperation locked away as I looked back at Samael, still refusing to grant him entry.

"And what do you want in exchange?" I asked bluntly. I sensed someone behind me shifting, but once again, I stayed focused on the demon.

He matched my tone. "I want to be spared. Once I have helped you slay my brother, my forces and I will be allowed to return to our world, where we will remain peacefully. You stay in your dimension, and I stay in mine."

Toward the end of his response, I felt my lip begin to curl. There was *nothing* peaceful about Samael's world, and if I had my way, I'd free all those broken and enslaved souls I had seen. The fact that he was so adamant about me staying away betrayed him—Samael was afraid of my power. Of what I could do.

But that wasn't the only problem with his proposal. I met the prince's gaze again and said, "Killing Lucifer isn't my only priority; I also plan to close the Gate. How am I supposed to promise your safe return if the way back is gone?"

"I am told you have discovered another way into Hell," he countered. A surprised breath caught in my throat. Hearing it, his eyes gleamed. We both knew what he'd just revealed without actually saying it.

Samael had a spy.

The only ones who knew the truth about the Unseelie Court were my people, Alexander Nørgård, and Viessa Folduin. Either one of them had gotten word to Samael, or someone had been listening to our conversations. My gut said it was the latter. There had been others in that cafe where I'd met Alexander, and any creature with enhanced hearing would've been able to eavesdrop. The passageways of the Unseelie Court weren't exactly full of well-intentioned faeries, either—any one of them could've betrayed the new, controversial queen.

Idiot, idiot, idiot, I thought viciously, hiding another scowl. This could put the entire Unseelie Court in danger, and if my world survived Lucifer, there was now a new threat to worry about.

Samael was still waiting for a response, along with everyone standing behind me. "If you want an answer right now, I can't give you one," I said finally.

I was stalling, but it was also the truth. Even if I wanted to, I couldn't agree to Samael's offer until I spoke to Viessa. Not only would demons need to go through the Unseelie Court to reenter their world, but they'd have to create some kind of opening to the surface . . . which brought on another slew of potential dangers. Agreeing to Samael's terms would once again expose humankind and this vulnerable world to the horrors of Hell.

He knew it, too, because he didn't try to press me.

"Very well. But I do hope we're able to reach a truce, Nightmare. I am willing to let bygones be bygones," the demon said. He held out his hand and attempted another smile. It looked false and unnatural on his face, as if someone had painted the friendliness onto his cheeks.

"You'll forgive me if I don't shake on it," I said coolly. Ally or not, I didn't forgive him, and I certainly hadn't forgotten what he was capable of. Sometimes I could still feel that cold altar beneath me as his demons swarmed all around, shrieking for my flesh like I was nothing more than a hunk of meat.

Hoping no one noticed the quake that went through me, I stepped back and closed the door, saying, "Good night, Samael."

If he answered, I didn't hear it—my heart was pounding too loudly in my ears. My fingers shook as I flipped the lock, and once that reassuring click filled the stillness, I turned to face the two males that had come to stand behind me. As if by some unspoken signal, the rest of my Court had made themselves scarce. Only Nym remained nearby. He sat on the bottom stair, holding what looked like a wristwatch in his slender fingers. I could hear him saying under his breath, "Tick tock. Tick tock."

I met Collith's gaze first, and Nym's mutterings faded into the background. I could tell from the unnatural brightness in Collith's eyes that he'd noticed my little shiver of fear, and there was a hint of something dark and feral in his voice as he said, "You know we can't trust him, Fortuna."

I didn't answer. I chewed my lower lip indecisively, studying Collith while my mind worked, considering every possibility. I hadn't seen Lucifer's brother in any of Nym's drawings. If he was really an ally, wouldn't there be some depiction of him at the battle? What if I agreed to spare Samael, only for him to turn on my people the moment Lucifer was defeated? What if he did exactly what the Dark Prince had planned, and consumed the world anyway?

"It was an act," Laurie growled. "The Dark Prince is just sniffing around, trying to find out whether you can close the Gate."

Once again, I said nothing. I was remembering the last thing I'd told Samael. *You're nothing more than second best. The eternal runner-up. I won't bother advising you not to forget it, because something tells me you never do.*

I'd flung those words in the demon prince's face knowing they would find their mark. I'd seen the hate in his eyes. In that moment, Samael would've killed me if he could have. Only a fool would trust his word, especially after I'd humiliated him.

But . . . we desperately needed the numbers he was offering. Even now, after all those knocks and visitors and vows, what our side had wasn't enough. Since the moment I'd realized that Gate was going to open, and facing the armies of Hell was inevitable, I kept thinking of the view from Lucifer's tower.

I had stared out at that view a thousand times, and no matter how long I stood there, the awe had never faded. The wonder at the sheer size of the First City and all its teeming, writhing, shrieking populace. The other city I'd visited had been no different, and there were five more I hadn't even seen. If I failed at shutting the Gate, and all those cities came pouring through, I would be responsible for snuffing out the lives of an entire world. Everything depended on holding back the tide and buying me time to pour my power into that tear.

And just as he'd said, there *was* one thing Samael wanted more than my life. One thing that made it possible he was actually telling the truth.

His brother's throne.

"What do you think, Nym?" I asked suddenly. I looked over at the Time Walker, hoping that we'd get lucky, for once, and he'd be experiencing a moment of clarity. To my surprise, he looked back at me, and his gaze was steady. My heart rose with hope.

But the moment Nym opened his mouth and spoke, it sank right back down.

"Tick tock," he said. "Tick tock."

CHAPTER TWENTY

The plan was simple.

Well, the first part, at least. Tomorrow was Olorel. Once we'd all eaten and gotten ready, those who were fighting would use the Door, and we would go to the Flint Hills. All of our allies knew to be there by sundown. According to Savannah, Lucifer was only safe behind his magical barrier until then, when he would be forced to lower it for the spell.

After that, we'd implement the second part of the plan, which was a little more complicated. There were a lot of variables, and magic was the biggest one. Wild, unpredictable magic. Our army would come at Lucifer from every direction, stopping the flow of soldiers and demons while I got to the Gate. I had no idea how close I needed to be, so I'd have to figure that part out as I went. Just like I'd have to figure out how Persephone and Olorel had used their power to manipulate the Door.

But what if I failed, just like I'd failed to kill Oliver?

"You seem distracted today," a gentle voice said.

I refocused on the human sitting across from me and registered her words. I thought about my response before I said it, as I always did during these sessions. I liked Consuelo, trusted her, even . . . but she was still human. She could never know the whole truth about my life, or it might put us both in danger.

"I guess I'm thinking," was all I said.

Consuelo tilted her dark head. "What are you thinking about?"

Once again, I paused to weigh my answer. I imagined myself as a house, and when I was with her, I allowed myself to open a window. I couldn't let her inside, or allow her to see all the dark corners. Only glimpses were safe.

But the fresh air was so, so good.

I spoke slowly. "People say that good always wins, in the end. That in the battle of good versus evil, the heroes will ultimately prevail. But what if . . . what if there are no heroes? What if there are only monsters fighting monsters?"

Consuelo considered this. It used to make me uncomfortable, the silence that sometimes fell between us. I would rush to fill it, even when I didn't want to, even when I had nothing else to say. It was the same reason I ran for miles in the woods or filled the loft with constant music—I was afraid of silence. In those still, quiet moments, there was only me left, and all the pain I'd been avoiding. The pain I had been afraid of my entire life.

"Even monsters have a reason for what they do. Hunger. Power," Consuelo said in a musing tone. Then she leaned forward in her chair, and her expression became more intent. "But let me ask you this, Fortuna . . . would a person who's truly evil care if they were?"

Her gaze was steady. For once, I didn't look away. The human's question tucked itself away inside me, and I felt my mouth purse in silent speculation.

My thoughts were cut short when Consuelo raised her delicate wrist and glanced at her watch. The hour was over. They passed so quickly now.

"Same time next week?" Consuelo asked as she unfolded her legs and stood.

I hesitated. It shouldn't have been a complicated question. But if I was being realistic, I'd have to admit that I probably wouldn't survive the battle. I was Fallen, and we were cursed with knowledge. But . . . I was also human. Humans tended to be reckless, and idiotic, and desperately delusional.

As Consuelo waited for an answer, something glinted at the corner of my eye. I found myself looking at that small unicorn on her desk. It glittered in a sunbeam coming through the window, kicking at the air with its front legs. I studied the play of light within the glass and how it shone brightest at the edges of those deadly hooves.

They reminded me of the kelpie's, I realized suddenly. But no therapist would have a sculpture of a kelpie in their office. Only a twisted person would admire such a vicious beast, and only someone desperately delusional would think about riding one.

And yet . . . I liked to think it was the delusional ones who changed the world most.

I tore my gaze from the sculpture and met Consuelo's gaze again. I nodded and said, "See you next week."

A few seconds later, I pushed the outer door open, and my focus quickly turned away from the conversation with Consuelo. The plan was simple, I thought again. Too simple if we really wanted to win. We were going into this fight blindfolded. We knew that killing either Lucifer or Oliver would end both of them, sure, but we still didn't know *how*. Every creature had a vulnerability. A balance.

"But what's yours?" I muttered, glaring at the sidewalk. I tried to remember every moment of my conversations with them, convinced there had to be something I'd missed.

"Are you talking to yourself?"

I lifted my head, somehow not surprised by the sound of Laurie's voice or the sight of him standing there, a shining figure at the end of the path. He waited in front of the trellis arch, hands in his pockets, head slightly tilted. If I had any artistic skill, it was a moment I would've liked to capture on canvas or film.

"I was until you interrupted." I sighed. "How did you know I was here? Do I need to search my car for a tracker?"

Laurie tapped a rectangular outline in his pocket. "Magic of the modern smartphone. You shared your location with me."

I gave him a suspicious look. "I don't remember doing that."

Laurie shot me an exasperated look back. "It's not my job to make sure you remember everything, Fortuna. I'm a *king*, or did you forget that, too?"

He wasn't serious, of course, but the question made a shadow pass over my mood. "Believe me, that fact is never far from my mind," I muttered.

Laurie cocked his head and studied me with his bright eyes. Eyes that saw far too much. "What's wrong, Firecracker?"

I started walking, and Laurie fell into step beside me. My brow furrowed in thought again. "I've read every book I could get my hands on about battle strategies and war. No matter which way I look at it, there isn't going to be some clever, surprising plan or tactic that will save us. The C-4 will slow them down, if the horde gets past our forces, but that won't mean anything if we don't close the Gate. Which, even if we actually manage to get to, we have no idea how to *do*."

They were all thoughts I'd had before, a hundred times, over and over. It wasn't even the first time Laurie and I had had this conversation. At this point, I was like a broken record.

But he wasn't. Instead of repeating what he'd said before, Laurie fixed his gaze on something in the distance. "What do you plan to do with our last night?"

The fact that he'd asked, the fact that he was *here*, told me everything I didn't want to know.

Laurie didn't think we'd survive tomorrow night, either.

I pursed my lips as we reached Emma's car, which she'd loaned to me for the morning. "It never ends, does it?"

"What?" Laurie asked, facing me.

"Being afraid. Feeling like something awful is waiting around every corner, or like the next fight for my life is always just seconds away. The constant, never-ending, relentless *struggle*." My voice broke at the end, and my grip tightened on my purse strap. "After everything we've survived, and how hard we've fought, it ends like this? I know that life isn't fair, especially for our kind, but . . . I really wish I'd done some things differently. A lot of things."

For once, there was no trace of mirth in Laurie's expression. His silver eyes looked gray beneath the shadow of the tree, and a breeze stirred the ends of his hair. The breeze brought hints of Laurie's scent over to me, and I tried to breathe it in without being obvious.

"No. It doesn't end," he said.

I made a humorless sound. "Wait, isn't this the part where you're supposed to give me some speech about why we keep fighting?"

"If you wanted that speech, you would've gone to Collith."

I quirked an eyebrow at him. "You found me, remember?"

"Did I? Are you sure?"

Normally I would have had a response ready, a retort that would make him smirk or volley back. But today, I couldn't do it. The part of my mind where I kept all my wit and sarcasm felt dim and hollowed out. But I mustered a smile for him.

"Okay, I'll play. Why did I come to you, then?" I asked.

"Because I'm an excellent distraction," Laurie said matter-of-factly. He paused. "I'm always the distraction."

Something in his voice had shifted. We kept ending up back here, I thought, looking away. Rays of sun broke through the leaves above me, and I squinted out at the street. I watched a car drive by without truly seeing it, my mind on this pattern we were trapped in. All three of us. We just went around and around, but I was so afraid to get off the carousel. I was so afraid of what came after.

The Seelie King hadn't interrupted my reverie. I forced my

gaze back to him, knowing that he deserved an answer. That he needed some kind of closure if we were going to break this endless cycle. "Laurie, I—"

I do love you, I'd been about to say. But the words stayed inside, just like they always did. I tried to think of something else I could give him that was safe and which I hadn't already said before.

"'Cowards die many times before their deaths. The valiant never taste of death but once,'" Laurie said softly. "There's your rousing speech."

The word *coward* made me flinch. Laurie's tone was neutral, yet somehow, his remark felt barbed. I didn't snap back. I just gave him another weary smile and remarked, "What did I tell you about quoting things at me?"

Laurie's throat shifted, and fear fluttered in my own. Then he said, his tone light again, "Actually, you've never said anything besides observing that I've done it."

The tension between us eased, and it felt as if we'd backed away from the edge of something. I fought the urge to heave another sigh. To hide it, I hurried to fill the silence. "You asked what I'm doing tonight. Everyone is meeting at the loft for another strategy session. You're welcome to join us."

"That's why I'm here, actually," Laurie replied. "You weren't answering your phone, and I volunteered to fetch you."

My curiosity piqued. "Fetch me for what?"

"There was a delivery this morning. A gift left by the Queen of the Unseelie Court herself."

Laurie wouldn't say more, and I was suddenly eager to get home. He walked with me back to the car, and I blinked in surprise when Laurie got in with me. But I didn't comment on it, and I put the key in the ignition. Music floated around us as I started the drive back to Granby. Laurie and I talked the entire way. An easy, surprising conversation that only made me love him more.

When I pulled into the driveway, some of my family members were outside. Danny and Damon chased Matthew around the yard, and my nephew's face was wreathed in smiles. It was his favorite game, but I hadn't seen anyone play it in a long time. Not since Finn.

The second I saw them, I forgot all about Viessa's gift. The sound of laughter rang through the air at the same moment I pressed on the brakes. I put the car into park and sat there for a few seconds, just watching them. My mind churned.

"I've seen that look before," Laurie remarked.

In response, I took my phone out of the cup holder. I unlocked the screen and opened my contacts list, where I'd saved one phone number without a name. I pressed CALL and held the phone up to my ear, my heartbeat slow and steady.

The ringing cut off abruptly, but no one spoke on the other end. I pulled the phone away from my ear to check the screen, confirming the call hadn't ended. Then I pressed it close again and said, "Tell Samael that he has a deal."

I hung up without waiting for a reply.

Laurie's voice was low. "I hope you know what you're doing."

"I do." I kept my gaze on Matthew, and my heartbeat was steady with certainty. "For once, I know exactly what I'm doing."

By the time the sun reached the opposite horizon, my entire family sat around the dining room table.

The surface in front of us was littered with boxes of pizza, grease-smeared plates, beer cans, and glasses, along with all the latest reading material Viessa had supplied. Letters, manuscripts, records, anything and everything that mentioned interdimensional travel or the Dark Prince. Viessa's other gift gleamed in the corner of the loft. It was a suit of armor fit for a conqueror . . . or a nightmare. A brutal kind of beauty, wrought not for ceremony, but for survival. Dusk-colored steel shaped into plates that echoed bone and shadow. Every edge spoke of violence, every curve of intent. I didn't need to try it on to know it would fit me perfectly.

I left the Unseelie Queen a voicemail to thank her, but I hadn't touched my phone since to see if she'd replied. I'd been a little distracted trying to save the world. I'd started reading the second I finished the voicemail to Viessa. Within a couple hours, everyone else arrived to help. Damon and Danny. Savannah. Emma, Lyari, and Collith. Gil and Seth. Cyrus and Ariel. Even Nym was here. Stanley panted in front of the fireplace, which I'd turned on because Emma had seemed cold. The only one missing was Laurie, who left hours ago, probably to spend time with his friends and say his own goodbyes.

At some point we'd all realized how hungry we were, and that's when things sort of dissolved. None of us had touched a manuscript since we'd finished eating. Savannah still held Matthew in her lap, and she bounced her knee, prompting happy sounds and smiles from him. The sound of his soft babbling floated through the dim room as I stood and stretched. How long had it been since I'd drunk any water?

I pushed my chair back, and the sound jolted Seth awake, who'd dozed off with his head on his hands. He tried to subtly wipe the drool off his chin as I left the table and padded into the kitchen. I stopped in front of the refrigerator and looked over my shoulder, reacting to the sound of Gil's voice. He said something that made Emma cackle while Cyrus choked on the bite of pizza he'd just taken. Gil had probably told them the same dirty joke he'd shared with me last week—it was *bad*. I winced in sympathy and turned to get the water pitcher from the fridge. When I turned back around, Seth was trying to shove Gil off his chair.

As I watched them, I felt a swell of protectiveness. It filled my chest and created a hot, unbearable pain. If I didn't stop Lucifer tomorrow, he'd come for them. Maybe not next week, or next month, but he'd come. I *had* to close that Gate. None of the weapons or armies would matter, in the end, if I didn't figure out how my predecessors had done it.

"I'm not sure if anyone has ever told you, but frowning is terrible for the complexion," someone murmured in my ear.

I turned quickly, my heart stumbling like I'd walked over an uneven surface. Laurie leaned his shoulder against the fridge. His hair hung loose and slightly wavy, as if he'd gotten out of the shower and run his fingers through it while it was still damp. He wore a soft but expensive-looking sweater, which was casual for him.

"Hi," I said with soft surprise. I set the water pitcher down and moved closer to Laurie. "Two times in one day. It really must be the end of the world."

After he'd greeted me with a small, secret smile, the Seelie King's attention went over my head. He took in the room and nodded at someone. "You mentioned this morning that you were hosting a last-ditch effort at finding a miracle. I like miracles."

"Oh, yeah?" I smiled back at him and crossed my arms, angling my body to follow his gaze. Gil was trying to convince Lyari to eat a piece of pizza now. She looked at him with a dangerously speculative expression, as if Lyari was considering how much trouble she'd be in if she killed him. My lips twitched, and I glanced up at Laurie. "What was the last miracle you witnessed? I could use a little hope right now."

Laurie didn't answer straightaway, and after a few seconds, I half-forgot what I'd asked. Gil was making airplane sounds now and carrying the pizza toward Lyari's face. I thought about warning him that it was a good way to lose his fingers, but I wanted to see how this would play out.

"You," Laurie said.

I made an absent sound, still watching my family's antics. "Me what?"

"The last miracle I witnessed. It was you."

I turned to look at Laurie and discovered that our faces were closer than I'd expected. My heart did that strange little thing again, but I didn't pull away. My eyes flicked between his. "What do you mean?" I asked quietly.

His breath was the barest whisper of cool air as he told me, "It was the night you killed Jassin, just after you'd won your queenship. You bent down and picked up the crown, and put it on your head. Then you stood there and looked out at the entire Court . . . do you remember what you said?"

Of course I did. That was not a happy memory for me, but it was one I'd never forget for as long as I lived. My gaze fell from Laurie's while my body filled with the cold, hard certainty from that night. Even then, I'd known what I was capable of.

If you fuck with me and mine, I will return the favor tenfold.

"I looked at you and thought, *This creature is a goddamn miracle*. I fell in love right then and there," Laurie concluded. My eyes snapped back to him, widening, but now Laurie was the one gazing off into the distance. I watched his lips curve with an amused smile. "Or maybe it was earlier, when I first met you in Collith's chambers. You looked like you wanted to kill him with your bare hands, and you asked if he actually had a plan for getting your brother back. God, the way you can take someone down with a single look. I'd never seen anyone get under Collith's skin like that, besides me. You were magnificent. That hasn't changed, regardless of whatever else has."

Laurie's voice softened, but he still didn't meet my gaze. Maybe he was afraid to. I couldn't exactly blame him—every time we opened this door, I slammed it in his face.

But tonight was different. Tonight could be our last chance.

A shriek from the table made my head jerk away, and then a sound escaped me when I realized that Gil's sleeve had erupted into flame. The vampire put it out instantly, his hand a panicked blur. He shot an indignant glare at Cyrus, who calmly bit into his pizza and didn't say a word. But judging from the begrudging, grateful look Lyari shot the silent dragon, I could guess what had happened. Another smile tugged at my mouth. I relaxed again while Gil clutched his arm and snapped something about a lawsuit.

"It took me a little longer," I said abruptly.

My gaze was still on the others, but I sensed Laurie's surprise. Maybe it was in the way he went still, or the swiftness of how he turned when he realized what I was saying. I kept my attention on the figures around the table as I continued, "I knew I was falling that night outside the tomb. You kissed me and went inside, and it felt like you'd taken my heart with you. But it wasn't until Germany, when we were in those tunnels beneath the city . . . that's when I fell in love with you. You'd just been stabbed a dozen times, and I held you in my arms while we waited for a healer. I didn't think you'd survive. That's when *I* imagined a world without *you*, and it was . . . unbearable. Just unbearable. Then the healer came, and she fixed you. You opened your eyes and looked at me, and you said something stupid. I'd never felt relief like that, or such a rush of happiness. Yeah, that was it. That was the moment I knew. I was a fucking goner."

Smiling, I finally looked at Laurie again, and he looked back at me. His throat shifted as he swallowed. The light in his eyes was almost childlike, as though he'd been told something he desperately wanted to believe.

"And there it is," he said softly. "Hope."

Before I could reply, Laurie pushed off the fridge and walked toward the chaos, rolling up his sleeves as he went. "All right," he declared, "let's focus, people."

"Laurie, dear, back so soon?" Emma beamed and began to stand up from her chair. Laurie quickly sifted and reappeared in front of her, bending to accept the old woman's embrace.

I moved to join them, too, and we got back to work.

The next hour crawled by. The one after that was even worse. I only lifted my head to drink water and stretch my neck. The words and images in front of me began to blur, but I pressed on, even when a headache pulsed behind my eyes.

The sound of Matthew's familiar cries finally drew me out of my task. Collith must've left the loft at some point, because when I scanned the room for him, he was nowhere in sight. The bathroom door was open and the light inside was off. Damon and Danny were gone, too, and I knew they were probably in the bedroom with Matthew.

Laurie sat back with a sigh. "This is pointless. We're not going to find our salvation in some old book."

"I thought you believed in miracles," I mumbled, staring at the empty coffee mug in front of me. I tried to muster the will to stand and refill it.

"I said that so you wouldn't give up hope. As for me, one of us has to be a realist." Laurie rubbed his eyes with his thumb and middle finger. He got to his feet and reached for his phone, saying, "I need to check in with my people."

On his way to the door, I saw him take a bottle of wine from the counter.

"I better get back," Savannah said. "I have some spells going at my worktable. I put a protection charm on your armor, Fortuna, but the ones I put on your body will have to be done tomorrow."

"I'll keep the walkie-talkie on me," I said, nodding.

She nodded back and crossed the room. It was going to be a long night for her, too. Savannah and the Tongue planned to put spells on all the Guardians and their weapons. We needed every advantage we could get. If it were any other witch, she'd probably be drained of magic for days, weeks. But Savannah was part of the Unseelie Court now, just as I had my Shadows, and the burden was not on her shoulders alone. She still planned to help the healers tomorrow, during the chaos of battle.

After she'd donned her coat, Savannah gave us another wave and went down the stairwell. My gaze fell, noting the object she'd left behind on the floor. "Shit, she forgot her basket. I'll be right back."

Truth be told, I was grateful for the excuse to take a break. I knew the others probably needed one, too. They were so tired that no one even looked up as I grasped the handle of Savannah's basket and hurried downstairs.

She was still crossing the lawn when I ran outside. I called out her name, and Savannah paused. As I handed the basket over she said, "Thanks, Fortuna."

"See you tomorrow, Sav. Thank you for the protection charm."

Hearing the sincerity in my tone, she gave me a weary smile before continuing on toward the woods. I watched her go, thinking about how much had changed since she'd killed Fred. Once, I couldn't have imagined trusting Savannah Simonson, much less becoming friends. Now she was one of my biggest allies in this fight, and she might very well be the reason we all survived.

After another moment, I turned back to the loft. I'd taken a few steps toward the door when raised voices echoed through the stillness. I recognized them instantly. Were Collith and Laurie fighting? For a moment, I wondered if I should just stay out of it. Then I thought, *Fuck that*. I lowered my body and crept through the trees the way Lyari and Finn had taught me, choosing every step carefully, walking on tiptoe. I followed the rising and falling crescendo of Laurie's voice, which moved through the shadowed trees like dark velvet.

Within a minute, I spotted two silhouettes standing in a dim patch of moonlight. I drew even closer. I wanted to know what they were fighting about, and whether or not I should intervene. I moved forward to creep over a fallen pine and duck beneath a branch. A moment after that, Collith and Laurie were in full view.

The moment I laid eyes on them, I realized I shouldn't have gone through the trouble of being quiet. They were so absorbed in each other that neither of them heard me. I heard a ragged sound, a soft *whoosh* of air that could only be a sob. The moon must've come out from behind a cloud—it cast brightness over the faerie kings, making them look unreal, not of this world. Both achingly beautiful.

Collith was embracing Laurie, his face buried in the curve

between his head and shoulder. His voice was muffled but the breeze carried the fragmented words to me: "... a million times ... I wish I could ..."

A knot formed beneath my heart. My hand fell from the tree I'd been using for cover, and I moved back. Witnessing this moment between them felt wrong. It didn't belong to me. I turned to go back the way I'd come, and it took all my self-control not to run.

I had barely taken a step when Laurie appeared.

An overwhelming, inexplicable sense of panic raced through my body. I turned again, and suddenly Collith was there, that stubborn lock of dark hair stirring in the wind. His hazel eyes were cast in shadow, making them fathomless. Fae.

As he moved closer, my fight or flight instincts kicked in, and I felt my body tense. Collith saw it and stopped instantly. He didn't speak, and neither did Laurie. They watched me silently.

"What are you afraid of, Fortuna?" Collith asked. His voice was husky, as if we were in the middle of an intimate conversation, rather than the start of one.

Once, I would've had a snarky response for him. I would've told him I wasn't afraid of anything. But that would be a lie—it turned out, I had a lot of fears. The more I allowed Collith and Laurie in, the more I had to be afraid of.

I shook my head as though I could banish the feeling inside me ... but I knew there was only one way to be free of fear. Only one way to break free of the cage we'd put ourselves in.

So I looked at Collith and Laurie and asked them, "What if we don't survive this? Or even worse ... what if we do?"

The question was barely more than a whisper. For a moment, Collith and Laurie just looked at me. The trees around us were still, as if a hush had fallen upon them. It felt like I'd stripped myself naked, and now I was standing there with all my secrets spilled on the ground between us. While I waited for one of them to answer, I kept fighting the impulse to bolt.

After another moment, Collith dared to draw closer. He

reached up slowly, and his cool fingertips were a whisper against my skin as he cradled my cheek. His earthy, masculine scent reached me, comforting and alluring all at once.

"Dear heart," he murmured, "haven't we proven yet that you can't drive us away?"

My hand rose of its own volition, and I held it over Collith's. He knew. Of course he knew why I was so desperate to avoid this, avoid *them*. Every choice I made led us closer and closer to some sort of conclusion, an inevitable choice, and I was terrified of losing this.

Laurie's voice whispered through my head. *Cowards die many times before their deaths. The valiant never taste of death but once.*

Finally, I looked at them both and said, "Yes."

Laurie didn't move, but Collith did. His long fingers grasped my neck, and he pulled me against him. I tipped my head back, hungry for his kiss. Collith was hungry, too. Heat coiled in my belly when I finally tasted him again after so much time apart. I'd missed this, I thought faintly. I'd missed *him*. I reached up and buried my fingers in his hair while Collith's hands slid down my arms, gripping them above my elbows. Then he propelled me backward, never breaking our kiss. I felt my spine press against a wide, solid tree trunk at the same moment Collith got down on his knees. When he undid the button on my jeans and tugged them down, along with my underwear, every thought left my head. Collith's gaze met mine, and he blew across my already-damp sex, teasing. Tantalizing. I bit my lip as he left a trail of lingering kisses toward the apex of my thighs.

Just when I was on the verge of begging, Collith sealed his mouth to me. He used the very tip of his tongue, flicking my clit over and over until I was moaning and saying his name. I clutched at Collith's lush, dark hair as if I were sinking.

Then . . . he stopped. I opened my eyes and saw that Collith's mouth still hovered near my folds. I could feel the faint touch of his breath, but he'd pulled back. My core was throbbing and my heart was a wild thing in my chest. I followed Collith's gaze, breathless. When I turned my head, a soft quake of awareness went through me. Laurie's arm rested above my head, and his face was a whisper away from mine. We were almost in the exact same position we'd been in earlier, in the kitchen. Except this time, Laurie didn't walk away. His eyes gleamed. He was enjoying this, I thought in a daze. I wanted to wipe that smirk off his face.

I reached for him, and my fingers collided with his massive, hard cock. Laurie's expression intensified, and his gaze dropped to my lips.

"I want to watch you come," he whispered.

"As do I," Collith growled. I looked down again, and he gave me a crooked grin. In that instant, I saw a glimpse of the person he'd been before. The playful, wicked side that had been buried underneath so much pain and darkness.

Before I could utter a sound, Collith bent his head and fully claimed my clitoris, sucking on it mercilessly. I bit my lip to contain all the sounds I wanted to make, then turned to Laurie again. His mouth came down on mine. It was too much pleasure all at once. I climaxed within seconds, uttering a jagged cry. My hips jerked with such force that I felt Collith's teeth scrape against the smooth skin of my mound. Laurie held me while my legs trembled. He gently lowered me to the ground. Collith removed the rest of my clothes while Laurie undressed, too. His perfect, naked body gleamed in the moonlight as he moved to join us.

Once again, I gave myself over to both of them like it was our last night on Earth, because it probably was. They kissed me. They kissed each other. Then Laurie and I undressed Collith together. Once I'd had a chance to familiarize myself with every inch of him again, I pushed Collith onto his back, intending to give him the same pleasure he'd given me. He stroked the sides of my face gently, looking at me with tenderness as I moved away. That tenderness quickly turned to ecstasy when I drove my lips down to the very base of him. Collith let out a sound that sent another burst of heat through my core. I continued my administrations, torturing Collith by skimming my tongue along the crown of his cock. I was dimly aware of Laurie kneeling behind me. His fingers fanned out over my hips. Realizing what he wanted, I spread my legs slightly wider and arched my back. A moan escaped me as Laurie slowly pushed his long erection inside, inch by inch.

"Finally," he sighed. The reverence in his voice made my toes curl.

While I brought Collith to the brink with my mouth, Laurie plunged into my wet depths. He moved his hips with that sensual skill I hadn't stopped thinking about since the last night we'd spent together. My fingers dug in the mossy ground just as Collith's wild cry echoed through the night. I felt how the sound affected Laurie, and his rhythm quickened.

Afterward, when all of us were sweaty and spent, still breathing hard from our efforts, Collith's hard body pressed against me from behind. I tucked my arms around Laurie, who lay in front of me, his forehead resting on mine. The night around us was cold, but the small place we'd made was warm. Part of me wanted to stay here forever.

I could already feel myself returning to reality, though. We needed to go back to the loft in case there were any developments from our allies. There were more tomes I needed to skim, since I still hadn't figured out what the last symbol on Michael's message meant.

I reluctantly turned my head to say something to Collith. Before I could say a word, his tongue claimed mine again. His kiss was deep, rough, and thorough. Within seconds, I felt his cock harden against me.

"Collith," I breathed, "I think we should—"

"For once in your life, Fortuna, stop worrying about should or shouldn't," Laurie whispered, his fingers stealing between my legs.

And then I didn't think again for a long, long time.

CHAPTER TWENTY-ONE

Smoke coiled through the air like a faded white ribbon. It created a haze around the three of us, and the hidden pocket we'd created for ourselves in the trees. Collith, Laurie, and I were tangled up in each other as if we had become part of the forest ourselves. All of us were spent, even Laurie. He'd only moved enough to retrieve a box of cigarettes from his pants and light one. As an afterthought, he'd grabbed the bottle of wine, as well. Then Laurie had sunk back down, still naked, and none of us had stirred since. The bottle was nearly empty now.

"I wonder how many impromptu love confessions are happening right now. It might be awkward for them if we actually win," Laurie remarked.

"Good thing the odds of survival are low, then," I murmured, watching as he moved his cigarette in lazy, graceful flicks of his wrist. He was drawing shapes, I realized. Using the smoke above our heads like an artist would spread ink on paper. I watched the wispy clouds swirl and dissipate.

"What are your biggest regrets?" Laurie asked drowsily.

Collith sighed. "It's late, Laurelis."

Laurie made a slow, dismissive gesture. "There's no need for love confessions here, since we all know how we feel about each other. So let us confess things that are far more interesting."

A breath escaped me, my lips curved as I continued to stare upward. "What do you consider more interesting?"

"I told you," Laurie replied. "Regret. My life is so lovely, you see, that sometimes I like to hurt myself just to keep things interesting."

"You *are* a masochist. I *knew* it," I whispered.

Collith's shoulder shook against mine. "Fortuna, darling, are you drunk?"

"She shall face the devil with a hangover," Laurie said airily, putting his lips around the cigarette again. "That's how the French do it, as well, and we should all strive to be more like the French."

Collith's voice was dry. "I think perhaps you're a little drunk as well, Laurelis."

"What poppycock. I do not get drunk, Lord Sylvyre. Not anymore."

I raised my eyebrows up at the tree canopy. "Is this the part where you finally confess how old you are, Laur—"

My words cut short abruptly.

Collith's voice penetrated the haze of concentration around me. "Fortuna? Are you all right?"

I was frowning, my neck arched as I stared at the smoke above us. "Do that again," I ordered.

Laurie's brow lowered. "What—"

"The cigarette," I said urgently, staring at the column of smoke still rising from that burnt tip. "Make that shape again."

"Shape?" he echoed. Under normal circumstances, his baffled expression would've made me laugh.

I leaped up from the warm nest we'd made. Laurie said something else, and Collith's low murmur joined in, but they'd become background noise. When I didn't answer, Collith shifted in my peripheral vision, probably to follow me. I heard Laurie heave a sigh. "Fortuna, normally I adore the dramatics, but now is not—hey!"

I'd yanked my shirt out from beneath him, since Laurie had been lying on it. I ignored his protests and kept searching through our clothes, finding my pants next. I pulled them on with shaking hands, my breathing uneven. Collith and Laurie must've heard it, because they'd started dressing, too. They moved in synchronous, graceful blurs, as if they had done this a thousand times. By the time I started in the direction of the house, they were right behind me.

I hurried through the darkness and the trees, ducking beneath branches, picking my way over thick roots. Collith and Laurie walked on either side of me and matched my pace. I caught them exchanging confused glances, but I didn't offer an explanation. Not yet. I emerged from the woods and charged across the lawn, making a beeline for the barn door, which I pulled open so hard that it made a hard, echoing sound. I heard Collith behind me as I rushed up the stairwell.

The moment I reached the loft, it was clear that everyone was asleep. All the lights were dimmed, the air still. But Lyari woke instantly from where she'd been resting on the couch, her face coming into view as she sat up. Her expression was alert. "What's going on?" she asked.

"Oh, nothing, Fortuna is just having a wee breakdown," Laurie told her.

I hurried over to the table without speaking to either of them. The drawing was exactly where I'd left it a few hours ago. I stared down at it with fresh eyes, mentally kicking myself. The ink was smeared. The fucking ink was smeared! That was the only reason I hadn't recognized it. Something about watching the smoke dissipate had helped me see it. I was barely aware of Collith, Laurie, and Lyari gathering around me.

"It's . . ." I trailed off in disbelief, then lifted my head. Horror gripped my stomach like ragged fingernails.

"What is it? What's happening?" Lyari demanded, her eyes flashing with impatience.

"Yes, what *is* happening?" Laurie put in. I still didn't answer; I was thinking about Olorel and Michael again. Their final conversation replayed in my head for the thousandth time.

Your power will not be enough.

No, it will not.

Don't do this, Olorel.

Michael's reaction finally made sense. I remembered feeling his shock, his dread. Not only had the angel tried to show me how to close the Gate . . . he'd also given me a weapon.

I jabbed my finger against the symbol that had been infuriating us for so long. "These marks. I finally know what they mean."

"What? How?" Lyari's gaze dropped to the map, searching desperately for whatever I'd seen.

"It's like we're not even here," Laurie muttered to Collith.

I ignored him and tapped the mystery symbol again. My heart was beating so hard that I swore I could feel its unsteady rhythm through the rest of my body. "I've seen this more than once in the texts we're reading. It's a bloodline crest," I told them. "The *missing* bloodline, which the fae just assumed went into hiding or were hunted to extinction. But Michael was there, and he saw what really happened. Olorel sacrificed them all to move the Door. To hide it from Lucifer and stop him from sending more demons through. Somehow Olorel was bonded to them, just like Collith with the Unseelie Court, Laurie with the Seelie Court, and me with my Shadow Court. He used that bond to drain them of their power, their energy, everything they had . . . along with his own."

I leaned back, my gaze darting between them to see who would figure it out first. At last, Lyari's eyes brightened. She'd put the pieces together, too. Her excitement only heightened my own. Now my heart was beating so hard it was almost painful. It was so obvious. Michael had given me a blueprint *and* his memories, and it had still taken me this long to figure out.

I looked at Laurie. "Save that conversation about regrets for another night, because the odds just turned in our favor. We might actually pull this off. We might actually save the fucking world."

"If it works," Lyari reminded me, but her eyes were gleaming with excitement, too.

For the first time since we'd failed to save Thuridan, I felt it—hope. I was almost giddy with it. I glanced at the clock on the stove. "Come on. I don't want to wait until morning."

I whirled away and rushed over to the hooks on the wall. When I turned, Collith stood behind me. His expression was calm. "Where are we going?" he asked.

I smiled up at him, my mind flashing back to the beginning, when I had once asked him the same question. I remembered his answer. We had come full circle, somehow.

"The Unseelie Court," I said.

Six hours later, Olorel dawned.

While the sun was still rising, its soft light turning all of Granby pink as cotton candy, I went to Adam's shop to pick up my sword, which he'd kept overnight to sharpen. The vampires must've woken from the sound of Emma's brakes as I parked, because Adam came outside without a word, waited for me to get out, and then drove the car into the bay.

He started working on the brakes, and while I waited, I noticed Seth shuffling around in the office. I'd intended just to get the sword and return home, but then Seth emerged and pressed a warm mug into my hands. When I peeked inside the cup, I saw that he'd made coffee exactly the way I liked it—far too much cream, with just enough caffeine to do the job and wake me up. Giving in, I sat down on the couch and took my first warm, overly sweet sip. My eyes drifted shut.

"Damn." I sighed. "I'm going to miss this."

None of the boys answered. I opened my eyes to look at them, and when I saw their grim expressions, I realized that I'd finally said what no one had acknowledged until now. This could be our last cup of coffee. Our last morning. Our last time being together. There was nothing I could say that would comfort them. Nothing that wouldn't be a lie, at least. My gaze fell, and I cupped the warm mug between my palms, trying not to worry about what was about to happen. There would be plenty of time for that later.

I took another drink and savored it.

With a Denver morning show playing from the radio, the four of us hung out in the garage, just like we had so many times before. There was nothing special about it, yet everything was special. Them. This. I watched Gil tousle Seth's mop of brown hair, and a hint of a smile ghost Adam's lips as he listened to them talk about Formula One.

Eventually, when daylight poured through the windows and the stillness of morning was long past, I forced myself to leave the couch. There were others I needed to say my goodbyes to, and more preparations to make.

"See you tonight," I said simply, nodding at Gil and then at Adam. My old friend nodded back in his usual stoic way, his dark eyes unreadable as ever. I didn't feel the need to say anything else to him, because that had always been the beauty of Adam. He didn't want the words. He knew that I loved him, which was enough for both of us.

My gaze went to Seth next, and I gave him a small, soft smile. He wouldn't be at the battle, so there was a possibility this was the last time we'd ever see each other. In this lifetime, at least.

"Seth," I said with a soft, teasing smile, "I'm really glad you decided to stalk me. Life wouldn't be the same around here without you."

The goblin's eyes flickered, but he gave a composed nod back. The simple gesture made my heart ache—he knew I hated it when people bowed. "It has been an honor being part of your Court, my lady," Seth told me.

I turned away quickly, because I didn't want his last memory of me to be tainted by the pain in my eyes.

After that, I stopped by the bar and had breakfast with Bea and Gretchen. I'd already warned them about what was coming. Despite the countless horrors and lives that had been already lost because of Lucifer, his war had brought one single, good thing into my life—Bea's forgiveness. Once we'd said our goodbyes, I chatted with some of our regulars, humans in Granby that I genuinely liked. Many of them had been kind to me over the years, in spite of my oddities. With yet another cup of coffee in my hand, I eventually left Bea's, too. I got back in the car and drove home.

It was all the same, and yet it wasn't. Usually people didn't know when it was the last time they did something. Yes, the knowing made it sweeter, I decided. I listened to the same music I always did, and I drove on the same road I always took home, knowing every bump and crack along the way. As the sun brightened, my eyes went to the rearview mirror, where the hilt of my sword glinted in the backseat. Then I deliberately looked away and focused on the horizon, my grip tightening on the steering wheel.

The knowing made it sweeter, and it was a reminder of how much I had to protect. In nine hours, everything could end. As long as I was leaving this world exactly as it was, every sacrifice would be worth it. In nine hours, I'd go to meet the devil and his army. I still didn't know how to close the Gate or whether I could stop Lucifer, but I did know one thing—I wasn't alone anymore.

As if the universe was sending me its silent agreement, a crow alighted across the road. Its small black shape cast a fleeting shadow, and I watched it soar into the blue beyond as if to say, *I'm ready. Let's go.*

And so we went.

CHAPTER TWENTY-TWO

Snow swirled across the battlefield.

The open space loomed far ahead, on the other side of the army that had gathered for Fallen and humans alike. They'd parted like the Red Sea when we arrived, and hundreds of heads swiveled as we passed. The final dregs of sunlight poured over the horizon and shone on their still faces. I couldn't decide if they were staring because everyone thought we were doomed, or because of the picture we made.

We did look pretty impressive, in my opinion.

Earlier tonight, Ariel had braided my hair back in several pieces that rested against my scalp. So it would be harder for someone to grab in the battle, she'd explained. I also wore the dark armor Viessa had sent over, which would make it even harder to fuck with me. It was lighter than it looked, and I'd already half-forgotten about it. The black plates made the slightest sound when they shifted with my movements, like whispers.

The final piece of my ensemble was the sword Gwyn's blacksmith had forged. It was secured to my saddle at the moment, and there was a sheath on my back for later. Those ornate etchings caught the light with every step.

But I knew it wasn't my face, my armor, or my sword that had everyone so spellbound.

No one had ridden a kelpie in thousands of years.

Sarod's enormous body rippled beneath mine, and he held his head high as we passed the throngs of wererats and fae, displaying the fins on either side of his skull. So far, we hadn't exchanged a single word since we'd found each other. I got the sense it was a kindness on Sarod's part, since he knew how much his voice hurt me. He was bigger than any horse I'd ever seen. Certainly bigger than he'd looked in the water. His coat was pure midnight black, and every so often, his scales caught the light in shimmers of purple and green. As we passed the rows of fighters, Sarod's white eyes roved over their faces, and he let out a deep sound that sent the closest figures skittering back. I gritted my teeth and held the reins tighter, as though that would make a difference if my mount did decide to help himself to a snack.

Luckily, the crowds kept a wary distance from us.

We continued riding toward the front—Collith, me, Viessa, and Nuvian. I craned my neck to search the crowd, looking for anyone familiar. There had been no sign of Lyari or Nym at the house and I'd assumed I would find them here. Cyrus and the others had left slightly earlier than me, but I didn't see them, either. My scan ended on the faerie riding beside the Unseelie Queen. He must've felt my gaze, because Nuvian glanced over at me with an ill-disguised expression of contempt. Unable to resist, I blew a kiss at him.

"Fortuna, stop torturing my brother," Viessa ordered.

Nuvian was openly glaring now. His expression made me think of Damon when we were kids, during one of the long road trips I'd teased him relentlessly in the backseat. My lips quirked, and I forced myself to look away. "But it's so much fun."

Viessa didn't respond. Tonight, she was the Ice Queen. Frost had spread over half her face, and her eyes shone such a bright, unnatural blue they almost looked white. Shards of ice grew from her shoulders like spiked armor. She'd left her fingers bare, exposing the black tips where she gripped her horse's reins. Her armor was similar to mine, and her horse—a dappled gray—must've been protected by a spell, because it didn't seem to mind the layer of frost that had spread over most of its hide. Its frozen mane clinked like eerie wind chimes with every step.

Halfway to the front, the sound of a neigh sliced through the air, and everyone turned in unison. The army had parted again, and a faerie rode toward us, sitting atop a gigantic white horse.

It took me a beat to comprehend that I was looking at King Laurelis of the Seelie Court.

He had never looked more like a fallen angel . . . or a faerie. He wore intricate, gleaming armor that rivaled even his moonlight hair. As Laurie drew nearer, I noticed there were delicate carvings along the edges of the breastplate, twining flowers and coiled vines that made me think of spring. A silver circlet rested upon the king's brow.

Laurie knew he had the attention of the entire field, of course, and he held it like he held his Court. Confidently. Dramatically. And maybe just a little arrogantly, too. Once he reached us, taking the spot on Collith's other side, Laurie drew back on the reins. A gust of wind stirred his hair.

"Sorry I'm late," he said.

I resisted the urge to roll my eyes, and I could tell Collith was fighting the same instinct. We all knew Laurie had planned his entrance down to the second. "Oh, are you? Are you really?" I drawled.

Nuvian muttered something under his breath.

As our small party continued toward that empty battlefield, the Seelie King's bright eyes moved down my body. He took in the hair, the armor, and ended with the beast I rode. Laurie's eyebrows rose with approval, and then he gave a slow shake of his head. "Fortuna Sworn . . . my work here is finished."

A smile tugged at my lips as I realized that was how we'd

started, Laurie and I—with the clothes, the looks, the messages I sent with an outfit or a streak of makeup. He'd taught me the value of such things, along with the knowledge that even a dress could be used as a strategy. I had also learned the benefit of restraint when the time came for it.

I was about to reply to Laurie when an unearthly scream tore through the night. The sound made me picture a creature with long teeth and flesh-tearing claws, and my smile died instantly. I turned my face back toward the horizon, wondering if I'd see whatever had made that noise against the fading sky.

"If you die, I'm taking your sword," Laurie said without looking at me. His tone was grim.

"I'd miss you, too," I said distractedly.

I didn't look at him, either, because we'd reached the front.

Despite my relentless training, in spite of my constant warnings to the others, I wasn't prepared for the sight before me. I searched the army Lucifer had amassed, feeling the slow rise of disbelief. It was so much worse than I'd imagined. There were so *many*. The devil's army writhed like a sea of wings and teeth, and the necrool soared above them, huge, winged carnivores that I had once watched from Lucifer's tower.

He'd kept so much from me during my time in Hell, I thought as I scanned the creatures that looked like they had crawled straight out of a nightmare. Every one of them probably had a different ability or power.

And those things weren't the only deadly opponents we'd face. Amongst the demons were Fallen, too. Witches, goblins, werewolves, shapeshifters. Creatures from my world that had pledged their lives to the Dark Prince and his cause. As far as I was concerned, they were traitors. I'd take no pleasure in their deaths, but I wouldn't feel bad about them, either.

I strove to sound like Laurie as I added, "If I do die, please donate all my organs to those in need. Except for my middle finger—give that to Lucifer."

My companions were silent, and the moment I finished speaking, I went quiet, too. Every single creature in the Flint Hills stared upward.

The Wild Hunt had arrived.

They came from the skies, just as they had when I'd been the quarry of this ancient, powerful force. The sounds the horses made were not the sounds of normal beasts. Goosebumps rose along my arms as ghostly screams echoed through the cold gloaming, but my prickle of fear was nothing compared to the relief I felt. I fought to keep a hard mask in place.

Gwyn had kept her promise. She'd shown up.

Although I couldn't sense any fear coming from across the field, I noticed many of those distant figures watching Gwyn warily while others shifted in agitation. Nervous chitters and shrieks echoed through the cold, and when I heard that, a flare of triumph lit up the gloom clinging to my thoughts. The Wild Hunt was infamous and feared. Gwyn's reputation might've held less sway in Hell, but to the Fallenkind fighting for Lucifer, this would be a terrifying development.

The huntress seemed completely unaware of the massive horde behind her. Without sparing them a single glance, she swung her leg over her dark steed and dropped to the ground, her boots landing with such force that a cloud of snow billowed up from the half-frozen soil. Laurie had made it a point to draw attention to himself, and I knew this was another show of power. I decided to make one of my own and nudged Sarod forward, going to meet the huntress. As she stalked toward us, the muscles in her thighs rippled with every step. Her hunters remained where they were, watching silently.

It was the first time I'd seen Gwyn in armor, but unlike Laurie's, her suit was simple and unadorned. She'd braided her hair similarly to mine, probably for the same reason, and the result was beautifully ferocious. A black line was smeared across her eyes.

The makeup was a stark contrast compared to my plain features—I hadn't painted my face today.

Today, I wasn't hiding.

Once we were within a few yards of each other, Gwyn stopped. I swung my leg over Sarod, dropped to the ground, and closed the distance between us.

"Glad you could make it," I said. I expected the faerie to make a sardonic comment or maybe offer a sensual greeting, based on our previous encounters, but Gwyn was silent. She finally turned in the direction of that menacing dark swarm and gave the devil's followers a long, hard look. A moment later, small bits of yellow appeared, leading all the way to the unsettled horde.

Flowers had sprouted up through the snow. I studied the ones around my boots, recognizing them instantly. Wood anemones.

Gwyn hadn't uttered a word, yet her message was loud and clear.

She was on the hunt.

Probably her last, I thought grimly, scanning the writhing mass of demons for the tenth time. It struck me, again, that people were going to die today. A lot of them. Maybe ones that I loved.

And I was about to lead the charge.

"Perhaps you should say something," Gwyn said.

Her tone penetrated the thick fog of dread that had started to gather around me. I tore my gaze away from the horde and met Gwyn's cool, ancient eyes, willing my heartbeat to slow down. Worried that others could hear it, I glanced toward the army to gauge their expressions.

With a startled jolt, I realized *everyone* was looking at us. The rats, the wolves, the fae, the nymphs. They stretched out in either direction, as far as the eye could see, and every single face was turned to me.

That was when Gwyn's words finally sank in: *Perhaps you should say something*.

A speech? But . . . I hadn't prepared anything. I swallowed a curse, mentally kicking myself for not expecting this. Why hadn't

I expected this? Oh, right. Maybe it was because I'd never led an army into a medieval battle before.

More panic rose from the pit of my stomach and crept through my veins. But the leader of the Wild Hunt was still waiting for a response, and she could probably tell I was scared shitless. Schooling my features, I nodded at her and said, "I'll remember this, Gwyn."

I didn't thank her, because she was a faerie, after all. A faint, knowing smile touched the huntress's lips, and I braced myself for her to say something ominous or taunting.

"As will I," Gwyn said. Then she added, "Thank you, Fortuna Sworn. You've been the most interesting thing to happen in this world for the better part of a century. For that alone, I am glad to fight by your side tonight."

She bent into a deep bow, and I found myself staring at her again, shocked by the gesture. When she straightened, I didn't know what to say other than, "I'm glad, too. Good luck, Gwyn. I . . . I hope we see each other on the other side of this."

Feeling her eyes on me, I returned to Sarod and climbed into the saddle a tad less gracefully than I would've liked. My face felt hot as I turned him back in the direction of our waiting forces. This time, I focused on Collith and Laurie. The sight of their familiar faces steadied me. Once I was close enough to call out to them, I drew on Sarod's reins again.

My stomach fluttered with nerves again. I took a slow, soundless breath and then raised my chin, silently defying the fear. Defying *him*. I kept my back to the nightmare across that field and fixed my complete focus on the people who had shown up to fight for us. They were all that mattered. I spotted Gil and Adam with the vampires. There was Zara, standing with a cluster of other healers, evident from the bags they all carried. I also found Narfu, and Nan, and so many more whose paths had crossed mine during the wild, winding journey to this battlefield.

Just as I opened my mouth to speak, there was another flurry of movement on the horizon. I raised my gaze, and when I realized what I was looking at, an awed breath caught in my throat.

Cyrus and Tabitha were here.

Two dragons approached from the east. There was hardly any light left, but the faintest glow shone through their wings as the enormous beasts descended. Horses made sounds of alarm or unease, shifting restlessly. Agitated breaths shot from their nostrils, and it was cold enough now that I could see them.

Luckily, Sarod was calm and still beneath me. His long face turned toward the new arrivals, and he hardly reacted when they landed just a few yards away from us. Tremors rumbled through the hill from the force of the beasts' landing. Clumps of earth went flying. Now the horses screamed in terror, and their riders shouted, grasping wildly at the reins. I didn't blame them.

I'd seen Cyrus in his true form before, but the sight still struck me with awe. His body was serpentine and scaled, ending with a deadly looking tail that flicked against the grass. The other soldiers must've felt the same, because they had given my friend a wide berth, and they scattered even farther every time he moved. Frills and spikes rippled around Cyrus's head as he stretched to his full height.

He was beautiful, I thought as I tipped my head back . . . and back. The dragon met my gaze calmly, his black eyes somehow older and wiser than they were in his other form. Unlike Tabitha, whose coloring was just as dark as I remembered, like a starless sky or a windowless room . . . Cyrus's scales were a deep scarlet. Like flames, and sunsets, and blood. His feet ended in sharp, curved claws that could cut through a man's torso like butter.

I gave Cyrus a nod of acknowledgment before my focus moved over the rest of our forces. I was still facing them. The sun had fallen, taking its warmth with it. Its absence left the Flint Hills in shades of black and gray.

Once again, I opened my mouth to speak. From the corner of

my eye, I saw one of the witches make a gesture, and whatever she did made my words echo over the hills.

"Our ancestors were called guardian angels," I called, my heart loud in my ears. "Today we are all Guardians, and we are all that stands between this world we've made our home and the ones who seek to destroy it. Everyone believes they have the right to a future. The right to peace. The right to life and happiness. We don't. We have a right to nothing except for the things we carve out for ourselves. So let's do some fucking *carving*!"

I raised my sword in the air, my voice echoing over the massive crowd. They began shouting something, over and over. My Enochian was good, but I didn't recognize this phrase. I frowned and looked over at Gwyn, who had returned to her horse and ridden across the field, stopping at my side. The rest of the Hunt streamed past us.

"What are they saying?" I asked.

"They're calling you the Queen of Shadows," the huntress replied, her tone amused. But her dark eyes were intent on me as the chant grew louder, spreading through the hills like thunder.

Something about that look reminded me what Gwyn was... and what she was capable of. I looked back at her in a way that would remind her of what I was, too.

Before either of us could say anything else, a new sound moved across the battlefield. I turned swiftly, reaching for my sword as my eyes roamed the length of Lucifer's army again. The sound happened again, and this time I recognized it—drums. Somewhere in that swarm, there were creatures playing drums. But they were nothing like what I'd heard in my world. This was slow, like a beating heart. I felt my own sink with realization. *No.*

It couldn't start right now! We were still waiting for some of our people.

I pressed my heels into Sarod's sides, and he must've felt my urgency, because he turned and broke into a gallop. The moment

I returned to my place at the front, I twisted around to search the sea of faces behind us again.

"What's wrong?" Collith asked quietly. Laurie stood on his other side.

I hid my frown, since I didn't want the army to see it, but I felt a small crinkle between my brows. "She's not here yet."

"Fortuna."

The sound of Laurie's voice made me turn. He was looking at something behind me. My head whipped round, and in an instant, the knot I hadn't even known was in my chest immediately began to loosen.

Lyari Paynore made her way through the crowd. She was on foot, both of her hands wrapped around a banner. The dark material flapped in the wind, and then it unfurled, allowing me to catch a glimpse of the shape sewn there.

It was a black rose.

Lyari reached us a few moments later. "Your Majesty," she said, inclining her head.

It felt like my heart was in my throat. "Lady Knight," I said back, because it felt right.

Her shoulders straightened, and she held her head a little higher. "I apologize for my tardiness. It didn't seem right that we should ride into battle without a banner."

"I agree. It doesn't seem right." I looked at the demonic army again. Lyari's arrival wouldn't save us, and we were probably still heading for certain death, but I felt stronger all the same. My voice was firm and clear as I said, "Thank you, Lyari."

And then Lucifer appeared.

He strode through the tangle of monsters, tall and shining in the dark. He wore white armor. The plates looked thin, delicate, every edge lined with gleaming gold. His hair had been cropped short, and the silken strands stirred in the wind, blowing past his blue eyes. The sword at his hip was long, black, and wicked. It was the biggest piece of demon glass I'd ever seen.

But I looked past the sword as if it were nothing, my gaze searching the swarm of demons again. Another whisper of unease went through my mind, like a cold exhale.

Where was Oliver?

Lucifer reached the front of his army and kept walking, clearly heading in this direction. My throat went dry as I realized he was coming to meet me.

It was time.

I hadn't expected to be this afraid. I hadn't been ready for the reality of seeing all these people, who were only here because I'd asked them to be. How many of them would die because I'd let the devil out of his cage?

"Hey," a familiar voice said softly. I looked over at Collith, my eyes wide and horrified. His expression was encouraging, one corner of his mouth tilted up, as if he'd just told me a secret.

He didn't say anything else, because there were no magic words that would ease the grim reality of what was about to happen. The army behind me may have responded to my rousing speech, but I could feel their fear in the air and taste a thousand flavors on my tongue.

No, it was in the way Collith looked at me that I found comfort. Steady, no trace of doubt, and maybe with a hint of that fae wildness he usually kept contained. Collith wasn't afraid.

Just as I had with Laurie, I thought of how we'd begun. The Collith I'd known was ruled by his fear. But now . . .

He had become the king he'd once longed to be.

Laurie rode to my other side. When our eyes met, his lips curled in a faint, challenging smile. I'd been considering whether I should tell them to stay put, but when I saw that smile, I swallowed a sigh and signaled to Sarod to move forward. Laurie wanted me to compromise? Fine, I could compromise.

Once we were close enough to make out the color of the devil's eyes, I stopped. I turned to Collith, then cast a hard look at Laurie over my shoulder to include him.

"Wait here," I said. It wasn't a request. Before either one of them could respond, I added, "You're close enough to help me if anything happens. But bringing you both would only add gasoline to the fire, and you know it."

Lines of tension deepened around Laurie's mouth. "The entire world is about to burn, Fortuna. I don't think a little gasoline is going to make much difference," he answered tightly.

"We'll be here," Collith put in. He nodded at me once, his gaze holding mine. But I knew I wouldn't be able to dissuade Laurie for long. Without another word, I dismounted from Sarod and left them behind. I lifted my gaze reluctantly to the King of the Underworld.

Gusts of wind scraped at my cheeks as we walked toward each other. Lucifer's expression was unreadable. His golden skin almost seemed to glow in the faint moonlight streaming through the wisps of clouds above. Closing the distance between us felt like a blink and a small eternity, all at once. Once we were so close that we could touch, Lucifer and I halted. The wind continued to push at me, making a hollow sound as it rushed past.

I was the first to speak. "The tradition is to wave a white flag, not wear white armor, but you're new here. I'll let it slide."

Lucifer didn't smile, or show any sign of irritation, which was what I'd really been hoping for. The angrier he became, the sloppier he'd get. I had seen the devil's temper, and I was one of the few who could get under his skin. I intended to utilize every weapon we had during this battle.

But Lucifer wasn't biting tonight.

"Last chance," he said. "Join us. Why die defending their world? Our true enemy created them, this place. He deserves to feel the pain we did when he cast us from our home."

For a moment, I just looked at him. Lucifer was still as beautiful as the first time I'd seen him in that mirror. Still a flawless, otherworldly thing that promised seduction and power. But now I felt nothing. Not temptation, or love, or even pity. My voice was hard with certainty as I said, "Because this is our world, too. And we *are* home."

Sorrow made the corners of Lucifer's mouth tighten. "So be it," he said.

We looked at each other for another beat, snowflakes and dark promises filling the air between us. His face had changed, somehow—he'd put away any part of himself that might actually care for me. Now only the devil looked back, and the devil did not love.

He just destroyed.

I was the one to turn away first. I felt Lucifer's eyes linger on me while I retraced my steps through the grass, my armor clinking softly. Moments later, I reached the point where I'd left Collith and Laurie. Collith had gotten off his horse, and both of them were staring toward that distant figure, who hadn't moved, I noted when I glanced over my shoulder. I put my back to him again and focused completely on the two males in front of me.

"Come on," I said quietly, inclining my head. "We'll deal with him when the time comes."

There was another beat of frozen, swollen tension, and then Collith finally shifted. We both got back on our horses. Laurie, however, kept looking toward the Dark Prince. A strange, small smile hovered at the corners of his mouth. As I watched him, a sense of foreboding gripped me, even stronger than the dread I'd already been feeling.

"Laurie," I said, more sharply this time.

He kept his focus on Lucifer for another beat, and then Laurie turned. He mounted his stallion and began walking back toward our forces, so Collith and I did the same. My gaze lingered on Laurie's profile, and I couldn't contain another flood of terror. Laurie was too brave, too defiant for his own good. As we rode away from the immortal he'd just taunted, his mother's words whispered through me. *He has a weakness, and I fear that it will lead to his ruin—his heart.*

We were nearing the army, and I knew it was important they didn't see any hint of fear in my expression. So I buried it deep inside me, just as Olorel had once hidden a magic Door—the Door that started all this. My jaw hardened at the thought. Tonight, I would fix Persephone's mistake, and I'd do it before it cost the lives of anyone I loved. I didn't allow myself to look at the males riding on either side of me as we rejoined our other companions at the front.

Sarod turned without any prompting and placed himself at the center. In an instant, I realized why everyone had gone silent, their gazes fixed in the same direction.

Something was happening across the field. The crowd was . . . shifting.

Dread gripped my stomach like ragged fingernails. A moment later, three figures emerged from an opening that appeared in the front line. Two of them were demons, some species with round horns that curved beneath their square jaws, fangs poking at their bottom lips.

The third figure was Thuridan.

The area around them was lit by torches, held aloft by more hideous-faced things that could've only been born in the dark. It allowed us to see clearly as the creatures holding Thuridan forced him to his knees. Even from a distance, it looked painful.

My hands clenched into fists around the reins, my muscles locking into place as I fought the urge to charge across the field. I searched the ground near Lucifer as if I could see the spell preventing me from doing exactly that. There was no sign of it, of course. Savannah had said there would probably be no way to discern the exact moment the barrier fell. The only thing we knew for certain was that it would remain in place until the Gate opened.

My thoughts were cut short when Lucifer shifted and an object glinted in his hand. I peered closer, concentrating so hard that I hardly noticed what his demons were doing. My heart quickened when I realized the object was a knife, and it looked identical to the one that had been next to the pool in Lucifer's tower. It was also similar to the knife I'd used down in the cells, where Lucifer tortured demons and souls alike. I'd been oblivious then, but now I understood what that black blade meant. Demon glass.

More demon glass.

Those fingers in my gut went deeper, sending a burst of torment through me. I knew what would happen next.

So did Lyari.

Without taking her eyes off Thuridan, she nudged her mount forward. Its hooves made dull sounds against the earth. Stiff with worry, I was about to go after her when Lyari pulled on the reins again and halted. She'd only gone a few steps—just far enough to put her back to us, and give Thuridan a chance to see her.

Don't look, Ly, I wanted to say. But I understood why she had to. If it had been Collith or Laurie across that field, I would've stayed, too.

Across the field, Thuridan stared back at Lyari. He didn't look away, even when a stooped old woman appeared. She seemed to be giving orders to someone. A moment later, two more demons came out of the crowd. They held something dark and bulky between them. When I figured out what they were carrying, my stomach lurched, threatening to upend everything I'd eaten earlier.

It was a cauldron.

Lucifer moved to stand behind Thuridan and placed the knife against his throat. Firelight flickered over the scene like a chilling painting. The demons, the fallen angel, the knife. I stood there, frozen, desperately trying to think of a way to stop this. Lucifer's lion eyes caught the light as he found me again. I felt a muscle in my cheek tic, but it was the only outward sign of my hatred and helpless rage. I knew that Lucifer would get off on any reaction, so I refused to give him one. I was done being his plaything.

The devil didn't look away from me as he drew his arm back.

He could've made the kill quick—he certainly had the speed and strength. Instead, Lucifer did it slowly. Drawing out Thuridan's suffering as the knife sliced over his throat. The horde roared and stomped its approval. They were so loud that I couldn't hear the sound Thuridan made as he died. But I saw the agony in his expression and the terror in his eyes.

When it was over, he just knelt there for a moment, that terrible dark gash across his neck staring at us like an eerie second smile. It didn't heal, just as we'd known it wouldn't—it only bled. The demons holding Thuridan tipped him forward so his wound spilled into the cauldron. Lucifer turned away to hand the knife to one of his followers, every movement infuriatingly casual, as though he were just walking around his study.

Then Thuridan toppled forward, released by his captors at last. His face smashed into the dirt, and the indignity of it made my stomach roll. We all waited, hopeful even now that he might recover, but Thuridan didn't move again. Moments later, a dark pool began to form beneath him.

A faint, strangled sound came from Lyari. I tore my gaze away from the sight of Thuridan's body and looked at her. She kept her face forward, but her throat worked. I could see the gleam of tears streaming down her gaunt cheeks.

Even though I still wasn't someone who touched another person easily, and even though Lyari wasn't someone who accepted comfort when it was offered, I urged Sarod forward. Once I was close enough, I reached out and put my hand on Lyari's arm. The faerie's face turned to mine. Wisps of hair blew in my eyes as I held her gaze and nodded, my nostrils flaring. Pain sang between us—pain and resolve.

We were warriors, and we would make him pay for what he'd done to us.

The snowflakes coming down were bigger now. I knew it wasn't my imagination that there were more, too. This was magic. I looked up, intending just to glance toward the clouds. What I saw made my entire body turn to ice.

The Gate was opening. It was visible now, just a tiny line of light far above where Lucifer stood, like a paper cut in the sky. It was getting wider by the second. Wind attacked us with a ferocity that burned my skin.

"'Something wicked this way comes,'" Laurie murmured.

"*Macbeth*? Really? At a time like this?" Collith said under his breath.

I lowered my gaze and scanned the ridge above Lucifer's side of the field. Still no sign of Savannah. What if something had gone wrong? What if we could no longer depend on her? Without the numbers she'd promised me, our chances of survival were significantly lower, and everything would depend on whether we reached the Gate. Another burst of anxiety seared through my veins.

Laurie's voice was as grim as I felt. He held his sword at the ready, staring at the legion across from us. "It's been a privilege torturing you both. Pity it must come to an end."

"Nothing ends, Laurelis Dondarte." I gave him a sad smile. "There are only continuations and beginnings."

Before he could answer, a blinding flash streaked over our heads—lightning. Then there were several more, all at once, erupting from the Gate that suddenly wasn't so small anymore. My braids blew back. In a matter of seconds, the opening became a vast hole, so huge that I could see something on the other side now. It felt like there was something burrowing into my stomach, tearing through all the layers of flesh as if my insides were soil.

"That thing has to be a half mile in diameter, at least," one of the soldiers behind us muttered.

Everyone stared up the crackling, gaping maw in the sky. There was only darkness within it, but somehow that blackness seemed deeper than the darkness of my world. More . . . absolute. As if it was a place where light simply didn't exist.

It was Hell, I realized with a burst of horror. We were looking at Hell. Lucifer had really done it.

My heart was pounding so hard that it affected my ability to breathe. I waited for a nightmare to come screaming out of that tear between worlds, but ... nothing happened. When several seconds passed and the Gate still remained empty, mad, wild hope streaked through me. Magic was unpredictable, even for someone like Lucifer. He couldn't have determined *where* the Gate would open on the other side, right? Maybe it had appeared deep in a cavern, just like the Unseelie Court. Maybe the creatures of Hell would never find it.

Indecision gnawed at me; I didn't know what to do. The Gate was open, which meant the spell barrier was down. Should we just keep waiting, or strike now while Lucifer didn't have the additional forces of Hell behind him?

I'd just started to glance at Collith when someone cried out, "What was that?"

Fear lodged in my throat, and I looked toward the Gate again. I still didn't see anything. But the creatures around me all stared upward as though they did. So I kept watching, too. Seconds passed, and I counted them, trying to control my heartbeat. *One. Two. Three. Four.*

At last, something emerged from the darkness.

It was too far away for us to hear the sounds of its wings, but in that moment, the battlefield was so still that I swore I could. When I finally got a good look at what the underworld had spit out, I held back a shudder. It was the strangest, eeriest thing I'd ever seen.

"A seraph," I heard someone behind me breathe.

I'd thought the seraphim were nothing more than ancient legend. A frightening story Fallen parents told their young, as humans did with their children about the Tooth Fairy or Santa Claus.

Apparently they were very real, and all this time, they'd just been in another world.

This one seemed to be alone. As the seraph flew over Lucifer's army, coming in our direction, I counted its wings—there were six. Two covered its face. Two covered what I assumed to be its feet. And the last two it used to fly, carrying a majority of its body weight while the others seemed to be more for navigation and support.

My thoughts had gone clinical, I noted dimly. That helped, sometimes, in moments of terror. But I could feel it edging closer, threatening to break through the careful wall of numbness I'd built.

Cool fingers slid beneath my chin. I was so detached from reality that I didn't jerk away when Collith tilted my head back. I focused on him, blinking. He'd moved his horse so close that its side nearly brushed Sarod. The wind rustled Collith's dark hair, and a tousled lock fell over one of his eyes, just as it always did.

For once, I didn't resist the urge to push it back. As I ran my fingers through the hair near Collith's temple, securing that wayward lock in place, my numbness and fear evaporated. A quiet, steady calm filled me, and the roiling sensation in my stomach went still. I let out a breath, shoulders slumping. I gave Collith a small, faint smile. "Thanks," I murmured.

When I began to pull away, Collith caught hold of my wrist. I raised my eyebrows in a wordless question. He stared at me intensely.

Then, for all the armies and kingdoms to see, he leaned over and kissed me.

I closed my eyes and kissed Collith back, softly startled when everything around us faded. Not because the world had gone silent, but because I'd stopped hearing it. I raised my hand and cupped Collith's cheek, breathing in his scent one last time. Savoring his taste and his quiet skin against mine. My entire body sang with love.

A fearsome roar echoed across the hill.

I jerked away from Collith, my heart lurching at that sound.

I spotted the dark figure instantly, a golden-haired silhouette standing out starkly against the gloom. Lucifer had risen into the air, his immense wings spread. I hadn't known he had wings; he must've kept them glamoured. They were white and immense, and any other day, I would've been fascinated . . . but right now it was the devil's face that held my attention. He stared at us with bright, fury-filled eyes. I gazed up at him and knew what would happen if Lucifer got his hands on me.

Collith knew it, too. Lightning erupted around his entire body and crackled from his hands. His eyes shone with a bright, unnatural light and strands of his hair lifted.

As if this was the unspoken signal everyone had been waiting for, all the other fighters prepared for battle, as well. Up and down the front, swords slid from scabbards and glinted as they were held aloft. Expressions hardened into resolution. We collectively tensed, every face turned toward the sky.

But Lucifer didn't fly at us or gesture to his army. The devil just stayed where he was, his wings flapping steadily, despite the ever-increasing wind. What was he waiting for? My hand tightened on my sword, and I started counting again, forcing myself to take a breath with every second. *One. Two. Three.*

This time, I didn't have a chance to reach four. Hundreds of demons came screaming out of the Gate behind Lucifer.

And then the world shattered.

CHAPTER TWENTY-THREE

Winged creatures took flight and soldiers burst into movement, charging forward at terrifying speeds. I screamed and squeezed Sarod's sides. Everyone around us did the same, and the din filled my ears as Tabitha and Cyrus soared overhead, already lighting up the field with their fire. Distant screams reached across the distance between us and the never-ending horde as they burned alive.

Lucifer's words slithered through my mind—a memory. *There's something so purifying about fire.*

My lips pursed with vicious satisfaction. I hoped, wherever he was, the devil was remembering those words, too.

The two armies collided.

I'd never known such pandemonium. The dying began instantly, on both sides, and if I hadn't been so consumed with trying to survive, I would've agonized over who I might've already lost. Pain-filled shouts and terrified screams battered against my ears while I struggled to stay in the saddle, swinging my glinting sword at the tidal wave of demons. Sarod sifted again and again, and every time we reappeared, the two of us worked in tandem. We were practically untouchable.

The sight of these creatures up close was horrifying. Laurie fought a pale-skinned, humanoid thing with no eyes and multiple rows of teeth. Narfu tore into a monstrosity that looked like a spider and spewed black tar. Collith flayed a creature with the head of a reptile and the body of a man. The smell of charred flesh stuffed itself up my nostrils amongst the stench of blood and horses. And everywhere I looked, someone needed help.

"Sarod, get the wounded to safety!" I shouted.

The kelpie's neck arched as he tore a goblin's head off with his teeth. His voice seared through my head. *I came here to kill, not to play nursemaid.*

"It wasn't a request." Driving my point home, I ripped through the kelpie's mind in an instant, giving him a taste of a Nightmare's pure, unfiltered power.

Before Sarod could respond, I yanked my feet out of the stirrups, swung my leg over his broad back, and thrust myself into the chaos. I landed with a jarring thud. There was no time to acknowledge the pain as I raised my sword to leap into the fray. I didn't look to see if Sarod had obeyed me.

At the same moment I swung my weapon forward, something grabbed my wrist in a vise grip. Ice coated my skin and left a trail of frostbite in its wake. I didn't even register the pain, but I lost my grip on my sword. It hadn't even hit the ground when I plucked one of my knives from its hiding place and twisted. I plunged the blade into the center of the demon's throat. It was beautiful, almost like the male version of Viessa. For a shivering instant its pale eyes met mine—there was no flicker of emotion, no fleeting glimpse of humanity. Coldly, I twisted the hilt and yanked it out at the same moment I heard someone shout a warning. I spun swiftly, ducking another demon's swipe. I tucked my knee under and rolled, coming up right in front of it. I reached for my sword, which was still on the ground.

But the creature turned faster than I'd anticipated, and a knife in its hand nearly sliced through my side. I jerked out of the way.

My opening appeared, and without hesitation I lifted my right arm and brought it down again, jamming the blood-coated dagger in and out of the demon's jaw. Wetness spurted out of the wound but I didn't linger to watch the thing go down.

It all happened in a matter of seconds, and another wave was already closing in, despite the members of my Shadow Court who were clearly trying to protect me. I finally snatched up my sword and took three demons down with one swift lash. More blood splattered. I whirled and confronted what looked like a horse-sized praying mantis. In a defensive response, it ejected some kind of glowing fluid from its face. I felt my own twist with disgust as I dodged it and, in the same breath, lopped off the demon's head. More of the glowing liquid burst from its neck like a faucet, and as the rest of its body twitched, the ground bubbled and steamed everywhere that vile shit had landed.

Noted, I thought. Then I went to kill something else.

I thrust, cut, and slashed my way through the battlefield. Sarod reappeared now and then, and every time, I sent him away with someone who had been freshly injured. I was able to focus better, knowing they were away from here. But eventually the kelpie lost me in the chaos of battle, along with my other allies. I didn't have trouble holding my own, at least until I spun to face a female with black lips. I recognized her instantly—the galbraith demon that had kissed me the night we'd tried to save Thuridan. My split second of hesitation cost me when she got close enough to reach for my face. I knew, even as I raised my sword, that I'd be too late.

Before the demon could make contact, she froze. Her eyes rolled into the back of her head, and she crumpled to the ground like a pile of perilously balanced rocks. I frowned and looked up. My gaze collided with that of a young witch. I nodded at her, and she nodded back. Then we both turned away to keep fighting. I stabbed the galbraith demon in the chest as I hurried by, making sure she was good and dead.

It wasn't long before I realized just how badly I'd underestimated Lucifer's numbers. While I was focused on killing one demon, more always attacked from the sides or behind. I kept trying to check on my weak spots, just as Adam and Gil had taught me, but no amount of training could have prepared me for the chaos of battle. Without Michael's power, I wouldn't have been able to endure the grueling, relentless pace. It was taking much longer than I'd thought it would to reach the Gate.

We'd gotten halfway across the battlefield when I forgot to check my blind spots. Just as I moved to behead the vampire I was fighting, fingers clamped down on my arm, biting and relentless. I tried to wrench myself free and the demon used my own momentum to swing me around. Two arrows lodged in its face, and then the fingers were gone. My head jerked to see who'd just saved my ass.

Sorcha Cralynn met my gaze.

Surprise shot through me, but I hid it as I gave her a begrudging nod. "Thanks," I muttered.

The shapeshifter tossed me a new dagger. "Don't mention it."

"Well . . . good luck." After an awkward pause, I began to turn away. Sorcha's voice stopped me.

"I was wrong about you. All of this . . ." She looked around, her beautiful face caught somewhere between bewilderment and awe. "You did something no one has been able to do since the Fall."

I'd hated Sorcha for so long that it was my first instinct to snarl back at her. I stopped myself and mumbled, "Yeah, well, Lucifer's arrival here was sort of my fault, so I can't claim too much credit."

I expected the faerie to jump on the chance to insult me or lay the blame at my feet. But Sorcha's mouth just tightened, as if she'd tasted something unpleasant. "He would've found another way in," she said. "You were just the easiest. Everyone knows you tend to open your legs for any pretty face that bats their eyes at you."

And with that, our nice moment was over.

There was no time for anything else, anyway; the tide was still coming. I forgot Sorcha and moved to rejoin the fight. Brandishing my new weapon, I threw it at yet another demon that was nearly on top of me. It embedded in the thing's face. I barely heard the sound of the creature's shriek as I moved on.

The ground ran blue, red, and black. The snow was long gone, turned to cold mud beneath our boots. Gore kept splattering across my face. Still we fought. Still we battled. The night went on and on. Sarod never came back, which meant that he was either dead or lost to bloodlust. Some part of me wondered if, later, I would be ashamed at how much death I'd dealt out. But right now, I was high. I felt a thousand years old, a creature of primordial power, swinging this way and that. Killing everything that dared to take me on. Silencing every voice that raised against mine. The violence—it couldn't compare to any movie, video game, or battle I'd fought so far—didn't penetrate the haze.

Images imprinted on my mind, though. Moments that part of me registered in the midst of all the adrenaline and chaos. A werewolf's innards hanging out. A fae male on the ground, legless and screaming while a swarm of dog-sized demons ate him. A black bear locked in battle with a female with tentacles shooting out of her mouth. I saw it all, and I saw none of it.

Time only stopped again when my gaze caught on a familiar face. I froze, my mouth thinning into a grim slash, and I instinctively held my sword a little tighter.

Iris.

She stepped over the water nymph she'd just killed, her eyes gleaming with anticipation as she looked back at me. We both knew this fight had been a long time coming.

"You hurt my friend," I said flatly, starting toward her. Because of this witch, Lyari had turned to Lucifer. She'd been tortured and isolated for months. Because of this witch, Bella O'Connell had come after me, which set off the chain of events that led to Oliver's emergence into the world . . . and Finn's death.

I was going to make this slow, I decided as I raised my sword, my lip curling. Slow and *painful*.

Iris raised her arms to do a spell when a familiar trilling sound pierced the air. The witch paused, frowning. I kept my eyes on her in case it was a trick. But a second later, several dark shapes slammed into her. Iris began screaming, and I heard the undeniable sound of tearing flesh. My eyes widened when I recognized Givi, who threw his head back to swallow the chunk of skin and muscle he'd just ripped off Iris's flailing arm. Then I spotted Salbrox, Tarek, and Ircuk, all of them feasting on the witch who had served their master for so long.

The gargoyles had turned on their own kind. For me. For my world.

I'd have to thank them later. Remembering my mission, I spun toward the Gate again. Two new figures reached the ground. I recognized them instantly, and my stomach sank yet again. *Oh, shit,* I thought.

The female was Lucifer's sister, Mammon. The male was his younger brother Asmodeus. I had spent time with Asmodeus. I'd liked him, even—in some ways, he seemed different from his siblings. But he was still a demon and a ruler in Hell, and he certainly hadn't come here to make nice.

We *needed* to close that Gate.

I looked around with sharp urgency, taking stock of who was nearby—someone from my Court or one of my allies always seemed to be within arm's reach. I blinked in surprise when I saw Gwyn and Lyari step over the demons they'd just killed. Viessa, too, finished cutting one down and turned my way. She swung her sword in a circle. It sang as it caught the light, ready for more.

"Shall the women get this done, then?" she called.

Gwyn smirked and flipped her own sword, bringing it upright

with an effortless movement. Blood flicked off the sticky-looking blade. "As we have since the beginning of time."

In unison, the four of us turned and started making our way toward Mammon and Asmodeus, and consequently, the Gate. It had gotten bigger since the last time I'd looked at it. The rip in the sky looked more like a diamond now, as though someone had peeled it open with both hands. I gazed up at the swarm of demons still pouring out like angry hornets bursting from a broken nest.

Then something else appeared in the darkness.

Terror exploded through the air like fireworks.

"What *is* that?" Lyari said. I heard the puzzled frown in her voice.

It came through slowly, its movements almost drowsy, as if this thing had just woken from a long, long slumber. The creature was so huge that its sides widened the Gate, and I questioned whether it even was a creature. At first glance, it bore no head or face, and it looked like it was made of rock and dirt. But then two great long shapes unfurled and cast shadows over the entire battlefield. Wings. Could it breathe fire?

I would call it a dragon, but other than its ability to fly, this thing bore no other similarities to my friends.

As if the thought had summoned him, Cyrus's roar echoed across the sky. With helpless horror, I watched as he flew toward the monster Hell had just spewed out. Cyrus was so small in comparison, but my friend was unafraid. Acting like a beast ten times his size, the red dragon drew his head back and let out a wall of flame. I held my breath, praying that it worked. Hoping this thing would cook alive before it could hurt any of us.

The dragonfire bounced off the monster and disintegrated into nothing. I cursed, but in the next moment, I was forced to turn my focus away from the battle starting overhead when a snake the size of a horse came at me. I kept glancing up as I fought, trying to keep track of Cyrus.

Realizing he wouldn't be able to fight this thing the usual way, Cyrus immediately switched to Plan B. His scales glinted as he changed his trajectory, flying over the monster's head to land on its back. The massive demon bellowed, and it tilted. For an instant, the shapes on its spine drew my gaze. I almost missed my opening to behead the damn snake, but I recovered just in time, and the edge of my blade found its mark just as the demon tried to recoil. Ichor sprayed my chest and neck as I glanced up at the strange shapes on the monster again. They looked like . . . volcanoes.

I had seen them before, I realized with slow dread.

My mind flashed back to the last time I'd laid eyes on those things. I had asked Lucifer about them. He'd acted all cagey and said, *That is where Abaddon resides. He has been asleep for several centuries. It wouldn't be good for my world if he ever awoke, not as he is now.*

Why? I'd asked.

Lucifer's tone had ended our conversation. *As Fallen have evolved in your world, so they have evolved in mine.*

I hadn't been the only one keeping a card up my sleeve, I thought grimly. Whatever Abaddon had "evolved" into opened its jaws—which apparently it did have—and flew at the small dragon again.

"Cyrus," I whispered, my heart bursting with terror. I searched the air wildly for Tabitha and found her locked in battle with a cluster of demons that looked like fucking pterodactyls. She couldn't help, and now I was afraid for her, too.

Just as I lowered my head to look for any ally with wings that could fly me to Cyrus's aid, I spotted a lion in the battle. It was the biggest one I'd ever seen, and as I watched, it took out a demon with a single blow from its deadly paw. The great cat could've been anyone, but I had a feeling in my gut, and I didn't question it.

"Nan," I shouted. The lion's head whipped round. Its bright, golden eyes found me instantly. I pointed at Cyrus and screamed, "Help him!"

The lion followed the direction of my hand and went still, as if it was concentrating. A moment later, its shape began to shift and bubble. Much like the transformation of a werewolf, torn flesh fell to the ground. Nan's body grew, and grew, and grew. She swelled and cracked until she was bigger than a house. Bigger than Cyrus and Tabitha. As massive, webbed wings stretched out on either side of her, tilting in a gust of wind, I realized what the shapeshifter was becoming.

A dragon.

Once the transformation was complete, Nan flapped those vast wings, dislodging some of the flesh and gore off her scales, and launched her body into the air. She went directly toward the battle between Cyrus and Abaddon, letting out a roar that shook the world. I watched her go, praying I hadn't just sent the queen to her death.

"Fortuna, look out!" a male voice barked. My head jerked toward Gil, and he lifted a crossbow. Reacting without thought, I dove away from the direction the arrow was pointing. Gil's aim was flawless, and the glass tip found its target, a humanoid thing that shrieked as it died.

Another demon out of commission. But there were still more, and one of them was reaching for me with huge, clawed hands. I had to trust that Cyrus could handle himself and that Nan had his back. I lifted my leg and gave the demon a hard kick at the same moment I lowered my sword and stabbed something coming up from behind, a creature with a foul smell and no hint of fear or reason within its mind. I heard the satisfying sound of a pained screech at the same moment the demon in front of me recovered. I dodged it again while I yanked my sword free, but I was a split second too slow in my reaction, and I hissed as a fresh cut opened on the side of my leg—it had gotten me right where my armor was weakest.

Luckily, despite the blow it had managed to land, the demon was big and graceless. I beheaded it and looked for my next opponent before the creature had even hit the ground. We were getting closer to Lucifer and the Gate. From the corner of my eye, I could see that splash of white. A bright glint of golden hair. My friends and I kept going, kept fighting, managing to stay close and form a line, of sorts, as we cut out way through.

At last, knowing we must've been nearly upon him now, I whipped round . . .

. . . and stopped.

My chest heaved. Pieces of myself drifted back. We'd reached the devil, just as we had intended. But Viessa was fighting Lucifer, and that wasn't part of the plan. A rush of terror filled my throat, and I lunged to cut down another demon in my way, trying to make a path to my friend. But Lucifer had surrounded himself with a species that, if they'd been from this world, I would've called giants. Even with all the adrenaline pumping through me, pain ricocheted through my arms with every blow. I wrenched my head toward Viessa every chance I got, making sure she was still alive.

Thankfully, the Unseelie Queen seemed to be holding her own. I'd just wounded the last demon that stood between us when Lucifer dropped to the ground, throwing his wings over his head as a stream of ice charged over his back. Roaring in pain, he lashed out blindly with his sword and managed to strike Viessa across her thigh. She snarled, springing back. Blue blood streamed from the gash. Just as Viessa started to raise her weapon, her leg gave way, and her knees hit the ground.

Lucifer must've struck an artery, or maybe there had been poison on the blade.

Panic blazed through me. I needed to reach her right *now*, I needed to help, but there was another demon between the three of us, and it was blundering toward me. I let out a snarl of my own and attacked the black-eyed giant with renewed, desperate ferocity, tearing through its oversized, dull mind while I dodged and danced around its skull-crushing swings. I found its fear within seconds—this massive *thing* was terrified of bajang, a small pest in Hell. My lip curled as I made them appear all around the demon.

The second my illusion made the giant go still, its club falling from limp fingers, I spun toward Lucifer and Viessa again.

My eyes met Lucifer's first. He stood perfectly still, and he held the edge of his sword across Viessa's throat. He'd been waiting for me to finish off the demon so I could watch whatever came next, I realized dimly. Viessa knelt in front of him, bleeding from a wound in her abdomen. Pain and defiance shone in her wintry eyes.

In that moment, I didn't care about my pride or how much I hated him. For her, I would beg, plead, and bargain. I would do anything.

Please, don't, I mouthed to Lucifer. *Please.*

He made sure that our eye contact never broke. Then he pulled his sword back, looking as if he barely made any effort, and Viessa's head fell to the ground in a spray of blood.

My scream echoed across the battlefield.

The need for vengeance burned through my veins. I killed another demon without sparing it a glance, keeping my eyes on Lucifer as we closed the distance between us again. When we reached each other, both of us came to a halt, just as we had at the start of the night.

I knew this would be the fight of my life.

Apprehension flitted through my stomach, but only for a moment. I leaned into my instincts, knowing I just had to trust myself. I'd trained for this. I put my right hand at the top end of the grip and the other at the bottom, closer to the pommel, just as Adam had taught me. I bent my elbows and put them close to my body. Then I looked at Lucifer with cold contempt, which was all I had left in my heart for him.

"Time to see if the devil bleeds," I said through my teeth.

He just gazed back at me with a bemused look on his face,

as if I were a child with a wooden sword. "Your move, my lady," Lucifer replied.

I didn't hesitate, because I knew that hesitation would get me killed. I immediately began with a feint, but Lucifer didn't fall for it. I went at him again. He blocked my assault as if he knew my every thought. I recovered quickly—with a circle parry, I caught the tip of Lucifer's sword and deflected it.

"Good, very good," he praised. He didn't even sound winded. "I see my brother left you a gift."

"That's not all he left me." I did a counter cut, stepping back and striking at his arm instead of his sword. Lucifer let out a hiss, but there was no pain in the sound. It was *excitement*. He couldn't help it.

"Oh?" he said. "How interesting. What else was there?"

I lifted my boot, aiming for his groin, but Lucifer swung out of reach. My breathing was only slightly uneven as I replied, "You'll see. Or maybe you won't, because you'll be fucking dead."

"Confident words for a fledgling." The look Lucifer gave me was almost pitying. "While my brother's power may have given you some advantages, you have existed but a blink, my lady. There is still much you have to learn."

Then he did a maneuver that I'd never seen before, faster than even my eyes could track. Our swords slid together and there was a hard tug I wasn't ready for. I blinked and suddenly Lucifer held both in his hands, the blades crossed at the center. In another blink, he pulled his arms back. The edges of the swords sliced through my sides.

I couldn't hold back a scream of agony as I crashed to my knees.

A ripple of awareness moved through the bonds of my Court—they knew I'd been hurt. I knelt in a puddle of my own blood, breathing hard. My head was already spinning, the world tilting back and forth like a seesaw, but I fought to keep one eye on Lucifer. It wasn't over yet. There was still work to do.

Lucifer took two steps closer, and I prayed he'd come near enough for me to ram a dagger into his heart. Unfortunately, the devil was no fool. He stopped just short of my reach and lifted the swords, putting those crossed tips on either side of my neck.

"Will you yield?" Lucifer asked. His voice was low and intimate, as if his bedroom walls were around us instead of violence and death.

My lip curled. I tipped my head back to give him better access and said, "Never."

Another ripple went through the bonds inside me. My Shadow Court could hear us. They could feel what was happening here, between me and Lucifer . . . and a few of them had noticed something else, too. An image brushed against my mind. Relief and excitement blazed through me. Following the direction of where my Court was looking, I glanced to the west.

Savannah Simonson stood at the top of the hill.

The sight of her made a faint smile touch my lips. In one hand, Savannah carried a compound bow, and the other was raised in the air. Two leather bands crossed her chest and she wore loose pants tucked into laced, leather boots. Every inch of her exposed skin was covered in whorls and words. Some of them would be protective markings, I knew. The same markings she'd put on me and the rest of my Shadow Court. Apparently no practice was too arcane when it came fighting the devil.

Too bad those markings couldn't protect me against demon glass, I thought with a wince as Lucifer's sword bit into the edge of my jaw. Then I watched Savannah kneel, and the pain faded. "Become what you were meant to be," I whispered.

Lucifer's eyes narrowed; he knew I wasn't talking to him. He may have given me those words, but I'd taken them back and given them to someone else. It was what I'd said to Savannah at the Unseelie Court last night, after I realized the symbol on the map was a bloodline crest—the bloodline Olorel had sacrificed—

and that all the strange drawings scattered across the paper were skulls.

Once I'd seen it, Michael's parting message was so obvious. He had practically left an instruction manual on how to kick his brother's ass. He'd *intervened*. The corner of my mouth tilted up at the thought. Maybe not all angels were heartless. Maybe it was just one.

As Lucifer's sword cut even deeper, I kept my gaze fixed on that distant figure, and Laurie's voice whispering through my head. *And there it is. Hope.*

The woman on the hill wasn't only a witch, or an apprentice, or a mother. Savannah Simonson was a goddamn necromancer, and a powerful one at that.

In the hours since we'd formed our new plan, I hadn't been able to stop thinking about it. The sequence of events that needed to occur, in perfect order, each one falling like a domino, to put us in this exact moment. If Jassin hadn't stumbled upon Damon in his garden and stolen him away, Savannah never would've become a necromancer. If Lucifer hadn't stolen the Horn and killed Michael, I never would've seen the angel's memories and learned the truth.

Don't do this, Michael had told Olorel on the day he tried to close the Door. The horror Michael felt during those final moments made sense now. Because he'd realized Olorel was about to use an entire bloodline's power, killing them in the process.

The bodies were buried under the very field Olorel had been standing upon when he'd tried to close the opening to Hell. He'd probably never intended for anyone to make use of them again. But once I made the connection, and figured out what was beneath the Flint Hills, I'd remembered something else Michael had said.

The remains of an angel never decay.

My thoughts cut short when Savannah brought her arms up. Others had seemed to notice her arrival, too, and after she moved, there was a moment of frozen, breathless silence on the battlefield. My heart hammered in my ears. What if the spell hadn't worked? What if—

A fleshless hand shot out of the ground at Lucifer's feet.

He shouted and jumped back. Just as an eyeless skull popped into the open, another pair of hands appeared nearby. They were *everywhere*, I realized, spotting at least a dozen more with a single glance. Within seconds, the screams started. The battlefield erupted into fresh chaos.

I looked around in awe as the dead crawled out of the ground in droves. The missing bloodline had risen again, every skeletal fighter with all the strength of an angel and none of the limitations. Magic held them together, brought back to life by Savannah's curse ... by her gift, I amended. Compared to the zombies that had killed Fred, these ones moved breathingtakingly fast, and they flooded the battle like locusts. I was still wounded, my sides drenched in blood. I couldn't defend myself, and yet, there was no need—the dead didn't come for me. The marks made sure of that, just as Savannah said they would.

The devil bore no such marks to protect him, though.

Lucifer had been driven several yards away. He cut three zombies down with a single blow and raised his gaze back to me.

"It doesn't matter," he shouted, a vein standing out in his forehead. "Whatever you do to this army, no matter how many of my people or my siblings you turn against me, there will always be more coming through that Gate! You can never close it!"

My nostrils flared. *Oh yes I can,* I thought.

In that instant, the rest of the battlefield faded, becoming nothing more than a distant ringing and moving, blurred shapes. The blazing pain in my sides eased. There was only me and him. I looked back at the Dark Prince and there was no love left in my heart, even now. All I felt was certainty. He thought he'd won.

But not only did I have the power of an original angel running through my veins ... I was a Nightmare. Magic was all about intent, and I already knew of one person who had used this magic to manipulate the fabric between worlds, *without* sacrificing any lives. Nym himself had confirmed it, and Lucifer's own words echoed back to me.

He saw how powerful one of her descendants would become. A power that could undo entire worlds.

As I scraped my strength together, the devil's voice whispered through my head again, trying to plant a seed of doubt. *She didn't know how much energy it would take. The price such powerful magic would extract.*

Resolve hardened my heart to stone. It was time to finish this. I *was* going to close that Gate, and I wanted Lucifer to watch. I knew what it might cost me, and I was willing to pay the price.

This time, I didn't ask myself how to do it, or question whether I could. Maybe some part of me had known how all along. Following a quiet instinct, I dragged one of my knees out from beneath me and knelt just like Savannah had. I kept hold of a dagger in case something nasty tried to attack, but my other hand curled in the earth. After a few moments, I sensed other fighters forming a protective barrier, fending off the onslaught while I focused on the Gate. Hard dirt lodged beneath my nails, and I replaced the mental image of Lucifer's face with one that was far better.

I remembered what Laurie had said to me the night I'd become queen. I could still picture that exact moment—how the light from a nearby flame flickered in his silver eyes.

Don't you know what strengthens a Nightmare's power? Unleashed fury. Pain. The things bad dreams are made of.

I took a deep breath, and then another. My fingers drove even deeper into the ground. I could feel every muscle in my body tensing as I began to amass the magic I'd need. What if I took too much? What if I killed everyone, just like Olorel had? Fear began to creep back.

Another memory whispered through my mind. Laurie's silver eyes became hazel, and his features melted into a face that was just as familiar. Collith's voice felt cool and calming in the heat of my hovering panic. *Fear is a seed. It can grow from pain or anger . . . or it can grow from something else.*

I let out one final breath. The air left my lungs slowly, and my shoulders lowered.

I was ready.

I didn't close my eyes, or fix my attention to the ground. Instead, I looked across the hilltop at Lucifer again. His voice was the last one I heard as the air prickled around me, practically thrumming with magic now.

Become what you were meant to be.

My gaze left Lucifer, and I all but forgot about him as I redirected all my focus toward the sky. The Gate loomed, bigger than ever. Demons were still pouring out of it like beetles from a broken, rotted log. I could make out more details now, like how some of those things had horns on their skulls or talons at the ends of their wings. Morning was coming. It was still a way off, but it was coming. Thankfully, I didn't need the blanket of night to accomplish this, or to be asleep. Those were just limitations I'd given myself. Desperate ways to keep the full extent of my abilities at bay.

The power I'd gathered began to build inside me, and for the first time in my entire life, I didn't try to quell it. I didn't search for ways to stop it. Instead, I *strengthened* it. I used my belief in the dreamscape. I used the power of my desire. I used the terror of failure.

The force rose like a dark, writhing maelstrom. Images seared through my mind—a dripping knife in my hand as I stood in Belanor's small, damp cell, a grassy clearing full of dead bodies, Collith's wide eyes going dim as the life slipped out of him—but I didn't flinch. Power was balance, I knew that now. The light *and* the dark.

And the light was incandescent.

A smile curved my lips when I thought of all the people I

loved. The memories stayed close to me as magic filled every corner of my being. Blood streamed from both of my nostrils and trickled over my lips. I barely noticed—the whole of my being was focused on the Gate. I could sense its magic now, writhing against mine, and it was repulsive. Unnatural. But feeling the Gate's power lent me a small understanding of it. This thing was made of dark energy, and creating it had caused an imbalance, just as Michael warned Olorel it would. To right the wrong, closing the Gate would require even more energy.

I'd trapped the magic inside me as if my body were a cage. Knowing what came next, I braced myself. The bonds to my Court brightened as I sent out one final, fleeting message, imbuing it with all the love they had given me. *Goodbye.*

Then I opened the cage.

Power streamed past me, through me, and the opening to Hell crackled. My braids whipped chaotically in the howling wind and someone shouted my name. But closing the Gate required everything, and I couldn't tear my eyes away, not even for a second. It felt like I was breaking something all around me and creating something else out of the pieces. Some vast, alien thing that I didn't fully understand. The Gate continued to roar and flash with streaks of light, as if it were sentient, as if it didn't *want* to close.

Well, I thought with gritted teeth. *That's too fucking bad.*

I sent every drop of power I had into the tear. When there was none left, I just kept giving, kept pouring, refusing to relent until lightning lit up the entire sky and the gaping hole began to shrink. The lower half of my face was caked in blood and my body ached as if I'd been beaten. But even that wasn't enough. The Gate needed more energy. It was still hungry.

And suddenly, I knew exactly what I could give it.

Following some dim, deep instinct, I imagined flinging myself inside that massive dark mouth trying to eat the world. Colors and sounds rushed past, everything blurring, as if I'd leaped through time.

"*Close!*" I screamed as I tumbled toward a terrifying, vast darkness.

Then... I was floating.

I felt the briefest flare of panic, which dimmed when I drifted a little further into the emptiness. Facts and names and details began to fade away like the darkness was swallowing them as they scattered behind me. All I knew was that I had to keep going. But at the very back of my mind, from some vaguely familiar place that I'd left far, far behind, I heard desperate cries. Voices, urging me to take power from them. To use them. There were so many. Infinitely more than Olorel had had on the dark day he'd hidden the Door, taking all those lives to do it.

It was the thought of Olorel that made me pause. Who was he again? Why did that name make me want to turn back?

When I focused on those faint, distant lights, they got brighter and clearer. They became images and thoughts. Within seconds, I could feel their fear, and everything else they felt.

And suddenly I could see their faces, too.

Love; this feeling came from a pale-skinned figure with dark hair, who swung his sword with desperate precision, trying to reach a distant female kneeling in the grass—me. I caught a glimpse of my own face in the faerie's mind as he fought. His name floated to me on a whisper of memory, some clinging shred of reason and the person I'd been before I stepped into the void. *Collith*.

Rage; the heat came from a silver-haired warrior who shouted my name while his drifted past me like a whisper. *Laurie*.

It was for them that I was doing this, I realized. They were the reason it was so important to keep going.

So I took some of their light and pushed harder. I plunged deeper into the darkness, and then there was nothing except my will and the power I'd brought with me. After a while, or maybe it was only a second, my body and the battle were completely gone. It felt like I was wandering through outer space. No tether to pull me back, no person to hear if I screamed . . . but I wasn't screaming. I just drifted, gazing into the expanse of eternal stars. I struggled to hold onto the reason I'd come here.

Close, I thought in a whisper, my eyes fluttering shut. *Close.*

Another second passed. Then I heard an agonizing noise, and another reality overlapped with this one. For several awful, shrieking seconds, I flickered between worlds, and my ears exploded with pain. I saw a flash of a torch. Stars. A stream of crackling light. *Heavenly fire,* I thought dazedly. Stars. The glint of a sword and a blurred figure. Stars again.

When I opened my eyes, I was back on the battlefield. Or part of me was, at least. That other reality still clung to my mind, so I saw both the chaos of the fighting and the pure, absolute stillness of those planets and pockets of darkness. I tipped my head back, too weak to stand. Did it work? Was it done?

The Gate had disappeared.

The sky overhead was just a sky now, smeared with clouds and snow. The demons pouring through had stopped, firmly trapped in their world.

A moment after I'd had the thought—and the bright, singing realization that my family was *safe,* along with everyone else—I noticed a tang of salt on my tongue. It wasn't fear, I thought faintly. Tears. I was tasting my own tears. I'd done it. I had actually done it. I swayed there on my knees, smiling. The stars kept twinkling around me.

"You *bitch,*" a voice snarled, echoing through space.

I remembered that voice. I frowned, and the worlds overlapped again. I saw a bright, furious face and heard a name. *Lucifer.*

No fear stirred in my heart. He didn't matter. I'd left him alive, but the others would end him. They had the demon glass, and each other. That was all they needed.

I tried to find those familiar faces, hoping for one last look, one final memory, but my vision had begun to dim. All the fighting around me was just shadows and blurred shapes now. The red-orange glow of a torch moved closer, and I fixed my attention on that spot of brightness, hoping to anchor myself.

It didn't work.

Someone shouted my name as air whistled past my ears. I felt a hard *thud*, and then I was lying on my side, unable to move. A rivulet of blood escaped my mouth and pooled on the grass in front of me. I heard my name again.

But I had died before; I knew what it felt like. My eyes drifted shut. *I'm sorry,* I thought to whoever was calling to me.

At long last, I surrendered to the dark.

CHAPTER TWENTY-FOUR

I opened my eyes to a vast, empty room.

The air was so still that I heard the hitch of air in my own lungs. I pushed myself up and looked around curiously. The place was beautiful and unfamiliar. The floors were made of shining tile, with golden walls on either side and an elegant, arched ceiling. A green skirt pooled around me, and I realized I was wearing a dress that I'd gotten over the summer. The last day I'd worn it had been a happy one. We'd had a barbecue.

Was this . . . Heaven?

I knew I should've been terrified or uneasy, but it felt like I'd left those emotions behind in all the mud, blood, and chaos. Slowly, I got to my feet, and the dress fell into place around me. I started walking, studying the intricate ceiling with awe. *Why this place?* I wondered. I had expected the dreamscape, but secretly, I'd been hoping I would wind up at that lake, with all its glittering water and cloudless blue skies.

The quiet shattered when shouts boomed from somewhere in the distance. The sound was muffled, as if it had come from beneath a blanket. I froze, holding my breath, worried that even the sound of my breath would make me miss something.

Moments later, I heard the unmistakable echo of wild, joyous cheers.

And that was when I knew for certain—it worked.

It *worked*. The Gate was shut. I'd achieved what Olorel couldn't, and I hadn't slaughtered an entire bloodline to do it. As the cheering went on, I smiled faintly. I imagined Gil clapping Adam on the back, and Laurie kissing Collith. Longing shot through me. I wished I could be there to see it, to take part in it.

But I didn't mind, I decided. I didn't mind that it had ended like this. My death had purpose, and more importantly, my family was safe. They were stronger than I had given them credit for, and they'd already proven they could survive without me. I could move on knowing they would be happy. That they would *live*. Air slipped between my lips and my shoulders loosened. I lowered my head to begin looking for a way out.

My mother stood in front of me.

All at once, those distant sounds went silent. My heart beat in my ears as I stared at her. I had to swallow before I could speak. "Mama? Is that really you?"

She pressed her hand against her mouth, muffling a sob, and ran toward me. I launched into a sprint, as well, tears already streaming from the corners of my eyes. We met halfway, and Mom's arms came around me without hesitation. She cupped the back of my head and we pressed into each other as if all those years of separation had never happened. As if I hadn't been responsible for her death.

The thought made me draw back, and a strangled sound left my throat. I bowed my head, composing myself, then forced my gaze back to hers. "Mama, I'm sorry, I'm so sorry that I—"

She held my face in her palms, and God, I hadn't realized how fiercely I'd missed this. Being with my mother. Smelling the oil she used to put on her hands. "Listen to me very closely, Fortuna," she said.

Here she paused, and we both smiled through our sorrow as we remembered how often she'd said that during our lessons. *Listen to me very closely, Fortuna.* And what had I always said next?

"I'm listening, Mama." My voice shook.

"Good. Good girl." Mom pressed her own trembling lips together. Then she took a breath and looked into my eyes. Her voice was firmer as she said, "You have nothing to be sorry for. Do you understand? What happened that night—the creature you created—is not your fault. We do not blame you in any way. You are infinitely precious to us, and we considered it an honor to be your parents in the time we were given."

I fought another sob. It felt like she'd pulled open the stitches of a wound I'd hidden away. "But if you hadn't had me, if I hadn't been born, you wouldn't have—"

"If you were so unworthy, Fortuna, you wouldn't have been given this chance," Mom cut in gently.

My eyebrows drew together. "What do you mean?"

She squeezed my hands. "I'm here because you have a choice to make, sweetheart. This is a special place, an in-between place. This is where powerful souls decide their own fate. The truth is, you're not completely dead yet, Fortuna. You still have the option to return to your body on Earth, and continue the life you have there. Or you are allowed to rest, if that's what you want. I can't tell you what comes next, because that is something everyone must discover for themselves, but I do know that it's peaceful."

I hesitated. The strange sense of calm I'd felt when I'd first arrived here was gone, and now my insides roiled with indecision. "Will I be with you and Dad?" I asked.

Mom gave me a faint, bittersweet smile. She reached up and tucked a wayward strand of hair behind my ear. "I don't know."

She didn't say anything more, and somehow, I understood that it was because I had to make this choice alone.

The enormity of it hit me. I thought of the ones I'd left behind.

They could survive without me, it was true. For once it wasn't a matter of survival. What did *I* want? Was I content to leave the story here, now that I knew there could be more? It was a good ending, I thought. An honorable one, even. I'd faced death too many times to count. Every time it came, I had been all too willing to accept the darkness. I'd played the martyr, when the truth was entirely selfish.

It was guilt, and self-loathing, and fear that had made me so eager to escape into oblivion.

But this was different. If I went back now I knew that I couldn't pull my old bullshit anymore. The constant excuses were gone. Damon was safe. The *world* was saved. Today, I had to ask the question—did I want to live?

Surviving had been so hard. But the part that came after might be even harder. Could I really let go of the past and move on?

I tried to imagine it, the life waiting for me if I returned to that muddy battlefield. I'd make more mistakes, that was a given. I'd probably laugh a lot more, too. There would be more Matthew, more Damon, more ... everyone. More barbecues and celebrations and sunny days after so many long, dark nights. The corners of my mouth tilted upward at the thought.

The uncertainty in my heart faded.

At last, I came back to the present. I wasn't sure how long I had been standing there. The light hadn't changed, and those distant sounds were silent now. Did that mean the battle was over? I refocused on my mother, reluctant to face what came next.

And even though she hadn't raised me, or had a single conversation with me in over a decade, Mom knew. She smiled again and said, "You've made your decision, then."

As she spoke, light passed over her features. I turned, looking for its source, and somehow I wasn't surprised to see a door of light.

It was time.

Urgency gripped me. I faced Mom and hugged her again,

holding her as tightly as I could without hurting her. My eyes squeezed shut, and I tried to memorize how she felt in my arms. What her perfume smelled like.

Mom cupped the back of my head again and whispered, "I am so proud of you."

I pulled back, searching her gaze through a sheen of tears. Sometimes there was nothing to say that would encompass the universe of feeling inside you. No combination of words to express all the contradictions that were making your heart come apart. So I kissed my mother's cheek and let her go.

This time, she wasn't the one to leave—I was. I turned away slowly, part of me tempted to change my mind. To hold on even tighter and travel to the next world together, wherever that might be.

But that was just the fear talking.

I kept going.

It was almost identical to how I'd passed through worlds before. I walked toward the light, and it got brighter and brighter, almost blinding. The air felt warm and thick, as if a storm was gathering. Just before the magic swallowed me, I glanced over my shoulder, wanting one final glimpse of my mother.

She stood there, young and shining and beautiful. This, I decided, lingering there. This was how I would remember her. I smiled, and she smiled back, raising her hand in a brief wave. I waved back before I faced the Door again. I closed my eyes, acknowledging the pain. Waiting for it to move through me.

Once it had passed, I took a breath and walked into that vibrant, looming beyond.

When I opened my eyes again, back in the midst of battle, Zara was crouched over me.

She was obviously in the process of healing my wounds. The

moment I became aware of it, the pain hit. I gritted my teeth and looked around, trying to get my bearings. Behind Zara, the Gate was still closed, and I almost sobbed with relief—part of me had worried it was a dream or a hallucination. Dying made you see such strange things, sometimes. My mother's face swam before me.

I told myself I'd have to think about that later. The Gate was shut, but the fighting hadn't ended. The hills were overrun with demons, and they were inching closer and closer, despite the Guardians that had formed a protective circle around us. Viessa was dead, along with countless others. So much loss. So much death. And for what? My jaw hardened.

It was time to finish this once and for all.

Zara was frowning. She leaned back, her hands covered in my blood, but the wound she'd been pressing down on was gone now. The skin beneath my pierced armor was smooth.

"What . . . what did you do?" Zara said. I didn't think I'd ever heard her so shaken before. "Wait, my lady, not so quickly!"

I sat up and got to my feet. The healer stood with me, her eyes dark with worry, but I just gave her a brief nod and replied, "Thank you, Zara."

She stared at me. I left her there and moved through the chaos, effortlessly drawing tidal waves of power to me. This time, I didn't cross the battlefield swinging a sword.

I walked.

I leveled Lucifer's army like it was nothing. Even the ones that belonged to Samael. Screams and moans followed in my wake. As if the thought had summoned him, the Prince of Solitude reared up in front of me.

"*We had a deal!*" he shrieked, spittle flying from his mouth, his eyes bulging with wrath. "*We had a—*"

With a single thought, I made the demon prince's entire body disintegrate.

While Samael's remains blew away on a cold gust of wind,

I continued on, snuffing out more lives as I went. I held my arms wide as though I were making my way through a summer meadow, and in my mind, I was. It felt as though part of me were in the dreamscape, back when it was a place of warmth and joy. I stopped seeing the horde as I ended their lives, and I remembered Oliver's sweet smile.

I finally understood what it meant to be a Nightmare, I thought, catching sight of my own reflection in a demon's sword as it ran at me. My red eyes shifted, fixing on the creature's birdlike features as I moved my arm with only a flick of effort, decapitating it in an instant. Meanwhile, all the demons around us continued to topple over like dominos. Onward I went, heading for a bright figure on the other side of the battlefield.

Over the years, my kind had been reduced to creatures with norms and limitations. Rules and boundaries, like vampires or werewolves. We had allowed it, maybe because we'd started to believe them, or simply to survive. But in the beginning, starting with Persephone, Nightmares could change reality. We could make thoughts and dreams into physical matter. We could create worlds and openings between universes.

And we sure as shit could take out one petty, bitter angel.

This time, I reached the devil in minutes. When our gazes met, he lowered his sword. He'd seen me coming, no doubt, and realized the futility of fighting. The screams of his dying army filled the air. But his surrender wasn't enough, I thought, as I continued stepping over all the bodies between us. Not even Lucifer's death would satisfy me now.

I wanted his dignity, too.

"Kneel," I said tonelessly.

Lucifer's knees hit the ground with such force that it sounded painful, and the moment reminded me of what he'd done to Thuridan. My heart felt like a piece of granite as I approached. The Dark Prince tipped his head back, his eyes flashing with fury. Fury . . . and fear.

"You would have been a god," he snarled. "And yet you chose these pathetic creatures. What can they give you that I can't?"

I didn't smile, but the corners of my mouth lifted. Wind whistled between us, tugging at a strand of my hair. "Everything," I said.

I bent down and put my face near his. Lucifer stared at me silently, but I could see the violence in his expression, the dark longing. I knew he wished we were in those cells beneath his tower, where he could do a thousand terrible things to me. Remove my skin, break my bones, hear the lovely cadence of my agonized screams. I knew all that because I was in his head, which was unguarded to me now. Not even the devil's impressive defenses could keep a power like mine out.

There was a reason we'd chosen fear, I thought as my nostrils flared, detecting a new scent. It was the easiest way to control our morsels.

It was also the most delicious.

And for the first time, I was tasting Lucifer's. The devil's terror tasted like blood. He wasn't afraid of light or death, I noted coldly. He was only afraid of failure.

My eyes met his, and then I crooned, "You lost, Lucifer. This world will live on. So will yours . . . especially when I go back and free every soul you put in chains. Your legacy will fade into nothing, and someday, you'll just be an old, sad story."

His throat worked, and he opened his mouth to respond. But before he could say another word, a fist burst through Lucifer's chest.

I wasn't sure who was more surprised—me or him. Lucifer lowered his eyes slowly. For a moment, he stared down at his own heart, and the blood dripping off the massive, clawed hand that held it. When Lucifer looked back up at me, I knew he wouldn't find any hint of regret or guilt. I couldn't read his expression, but I recognized the faint smile curving his lips. It was the same one he'd given me that last night in Hell, while we were flying through a black sky, rain shining on our skin.

He was saying goodbye.

At the same moment Lucifer opened his mouth to speak, his killer pulled their fist out. The devil's body jerked, and blood burst from his mouth. A glassy sheen entered his eyes. The sun shone through the hole in his chest, bright, streaming ribbons of light. Then Lucifer tipped over and landed on his side, his armor making a dull sound against the earth.

As he died, it felt like something inside me gave way. As if I'd been holding my breath for months, and now I could finally let air back into my lungs. Lucifer was gone. He couldn't hurt anyone else, and for the first time in years, it felt like my family was safe. I held a hand against my stomach, making a strange, strangled sound deep in my throat. Relief, and pain, and release all at once. I was free. I was *free*.

Oliver stood over Lucifer's body. He was still in his Beast form, and he clutched the devil's heart as if he wanted to crush it into a mass of ruined flesh. But the way he looked at me was entirely Ollie, and I wondered if the ichor coating his skin meant that he'd turned on the demons he was supposed to fight alongside. No wonder I hadn't seen him during the battle.

I felt a jolt of terror when I realized what Lucifer's death meant.

Michael's voice whispered to me, and suddenly the words felt like a vicious, dark taunt. *What happens to one happens to both.*

Oliver had known, of course, and he'd killed Lucifer anyway. We stared at each other, waiting for something to happen. But as the seconds passed, one after the other, he still stood there, whole and alive. I stretched out my hand.

"Ollie," I said softly, daring to take a step toward him. "Ollie, this could be—"

Suddenly his gaze shifted, and any trace of the man I loved vanished, leaving only the Beast. Whatever Oliver saw behind me made his wings snap out. Without a word, he launched into the air, and the force of it blew my braids back. The dark shape of the Beast flew into the horizon, and the light-tinted clouds swallowed the sound of his distant roar.

I stood there long after he was out of sight, wondering if I'd just made another mistake by letting Oliver go. Slowly, I became aware of the rest of the world again. Dawn streamed into the world like a golden river. It spilled over the hills and shone across the crushed, bloodstained grass, lending a dreamlike feel to all the carnage.

But I felt like I was waking up. Suddenly I could feel how much power I'd expended, and in that moment, I wanted nothing more than a hot shower and my warm bed. I reminded myself that there was still work to be done.

Swaying on my feet, I took stock of who was still alive. Adam was nearby. Overall, he looked no worse for wear. There was a cut over his eyebrow and someone had ripped a piece of his beard off, but his visible wounds—inflicted by demon glass, no doubt, which explained why there weren't healed—all seemed superficial. Lyari appeared unharmed, as well. Along with Cyrus, Ariel, and Gil.

Tension eased in my chest, and I continued my search of the battlefield. There was Laurie, standing with his inner circle. Tabitha had also changed back to her other form, and she held a saddle blanket around her naked body, nodding at something her king said.

Once I knew they were safe, my thoughts moved to my allies. I spotted Alexander Nørgård off in the distance, and Cora was with the wolf packs. There was the Rat King, Savannah and the witches, and the fae of both Courts. I didn't see Nan, though. Had she survived her battle with Abaddon?

The wind carried another soft sound to my ears. I turned, and I wasn't surprised to see Collith standing nearby. Oliver must've seen him, too, and that was why he'd left so abruptly. Collith's eyes met mine. In the light of morning, they looked startlingly green.

"You turned on Samael," he remarked.

I'd all but forgotten about that. I made a vague sound and looked down at a dead faerie. She wore the armor of a Guardian, and it looked like her throat had been ripped out. Blood coated the grass beneath her and most of the faerie's lower face, which was frozen in an expression of horror. Her beautiful eyes were open and vacant.

As I bent over to close them, I answered Collith.

"I was never going to tell Samael about the Unseelie Court. The moment I made that phone call, I knew I was going to double-cross him, and I knew what I was risking." I straightened and stepped over the fallen warrior, moving to stand next to Collith. My gaze went back to my friends, who were still gathered close by. Something tight and hard inside me loosened when I saw Gil removing what looked like porcupine needles from Lyari's back. She was grimacing and cursing, but she didn't move away from him.

My voice softened as I finished, "I decided they were worth it—eternal damnation. For them, I would cover my soul in a thousand stains. And I'd do it again in a heartbeat."

Collith looked at me for a long moment. I couldn't read his expression. "You sound like Laurie," he said.

At the mention of the Seelie King, my eyes found him again. Laurie had left his companions, and he stood on his own now, staring up at the sky. There was something in the set of his shoulders that made it clear he wanted to be alone. I knew that he was grieving the ones he'd lost today, and I thought of my own losses.

"He's right about one thing," I murmured. "We're not human, Collith . . . and sometimes the monster does win. Today, it was just the better monster."

There was no bitterness in my voice, but I couldn't bring myself to say anything else. And though I longed to go to those people waiting for me, to celebrate and exalt in the miracle of another dawn, and the fact that we were alive to see it, I couldn't bring myself to do that, either.

Instead, I turned away. I began to scan every face I passed, leaving Collith to pick my way through the sea of dead.

I had a body of my own to find.

CHAPTER TWENTY-FIVE

*I*n books and movies, it never seemed to show what came immediately after the big battle.

I was unnerved to discover that, after such a rush of fear, adrenaline, blood, and pain, everything that followed was ... ordinary. Quiet.

Awful.

Sunlight bounced harshly off all the armor and weapons. I squinted as I picked my way through the dead, looking at every face, dreading that I'd see more I recognized. So far I had found Narfu and Sarod. In the distance, I could see Luther's huge frame doing the same thing I was. Every so often, he bent over, flung a body over his broad shoulder, and carried the fallen soldier to a waiting cart. The wheels squeaked as they rolled over the uneven ground. I watched the one closest to me go for a moment, knowing the rats would have several more loads before they were done.

They hadn't been the only ones to suffer huge losses. There were a dozen other carts scattered over the hills as others did the same with their dead.

A hawk shrieked overhead, drawing my gaze away from the

carts. I continued my search, and a few minutes later, I finally found the body I'd been looking for.

I closed a door inside myself, then settled on the ground. With ash-covered hands, I lifted Viessa Folduin's head and placed it near the rest of her. She was as cold as ever, but the magic had left her body, leaving a beautiful, terrible shell. I closed Viessa's eyes and sat back, feeling heavy and hollow at the same time.

"Thank you for being my friend," I whispered.

A shadow fell over us. After a moment, I tipped my head and looked up at Nuvian. His back was to the sun, but I could still make out his expression. For once, there was none of the hatred or disdain I was used to seeing—there was only pain. He didn't say a word, and neither did I as I stood. Nuvian sank to his knees on Viessa's other side.

I left him to grieve alone.

More time passed. I didn't track the sun's progress as it began to move overhead. I helped the rats, the faeries, the nymphs, and the shapeshifters. Body after body I put in those carts. They got heavier and heavier, but still I went on. Even when another shadow fell across me and I caught that wonderful scent, I kept my head down, my focus completely on the task at hand.

"Go home," a familiar voice said. Then Collith added, because he knew I was about to argue, "Please."

I shook my head without looking at him. I bent down to grasp a dead water nymph's wrists. "I need to help with the cleanup."

"You've given enough. We all saw you close that Gate. We felt it." When I straightened to respond, Collith stepped closer and pressed a slow, tender kiss to my forehead, utterly disregarding the dirt and blood coating me. He spoke against my skin, murmuring, "Fortuna, please. You're about to collapse, and then I'll just have to carry you back anyway."

I knew he was right. I still really hated it when he was right. "Okay," I said faintly. "Fine."

Collith studied me with a faint look of surprise, but he didn't question it. "Do you want me to come with you?"

I considered the question for a moment before I cast another look around us. So many of the bodies were fae. These were his people, and no matter how sincere he was, I knew Collith would want to help put them to rest.

"No," I said numbly. "I'll just see you back at the loft when you're done."

I felt his eyes on me as I walked away. It took me at least an hour to get to the place where we'd parked all our cars. I'd hidden the keys behind one of the tires, and thankfully they were still there. They jangled in my hand as I unlocked the trunk. It took me a couple of minutes to peel off my gore-covered armor and put it inside. Once I'd rubbed most of the blood off my face and arms, I got in the car and started the engine. I was barely aware of the sound it made. I was barely aware of driving to the closest town, where the Door awaited. Barely aware of leaving the car, or using the Door, or making my way through the woods. Barely aware of climbing the stairs to the loft. Of greeting my family. Of Emma hugging me, Danny and Damon standing nearby with a happily babbling Matthew, as she said, "Oh, thank God. Thank God."

I let Emma fuss over me for a few minutes, and then I told everyone I was tired. They nodded and reassured me they would tell the others we'd won. Bea and Gretchen. Seth. I was so detached that even the thought of them caused no reaction.

"Oh," Emma said as I walked toward my bedroom. I slowed, then stopped in the doorway, as if my body was two seconds behind the commands coming from my brain. I looked over my shoulder at Emma, whose brows were drawn together with worry. "Was anyone hurt?"

"Yes. A lot of people were hurt." My hand fell from the doorframe, and my voice was still empty. "Viessa died. Narfu is gone, too."

Her hand went to her mouth, and tears filled her eyes. "Oh," I heard Emma say softly.

But I'd turned away again. I couldn't bring myself to say anything else. I continued going through the motions, because I didn't know what to do. I took off my armor, then the sweaty clothes beneath it. I showered. I brushed my teeth and got into bed. Hello jumped up, purring, and curled into a ball on my stomach. I rested my hand on her tiny spine and stared up at the ceiling.

I didn't expect to fall asleep. It did take a while. The battle replayed in my head, over and over. I wondered if I'd really spoken to my mother. I absorbed the aches and pains in my body. I relived the vivid scene of Lucifer's death. When I finally drifted into the darkness, I was still thinking about him.

And then I saw him.

He was in his study. His head was bent, his shoulders slumped. But a moment later, he let out a bellow of rage and swept an arm across his desk. Everything went crashing to the floor, the lamp, his computer, all of it. Cords yanked and sparked, and the light went out.

Lucifer moved to stand in front of the window, his chest heaving, fists clenched at his sides. He stared at his reflection in the glass, and suddenly his eyes narrowed. A chill went through me, as if I were standing on the other side of the glass looking back at him.

Could he . . . see me?

I want to wake up, I thought, making it a hard command instead of a hysterical burst. *I want to wake up* right now.

I woke up in my bed, drenched in sweat.

The first thing I noticed was that Hello was gone. In a rush of worry, I searched the dim room. I spotted her on the floor—my cat was pressed against the door, glaring at me with bared teeth. Her back was arched, her fur spiked. I studied the poor thing, my heart rate still uneven. She looked like she'd been threatened. Like she'd sensed something else in the room with us.

And I knew. What I'd seen hadn't just been a dream.

It wasn't over.

Steam rose from the coffee cup in my hand.

We'd all gathered in the kitchen. I sat on one of the barstools, and Emma occupied the one beside me. Collith and Laurie stood to my left while Cyrus and Ariel had claimed the space on the other side of the island, their arms wrapped around each other. Damon and Danny had done the same across from where I sat. Gil leaned against the refrigerator, his arms crossed, and Seth was nearby pouring himself a cup of coffee. Lyari had come, too, but she stood in front of the sink and stared out the window. The baby monitor rested silently in the middle of our tension, its small lights dim.

"We really need to work on your poker face, love," Gil said to me.

Shit, I thought, gripping my cup tighter. The bad news was probably written all over my face, and staying quiet about it certainly wasn't helping. I'd just been waiting to see if Nym would come. He hadn't been in his room, of course, so I had tried texting and calling, none of which went through. The fact that Nym didn't have any signal was a solid indication that he'd gone back to the Unseelie Court, and I didn't blame him.

The battle for the world might be over, but with Viessa gone, the fight for the throne had just begun anew.

Seth finally left the counter, holding one of Emma's coffee mugs between his palms. As our eyes met, I knew I was out of excuses. I just didn't want to see the expressions on their faces when they found out it wasn't over. But we were all in danger—again—and keeping them in the dark wasn't an option. Steeling myself, I rested my weight on my elbows and looked around at the people I loved.

"He's alive," I told them. "Lucifer is alive, and he's back in Hell. I saw it in a dream."

At first, no one reacted. Their expressions didn't change, and neither did the tension. "Good riddance. Let him rot, just as the Lord intended," Emma declared.

I gave her a strained smile. Gently I said, "The problem is that he still has connections here. Ways to reach his followers and give them orders . . . like killing us. Even in Hell, he's dangerous."

"Then we're right back where we started," Lyari said grimly, turning from the window.

"We didn't know about demon glass before," Ariel volunteered.

Lyari's eyes flashed. "And how do you propose we use it on him?"

Her tone made Cyrus bristle. Before he could intervene, I said quickly, "Ariel is right. We do have an advantage we didn't last time. Several, actually. Maybe we could talk to Gwyn. If she's not willing to help, what happens to one happens to both, right? Lucifer may be in Hell, but . . . but Oliver isn't. Does he still have the tracker on him, Laurie?"

Laurie nodded at the same time someone said, "Haven't we already established that the Beast is invincible?"

My attention had gone elsewhere, though. Nym now stood near the counter, and the others hadn't seemed to notice him. He stared at me silently. I gave the faerie a quizzical look. "Hi, Nym. Do you want to say something?"

"Time," he said, as if that was an answer.

"Oi. You hear that?" Gil muttered. Everyone went silent, and stillness rang in the loft. I glanced at Gil, on the verge of shaking my head in confusion, but then it hit me—the stillness. It was *never* this quiet, even when I was here alone.

The clocks, I thought suddenly. All of Nym's clocks had stopped. They weren't broken, as they'd been in that dark, dingy room at the Unseelie Court. I turned in my chair, finding each one. Many were scattered on surfaces throughout the room, and there were several mounted on the walls because we'd started running out of places to put them. Nym had been bringing the clocks home gradually these past few months, filling the loft with them, and Emma had happily helped him find a spot for every new find. If a stranger was to come in, they would probably think an old man with an obsession for antique clocks lived here. The constant sounds they made had become so normal they'd become background noise to me.

But now, all the ticking and moving hands had just . . . frozen.

I refocused on Nym, and my heart picked up speed, pounding in my ears. "What does this mean?" I asked.

The faerie rested his palm on my shoulder, pressing down briefly, as if to say, *Wait*. Then he looked at the door. We all followed his gaze, the air thick with tension.

Savannah Simonson stood in the doorway.

The necromancer wore a grim expression, and she was dressed all in black. The outfit reminded me of what I had put on for my battle with the Leviathan. I looked between Savannah and Nym, my brow furrowed. She fixed her gaze pointedly on the Time Walker, as if they'd agreed that he would handle all the questions.

"We are going back," Nym told me.

"Going back?" I frowned and shook my head. "Going back where, Nym?"

He held his hand out to Savannah, who crossed over to us and took it silently. Then Nym looked back at me and just repeated, "Time."

Did he mean . . . time travel? Right now? As I frowned at him, I remembered what Nym had said when I'd asked him to save Finn. *I have one more journey to make.*

My gaze lowered to where he still held Savannah's hand, and understanding flared in my mind. "Wait, you can take people with you?" I blurted.

"Now wait just a second—" Laurie began.

Before he could even finish his sentence, Nym's other hand fell from my shoulder. I had a second to register the sensation of his cool fingers wrapping around mine before the world imploded. Everything fell away in a rush of color and white noise, and we were moving so fast I couldn't even scream. Vomit spewed from my mouth and I felt like I was tumbling through nothing like Alice in Wonderland. *Nym*, I tried to say, but all I could do was hold onto his hand like it was a lifeline.

Pain vibrated through my knees as I landed on all fours. A small groan slipped past my lips, and I swayed there for a few seconds, trying not to throw up again. My eyes were squeezed shut, but I heard soft sounds around me—hopefully that meant Nym and Savannah had gotten here, too. Wherever *here* was. Once I felt strong enough, I leaned on my haunches, holding a hand against my forehead. I took in the room we'd arrived in, and though my skull was pounding from the shock of time travel, I recognized it immediately. A fire crackled on one side of the room, and a huge desk stood on the other.

We were in Lucifer's study . . . in Hell.

My stomach dropped. I looked around again, half-convinced this was a hallucination or a dream. Maybe I was dead. But what if I wasn't? What if Nym really had brought us to another dimension? If this *was* real, I'd never fully realized what an awesome power he had.

The thought made me pause. Some of my awe faded as something else occurred to me. I whirled on Nym, my eyebrows lowering in confusion again. "If you could do this the entire time, why—"

The door opened. All three of us turned in unison, and I froze at the sight of Lucifer. He froze at the sight of me, too, his brow knitting with confusion.

Nym recovered first. He moved faster than I'd ever seen him, producing a knife that glinted in the firelight. He went straight for Lucifer's heart. The taste of Savannah's terror filled my mouth as I cursed and launched across the room to help. Lucifer deflected the faerie's assault effortlessly. Nym was in no physical state to fight, I thought as I snatched up a poker.

Guess it was a good thing he'd brought me.

But I was still just a breath too far away, and as Lucifer's hand rose, I knew he was about to rip my friend's head off.

"No!" I shouted, shoving the closest thing I could reach to buy me precious seconds. The sound of the chair slamming to the floor drew Lucifer's focus for an instant, and that was all I needed. I flew at him and swung the poker at his head. Nym fell backward while Lucifer dodged my blow. At the same time, he grabbed my wrist and wrenched my entire arm around. I bit back a cry, but air hissed through my teeth as he let go. I cradled my arm against me and whirled to face him again. Lucifer's eyes flashed with something—regret, maybe—but then Savannah appeared, taking advantage of his distraction. Her hand flew out, and a cloud of dust hit the devil in the face.

He stumbled back, his face going slack, his eyes dulling. Everything seemed to slow down again, and I watched in stunned silence as Lucifer sank to the floor. His breathing was fast. Perspiration gleamed at his temple. After another moment or two, he curled onto his side like a child.

In exactly the position my other self would find him.

Awareness shot through my veins, and I couldn't contain a faint, startled breath. That night I'd assumed Lucifer was crying out from a bad dream, a night terror. When I'd gone in to comfort him, he hadn't corrected me.

Another truth tore through my mind like a bright, roaring car on a dark night. Lucifer had to have known he would lose me after this. He must've known the entire time we were together.

But that didn't matter right now. With effort, I refocused on the task at hand. Savannah bent over Lucifer, and there was a brief stillness as she did something I couldn't see. My gaze kept darting to the door. It took everything I had to stay still knowing that, any second now, another Fortuna would come in. I couldn't shake the sense that I was supposed to be *doing* something. Agitation roiled in my stomach, and I held my injured arm so tightly that pain shot through it.

In a matter of seconds, Savannah spun around and darted past me. "Got what we need. Let's go," she said.

What we need? I thought, nonplussed. There was no time to ask her about it. I began to follow, but that feeling inside me only got worse. I slowed, frowning. "Hold on, guys."

"If we don't go back now, we don't go back at all," Nym said, his voice surprisingly firm.

Ignoring him, I ran over to Lucifer's desk. I still didn't know what I was doing or what I was looking for as I opened the top drawer. But then I looked down at what was inside . . . and I knew. Instinct guided me now, and I pulled a piece of paper out, along with one of Lucifer's fancy pens. I put the dark tip to the blank surface. I didn't think about it. I didn't question it. The words appeared in my head like magic.

Don't trust him, I wrote.

Then I crumpled the paper into a ball, spun from the table, and tossed my message onto the floor, next to the door, where I knew my past self would find it. If this played out exactly how everything happened the first time around, I knew my note would end up in the fire eventually, burned completely to ash, but that didn't matter. It would plant a seed of doubt. It might've even been what kept me from giving myself fully to Lucifer, even when we were at our happiest.

"*Fortuna!*" Savannah hissed. I rushed back over to them.

No wonder I hadn't been able to read my own handwriting, I thought as Nym grabbed hold of me again. I'd used my left hand.

Then I felt that terrible whooshing sensation again, and Lucifer's study was gone. But the feeling only lasted for a second. When we stopped again, I looked around in bafflement. We were still in Hell. We were still in Lucifer's tower, in fact. Nym had brought us outside to the column-lined walkway, and familiar red skies churned beyond.

"I apologize," the faerie said thinly, pressing his fingers against his chest. "I am . . . I am having difficulty . . ."

Savannah and I reached out at the same time to steady him, and we both held Nym beneath his arms as he leaned against the wall behind us, trying to catch his breath. A line of perspiration gleamed at his temple. He was in no shape to travel, much less take two passengers with him. The realization made my stomach sink. What if we were stuck here? What if Lucifer captured us?

Fuck. We were screwed.

"Fortuna," Savannah whispered. The obvious terror in her voice made my head jerk toward her, but Savannah wasn't looking at me—she was staring at something over my shoulder. I looked back quickly, my arm half-raised to defend myself.

But it was only a lone gargoyle perched on the railing. The creature peered around a pillar cautiously, its eyes bright with curiosity.

"Givi," I gasped. At the same moment I said his name, an idea crackled through my mind with such bright, hot intensity that I almost gasped again. Gwyn's voice echoed back from the future.

Several months ago, I received an intriguing summons. A small creature from another world. It led us to a place full of stones.

There was another reason I'd come back to Hell.

I resisted the immediate urge to rush up to the small gargoyle. Instead, I looked in both directions, making sure we were truly alone before I crept over to him. Savannah hissed my name again. I could taste more fear on my tongue, but it would cost us precious seconds to give her an explanation. I ignored Savannah and focused solely on Givi. My voice was low and calm as I said, "Givi, I need you to get a message to someone. To Gwyn of the bloodline Nudd. She can be summoned by using her name. Tell her about the demon glass. Tell her that it's here in the city."

The gargoyle cocked his head, looking for all the world like some weird cross between a prairie dog and a creature from a child's bad dream. He made a chittering sound and stared at me with his round, black eyes as if he'd asked a question. Anxiety ebbed through my chest. What if he had no clue what I'd just said? I had never been able to figure out how well the gargoyles understood me.

I reminded myself that it *had* worked, because in the future, Gwyn got the glass and forged the weapons. We'd won the battle because of them. But just in case, I lowered myself down, putting my face right in front of Givi's whiskers. The gargoyle went completely still.

"Gwyn," I repeated softly. "You must summon Gwyn of the Wild Hunt. You must tell her about the demon glass. The mines are near the tower—at least the ones I know about—so she'll have to be careful. Mines. Tower. Do you understand, Givi?"

As I waited for some kind of response, another memory struck me. I remembered the stone Givi had given me during my final days in Hell. *Holy shit,* I thought.

That must've been demon glass, it had to be. I didn't have the stone with me now, of course, but I allowed my desperate hope to guide me. I reached for Givi's small talons and mimed putting something inside it, just as he had on the roof that night. It hadn't happened yet, but maybe that had been the gargoyle's way of saying he'd got my message. I stared into his eyes again and repeated, "Demon glass. Gwyn Nudd. Stones."

"*Fortuna,*" Savannah hissed.

Praying Nym had enough time, I spun from Givi and hurried back over to my companions. Nym pushed himself off the wall, still looking far too weak and pale. Part of me didn't want to take his hand, because the moment I did, he'd push himself to the limit to get us back. But I knew we didn't have a choice. We couldn't stay here. I forced myself to reach for him.

Once again, the Time Walker's cold fingers wrapped around mine, and Hell rushed away. We fell through red skies and a screaming stream of images and sounds. I felt my body stretch like taffy while my brain exploded with agony. I tried to say Nym's name, and I heard someone else say mine, but I couldn't answer.

After a blink and an eternity, I hit the floor of the loft with a hard jolt.

Pain flared in my wrists and knees. I lifted my head instantly, desperate to make sure that we'd actually returned to our world. The walls of Nym's room looked back calmly, and I let out such a strong breath of relief that it felt like my entire body deflated. Home. We were home. Hell was far, far away and Lucifer couldn't touch us.

The adrenaline was slowly leaving my veins. I sat back but remained on my knees, gazing across the space at Savannah. She knelt on the other side of the rug, looking just as shaken as I felt.

"What was that? The dust you threw at him?" I rasped.

Her throat worked, and I knew why, because my own was aching like a literal cry for water. It felt like I'd been in the desert for weeks. But Savannah's voice sounded worse than mine as she said, "A spell that makes you relive your worst regrets. I figured a person like him must have a lot of them."

A bitter smile touched my lips. "Not as many as he should. A little warning would've been nice, by the way," I added. "Next time you and Nym decide to go on a super fun trip to Hell, give me a heads-up. It would also be nice to know *why*."

"We were instructed not to."

"Instructed?" I repeated as I shakily got to my feet. "By who?"

Wait a minute. My mind was clearer now, and the urge to vomit had passed. I frowned, casting another glance around the room. Where was everyone? Where was Nym?

"I'm sure he's fine," Savannah said quickly, seeing the flare of worry in my eyes. "He must've sifted as soon as we got back."

"We need to do something. Collith!" There was an edge of hysteria in my voice.

I'd only taken one step toward the door when Nym reappeared.

In an instant, I knew something was wrong. The faerie's skin was like paper, and his eyes were unfocused as he stumbled.

He tried to regain his balance by putting his palm on the bed. I rushed over to him and grabbed his arm without hesitation, holding him upright. "Nym, what's happening? What can I do?"

He sank onto the bed without answering. I moved in a blur and grabbed Nym's narrow shoulders to stop him from lying face down. He didn't make a sound as I adjusted his limp form, putting him on his back, his head resting on the pillow. When my gaze returned to Nym's face, a shock went through my chest. It was quickly followed by a rush of pain.

No. I couldn't bear this again. Not again.

Blood flowed from his ears, his eyes, his nose. It was blue as the ocean. Blue as the deep dusk. I lowered myself to my knees and tried to wipe the blood away with the balls of my thumbs, even though it was useless, because more just kept replacing it. I knew there were tears pouring down my face, I could taste them, but the bitter flavor felt like a hazy, distant detail.

I sensed Savannah standing nearby, and the fact she wasn't trying to help Nym spoke volumes. Swallowing, I reached up and pushed his wild hair back, revealing the Time Walker's emaciated features. They'd always been gaunt and pale, but now his countenance lacked the spark, the inner light that was entirely Nym. Even when he'd been at his worst and unable to remember who I was, there was still a small part of him in there. And now I was seeing it fade before my eyes.

"What did you do?" I whispered.

"I used the strength I had left to come back to you," he said simply, smiling up at me. There was something childlike in his face, as there so often was, but it was different now. Less broken.

I forced a smile to my lips. "I'm so glad you're here. It . . . it doesn't feel completely like home until I know you're in your room, scribbling away. Ruining all our clocks. God, Nym, have I ever mentioned how annoying it is? You broke the *stove*."

I laughed, but it didn't feel like I was the one doing it, somehow. It felt like the real me was screaming, shrieking, sobbing, and my body had gone on autopilot. Nym must've seen the truth, though, because he gave me a sad smile. "I am sorry to cause you pain, my lady."

"You're worth it," I told him, trying to smile back.

His eyes drifted, roaming over the ceiling as if he saw something there I didn't. His voice became even hazier as he said, "You asked me, in the Dark Prince's realm, why I waited until that moment to intervene. Every decision, every action has a reaction, Lady Sworn. I knew I could only make the journey once, so I weighed my decision carefully. Time is such a tricky thing, wouldn't you agree? Too late, and the world would cease to exist. Too soon, and *you* might not exist. I knew we'd be friends, you see. I saw how kind you were. Perhaps I was a bit selfish in the timing I chose . . . just a bit. But the Maker can forgive me that, I would think. Such a small thing, and we did win in the end, after all . . ."

His voice drifted. I kept my eyes on Nym's face, afraid that I might miss him saying something else, but at the edge of my vision I saw the movements of his chest slowing. Slowing. Slowing. As Nym's eyes closed, the tension seeped out of his entire body as if he'd let out a long, deep exhale. A quake went through those bright, invisible threads between us, and my grip on him tightened, responding to the flash of pain.

And then, for the first time since I'd met Nym, he was completely, utterly still.

He was gone.

Several more seconds went by, and they were unbearably silent. I sat there, absorbing the blow of yet another loss. It wasn't a sharp, hot pain like I'd experienced after Finn's death. This pain was cold and quiet. I looked at Nym's face and prayed the peace I saw in his expression wasn't just wishful thinking. I committed this moment to memory, too, just as I'd memorized so many others, accepting that the remembering would hurt. Nym really was worth it, I thought as I lifted my head and looked at Savannah.

"We should get a message to the Unseelie Court," I said tonelessly. "His bloodline will want to burn the body."

Her eyes were bright with grief. She nodded. "I have the walkie-talkie. The Tongue agreed to use it after I started seeing Matthew again."

I said something back to her, but I was barely aware of the words coming out of my mouth. As Savannah left the room, I reached for my phone to call Collith—the fact he hadn't come when I'd shouted his name made it clear he wasn't at the loft. A glance at the lock screen told me that only an hour had passed since we'd left. Relief spread through my chest, and the line began to ring in my ear. Time worked differently in Hell, so part of me had started to worry we'd been gone too long.

"Hi," he said.

I held the phone tighter, swallowing down a rush of pain. I was still kneeling beside the bed, staring at the pale, empty shell that used to be my friend. "Hi."

Things got even murkier after that. I felt like I was underwater, the entire loft filled with it, shimmering in front of my eyes. I didn't remember talking to Collith or leaving Nym's side.

When I came back to my body again, I was standing in the kitchen.

I held a pitcher of water in one hand and two glasses in the other. Savannah sat on one of the barstools. Her expression was troubled, but her gaze was fixed on the counter in front of her, and there was a stillness around us that felt as if it had been undisturbed for a while. Like the glassy surface of Finn's lake at dusk.

Recovering, I moved over to the counter and set the glasses down. I tilted the pitcher to pour, and the sound of trickling water floated through the dim loft. I filled each glass and gave one to Savannah, who took it with a wordless nod of thanks. I took a long drink, then set the glass down with a jarring, hollow sound.

"Why did we go to Hell?" I asked dully. My gaze shifted past Savannah to the hall behind her, peering in the direction of Nym's room. His door was out of sight, tightly closed, but I could still perfectly picture the quiet, pale body we'd left in the bed. Waiting for his family to come get him.

His other family, I thought distantly, my fingers tightening around the empty glass. We'd loved him, too. He'd been part of my Court, and I knew all of us felt the torn threads reaching into empty space, the gaping hole that Nym had left behind when his death broke the bonds. My Court would be back soon, along with everyone else. I could feel them drawing nearer. I still wasn't sure why they'd left. Collith had probably told me, but all I could think about was Nym. About the question I'd asked.

Why did we go to Hell?

"I needed the Dark Prince's blood to do a spell. One that would attach his life to someone else's," Savannah answered finally, the sound of her voice bringing me back to the present. I pulled my eyes away from that shadowed hallway and refocused on the necromancer sitting across from me.

Once I had registered what she'd revealed, my jaw tightened. "And you didn't tell me because you knew it was a death sentence. Not just that—it's fucking murder, Savannah. I mean, we could pick someone obvious. Someone already on death row, or one of the faeries in the Unseelie dungeons that actually deserves to be there. But I've played God before and it always bites me in the ass. Always. If you *had* bothered to talk to me about it, I would've told you it was a bad idea."

Savannah licked her lips and raised her glass abruptly, taking such deep gulps that she half-emptied the glass. As she set it back down and raised her face to me, I sensed the faintest hint of fear in the air. "We already bonded his life to someone, Fortuna," she said.

My eyebrows drew together, and I replayed her words, certain

I'd misunderstood. But the second I actually processed this revelation, a thousand questions roared through my head and spilled out of my mouth. "What? What do you mean, you already did it? How? And *who*?"

"It was not my decision. There was another meeting of the Order," Savannah said.

My frown deepened. "The Order is gone."

"It has been remade. They had a meeting, during which they summoned me and Nym. One of the members knew about the bonding spell, and they commanded Nym to bring me back so I could perform it between the Dark Prince and one individual."

One of the members. It didn't take a genius to figure out who that might be.

Dracula and his tricks, I thought with a grim, tight-lipped smile. I'd been so focused on Lucifer that I had forgotten to worry about the Order. Nan said there were contingencies in place for certain events. But why would they get involved with this?

That one wasn't hard, either. The Order only had a single purpose—to keep the secret. To ensure our kind remained hidden and unknown. It was all Dracula cared about. Despite the Dark Prince's defeat, there was still one loose end. One threat to the great secret they had guarded so fiercely for as long as we'd been in this world.

I raised my gaze to Savannah again, and I saw my resignation reflected in her eyes.

"Who did they pick?" I forced myself to ask. Whose death warrant had they signed by connecting their life to Lucifer's?

But I already knew. It made perfect sense, no matter how much I wanted to be wrong. The inexplicable bond between them. The way Lucifer had been able to control him. All of it led back to this moment.

Savannah remained silent, which was as good as a confirmation.

Another crack burst up inside me, fissuring my heart into

more pieces. We'd been such fools. We thought he had escaped his fate, when in truth, it just hadn't happened in the moment we'd expected it. The imbalance had righted itself—that's what Michael would've said.

As the pain whispered through my chest, I remembered that dark promise for the thousandth time. *What happens to one happens to both.*

His name traveled alongside those words like the tail of a falling star.

Oliver.

CHAPTER TWENTY-SIX

My family slept around me.

They were exhausted from the battle, and undoubtedly from worrying about me after I'd pulled that vanishing act. I hadn't had the energy to tell them the full story of what had happened after Nym had grabbed my hand. All they knew was that Nym was dead and he'd taken me to another time. I had decided to reveal the rest after they'd gotten a chance to recover. Or a few hours of sleep, at the very least.

I'd braced myself for their nightmares, but all the minds around me were quiet after everything we'd been through. Collith was on the couch, exactly where he had been all summer. But everything was different now. For the first time, Collith and I were truly *free*. We should've been celebrating, or at least together. Yet there we were, a wall still between us, each of us sleeping alone. Well, Collith was. I wasn't sleeping at all.

I lay there with one arm slung restlessly above my head, staring at the dim ceiling. I kept going back, going around, remembering every moment and choice that had led me here. I yearned for a different ending, because I knew what came next. What I had to do. No amount of regretting or bargaining would change that. It was why Collith was on the couch instead of in bed with me.

When I finally drifted into sleep, I went to Oliver in a dream.

It was easy now, controlling my power. Understanding it. I couldn't recite a list of rules or ingredients like a spell, but the magic was ... me. It existed in every part of my body, in every cell and thought. It moved and changed as I did. Fighting myself and being afraid was what had caused so much chaos for so long. Now, after a lifetime of struggle and self-loathing, I finally felt at peace.

Well, I amended, gazing at the dark house in front of me, *not totally at peace.*

The sky overhead was black and starless, but I didn't need light to recognize the house that loomed over my head. I had committed every detail to memory the night I'd come here. And so, apparently, had Oliver.

Nothing moved beyond the windows, but I knew he was inside. I wouldn't have been here otherwise.

Neck arched back, I stood there for a while, long enough that I imagined my feet sinking into the dirt and becoming one with the ground. It all made sense now, I thought as I gathered my courage. Lucifer had been fascinated with Oliver from the moment they'd met. I'd seen the bond between them, even if I hadn't known what it was.

For the hundredth time, my mind went back to my conversation with Savannah. Even in sleep, I couldn't stop thinking about it. I remembered how the kitchen lights had shone down on us like a spotlight, casting shadows beneath Savannah's eyes as she'd lowered them.

"How could you do this without even talking to me about it?" I asked. My voice was still dangerously calm.

Savannah was calm, too. "They made the choice so you wouldn't have to."

The Order hadn't made the choice for me, I thought, simmering with barely checked rage. They'd taken it from me. I raised my gaze back to Savannah. "When did you see Oliver?"

"I didn't," she answered quickly. "Nym finished the spell, actually. We'd gone over it together, and he knew all the steps. After we went to Hell, and he brought us back to the loft, he made another . . . stop. The original plan was to take me with him and I'd do it, but Nym was too weak after we traveled to Lucifer. So he improvised."

Realization seared through me. It had taken Nym longer to come back to the loft, I remembered. I thought he'd gotten lost in time, or we'd left him behind in Hell. Savannah had let me believe it, probably because that was exactly what Nym instructed her to do. He knew I wouldn't have let him do that to Oliver.

The ramifications of the spell were still sinking in. Nothing had changed, not at the heart of it, but I felt the slow trickle of pain. Soon, it would become crashing waves of anguish. Oliver had to die, just as he'd always had to, and I couldn't waver. Not anymore.

Once again, I lifted my head and refocused on Savannah. My voice became dull as I said, "How did Nym even pull it off? Oliver would've overpowered him in a second."

Her eyes drooped at the corners, as if she felt sorry for me now. She nodded slowly. "Nym thought of that, too. That's why he went further back."

I frowned in confusion. "What? Further back would be impossible. Oliver didn't exist until this year."

Savannah's pulse visibly feathered against her throat. Her fear was all over my tongue, a familiar flavor that I hadn't tasted in a long time. She was terrified of how I'd react to this final truth, and her reaction heightened the sense of dread creeping through my heart. But Savannah looked back at me bravely. There was only the slightest tremble to her lips when she answered, "He traveled to a place the Beast lived before."

Before? I shook my head, trying to understand. Before I'd brought Oliver into the world he'd only been in the . . .

"He went to my dreamscape? It's real?" My voice was faint. Breathless.

"You made it real, Fortuna."

Savannah said it quietly, but I still stared at her as if she'd shouted the words at me. I'd known the magnitude of my own power, of course. It was hard to deny after I had closed the Gate to Hell and leveled the devil's army. But the ability to create entire worlds . . . my own pulse felt unsteady now.

Then I reminded myself that I did have limits.

"There's one glaring flaw in your plan. I have no idea how to kill Oliver. Maybe you missed it, but we already tried to do it a few times. He's as immortal as Lucifer. Which I'm now realizing is your fault, because you did the fucking spell that tied their lives together!" *A hysterical laugh burst out of me.*

As if Savannah was reading my mind—hell, maybe she was with another twisted, fucked-up spell—her jaw tightened. "I didn't make Oliver a monster, Fortuna. He'd already killed your parents when my spell took hold," *she told me.*

"How far back did Nym go?" *I asked sharply. Knowing the exact moment wouldn't make it more bearable, but it felt important. When had they doomed my best friend and sealed his fate forever? When had we lost any chance at happiness? And why hadn't I even noticed it happen?*

Savannah swallowed. "I have no idea. We didn't talk about that. He went to whenever the Beast was most vulnerable, I would guess."

Most vulnerable. *My mind halted on those words. I had an idea. A pretty good one, actually.*

In the beginning, back when Oliver had first started appearing in my dreams, he hadn't been the lovely, kind boy I would eventually fall in love with. At his birth, Oliver had been comatose. Pale, thin, unremarkable. A broken thing that could not bear the shock of existing. It was only later that Oliver became strong and beautiful and golden. He began to paint. He started to manipulate the dreamscape. He grew into something intelligent and powerful.

My stomach dropped as another realization hit me. No wonder I'd fallen for Lucifer so hard, so quickly.

I'd already been in love with the parts of him that lived in Oliver.

I raised my gaze back to Savannah, and now I wasn't sure who I resented more. Her, Nym, Lucifer, the Order . . . or myself. "You damned *him," I said thickly. "He was just a little boy. A weird little boy, maybe, but after I put him in the dreamscape, that's what he became. And you damned him. Any chance he might've had at a life . . . it was all gone the second you helped Nym with that spell."*

This time, Savannah's voice was steady. "Yes," she said.

Another silence swelled in the room. The air was so cold and tense that it made me think of the snowy battlefield we'd just left behind. The ticking of all Nym's clocks was gone now, and in their absence, Savannah's fear and my fury were all that was left. I could still sense that flavor, but there wasn't as much as I would've thought. Savannah had seen me at my worst—she knew the risks of pissing me off or betraying me. I looked into her eyes and I saw that she'd accepted the consequences of this choice she'd made.

Tension thrummed between us like a heartbeat.

Then I walked away.

I was still staring up at the house as the memory faded. I didn't feel ready to go in yet, but I suspected I never would. I couldn't wait any longer. So I walked up the path and climbed the porch steps, each one letting out a whimper as I went. The front door was slightly ajar. It opened with the slightest push, revealing the same dark hallway I'd seen before. The same awful smell.

I found Oliver in the living room.

His back was to me, his wings drooping. The ends trailed along the floor, leaving a line through all the blood. I stepped over the bodies and moved to stand in front of Oliver, deliberately keeping my eyes on his face. The corners of his mouth turned downward, a faint line appearing between his brows. He looked at me as if he wasn't completely certain I was there.

"Fortuna?" Oliver said. His voice was faint and confused.

Ignoring the carnage all around us, I reached up and cupped his blood-flecked cheek. "Come with me," I managed.

There was wariness in Oliver's eyes, but he followed easily enough. I led him out of that reeking house and into the fresh air. The second we reached the bottom of the steps, I cast my gaze toward the sky. Suddenly stars glittered above us, cheerful guides as we stepped into the woods, where life had always felt so much simpler.

Once the house was out of sight and there were only trees to witness us, I faced Oliver again. I didn't question if what we were about to do would work. I was a Nightmare, and we created our own reality.

"Picture our place," I told him softly. "Picture home."

I didn't wait for an answer; I wasn't even sure he could give one. I held Oliver's clawed fingers without flinching and thought of our childhood. Echoes of laughter sounded in my ears, and I felt the spray of the sea against my face. When I opened my eyes, familiar golden grass rustled around us.

We were back in our meadow. Back in our place, where I'd known such love and safety it truly could only have been a dream. It seemed fitting, that we should end in the same place we'd begun.

But I wasn't ready to finish it. Not yet.

Oliver's gaze roamed the dreamscape. He already seemed more like himself. His eyes were normal again, and all those black veins had faded as if they'd never been. "Fortuna, did you say something? I feel like . . . like I'm just waking up from a dream. Did something happen?" he asked me.

Seeing the worry in Oliver's eyes, the hint of apprehension in his voice, made the ache inside me widen. Once again, I avoided the question.

"No. Not at all," I lied.

Before he could say anything else, I went into Oliver's arms. As always, they tightened around me instantly, and it felt like my bones turned to liquid. My eyes fluttered shut again, and a single thought filled my being from corner to corner. *Home*.

Just as quickly as it had come, the slow warmth of joy began to go cold. Oliver's voice whispered through my head. *Is the bliss and the beauty worth the absence and the sorrow, Fortuna?*

I must've stiffened or flinched, because he drew away. "What's wrong?"

I still couldn't bring myself to tell him the truth. Not in words, at least. I looked up at Oliver silently, knowing he would see the pain in my eyes. I couldn't hide it from him—even now, after everything, he was my best friend. My first love. We may have begun with death and fear, but we got to choose our ending.

He frowned and cupped my cheek. "Fortuna, what is it?"

I just shook my head and wordlessly reached for the bottom of his shirt. I pulled it over his head, then I did the same with mine. I removed our pants, too. Once I'd laid all our clothing on the ground, I took Oliver's hand again and led him into the sea. The waves lapped at our waists as I faced him.

I could feel Oliver looking at me in silent puzzlement, but I still kept my focus on the movement of my hands as I reached down and formed a cup with my palms. I raised it to Oliver's chest, letting it trickle down his body. I did this again and again until I'd washed all the blood away, letting the water claim it, along with everything else.

When I finally lifted my gaze, Oliver's eyes burned with familiar intensity. He lowered his head, and his mouth hovered near mine. Waiting. I wrapped my fingers around the back of his neck and closed the breath of space between us. The kiss was hungry and tender all at once. Oliver reached down and lifted me into his arms. He carried me out of the cold and strode back to the grass, where he laid me down and reclaimed my mouth. My knees clamped against his rib cage and I felt him harden against my core. Arousal shot through me. Never breaking away from Oliver, I reached down and wrapped my fingers around him, guiding his cock to my slick, ready opening. Oliver made a low, masculine sound and pressed my wrists against the ground.

When he thrust inside of me, I felt the same pure strength in his hips that lived in his heart. I linked my ankles behind Oliver and began to meet him. He breathed my name, and I cried out his. We made love for the last time, losing ourselves in each other, losing all sense of time. Then Oliver's movements became harder and faster. His body went rigid, and he climaxed with a long, blissful moan. His entire body shuddered while I ran my fingers through his hair.

Afterward, I expected him to pull back, but Oliver laid his head on my chest. We lay there, drowsy and silent. I ran my fingers through his silky hair. In that moment, I was happy. Truly happy. It was like reaching the end of a long, exhausting journey. Nothing else mattered. Nothing else existed.

"I love you," Oliver murmured.

"I love you, too," I whispered back. No four words had ever been the easiest and the most impossible to say. My heart throbbed like an old wound.

Oliver's eyes glowed with happiness. In that instant, he was more trusting and vulnerable than he'd ever been. His guard was completely down.

That was when I knew—it was time.

I took a mental breath and slipped inside his head. Oliver didn't even notice. He didn't feel or sense me as I sifted through his innermost thoughts. Every creature had a weakness. Something they were afraid of. I'd know that better than anyone.

When I finally found Oliver's greatest fear, I felt my heart shatter.

"Oh, Ollie," I whispered, my lips trembling. I pressed them together.

He smiled at me like a child, so innocent and trusting. "Yes?"

Tears ran down my face—I tasted one, hot and bitter. I knew what Oliver was afraid of now. I knew how it had to be done. I held the knowledge of my best friend's undoing delicately, as though it would break at the slightest touch.

It was me. Or rather, seeing me in pain. Watching me die. Living in a world without me in it. Oliver's mind was a dark maze, something monstrous and hungry around every corner.

But in the center, there was a bright light, a single shining beacon. Me.

He'd been telling the truth all along. My mind flashed back to the day I'd asked him, point blank, *Can you be killed?*

Yes. I already told you how, once.

And he had. He'd told me back at the very beginning. I was Oliver's demon glass.

My chest quivered with pain as I leaned down to press one last kiss to his lips. Oliver kissed me back, smiling against my mouth. He was still smiling when I stood up and moved away, putting some space between us. I used my power to make the clothing reappear on our bodies, because I wanted Oliver's ending to be dignified.

"I'm sorry. I've never been very good at goodbyes," I said, my voice shaking.

Oliver sat up to watch me. He wore a faint look of confusion now, but he still didn't realize what was happening. "Who are you saying goodbye to?"

"Someone has captured me," I whispered. Oliver's serene expression turned to terror. I forced myself to keep going. "A werewolf. He's holding his claws to my throat. One move, and he'll tear it open."

My best friend's nostrils flared in fury. He got to his feet, and his eyes had hardened into ice. His voice became a dangerous, familiar rumble as he said, "If you hurt her, I'll—"

"Threats are useless," I cut in flatly. As quickly as they'd appeared, the black veins along Oliver's throat began to retreat, his claws retracting. I swallowed the sob that was lodged in my throat and kept going, my voice still hard and pitiless. "This time, you only have one choice. Take your own life, or sit there as the werewolf ends mine."

Oliver wouldn't be defeated so easily. He struggled against my will, trying to find his way back to reality. Something inside him knew this wasn't right.

Another day, another Fortuna, he might have won. But too much blood had been shed. Too much had happened. I merely tightened my grip on Oliver's mind and made the image worse. The werewolf flicked a single claw, and a deep cut opened across the other Fortuna's skin.

Oliver made a sound of horror. He tried to launch himself at me, but suddenly there was an unbreakable glass wall between us, stretching as far as the eye could see in both directions. The top of the wall reached up and disappeared into the gathering clouds, so that way was out, too. Oliver bounced off the glass and hit the ground, his eyes wide with shock and confusion.

Help me, the other Fortuna whimpered, pressing her palm against the clear barrier.

"Stop this," Oliver roared, throwing himself against it. "Take me. *Take me!*"

The werewolf flashed a grin, all pointed teeth and barely contained glee. *No trades. You must choose.*

But Oliver kept trying to break the wall, putting all of his considerable strength behind each attempt. The glass held, not even a spiderweb crack appearing along its smooth surface, because I willed it so. Tears streamed down my cheeks as I watched Oliver beat and batter himself, knowing he needed to believe there was no way to save me.

Eventually he did stop. He stood there, chest heaving. His furious, helpless gaze went back and forth, from my face to the werewolf. The werewolf gouged a second claw into the other Fortuna's flesh, and she screamed, her knees buckling. The werewolf used his free hand to keep her upright.

And finally, Oliver broke.

"Enough," he rasped, pressing his palm against the barrier. "*Enough.* I'll do it. But first, let her go."

The werewolf shook his shaggy head. *Sorry. That's not how this works. Guess you'll just have to take my word for it—she goes free the second your heart stops beating.*

There was a moment of terrible stillness. I could see it in Oliver's eyes, the realization that he was about to die. Slowly, he took something out of his pocket. He held the object so tightly in his fingers that it took me a moment to figure out what it was. But as his hand rose, I caught a glimpse. Pain streaked through me when I realized it was a paintbrush. I'd painted the blue flowers along the handle myself, and had given it to him as a gift. We'd been twelve years old. He'd kept it all this time?

Oliver did it so quickly that, once again, I didn't register what I was seeing at first. One moment the paintbrush was in his hand, and the next it was poking out of his chest, so deeply embedded that only the bristles were visible. When my mind registered the blood beginning to slide down the center of my best friend's stomach, a small sound escaped me. The sound itself had no name, but the pain in it was unmistakable.

For an instant, just an instant, I wished I could take it back. Doing this to him.

Oliver kept his gaze on mine. Even now, I didn't let myself release the anguish filling my throat, but I felt more tears dripping off the edge of my jaw. *Love you*, I mouthed.

He couldn't say it back, because Oliver was gone. His eyes were glassy and vacant as he fell.

To block out the sound of him hitting the ground, I thought of his smile again. The way he held his arms up on a roller coaster. How sweet he looked with sugar clinging to his lips.

If you died, Fortuna, I'd follow you into whatever afterlife there is. The rest doesn't really matter, does it?

When I opened my eyes again, Oliver and the dreamscape were gone.

I was back in my bedroom at the loft. It was early, almost seven. Gray light came through the windows—I must've forgotten to close the curtains last night. It was pouring, and the rain drummed softly against the roof. Water sluiced down the windows and cast trembling shadows across the floor. I turned onto my side and stared out at the cloudy, storm-smeared sky and wondered if Oliver was out there somewhere, flying between worlds.

"See you in the next life, I hope," I whispered.

Only silence and the storm replied.

Normally the silence would've driven me out of bed. I would've been brimming with energy and the ever-constant restlessness that lived in my veins. A restlessness that sent me on long runs through the woods or rushing to town, where I could find an abundance of distractions and ways to keep my mind occupied.

But today, I was a dim light. Today, I just looked toward the window, where that barest crack of day shone through, and I had no interest in it. I turned my head and sank deeper into the bed, pulling the covers up to my chin because I was cold, even though Nightmares didn't get cold.

For the next several hours, I drifted in and out of a semi-conscious state. Never fully waking, never completely falling asleep. Fragmented images flitted through my thoughts like pictures on an old projector. I saw the awful things that had happened in battle, the terrible things I'd done . . . and I saw Ollie.

It always came back to Ollie.

But eventually something did stir me awake. The low hum of voices floated through the stillness. When I heard my name, I felt a faint spark at the back of my mind. Not curiosity, exactly—maybe only a dull sense of obligation. Had something else happened? Was someone else I cared about in danger?

I forced myself to leave the warm bed and slip across the room. I still felt detached from reality, as if I were a ghost. I opened the door half-expecting my hand to pass through the knob. When I emerged into the loft, I immediately spotted Laurie in the doorway to the stairwell. His back was to me, and he'd turned in a way that I knew meant he was about to sift. Collith had taken a single step after him, his hand around the edge of the door, probably to pull it shut behind him.

"What are you doing here?" I asked. Although I spoke quietly, my voice cut through the stillness like the harsh, whistling wind of the Flint Hills.

Both of them paused, their faces turning in unison. When the faeries saw me, they exchanged a single glance, and I watched a silent communication pass between them. Any other day, I might've been annoyed, but right now I could barely muster the will to stay on my feet. I wanted nothing more than to drift away, back to that warm, silent darkness. I was about to do just that when Laurie moved to stand beside Collith, his next words directed at me.

"One of the witches in my employ had news," he said. His eyes gleamed with triumph. "Savannah confirmed it. Word in Hell is that the Dark Prince is dead."

Damn, word traveled fast. "Guess it worked, then," I said bleakly.

Collith frowned. "What do you mean?"

I couldn't bring myself to say the words. I swallowed and looked at the time displayed on the microwave. It was almost six. I hadn't eaten all day, but the thought of food was so unappealing that it turned my mouth sour. My gaze shifted toward the water dispenser in the refrigerator door. Without a word to Collith and Laurie, I went to the cupboard where we kept our glasses. I felt their eyes on me, cataloguing my every move as I took one down and walked over to the fridge. My motions were automatic. Slow.

Once the glass was full, I turned and took a long drink, thinking about how to tell them everything. I kept my gaze on the counter as I relived it all. God, there was so much. I decided to keep it as simple as possible.

"The Order has reformed," I said finally. "Apparently they summoned Savannah and Nym, and commanded them to bond the Dark Prince's life to Oliver's. When I disappeared, Nym took us to Hell, back to the time I'd been there. He didn't tell me anything, and neither did Savannah. Not about the Order, or the spell, or that it was Oliver they were bonding Lucifer to. I'm guessing they needed me so I would distract Lucifer, or maybe because I knew the layout of the tower. Either way, they did the spell, and last night . . . last night I killed Oliver."

I laid it all out like bullet points, hoping that would make it easier. But the second I uttered those final words, I felt my stomach lurch. I made a choking sound and bolted for the stairwell. I was outside, the barn blurred past, and then I was bending over the lawn. Whatever was in my stomach hurtled up. Gentle hands held my hair back. I was dimly aware that it was raining again as I gagged, the sour taste of vomit coating my mouth.

When I was able to stand up straight again, Collith and Laurie were there. Laurie held out a water bottle, but I didn't reach for it.

"I confess, I didn't really think you'd do it," he said, lowering his arm. His expression was blank. Pleasant. Fae.

"He had to die." My voice was still dull. "He killed Finn."

Oliver had killed so many others, of course. My parents and all those people. But . . . he'd killed Finn. For that alone, he had to die, no matter how much I loved him.

Suddenly a laugh bubbled up inside me. It filled my chest and throat, high and hot, until I couldn't contain it anymore. It exploded from my body like a physical force. I stood there with my head tipped back, arms hanging at my sides, laughing so hard that my sides ached. Water pounded down from the sky, sliding between my eyes and beneath my clothing. I hardly felt it.

When I finally lowered my face, Collith was staring at me. His expression was pained and helpless. He didn't ask me what was so funny, and slowly, my laughter faded. Thunder made the ground tremble.

Without really knowing why, I lowered myself to my knees. The ground sloshed beneath me as I looked back to the sky, where it was nothing but darkness and the occasional flash of light. Slowly, I lifted my arms. I could *feel* Oliver's blood on them, and I willed the rain to wash it away, just as I'd washed him in the sea.

But I knew that even if it did, I would never feel clean again.

Gone. My best friend was gone. A vital part of me ripped out forever. Lightning flashed as I pictured Oliver's freckles again.

I gathered air into my lungs and sent it back up as a scream.

CHAPTER TWENTY-SEVEN

My throat felt raw and acrid. Rain pelted my skin like needles. I was still on my knees, but I was shivering uncontrollably now, still staring up at the sky as if I'd find answers there, written in the roiling clouds. I was in shock, I thought dimly. Part of me knew I should probably get up, get out of this storm that I suspected I was responsible for. But . . . I couldn't bring myself to care. There was only the dull roar in my head, and the white-hot sensation burning through my veins.

Suddenly it felt like everything was tilting. I leaned forward, breathing heavily, and flattened my palms against the cold, wet ground. A moment later, I felt someone help me lean upright. When I just knelt there, swaying, those same hands slid beneath my knees and behind my back. A moment later, I was tucked firmly against someone's chest. My only response was to shiver, and then my teeth started to chatter.

"Goddamn it, Fortuna," a voice muttered. Probably Collith.

"Think we need to call Zara?" another voice asked. *Laurie*.

"Not yet. But we do need to get her out of these wet clothes."

I was regaining some of my senses now, enough to register that Collith was pulling off my shirt while Laurie bent to remove my shoes. I didn't want their tenderness. Not so soon after leaving Oliver. I saw that look on his face again—the pure anguish—as he'd died. Grief tore through me. I pushed Collith's hands away, shaking my head as I retreated. I held my arms against my chest and balled my hands into trembling fists.

"I'm sorry," I whispered. "I'm sorry."

I didn't know who I was apologizing to, or why. A moment later, my spine hit a hard surface, and I stared blankly at the familiar details of my bathroom. The bottle of perfume on the counter. The sticky note on the mirror that Emma had left one day, which said in her surprisingly neat handwriting, *You are loved*. The framed map of Granby on the wall. All of it was achingly familiar, and yet, I felt like a stranger in someone else's space.

Collith turned his head toward Laurie and said something quietly. Laurie nodded and disappeared. My teeth were chattering now, I realized, and I was shivering again. Or maybe I'd just never stopped. I didn't move as Collith turned on the shower. Within seconds, steam clouded the air over our heads. Then Collith crossed the room in three strides and reached for me.

I shrank away. "No," I said.

Collith immediately pulled back, and I heard the sound of soft footsteps. The door opened and closed. I stayed where I was, still staring at those objects blankly. The perfume, the note, the map. Then the door opened again, and I heard Lyari say, "We're coming in, my lady."

I didn't look up, but I sensed her drawing near. I felt a careful touch on my arm. The silent question got through to me somehow, and this time, I went willingly. A second figure appeared on my other side, supporting me around my waist. Emma and Lyari guided me over the lip of the tub and into the spray of the water. One of them stepped in with me while the other helped from the side. I felt gentle fingers in my hair, and the familiar scent of my lavender shampoo permeated the air.

Afterward, they dressed me and put me to bed. I shifted onto my side and clutched the corner of the pillow. Someone sat in the chair beside the bed while the other person stretched out on the floor. I stared unseeingly at the wall again, picturing that soul-rending moment. *Take me. Take me!*

"He's gone." My voice was hardly more than a whimper.

"Yes, he is," one of my companions said gently. "But we're here. We're not going anywhere."

A hand took mine in the dark. I didn't know whose it was, but it didn't matter. My fingers curled around theirs. "It hurts," I whispered.

"I know," someone murmured back. They squeezed my hand, as if to say again, *We're here*. A small, faint voice at the back of my head urged me to let go.

I held on even tighter.

"Fortuna? Did I lose you?"

The sound of Consuelo's voice was jarring. I pressed my eyes shut, hard, and forced all my thoughts back. To make sure they didn't sneak in again, I envisioned locking a door. Swallowing, I refocused on the woman across from me and muttered, "Sorry."

The clock on the wall told me that I hadn't said anything for almost a minute. Strange. It had only felt like a few seconds. Ever since I'd killed Oliver, time had moved strangely. Or maybe the damage had been done before that, when Nym brought me to Hell. I still didn't have an explanation for why all the clocks at the loft had stopped, not really. There were so many things I'd never get answers about.

"You have nothing to be sorry for," Consuelo said.

The human sat in her usual chair. Her legs were crossed, her head tilted in the way it always did when she was listening to me. Her office was lit by the gentle glow of a lamp, and dusk poured through the window shades.

"Where did you go just now?" the human asked softly.

I wasn't sure how to answer her, or whether I even wanted to. But Consuelo had taught me the value of silence. It had become easier to pause, and stop, and consider before I responded.

As I thought about what to say, my eyes roamed the room again. For the hundredth time, I noted the exits and the potential weapons. It was an instinctive thing—Adam's lessons had gone too deep. Me and my family might be safe now, but I would always catalogue every place I passed through. Assess for threats.

Everything was exactly as it had been last week, and the week before that. All that ever changed were the minute, insignificant details. Today Consuelo wore a cream, V-necked sweater and crisp-looking jeans. A thin, golden bracelet encircled one of her wrists.

What had she said to me? I wondered. Oh, right.

Penny for your thoughts.

"I was thinking about Collith . . . and Laurie," I confessed. Consuelo stayed silent. I shifted on the chair cushion, and in my agitation, some of those locked-away thoughts slipped through again. "Neither of them have asked me to choose, but I feel like I need to. Soon. It's been a few weeks since . . . since my friend died, and their patience is going to run out. We can't go on like this. Well, I can't, at least. Being with more than one person . . . it's just not who I am."

Consuelo regarded me for a moment, and although her eyes were as gentle as ever, they still felt piercing. She was one of those humans who seemed to see just a little better than the rest, and I fought the urge to fortify inner defenses against it. Consuelo had earned my trust. Sometimes the old fears crept in, wounds that were still scarring over.

When Consuelo responded, her lilting voice was thoughtful. "It may not be who you are right now, but that doesn't mean it always has to be that way. It's okay not to be ready for something."

In a burst of restlessness, I leaned forward and rested my elbows on my knees. "I need to choose," I repeated.

Consuelo watched me with a kind look on her face. "Do you know who it's going to be?" she asked.

"No. I love them both, in different ways." I swallowed again, my eyes wide and tormented. "But no matter who I choose, someone will be hurt."

The human gave me a wistful smile. "That is *life*, Fortuna. You can't be afraid of causing someone pain—pain is inevitable. It's the risk we take when we forge a connection with someone. The real cruelty would be to withhold the truth from them if your desires don't align."

Consuelo didn't seem to be judging me. She didn't know that we'd just faced the apocalypse, though. After everything I'd been through, after what the world had been through, this entire conversation felt ridiculous. Maybe that was why it did matter. Consuelo was right. These were things that people cared about not when they were surviving, but living.

There was a jab of pain toward the center of my chest, caused by the realization that she was right about something else, too. Pain was inevitable. It meant that I really was going to lose one of them. Forever.

I couldn't speak for a moment, and I turned my face away, wanting privacy as I regathered my composure.

"There is a third option," Consuelo said slowly. I looked at her and waited, still not trusting myself to respond. Consuelo gave me a small, kind smile. "You could choose yourself, for once."

I scoffed. "I choose myself all the time."

Her eyebrows half-rose, softly challenging me. "Do you?"

She really had no idea, I thought grimly. I tried not to think about all the turmoil and pain I'd caused, hearts and lives littered behind me like a road of debris. As I began to form a response, my eyes went to the clock on the wall.

"That's time," I said. I got to my feet and smiled politely. "Thanks for the chat. I'll see you next week."

Consuelo said goodbye, but something about her expression was solemn, as if my response had worried her. I left without offering any reassurances. I didn't want to lie, but I also didn't know what the truth was. The only thing I was certain of was that I loved Collith and Laurie, but sometimes, love wasn't enough.

Outside, I encountered a crow on the path. As soon as I came into view, it alighted into a nearby tree.

I hadn't seen Nan since the battle. I'd texted Dracula about her, who reassured me the shapeshifter queen had survived, but the fact she hadn't visited planted a seed of worry that grew with each passing day.

"Is that you?" I called to the crow, trying to hide a rush of relief and annoyance. Why did the entire supernatural world seem to know exactly where my therapy sessions were? Talk about an invasion of privacy.

The crow cocked its head at me. Then, an instant later, it turned around and hopped up to a higher branch, cawing as it went. *Great*, I thought. I was talking to birds now.

Feeling a twinge of embarrassment, I quickly turned and continued down the sidewalk. My keys jangled in my hand. I'd only gone a few steps when something made me pause again. I glanced behind me, looking over my shoulder. I realized the crow was back on the ground, and it had ventured so close that I could make out the grooves of its beak.

When my gaze landed on it again, the small animal bent into a deep bow.

"It *is* you," I said. Nan just flicked her tail feathers and launched into the sky. I called after her, "You're kind of a creep, you know that?"

Her answering caw echoed through the air. I arched my head back to follow the crow's progress, squinting against that distant, dying sun. The creature flew directly into the light, feathers gleaming like bits of stars. Those wingbeats didn't slow or hesitate, and soon, the rapid sound faded, leaving stillness in its wake. I reached the end of the sidewalk and turned right, heading for the new car I'd just bought.

At the curb, I turned and looked back at Consuelo's house, my lips pursed thoughtfully. The comment she'd made echoed through my mind. *You could choose yourself, for once.*

I turned and got into my car, closing the door so hard I felt it in my bones.

CHAPTER TWENTY-EIGHT

The vibrant colors of autumn gave way to the dull, solemn hues of winter. Days became shorter, and the hum of the cicadas was replaced by frost-edged, hollow gusts of wind.

The world had never felt so quiet. While the Unseelie Court fought over the throne like rabid dogs below, life on the surface was ordinary. Humankind went about their busy lives in the sun, and Fallenkind hid in the shadows as we always had. As we always would.

I'd gone back to working at the bar. It was strange to be doing something as mundane as waiting on tables after fighting the devil on a bloodstained battlefield, but there was also comfort in the familiarity.

Some things had changed, though. Bea no longer looked at me with fear in her eyes, and Gretchen protected my secret whenever I encountered someone dangerously perceptive, or a customer showed intense signs of interest.

Cyrus stood a little straighter in his kitchen, and he talked more than he used to. Once, I caught him manipulating the flame on one of his burners, the outline of scales brightening along his neck.

There hadn't been the faintest hint of fear around him.

The rest of my family was healing, as well. Damon and Danny began planning their wedding. They asked Emma to officiate, and Matthew would be their ring bearer. Watching them practice with him became the highlight of my evenings, and every night, the sound of scattered laughter floated through our warm loft.

When Damon requested that I stand as his best man, the outline of his face blurred a little as I told him I'd be honored.

Savannah continued her training at the Unseelie Court. She had become so renowned in her reputation as a necromancer that she'd begun getting letters—people pleading for her to bring back their loved ones, or teach a new necromancer how to control their power. But Savannah clung to her quiet life in the ground, emerging only to make the walk to our house, where she visited Matthew and caught up with everyone. More often than not, she stayed for dinner and lingered long after Matthew had gone to bed.

Laurie, of course, had his reign at the Seelie Court. He'd gone back to keeping his distance, but he still stopped by now and then to flirt with Emma and ask for Collith's advice on a variety of topics. He always made sure to smile at me, or kiss my forehead before he left.

Emma got approved for a bank loan to open a dispensary. Everyone drove into Denver for a celebratory dinner, and she listened to our toasts with shining eyes. At the end, we took a group picture with Emma in the middle holding up her paperwork.

The name across the top of her proposal had simply read, *Fred's Place*.

Ariel officially moved in with Cyrus, and she commuted to Denver for a new marketing job. She adapted to life as a human so efficiently that most days, I half-forgot she wasn't one. She remained as vibrant as ever, walking around with a smile stretched across her face, those dark curls bouncing with every step.

As for Lyari . . . Lyari had disappeared again.

I knew she was grieving for Thuridan, so I didn't push her to come home. We all dealt with that pain in our own way. But I took a page from Collith's book and sent messages now and then. Not of passages or quotes, since neither of us were huge readers. They were mostly pictures I took on my phone, along with texts that I hoped would make her smile.

The play of sunlight off a puddle in the parking lot. *Contemplating whether or not I can drown myself in this. That's how much I miss your stupid face.*

A selfie of me and Gil at Adam's garage. *Better come and insult the vampire soon. He's starting to develop some self-esteem.*

The horizon over the trees, with Stanley a small shape in the foreground as he took a morning dump on the lawn. *How I feel about you not being here. Everything is great, and it would be pretty close to perfect, except for that one pile of shit.*

No reply ever came, but I remained gently relentless, just as Collith had been. Sometimes I found myself half-wishing something *would* attack me, like that night with the demon. Lyari had certainly come running then.

But there had been no more attacks, Fallen or otherwise. No one came to the house or the bar who wasn't supposed to be there. Whatever enemies I still had in the world stayed away, and slowly, I stopped looking over my shoulder everywhere I went.

For the first time since my parents had died, I started looking forward to Sundays again.

Everyone in the family made sure to get that day off, no matter what. Me. Cyrus and Ariel. Damon and Danny. Emma. Seth and Gil. Savannah. Sometimes Adam came, or Bea and Gretchen, if they had enough staff at the bar. With the sounds of a football game always drifting through the room, we filled the corners of the loft with warmth and light. We ate, we drank, we talked, Hello usually curled in my lap and a fire burning beneath the mantle.

On those nights, I didn't mind taking a sleeping pill—reality was better than anything I could conjure up. What need did I have for dreams?

But despite all the joy, despite the hard-won peace that we'd fought and died for, I couldn't ignore another feeling deep inside me. A niggling sense there was still something missing. Not Finn, Viessa, or Oliver, though I missed them every day. This was something else. I just couldn't put my finger on it. Shouldn't I be happy now? Wasn't this what a happy ending looked like?

The answers evaded me, and the questions only got louder.

One Sunday, two months after our battle at the Flint Hills, Emma entered the loft with a box in her arms. "I stopped at a garage sale on the way home," she declared.

Gil was sitting with me on the couch, and Danny and Damon were on the floor with Matthew. When my nephew saw the box Emma was carrying, the little boy made a sound of intrigue. Damon imitated it and bent to hold my nephew's hand as they walked toward her together. Danny stayed behind to pick up the game they'd been playing.

Damon and Matthew were about to reach the table when Emma yanked her arms out of the box, revealing a squirt gun in each hand.

"Admit that I am Queen of the Loft, or get soaked to within an inch of your life!" she declared.

Damon's hands shot up, his wide eyes darting from Emma's face to the neon green toy she held. After a moment, he looked down at Matthew. My nephew's eyes were wide with delight. Damon looked back at Emma and raised his chin defiantly. *"Never,"* he swore.

"Big mistake," Emma replied. Then she tipped her head back and made a high, unintelligible noise that was probably supposed to be a battlecry. Her fingers closed on the plastic triggers, and streams of water shot toward her targets. Emma ran at the boys, shooting relentlessly. Damon cried out in exaggerated terror and swept my nephew up in his arms.

"I'll save you!" he shouted, cupping Matthew's silken head to shield it from the water. They ran through the loft, Matthew's squeals bouncing off the walls.

Grinning, Danny went over to the box and took out two more squirt guns. He threw one to Gil. I smiled in a wordless thanks but shook my head—I wanted to watch. Gil launched at Damon, and while the vampire's back was turned, Danny completely soaked him. Emma gently touched my arm just as I heard a British voice cry out, "Traitor!"

While the threats and screaming went on around us, I let Emma lead me into the hall. "I got a text," she said. "Apparently you're not so good at checking your phone, honey. There's someone here to see you."

I opened my mouth to ask Emma who was waiting, but at the same moment, Gil found us and aimed his squirt gun, shouting from the end of the hall. Emma screeched and ran past him, holding her hands up to protect her newly dyed hair. Gil went after her, a trail of water forming behind them as he pumped the toy gun. Matthew's giggles filled the air as he toddled after the vampire. Damon wasn't far behind, his arms extended toward his son, ready at any moment to catch him if he fell.

That was how I left them.

I walked outside expecting to find Collith or Laurie standing there. Maybe even Gwyn or Dracula. But it was someone else.

Standing on the other side of the driveway, Lyari Paynore turned at the sound of my approach.

She looked so different, and I struggled not to stare as I drew to a slow halt. My friend's hair had been cut short, and her face was narrower, making the ridges over her eyebrows even more pronounced. She wore modern clothes again, and the hilt of her sword rose up behind her. I liked it, I thought silently. I'd never seen this version of Lyari, but somehow, it was the one that suited her the best.

We faced each other across the narrow strip of gravel. For

a few seconds, the only sound in the world was a lone, forlorn wind. At last Lyari said, her tone as dry as the leaves littering the ground, "Did you call me a pile of shit in your last text message?"

Startled, I felt my lips twitch. "No. Well, sort of. But you're *my* pile of shit, you know?"

Lyari shook her head, and there was a slight tilt to her mouth, too. "You are so strange, Fortuna Sworn. Have I ever told you that?"

I shrugged. I was smiling freely now. "Maybe once or twice."

Neither of us moved, but the tension between us had eased. There was so much I wanted to say ... and so much I knew I couldn't. Lyari was still in the throes of her grief. I could see it as plainly as she'd seen mine, that night in the shower. The night she'd been there for me, helping me through my pain while her own must've been excruciating.

I wanted to ease it, just a little.

"Can I ask you something? About Thuridan?" I ventured, hesitant. Lyari moved her head, a subtle shift that told me she was listening. I kept my posture loose, my expression free of judgment as I asked, "What was he like? Before he became a Guardian and left Court."

Silence met my words, and for a moment, I was terrified that I'd made a mistake. The last thing I wanted was to drive Lyari away again. I was just trying to understand her better; I only saw the cruel, hard-faced version of the warrior she'd loved. Toward the end, I caught a glimpse of something different. Who had Thuridan Olorel been, really?

When the quiet stretched on, I bit my tongue and reminded myself to be patient. Some questions took time to answer. Some just didn't have an answer at all. I knew that better than anyone.

Lyari turned her head and watched the snow come down. Her eyes trailed the progress of a snowflake all the way to the ground, then moved upward again, latching onto a new one. When she spoke again, her voice was soft. "A long time ago, the other children at Court avoided me. I was the mad one's daughter. Weakness was in our blood, and associating with us made others look weak, too. But Thuridan didn't care about that. For many years, he was my only friend."

She met my gaze, and the ends of her short hair lifted in a gust of wind. She went on. "He was quieter, then. Kind. He made my first sword, as a way to defend myself when the others decided to stop ignoring me, and started beating me instead. Most evenings, I would hide in his room. It was a haven from the beatings, and my father's endless parties, and my mother's screams. Thuridan read out loud to me, or taught me how to use the sword. It was those lessons that prompted me to become a Guardian. But then a change happened in him—without any explanation, he became cold. Distant. Thuridan left shortly after, and ignored my attempts to see him. The first time our paths crossed again was the day he returned to Court and accused you of murdering the king."

"He distanced himself to protect you," I said, but of course Lyari already knew. She nodded, her eyes skittering away again. Another silence fell.

I considered walking toward her. After a moment, I held myself back. It was obvious Lyari wanted space, and I had to respect that, no matter how much I was tempted to forcibly close the distance between us. But that didn't mean I couldn't try to offer comfort.

I crossed my arms and peered up at the sky, remembering something the devil had once told me. "We get to choose," I said. Lyari's attention shifted back to me. I sensed her silent question and continued, "Being Fallen isn't a one-way ticket to Lucifer's torture chambers, like all of us believed. *We* get to decide, Lyari. Our souls go where we truly believe we deserve to be. You and Thuridan may not be together in this life, but he could be waiting in the next one. You know, if you ever figure out how great you actually are and realize you belong in a good place, too."

I gave her another small, teasing smile. Lyari didn't react. I studied her, unable to tell if my words had helped or caused her more pain. I knew all too well what that pain felt like, and my voice dropped to a near whisper. "I'm so sorry you lost him, Lyari. I wish you two could've had the future you deserved, and it's so unfair that you didn't get to."

Something trailed down her cheek, barely perceptible in the dim light—a tear. Lyari wiped it away with a rough, impatient movement. Without another word, she briskly crossed the driveway and stopped beside me, arching her head back to look at the loft. Light shone through the windows. A moment later, we both heard the sound of a distant laugh.

"I can't come back here," Lyari said. Her smile was gone, her eyebrows drawn together with regret. "This is not where I'm meant to be."

Sorrow cut through me. I didn't let it show on my face, though. Lyari didn't need any more guilt, since I had no doubt she was already feeling plenty of her own. "Where are you meant to be, then?" I asked.

A frown hovered around her mouth, her dark brows knit together. "I'm not sure yet. But I intend to find out."

I watched her with a small, soft smile. "I have no doubt that you will."

Both of us fell silent after that, and for a while, we just stood there together. Absorbing the fact that everything was about to change. It already had, a long time ago if I was being honest, but we'd never truly acknowledged it. Grieved it. The day was nearing its end, but it wasn't quite dusk yet. The periwinkle sky loomed quietly above us. Not even the crows came to disturb us.

Then Lyari turned to me and said, "It was good to see you, Fortuna."

At the sound of my name on her lips, a small jolt went through me—she used it so rarely. I swallowed the knot of emotion filling my throat. "It was really good to see you, too, Ly," I said.

With a final, parting smile, she began to walk away.

"Hey," I called after her. Lyari turned. "Any interest in sticking around for a drink?"

"I would, but there's someone else who needs to speak with you," she said. I frowned in a silent question. With a knowing look in her eye, my friend just retreated, leaving slight marks in the snow. Then she ran. She might've been a goblin now, but she still had the speed of a faerie. In seconds, she was out of sight.

I opened my mouth to call her back, demand that she at least give me the chance to say goodbye. Lyari was already gone, though, and her threshold was as limited as mine when it came to vulnerability. Deciding to let her go, I searched the trees for this new visitor she'd mentioned.

I would've been terrified by Lyari's parting comment—I didn't exactly have a good track record with nightly visitors—were it not for the feeling in my chest. Like the tiniest, almost imperceptible pressure had eased. Like a small part of me that had been far away was back now. As I turned, I knew as I always did, somehow, that Collith would be standing behind me.

I started to give him a warm greeting, but something about the way he stood made alarms go off in my head. I felt my welcoming smile fade. "Hey. Everything okay?"

Collith was expressionless as he said, "The bloodlines have decided. The throne will return to the Sylvyre bloodline."

I let the words sink in for a moment. It felt like my heart had turned to lead. My mind flashed back, lingering on an image of Collith sitting on that gnarled throne, cold-faced, his ringed fingers curling over the armrests as he looked out at his Court. "You're going to be king again," I said.

Collith just nodded. His eyes were riveted to my face, watching my reaction carefully. Trying to figure out how I felt about it, probably. Hard to do when I didn't even know. His tone was still neutral when he asked, "The coronation is tomorrow night. Will you come?"

My gaze lowered. A war raged inside me, tearing my insides to ribbons. Confusion, frustration, terror. Collith could taste it, no doubt. For the first time, I wondered if my fear had a flavor to him.

"Do you want to go upstairs?" I asked abruptly. "I'm cold."

It was true. The winter's bite shouldn't have bothered me, and maybe it was all in my head, but the pain of its teeth had sunk into my skin. Collith nodded again. I walked over to the door and held it open for him before I went inside too, sighing in relief at the warmth already seeping through my clothes. We went up the stairs silently, unspoken words swelling between us in the dark.

When we entered the loft, I expected to find chaos, but it was quiet. I must've been talking to Lyari for longer than I'd thought . . . unless Emma had seen me and Collith out the window and conveniently decided it was time for everyone to go to bed. *Meddling old woman,* I thought.

I went into the kitchen, more out of habit than anything, and Collith followed. Neither of us sat down or went to the cupboards. We just stood near each other. The silence still felt strange to me—I'd gotten so used to the sound of Nym's clocks. Maybe I'd get another one, just one. Nym would've liked that, I thought.

"To be honest, I'm a little surprised you're inviting me," I said at last, continuing our conversation from outside. "My presence might be a distraction."

Collith's hand rested next to mine on the countertop. "I don't want you to come as a guest," he said. "I want you to sit in the chair next to me."

My gaze snapped up to his. I waited for Collith to say something else, because what he was asking wasn't that simple. But he just looked at me and waited. Finally I replied, half-shaking my head, "You'd really want that? After everything?"

"Do you truly have no idea?" Collith asked, staring at me as if I'd said something ludicrous. I stared back blankly, and I didn't answer, because I didn't know how. Collith uttered a soft laugh, but it was as if he was reacting to a secret joke. He shook his head, smiling faintly. Then, before I realized what he intended to do, he closed the distance between us and cupped my face. His scent surrounded me in a rush of earth and spice and pure *Collith*. My toes curled in my shoes.

He bent his head, and his hazel eyes held mine as he said, "Fortuna Sworn, from the moment I saw your face on a piece of paper, nothing more than lines of charcoal and a vague idea, I have belonged to you. You are my first thought when I wake up and the one I carry with me into dreams every night. Decades ago, I set out to correct my father's mistakes and wrongdoings, but now, all I want is whatever life allows me to be at your side. I've made mistakes, I've been a fool, and you probably have more reasons to walk away from me than to stay. But I love you, in every way one soul can love another. When this world turns to ash, and all the stars are dust, and all the other worlds are gone, too, I will still love you. So yes, I really want that. I want *you*, all of you, forever."

The way he looked at me made my entire body feel like a live wire. Part of me *ached* to say it back ... but even now, doubt reared its ugly head. I opened my mouth to argue. To remind Collith of all the mistakes I'd made, too, and all the reasons we were bad for each other.

Then I thought of my conversation with Lyari. I remembered the shining pain in her eyes and how there were no guarantees or tomorrows.

I relived the sound she'd made as she'd watched the love of her life die.

Banishing Lucifer from my mind—he was the past, and I was keenly interested in the future—I cupped Collith's dear, familiar face. I knew it better than my own now. This beautiful creature had loved me from the beginning. Through every fight, every betrayal, every straying. Our story was long, convoluted, and damn near illegible at times. All I knew was that, by the end, it was the two of us again. And I wanted him, just as he wanted me.

"Will you sleep in our bed tonight?" I asked softly.

For just a moment, Collith's hazel eyes, framed by lashes so long and dark they almost looked fake, stared at me, taking me in, probably contemplating whether I was serious.

Instead of convincing him with words, I decided to show him. I took Collith's hands and led him into the bedroom he'd built for me, nudging the door shut behind us. When we reached the foot of the bed, I reached for the top button of his shirt. I slipped it free and moved on to the next, and the next, and the next. Collith's eyes never left my face as I worked, and the heat of his desire made me clench with need. Once every button was undone, I opened Collith's shirt and slid my hands down his taut stomach, landing on his belt. I undid that, too, finally raising my gaze to look back at him. A jangling sound floated through the stillness as I grasped the waistband of Collith's briefs and used them to pull him closer. My fingertips brushed against his hardening cock. I tipped my head back in a silent invitation, but he didn't move. I knew he was tempted. Why was he hesitating?

"You haven't answered me," Collith murmured.

My only response was to kiss him. Collith made a brief, frustrated sound, but he stopped resisting. His tongue entangled with mine and I moved my hands to his smooth, muscled back, exploring every inch of that, too. Now that I'd started, I couldn't seem to get enough of touching him. Luckily, the feeling was mutual.

"You drive me crazy," Collith groaned.

I smiled against his mouth. "Prove it."

Collith buried his fingers in my hair, tugging slightly at the roots. I lost myself to his taste and his scent while he made short work of taking off my clothes. I sat on the edge of the bed, then pulled away to move backward, putting my weight on my elbows. Collith took off his jeans and briefs and leaned over me. When he bent to kiss me again, I felt his hardness lodge between my thighs. The tip slid through the folds of my clitoris. I was already wet and aching. I moaned in Collith's mouth. The sound made his erection swell even harder against me, but he still didn't give in. Instead, he pinned my arms above my head and began to kiss the tattoos that only we could see, the tip of his tongue caressing and teasing my skin.

Finally I couldn't take it anymore, and I ground against him. "Don't make me wait any longer. Please," I whispered.

"*Fuck.*" Collith claimed my mouth with another hard kiss, then he drove inside me with a strong, single thrust that filled me completely. I would've gasped if my mouth weren't already so occupied. I made a deep sound instead, the vibrations of it moving through Collith. He thrust his hips harder, his fingers moving between my legs, where he found my clitoris again. He touched and teased me while we moved together in a perfect rhythm. Moans and breathy gasps escaped me, floating through the blue-black dark. I felt a familiar heat building.

"I'm still not coming. Not yet. You first," Collith growled. He plunged again, roughly, and I threw my head back as the orgasm took over, a rolling crescendo that had me biting my lip to hold back sharp cries. My thighs shook as Collith pressed into me one last time, and suddenly I could no longer see or hear, my mind filling with color and light. A moment later, Collith groaned, the sound low and masculine. It only heightened the intensity of my climax, and we finished together.

Long after our bodies had stopped quaking, Collith and I stayed there, clasped together. But his question still hovered between us, even after all we'd done. *Will you come?*

"Okay," I whispered.

Collith drew back slightly. I could barely make out his expression in the dark, but I saw the cautious hesitation in the set of his brow. The barest glimmer of hope. "Okay?" he repeated.

I mustered a smile. "Okay."

Joy lit Collith's eyes, and he bent to kiss me. I'd never seen that look on his face before. Anything that could make him so happy had to be the right choice, I thought to myself, kissing him back fiercely.

It had to be.

CHAPTER TWENTY-NINE

The dress was simple this time.

I stood in my room at the loft, studying my reflection with a troubled expression. I didn't exactly have access to the clothing at Court, and I wasn't about to ask Laurie for handouts, so I'd gone shopping in Denver. I had found a small boutique with gowns that wouldn't cost me a month's rent. The one I'd chosen was a sleeveless green satin, with a layer of golden flowers and a deep V-neck. The train was made of tulle, and there was a long slit that showed glimpses of my bare leg.

If this were a human event, I'd be fine. But it was a coronation at the Unseelie Court, and this dress would make me the laughingstock of the fae. Luckily, I didn't really care what they thought—it was Collith who I wanted to look right for.

I'd even put on the sapphire he had given me when we were mated.

That night seemed like a lifetime ago. My last memory of the necklace was when I'd taken it off during Viessa's coup, using it to humiliate Collith and break his heart. Maybe wearing our sapphire to the ceremony tonight was bad luck, instead of the new beginning I thought it was. I touched the jewel with my fingertips and watched my frown deepen.

This made sense, didn't it? This was the next, inevitable part of our story. Collith and I loved each other, and he wasn't the same male I'd ruled with before. I wasn't the same person, either. We had learned from our—

Emma appeared in the doorway and cut my thoughts short. My gaze flicked to her in the mirror. I lowered my hand and quickly pasted a smile on my face. "Oh, is he here already? I thought I had a little more time."

Emma smiled back, but there was a shadow in her eyes. "I haven't seen Collith yet, don't worry. Someone else has stopped by to see you, though. I left him standing in the driveway, since he was adamant about not coming up."

My awareness sharpened. "Who is it?"

Her brows lowered. "You know, I forgot to ask his name. I'm sorry, dear. I've been testing some new product."

Moving in a blur, I turned my back on the mirror and made a beeline for the nightstand. Emma watched without comment as I hid multiple knives beneath my dress. Human visitors tended to text before they showed up, which meant there was something supernatural standing outside. The battle had established that I had allies in the shadow world, so it could be a friendly meeting . . . but I was still a Nightmare, which meant there was always danger. Power attracted power. I still had plenty of enemies, too.

"Fortuna."

Emma so rarely used my full name that I drew up short at the sound, and I paused in the doorway of the stairwell. "Yes?"

"About tonight," she started, but then Emma stopped. Hesitation was unlike her, too. I was starting to feel true concern when Emma said, "You know, I used to think that happy endings included another person. But lately I've come to realize that we can still have happy endings with or without someone to share it with. There are many different kinds of love, and I was so focused on what I knew that I almost missed the others."

She paused again, and remorse shone in her eyes. "I pushed you toward Collith because I thought you were just afraid to want him. But . . . if your heart is telling you something, Fortuna, it's all right to listen to it."

"Thanks, Ems." I pursed my lips to hide how they trembled. As I tried to think of what to say, I realized I didn't want to talk about this. I wanted to be with Collith, so I'd made my decision. I gestured toward the stairwell behind me. "I should . . . I should see what this visitor wants. And then I need to go. Collith will be here any second."

Emma nodded. "Are you sure you don't want me there?"

"No," I said quickly. Too quickly. But the thought of small, frail Emma entering a room full of fae made my stomach churn. I gave her a reassuring smile and shook my head. "The Unseelie Court isn't a safe place for humans, trust me."

"Okay, then. Good luck." Emma smiled back. "Not that you'll need it . . . Your Majesty."

I turned away to hide my wince, taking my coat off the hook. When I got downstairs and opened the door, I spotted him immediately, standing exactly where Lyari liked to whenever she was waiting on me. It was the last person in the world I would've expected to seek me out, and I stepped outside cautiously, meeting his unfathomable gaze across the driveway.

Nuvian Folduin.

"What do you want?" I said, but there was none of my usual bite when I talked to him.

The faerie didn't answer. He stood there for so long, in fact, that I normally would've gotten annoyed or said something, were it not for the look on Nuvian's face. But I recognized that look. I knew the pain he was feeling. So I stayed silent and waited. For a few seconds, the only sound between us was the scrape of a leaf as a breeze dragged it away. When Nuvian finally spoke again, his voice was raw, as if someone had ripped all his armor off.

"I got caught in the tide of battle. I looked away, just for a few seconds, and then she was . . . I didn't even . . ." Nuvian stopped, his throat working. "I was hoping you'd . . . "

"You want to know how she died," I said softly.

Nuvian's eyes met mine, and he nodded once, jerkily, the abrupt movement unlike his usual grace. I couldn't bring myself to deny his request, however much I disliked this faerie. But what was the right way to tell him? What would Viessa have wanted me to say?

Buying myself some time, I walked past Nuvian—he moved out of the way quickly, as if touching me would burn him—and leaned against a tree trunk. The ridges of the bark dug into my palms. I fixed my eyes on the ground and thought about the friend we'd both lost. Our shared grief was something I never could've predicted a few months ago.

"You know," I said quietly, "getting thrown in the cell next to Viessa's was one of the best things that ever happened to me. I've never had a friend like her. Someone who could get me to dance and laugh, even when there was nothing to celebrate. *Especially* when there was nothing to celebrate."

"She was like that for me, too." Nuvian's voice was soft with remembrance.

"I'm guessing you already know that she faced Lucifer. What you don't know is how much she surprised him. Viessa took on the devil himself without any hesitation, and where most warriors would've been pissing themselves, she was absolutely fearless. Like, it didn't even *occur* to her to back down, you know?" I shook my head slightly and felt my lips curve in a soft smile. But then my smile faded. I realized that I couldn't tell Nuvian exactly how it had ended. He didn't need to know about that awful moment or the terrible pain. All he needed was the truth. I met his gaze and said, "Viessa Folduin fought like a queen, and she died like one, too."

Nuvian's face shifted toward the horizon. The golden strands in his locs caught the light and shone on the planes of his perfect, hardened features. "I never wanted it," he said. "If I'd had my way, the two of us would've slipped away from Court a long time ago."

His words made my eyebrows rise. We had something else in common, this faerie and I. Both of us had chosen this life for the sake of someone we loved. I wondered how things would've turned out if he'd gone down a different path. For some reason, my mind picked that moment to remember what Consuelo had said to me at the end of our last session.

You could choose yourself, for once.

A moment later, I felt it. The familiar, telltale prickle that told me Collith was near. It didn't make sense, since there was no mating bond between us, and he wasn't part of the Shadow Court. Some things, I thought as I turned, were simply unexplainable.

He was standing there, just as I'd known he would be. I walked toward him, and my voice was soft as it floated through the stillness. "Hi."

Collith smiled. "You look beautiful."

"Thank you." I mustered a weak smile for him before I turned back to Nuvian. "Are you coming?"

"No. I won't be returning to Court," he answered, nodding at Collith. As Collith nodded back, I realized a conversation must've taken place between them already. A Guardian could only leave their post if they'd gotten approval from the king or queen.

"Then I guess this is goodbye," I said to Nuvian.

"I suppose it is." The faerie bent in a stiff bow and turned to leave. But then he paused, as if he'd heard something or had a thought. After another moment, Nuvian moved his head. He kept his gaze fixed on the ground as he said over his shoulder, "She loved you, too."

My throat worked, and I watched him disappear into the trees.

After a few seconds, Collith stepped closer and touched my waist. "Do you have everything you need? We should go. My guards are waiting for us just beyond the trees," he said.

He had guards again. Because that was part of the deal when you became the king and queen. I nodded silently and started walking toward the trees, as we had a hundred times before. We walked all the way to the Door tucked away in the dusk-tinted forest, as we had a hundred times before. We made our way through the tunnels and down to the throne room, as we had a hundred times before. Then we reached that towering set of doors, as we had a hundred times before.

I stopped near the threshold. I stared at those distant thrones and couldn't bring myself to take another step. Collith murmured something to the guards, and I sensed them retreating. The courtiers had already started to gather. None of them noticed us yet. I didn't want to embarrass Collith, and I silently commanded myself to move forward . . . but my feet wouldn't move. I could feel Collith studying me.

"You don't want to do this." It wasn't a question, but he still waited for an answer. I turned toward him. Silence swelled between us. When I didn't deny it, Collith bent his head so I couldn't see his expression. Pain clawed deep into my heart.

"I do *love* you, Collith. More than I can say. This doesn't . . ." I faltered. My hands curled into fists. As I struggled to form a response, I thought about the conversation I'd just had with Nuvian. I exhaled and spoke slowly, deliberately. "It feels like I'm stepping into someone else's story, just when I was finally given the chance to write my own. You may have been born to be a king, but sitting on a throne isn't for me, Collith. It's not just because I don't trust myself not to let the power go to my head again."

"You could learn . . ." he started desperately. I was already shaking my head.

"I don't *want* to learn, Collith. This isn't the life I choose. I choose happiness. I choose myself. And that's okay, I'm not ashamed of it." I stopped, swallowing. "This whole summer, whenever I was with you and Laurie, I felt a little sad. Even when I was happy, it was there. I think I've known for a long time what's right for me. What I need to do."

I raised my gaze. It felt like someone was beating at my heart with their bare fists. I was about to continue when Collith looked away, his jaw working. I'd have thought he was angry were it not for his eyes, or the faint flavor on my tongue.

"I can't do this without you, Fortuna," Collith whispered. "Before we met, I accomplished nothing. You did more in one month than I did in one decade."

"Hey." Suddenly I didn't care who was watching us. I moved closer and cupped Collith's face in my hands, my fingers resting gently on that jagged scar. "You are *not* the faerie I met that day in the black market. You don't have to be as . . . brutal as I was, but I don't think you're capable of just sitting there anymore. It's more than a big, creepy chair now."

His gaze traced my features while his own eyes shone with pain. "I love you," he said.

I smiled sadly. "I know."

Collith bent his head. I expected a chaste kiss, but his hands slid around my waist and pulled me close. He claimed my mouth without hesitation, without restraint, reminding me exactly what I'd be missing. It was one of the first things I'd liked about him, I remembered as I wrapped my arms around Collith's neck and kissed him back.

When Collith broke the kiss and pulled away, he didn't say goodbye. He'd promised me a life of hellos, after all. And technically, I was the one leaving.

I turned from him just as the drums started. I kept the image of Collith there in my mind, memorizing every detail. I heard footsteps and voices as the guards moved and the crowd spotted their king.

I told myself I wouldn't look back, but when I reached the far doorway, I gave in to the urge. My vantage point was perfect. From where I stood, I could see Collith walking through the crowd, that gnarled throne looming.

The mural above him snagged my attention. It took me several moments to pinpoint what had changed—someone had added to it again. The painter's skill was considerable, and it was obvious the face staring out from above the doorway was my own.

Then something moved, drawing my gaze back downward. Lyari stood beneath the archway now. She wasn't wearing her Guardian armor, which meant she'd probably just come to witness the return of a Sylvyre to the throne. I could still see Collith behind her, and the drum filled my ears. My heart beat in tandem with its steady rhythm.

I want to leave, I realized suddenly. *Right now.* In the past year, I'd experienced every kind of torture and pain imaginable. Watching the person I loved make vows to a crown instead of me was one I would spare myself.

As I prepared myself, my gaze returned to Lyari, and she nodded at me. Smiling faintly, I nodded back.

With that, I walked away from the throne room again, and this time I didn't stop. The train of my dress dragged behind me, and I put the Unseelie Court behind me. Not a queen, not a mate, not a player. Just . . . Fortuna. And that was okay. More than okay.

The earthen walls swallowed the sound of my footsteps as I left the Unseelie Court for the last time.

When I emerged from the trees, Laurie's slender form stood in the distance.

His back was turned to me, to the loft. Of course he was standing directly in a beam of moonlight, because Laurie was drawn to any spotlight within a mile radius. I couldn't bring myself to mock him, though. I walked the rest of the way to the Seelie King, then stopped beside him. His nostrils flared, and I knew what he was scenting on me. On my dress. On my skin. But Laurie's expression didn't reveal anything.

"So you chose him," he remarked. "I'd heard as much. Not from you, of course. Tabby mentioned it."

"Well, Tabitha's information is outdated. I actually chose myself." I tipped my chin toward the sky, admiring a sprinkling of stars. "Will you be paying a visit to the Unseelie Court to congratulate the new king?"

Laurie was silent for a beat, as if I'd surprised him. "No," he said finally. "My days of lurking around that place are finished."

I was tempted to ask why, but I also didn't want to know. I needed to walk away from both of them, and I wouldn't be able to do that if I kept making the same choices. At least for a while.

Maybe Laurie had already guessed what was coming. As we stood there, he didn't ask any questions or try to whisk me off to some country or other. He was dressed more conservatively than usual, too, in simple dress slacks and a button-up shirt with the sleeves pushed to his elbows. I longed to lean my head on his shoulder, but the time for leaning on Laurelis Dondarte had come to an end, like so much else.

"Hey, if neither of us are married by the time we're nine hundred, how about we just marry each other?" I suggested, hoping to lighten the mood a little.

Laurie did smile, but it wasn't the one I'd been hoping for. This smile was the shadow behind the sun, the dark side of the moon. "I knew the moment I laid eyes on you, Fortuna Sworn, that you were a heartbreaker. And I consider it an honor to have had mine broken by you," he told me.

"Laurie . . ." I swallowed. "I was scared, but I was also being selfish. I didn't want to let you go. I didn't want to lose this."

Once again, the Seelie King fell silent. Somewhere in the trees, a bird began to sing. Its call echoed over the dim yard. I searched for the flutter of wings, or any sign of the small creature hopping from branch to branch, but it was too dark.

"Nothing ends, Fortuna Sworn," Laurie said at last, drawing my attention back to him. "There are only continuations and beginnings."

He'd first said those words to me when I was at the Unseelie Court trying to save my brother. Laurie and I had been strangers then, and hearing him say it now felt like a cut and a kiss. In a way, he was right. He and I had come full circle, just as I had with Collith. And now, finally, there was nothing left to say. No more arguments, no more confessions.

Well, I amended silently, maybe there was one more.

"I love you," I told Laurie.

He went still. Then he turned, taking his hands from his pockets. I expected him to kiss me. Instead, Laurie wrapped his arms around me, his grip fierce and gentle at the same time. Recovering, my eyes fluttered shut and my hands slowly rose to hug him back. I pressed into his body and breathed in, knowing this would probably be the last time I'd be able to for a long, long time. That springtime fragrance assailed my senses.

"I love you, too," Laurie said huskily, cupping the back of my head as if I was something infinitely precious. I felt his chest move like he was memorizing my scent, too.

And then I was holding onto nothing, my arms embracing nothing but air. They fell to my sides, empty. I tipped my head back and peered up at the barn. That was my last goodbye, I thought. I'd said my farewells to everyone else. No one was expecting me back, since I'd assumed I would stay at Court after the coronation. I could've kept living at the loft part-time, like I had before, but I didn't want to do anything at half-measures anymore.

There was one thing I needed, though. I headed for the barn and slipped inside, moving quietly so I wouldn't wake anyone.

Five minutes later, Hello yowled her displeasure as I put her in the backseat. "I know, I know," I crooned at her. "Who's such a good kitty?"

When I straightened, I jumped at the sight of my brother leaning against the side of the car. "Damon, what are you—"

"Don't bother," he said.

Whatever I'd been about to say faded as his meaning became clear. It was the same thing Damon had told me on my eighteenth birthday, when I was leaving Dave and Maureen's. Even now, all these years later, I could picture him in that moment, his young face so determined and earnest. So completely Damon. *Don't bother. I'm going with you. We made a promise, remember?*

I was about to speak when my brother added, straightening from the car, "I just need some time to get ready. I'll need to pack a bag for Matthew, too."

He didn't ask why I wasn't at the Unseelie Court getting crowned with Collith. He didn't mention Danny, or his job, or any of the other reasons why he couldn't come this time. But the fact he was willing to leave it all behind for me, even temporarily, made a lump swell in my throat. I stepped forward and held Damon's elbows in my palms, smiling up at him.

"Things are different now, little brother. You have a family of your own to look after." I stood on tiptoe and pressed a soft kiss against his cheek. "I'll be all right. I promise. Nightmares may be lies, but we don't have to—

"—be liars," Damon finished. He knew I was right, but a struggle still shone in his eyes. "Are you sure?"

I gave him another soft smile. "I am."

"Okay." He looked down at me for a moment, as if he was trying to read my mind. Then Damon nodded and said again, more firmly this time, "Okay."

To hide the pain in my own eyes, I stepped closer and embraced him. Damon was so startled that he froze for a moment. Then his long arms wound around me, and for a few seconds, we stayed like that. "I'll miss you," he murmured.

I pulled away. I felt a tugging sensation within me, and I knew if I didn't leave now, I never would. "I'll call you from the road. And I'll send you guys so many updates you'll probably get sick of me."

"Not possible." Damon moved back, his expression solemn as he watched me reach for the small bag I'd packed.

I circled the car and opened the door, tossing my bag into the passenger seat. Just as I put my foot inside, I paused. I tipped my head back and looked up at the barn. Then I looked at Cyrus's house, and those far off trees I'd walked through so many times during the seasons we had lived here. I knew, no matter where I went or how many people I met, this would always be home. Some things embedded not just in your heart, but in your very soul, and there was no way of removing them. Not time, not distance. Not even death.

My throat filled again, and I lingered there, holding the door with white fingers. I was afraid. Afraid to actually get in that car and drive away, move on to somewhere different and unknown.

But I was a Nightmare. I knew what fear did to people.

So I got in the car, and I drove.

CHAPTER THIRTY

ONE YEAR LATER

Condensation rolled down the plastic sides of my iced coffee.

It rested beside me, all but forgotten as I frowned at a textbook splayed open on the table. I held a highlighter in my other hand, and I fidgeted with it absently, my lips twisted in concentration as I clicked the cap on, off, on, off. A dry breeze stirred the end of my ponytail. Moments later, I briefly raised my eyes from the page, distracted by the trilling sound of a cyclist ringing their bell as they passed.

After the bike was gone, I allowed myself a temporary reprieve, my gaze lingering on the street. I sat at one of the tables along the sidewalk, and all the windows and doors to the cafe were open behind me, allowing the sounds and smells to come through. Clinking dishes, the hiss and spit of the espresso machine, music crackling from the speakers. Contentment rested in my chest, a small, comforting weight that I was still getting used to. There was a lot I was still getting used to, despite all the months that had passed since coming here.

It was a year ago today, I realized with soft surprise. I stared out at the street without really seeing it now, my mind wandering. It was a year ago today that I'd gotten in my car and driven into the horizon, leaving everything familiar behind. And even though I missed so much about that old life, all the change was easier than I'd thought it would be. I liked Tucson. I liked the heat, and the sunlight, and the endless blue skies.

And I liked the strange, new person I'd become.

If anyone in the world of Fallen came looking for me, this was all they'd see—a girl. A quiet, pretty girl who went for jogs every morning and attended classes every afternoon. A girl who worked at a bar part-time. A girl who seemed to have many unique-looking friends, like a pale man with bleached hair or a boy with horns growing from his head—Seth no longer wore his glamour.

A girl who didn't laugh or smile very often, but when she did, it was genuine.

I wore that faint smile now as I finally refocused on the textbook. I'd just skimmed the first sentence when a shadow fell across the page. A moment later, chair legs screeched over concrete as someone pulled out the other seat, then sat in it. I lifted my head again, annoyance dimming my good mood. I opened my mouth to tell the bold stranger to get lost.

When I saw who was sitting there, the sharp words on my tongue faded. It felt like the ground had dropped out from underneath me, and my stomach hollowed out in shock.

"Nym?" I breathed.

He smiled, a breeze stirring his dark bangs. "Hello, my lady."

A million reactions rushed through me. Disbelief, joy, hope. Such wild, wild hope. *Nym was alive.* I kept staring at him—this was a version of my friend I'd never seen before. He was still slender, but there was none of the gauntness that had clung to him before. The constant haze in his eyes was gone, too, and Nym looked back at me with a clear, steady gaze that was almost unnerving. He wore the clothes of a faerie courtier, and every button on his brocade vest was neatly done. He was even wearing *shoes*.

A second after that, it felt like my mind thawed. I'd been frozen there, gaping, but now I launched across the table and hugged him.

Nym made a soft, startled sound. He raised his arms slowly, and then I felt his hands rest on my back, the touch light as butterflies. The street behind him blurred as tears sprang to my eyes. I blinked rapidly, and I made sure I'd cleared them away before I settled back in my chair. Nym watched me, probably waiting for me to ask one of the thousands of questions racing through my head. We both knew what the first one would be.

"How?" I said finally.

He gave me another smile, but this one was sadder. "I have not come back to life, my lady. I'm merely breaking a rule or two."

It took me a couple seconds to realize what he meant. The hope in my chest shriveled like a dying flower, and in some small, awful way, it felt like I'd lost him all over again. "You're from the past?" I asked.

"That is correct, my lady."

Something else occurred to me, and panic surged through my veins. "Doesn't it cost you to Timewalk? Even one visit can affect your sanity."

"I've come to tell you something," Nym said. He spoke so firmly that my protests faded. He rested his hands atop his knees, which were primly crossed, and I was struck anew at this strange version of the chaotic faerie I'd known.

"Okay," I said with a touch of apprehension. I realized I'd dropped my highlighter on the table, and I put the cap back on, knowing my studying was officially done for the day. "What is it?"

There was a softness in the way Nym looked at me then, as if he was memorizing this moment, too. "Collith Sylvyre did not accept the crown," he answered.

"What? Are you serious?" I stared at him again. My mind raced, thundering with wild questions, and my heart became a herd of horses in my chest. Collith wasn't the king? Why hadn't he told me? What had he been doing all this time if he wasn't ruling the Unseelie Court?

But I hadn't heard a thing from Collith since I'd left the coronation. Not even a text. Same with Laurie.

I started to consider whether their silence indicated they just hadn't *wanted* to talk to me, but almost immediately, I dismissed that fear. I knew better now. I knew the depths of how much Collith and Laurie loved me, because I felt the same for them. It had no limits. Not death, not distance, not time. They'd only stayed away because they thought it was what *I* wanted.

My thoughts came to a screeching halt when I realized I hadn't asked the most obvious question of all. I refocused on Nym and leaned forward, my voice low with urgency. "Wait. Who rules the Unseelie Court, then?"

This was the part Nym had been waiting for—his arm moved. A moment later, he set a picture down on the table and said, "All hail Her Majesty Queen Lyari of the Unseelie Court. Long may she reign."

My gaze latched onto the image, and I stared down at it for several seconds. I touched Lyari's solemn face with the barest brush of my fingertips. She sat on that twisted, gnarled throne, the crown resting on her head. "No fucking way," I breathed.

"Collith Sylvyre was the one who suggested it," Nym said, nodding. "He told the entire Court he'd never seen a fiercer warrior or a better protector. Then he walked over to Lyari and put the crown in her hands."

I absorbed this with another awed silence, still unable to take my eyes off the picture. The first goblin queen in Fallen history. The first Paynore.

The fact this photograph existed spoke volumes—Lyari hadn't just broken the rules she'd once lived and breathed by, she'd tossed the rulebook out altogether. I touched her face again and shook my head wonderingly. My voice was soft. "Well, I'll be damned. Good for her."

"It seems the Unseelie Queen is not the only one who deserves congratulations," Nym commented. As he spoke, the faerie's eyes flicked toward my textbook.

I smiled. "Thanks. I'm not sure it's something worth congratulating, or at least not yet. I just finished my first semester at the University of Phoenix. Pre-med. I still have a long way to go."

"Going to be a doctor, then?"

"Veterinarian, actually." My smile grew as I said it.

A car passed with all the windows down, music blasting through the hot afternoon. Once the noise had faded Nym asked, "Why Arizona?"

"Because of someone I used to know." I propped my chin on the heel of my hand, thinking of the man who had been so kind to me. "His name was Fred. I grew up listening to him talk about it. 'When I get to Phoenix' this and 'Thank God I'll be living in the desert' that. I guess it was always at the back of my head, and that day I got in my car, it just . . . came out."

Nym smiled at whatever he saw in my expression. He'd never looked at me that way before, and I found myself wishing I'd gotten the chance to know this person more. It was a strange thrill, meeting Nym's gaze and knowing he was actually looking back at me. Seeing me. It was addictive to hear his voice without any of the pain or the confusion it had always carried before.

But I loved the Nym that I'd known, too. Along with the rest of my Shadow Court, no matter how much had changed since the last time we'd all been together. My eyes dropped back to the picture.

"I still can't get over the news about Lyari." I shook my head again. "It works, though. It fits. She'll make a good queen."

"They added her to the mural. Viessa, as well. Our historians are calling it the Year of Three Queens," Nym told me.

"They always were so original with naming things," I remarked dryly. My voice went soft again. "Still. I think I'd like to see that sometime."

The prospect of going back didn't disturb me like it used to. In the dirt passageways of the Unseelie Court, I'd experienced fear and pain, yes. But it was also the place I'd met Nym and had become friends with Viessa. It was where I had started to fall in love with Collith. It was where I'd made love to Laurie for the first time.

"I am certain Her Majesty would welcome you back," Nym said.

But he wouldn't be there, I remembered with a pang. I refocused on the faerie sitting across from me, wishing some things could be different, no matter how content I might've been with how it had all turned out. "I'm sorry about what happened to you, Nym. I'm so sorry."

"I've seen how it ends for me, my lady. I am content with my choices," he said simply. He paused before adding, "But there's something I won't be capable of telling you by the time we meet. Every time I come back, and I lose a little more of my mind, there will be one memory I never forget—the first time I saw you."

The first time he'd seen me? I thought of all the drawings Nym had done, and my mind's eye filled with a memory of his bedroom wall. "Was it during the battle?" I asked.

Nym shook his head. "Quite the opposite, actually. It was during one of the quieter parts of your life. You were only sixteen years old. You didn't seem to have many friends, and you didn't say much, so I continued to watch you for a while. One day, you walked past a human who had just dropped her book. You stopped, and you bent down, and you picked it up for her. She thanked you and you continued on your way. Such a simple thing. Some might not even consider it consequential. But I knew the world had been cruel to you. You could've let it harden you. You could have ignored that woman, like most people would have. Yet you were kind to her.

"That was when I knew Lady Persephone's fears were unfounded," Nym concluded. He gave me a sweet, tender smile. "You were well worth the wait, Your Majesty."

My chin wobbled, and I knew I was staring at him again. I didn't care. I wanted to remember this moment, every detail of it. Nym had been part of my family. He knew the shape of my soul, the secret fears that hid inside it. And here he was, telling me he had no regrets.

Even after all this time, the loss of him hurt. Grief laced my voice as I whispered, "I love you, Nym."

"Being loved by you is an honor, my lady. One that is entirely worth dying for," he replied. He took my hand, which had been resting on the table, and pressed a gentle kiss to the back of it. Then Nym stood from his chair, the legs making a slight scraping sound on the pavement. As he pushed it back in, the Time Walker's gaze met mine again. "You're wasting it, you know."

"Wasting what?" I asked, my head tilted back to keep my eyes on him.

Nym slid a piece of paper toward me. "Time."

With one last smile, he turned away from the table. He put his foot out as if he were taking a step, then sifted before his shoe even touched the ground. Another whisper of pain went through me as I realized it was the last time I'd ever see my friend.

Swallowing, I pulled the piece of paper closer and unfolded it. I'd half-expected it to be a letter, but there was just an address written in the center. It was on the East coast. I unlocked my phone and typed the address in. I'd have to use a Door to get there. Luckily, there was one right in Tucson.

Well, no time like the present, I thought.

I packed up my things and pushed away from the table, then followed Nym into the bright unknown.

I arrived just as daylight was beginning to peek over the horizon.

For a few minutes, long after the engine had gone silent, I just sat there and looked up at the house. I'd never seen the front of it, since my visits had only been in dreams, but it suited him. Beautiful, reserved, the darkness broken by spots of light.

Hello shifted in her crate, which I'd strapped in beside me. The sound pulled me out of my reverie. Taking a breath, I unbuckled and finally climbed out of the car. I clutched the corner of the door in my hand, one foot in, one foot out. Nothing stirred beyond the glass of those gently lit windows. I glanced toward the garage doors, wondering how many cars were parked inside.

That was when something else occurred to me. Something I should've thought of at some point during the trip here. What if he wasn't alone? What if he'd moved on? I could hardly blame him if he had—I'd been the one to walk away on the day of his coronation. Uncertainty gripped my heart, and I couldn't bring myself to move.

I was still standing there when the front door opened.

The sight of him didn't bring back a rush of memories. Instead, it only brought one—our wedding ceremony. When we were two strangers, standing in those twilight woods, making promises to each other that we'd both break. It wasn't so long ago, in the grand scheme of things, but every time I pictured those people we'd been . . . I thought about how young they were. How guarded. How hopeful. We hadn't been looking for each other in a physical sense, but we'd been looking for each other nonetheless. Then we'd screwed it up, over and over, because we were alive and life was a fucking mess.

Did that mean it was too late to fuck it up one more time?

I looked up at him, still remembering those vows. Reliving the part that I'd kept with me, tucked inside like a secret, taking it out on the nights I was alone. *I will never tell you goodbye, because*

I will never leave you. I will do my best to give you a life of hellos, Fortuna Sworn.

When those final words echoed through my head, it was as if something clicked into place. For the first time in my life, I had the right words.

"Hello," I said.

Collith smiled. The tilt to his lips was subtle as ever, but the light reached his eyes, spreading from the corners in small lines as he walked toward me. "Welcome home," he replied.

A sensation darted through the edges of my heart. It felt like something was being built, or like two things were being knit together. For once, I didn't hesitate. I stepped forward and wrapped my arms around Collith's neck, burying my fingers in the soft curls against the back of his neck. His achingly familiar scent washed over me, dark and rich and masculine. I hadn't realized just how much I'd missed it.

"It's good to be back," I murmured, just before Collith bent his head to claim my mouth. There was nothing hesitant in the heat of his kiss, no hint of the year we'd been apart. I thrilled in his taste. Being able to touch him again. I could have an entire lifetime of touching him, and it wouldn't be enough.

Without breaking away, Collith shifted and yanked me off my feet. I tipped my head, laughing, but I caught hold of his shoulders for balance and didn't fight his hold. He began walking toward the front door of the house.

Halfway up the path, though, Collith paused. He met my gaze again, and suddenly there was a shadow of uncertainty in those hazel depths. "Laurie is inside. We . . . we were just starting to make breakfast," he told me.

A breeze whistled between us. Dawn warmed my skin, yellow streams of light over the horizon as I gave Collith a slow, wide smile. "That sounds absolutely perfect."

He gave me a look of such pure joy that I felt an answering, giddy flutter. Without another word, Collith carried me inside. A rush of warm air greeted us. It smelled like fresh coffee and melting butter. My mouth began to water just as a familiar voice called, "It's about time, Firecracker!"

I grinned, and Collith kicked the door shut behind us.

THE END

ABOUT THE AUTHOR

K. J. Sutton lives in Colorado with her two rescue dogs. She has received multiple awards for her work, and she graduated with a master's degree in Creative Writing from Hamline University. K. J. also writes young adult novels as Kelsey Sutton.

When she isn't writing in a coffee shop, K. J. spends her time travelling the world and working at a vet clinic. She is best known for her Fortuna Sworn series.

CONTENT WARNING

Please be aware this novel contains scenes or themes of profanity, gore, violence, death, murder, decapitation, and sex.

HOW THE OTHER HALF KILL

P. C. ROSCOE

HODDER CHILDREN'S BOOKS

First published in Great Britain in 2026 by Hodder & Stoughton Limited

1 3 5 7 9 10 8 6 4 2

Text copyright © Pippa Roscoe, 2026
Cover design by Lisa Horton
Cover images © Shutterstock.com

The moral right of the author has been asserted.

*All characters and events in this publication, other than those clearly
in the public domain, are fictitious and any resemblance to
real persons, living or dead, is purely coincidental.*

All rights reserved.
No part of this publication may be reproduced, stored in
a retrieval system, or transmitted, in any form or by any means, without
the prior permission in writing of the publisher, nor be otherwise circulated
in any form of binding or cover other than that in which it is published
and without a similar condition including this condition being
imposed on the subsequent purchaser.

A CIP catalogue record for this book
is available from the British Library.

ISBN 978 1 444 93458 8

Typeset in 10.75/15.5pt Adobe Caslon Pro by Six Red Marbles UK, Thetford, Norfolk
Printed and bound in Great Britain by Clays Ltd, Elcograf S.p.A.

The paper and board used in this book
are made from wood from responsible sources.

Hodder Children's Books
An imprint of
Hachette Children's Group
Part of Hodder & Stoughton Limited
Carmelite House
50 Victoria Embankment
London EC4Y 0DZ

The authorised representative in the EEA is Hachette Ireland,
8 Castlecourt Centre, Dublin 15, D15 XTP3, Ireland (email: info@hbgi.ie)

An Hachette UK Company
www.hachette.co.uk

www.hachettechildrens.co.uk